PENGUIN CLASSICS

AMERICAN LOCAL COLOR WRITING

Elizabeth Ammons is the Harriet H. Fay Professor of English at Tufts University. She is the author of *Edith Wharton's Argument with America* (1980) and *Conflicting Stories: American Women Writers at the Turn into the Twentieth Century* (1991). She is the editor of *Critical Essays on Harriet Beecher Stowe* (1980), *How Celia Changed Her Mind and Other Stories by Rose Terry Cooke* (1986), *Short Fiction by Black Women, 1900–1920* (1991), and, with Annette White-Parks, *Tricksterism in Turn-of-the-Century American Literature: A Multicultural Perspective* (1994).

Valerie Rohy received her Ph.D. at Tufts University. She has published an essay on James Baldwin and is the author of a book-length study of female sexuality and representation in American literature.

AMERICAN
LOCAL COLOR WRITING,
1880–1920

EDITED WITH AN
INTRODUCTION AND NOTES BY
ELIZABETH AMMONS AND VALERIE ROHY

PENGUIN BOOKS

PENGUIN BOOKS
Published by the Penguin Group
Penguin Putnam Inc., 375 Hudson Street,
New York, New York 10014, U.S.A.
Penguin Books Ltd, 27 Wrights Lane,
London W8 5TZ, England
Penguin Books Australia Ltd, Ringwood,
Victoria, Australia
Penguin Books Canada Ltd, 10 Alcorn Avenue,
Toronto, Ontario, Canada M4V 3B2
Penguin Books (N.Z.) Ltd, 182–190 Wairau Road,
Auckland 10, New Zealand

Penguin Books Ltd, Registered Offices:
Harmondsworth, Middlesex, England

First published in Penguin Books 1998

1 3 5 7 9 10 8 6 4 2

Copyright © Elizabeth Ammons and Valerie Rohy, 1998
All rights reserved

LIBRARY OF CONGRESS CATALOGING IN PUBLICATION DATA
American local color writing, 1880–1920/edited, with an
introduction and notes by Elizabeth Ammons and Valerie
Rohy.
p. cm.—(Penguin classics)
ISBN 0 14 04.3688 X
1. American fiction—19th century. 2. United States
—History, Local—Fiction. 3. American fiction—20th
century. 4. Short stories, American. 5. Local color in
literature. 6. Regionalism in literature. I. Ammons,
Elizabeth. II. Rohy, Valerie. III. Series.
PS658.A45 1998
813'.40932—dc21 97-18115

Printed in the United States of America
Set in Stempel Garamond
Designed by Virginia Norey

CONTENTS

INTRODUCTION

FROM 1868, when Bret Harte published his local color stories "The Luck of Roaring Camp" and "The Outcasts of Poker Flat," until the First World War, literary regionalism enjoyed enormous popularity in America. Supported by magazines such as the *Atlantic Monthly*, *Century*, the *Colored American Magazine*, and *Land of Sunshine*, it was championed by influential writers such as William Dean Howells. There was never a single local color or regionalist tradition, as suggested by today's debate about which term best names the tradition. Instead, the genre includes a wide range of writers and texts, spanning not only different parts of the United States but also many cultures and ethnicities, genres and forms, goals and ideologies.

While the perspective of this volume is multicultural, turn-of-the-century published definitions of local color appear chiefly in work by successful white authors. Hamlin Garland's 1894 essay "Local Color in Art" describes the local color novel as a text that "could not have been written in any other place or by any one else than a native" (53–54). Mary Austin offers a similar definition in "Regionalism in American Fiction" (1932), praising novels that pass "the regional test of not being possible to have happened elsewhere" (100); such novels, she argues, are grounded in a particular place and describe "life as it is lived there, as it unmistakably couldn't be lived anywhere else" (104–105). Local color celebrates the lived experience of what Garland calls the "native"; as Austin notes, it valorizes "authenticity" (106) above all. But in doing so, regionalist writing poses important questions for us today: What is authenticity? What is at stake in the documentation of regional differences? In a period of rapidly increasing United States imperialism, nation building, and racism in the later nineteenth and early twentieth century, why did the construction of "America" and of an "American tradition" require the representation of cultural diversity? And at a time of signal shifts in notions of gender and sexuality, what sexual ideology or collective fantasy motivated American writing to seek out the peculiarities of regional life?

CULTURE, NATION, AND EMPIRE

The relationship of local color writing to structures of dominant power reveals a number of complexities. Questions of representation and authority arise, and the lines separating the local from the national and the global lack precision. As the literary theorist and critic Mary Louise Pratt suggests in *Imperial Eyes: Travel Writing and Transculturation* (1992), it might be useful to conceptualize the place where cultures meet not as a frontier, a line that gets drawn and redrawn, but as a contact zone, a space in which reciprocity and exchange occur, albeit within power differentials. Also relevant to local color is Pratt's addition of "autoethnography" to the concept of ethnography, both of which are helpful in thinking about regionalist fiction. Pratt uses autoethnography "to refer to instances in which colonized subjects undertake to represent themselves in ways that *engage with* the colonizer's own terms. If ethnographic texts are a means by which Europeans represent to themselves their (usually subjugated) others, autoethnographic texts are those the others construct in response to or in dialogue with those metropolitan representations" (7). As ethnographic texts, certain stories in this volume, such as those by Joel Chandler Harris and Jack London, can be seen as attempts to capture and render the experiences of people unlike their author. To what extent such pieces colonize their subject emerges as an important question. In contrast, most of the stories in this collection, as autoethnographic texts, perform significant decolonizing acts; they destabilize the master narrative. Offering fictions at once obvious and subtle, many of the authors challenge the dominant culture's ability to authenticate, categorize, map, and control all those falling under its gaze and thus supposedly in its power.

These issues of social control, self-determination, and conflicting definitions of Americanness in many ways dominated the United States at the turn of the century. If the Civil War had settled the question of whether the country would remain unified despite strong cultural and political differences, patterns of

immigration and migration during the second half of the nineteenth century continued to test assumptions about American
identity. Between 1870 and 1920 one quarter of the population
abandoned farm life to live in towns and cities. Between 1880
and 1914 more than 20 million immigrants arrived in the United
States, most coming from Ireland, Italy, and eastern Europe and
most of them Catholics. With the failure of Reconstruction in
the late nineteenth century, tens of thousands of black Americans left the South to find work in the North. It is not surprising
that urbanization, rural depopulation, immigration, racial and
ethnic tensions, and internal migration were important themes
in local color fiction at the turn of the century, for the rate and
magnitude of change in the United States were staggering.

This change extended to the very boundaries of the nation,
with the United States Census Bureau declaring in 1891 that the
frontier had ceased to exist. Two years later the historian Frederick Jackson Turner offered his famous "closing of the frontier"
thesis, which held that American character had been shaped by
the clash between "civilization" and "wilderness" on the frontier, where the European had been transformed into "a new
product that is American." Now new challenges would have to
form and produce Americans. As the historian Ronald Takaki explains in A Different Mirror (1993), "The world that
Turner inhabited was immensely different from the America that
Thomas Jefferson had envisioned—a nation of a racially homogeneous people covering the entire continent. Here in the
making was a multicultural America composed of an increasingly
polymorphous 'giddy multitude'—blacks, Indians, Irish, Mexicans, and Chinese as well as new groups, including Jews and
Japanese" (227).

Of course, a racially homogeneous America had never existed
on the North American continent after European contact, despite Jefferson's fantasy. Indians, Africans, northern Europeans,
Spaniards, and Mexicans had been living and fighting with each
other for several hundred years before the turn into the twentieth century. However, what was changing rapidly as the new
century approached was the unquestioned hegemony of Anglo-
Saxons in America. With the immigration of large numbers of
Italians, Irish, and eastern Europeans, especially Jews, to the

United States, in addition to the migration of emancipated African Americans to all the major cities of the North and the presence, especially in the West, of Chinese immigrants and Mexicans, the nation was becoming more and more ethnically and racially diverse.

One sign of the increasingly multicultural composition of the United States was the proliferation of newspapers and magazines published for particular ethnic audiences. As Werner Sollors explains in *The Columbia Literary History of the United States* (1988), as early as 1870 the first Yiddish periodical, *The Post*, was published in the United States. It was followed by many Yiddish papers, as well as sketches and stories about Jewish life in mainstream publications such as the *New York Sun and Press*. Even older was the African American periodical press, which predated the Civil War but burgeoned at the turn of the century. In 1900, for instance, the *Colored American Magazine* appeared, edited in Boston by Pauline Hopkins, whose stories appear in this volume; in 1910 the *Crisis* was created, edited by another author in this volume, W. E. B. Du Bois, as the official publication of the National Association for the Advancement of Colored People (NAACP). Spanish-language periodicals such as *La Revista Hustrada de Nueva York* existed at the end of the nineteenth century; and it is thought that the first Japanese papers and magazines, *Nineteenth Century* and *Ensei*, appeared in the United States in the 1890s. Most abundant were German-language papers and magazines. They numbered in the hundreds and were often identified with a local German American community, such as the *Cincinnati Republikaner* or the *Philadelphische Zeitung*. Finally, the Potawatomi writer Simon Pokagon distributed his pamphlet *Red Man's Greeting* at the 1893 World's Fair in Chicago. As Sollors summarizes, the pamphlet aimed to "remind Americans that 'the land on which Chicago and the Fair stands, still belongs to [the Potawatomis], as it has never been paid for' " (575).

As many of the stories in this volume illustrate, distinct, strong ethnic communities were growing in visibility, self-definition, and influence at the turn of the century. At the same time, the popular ideology of the United States as a "melting pot" captured the national imagination. Rather than preserving and nurturing cultural diversity, Americans should come together as one people, dissolving differences of heritage, language, and values to form one unified culture: English-speaking, capitalist, and characterized by the Protestant work ethic. Advances in transportation and communication during the second half of the nineteenth century greatly aided the success of this national agenda. As early as 1869 a transcontinental railroad connected the Atlantic and Pacific Oceans, and by the turn of the century, railroads laced the country, with the amount of track increasing from 35,000 miles in 1865 to 200,000 miles by 1890. After the Civil War, cheap, fast printing and publishing technologies made it possible to issue large numbers of affordable books and magazines. The result was the birth of mass market popular culture, with ideas, products, and entertainment much the same from New York City to Los Angeles.

Inexpensive popular novels, for example, allowed hundreds of thousands of people to share the same narrative, much as mass culture is promulgated through television today. The Ragged Dick series of Horatio Alger novels sold at the rate of about a million books a year by 1910, and this does not take into account the number borrowed and traded among friends and acquaintances. Like all popular culture, the books were formulaic and stereotypic; they glorified masculine lust for adventure and action, making material wealth the reward, and praised highminded, virtuous women. Because of improved transportation (railroads, canals, better roads), the appeal of regional music such as ragtime spread throughout the nation; and traveling entertainments such as Buffalo Bill's Wild West Show reached tens of thousands of audience members.

As a theme that shaped national popular culture, local color extended to the cinema, which entered the American mass market around the turn of the century, beginning with short vitascope films. While full-length movies would offer images of heroic Anglo cowboys, villainous Mexicans, imperiled white women, lust-driven black men, and glorified Ku Klux Klan vigilantes, early cinema provided glimpses of exotic scenes within and outside the United States in popular short films called "Local Views." Like local color writing, early cinema often focused on regionalism and the exotic: in 1898 filmgoers could see orange groves in California and a bullfight in Mexico, and in 1911 they were invited to tour "Ranch Life in the Southwest." Such short films were instrumental in the rise of tourism among middle-class Americans, and many were sponsored by railroad companies to promote tourism; indeed, a conventional shot placed the camera at the window of a moving train.

While the development of regionally inflected national entertainments responded to middle-class tastes and values, vast economic inequities and violent confrontations between labor unions and bosses made the turn of the century explosive. With no income tax, the rich got richer. Industrial barons lived in mansions often modeled on European palaces, traveled the globe in luxury, employed many servants, and spent their millions on clothes, jewels, art, European titles, and, in some notable instances, philanthropy. Meanwhile, sweatshop and factory workers, whose numbers were growing exponentially, found themselves working sixty or more hours a week in unsafe conditions for low wages.

Clashes between labor and bosses became common. In 1886 demonstrations in Chicago for an eight-hour workday erupted into what became known as the Haymarket Riots, resulting in a number of deaths, including those of seven police officers. Charges of anarchy were brought against eight demonstrators, and their trial, which resulted in the execution of four of them, led even the moderately liberal writer and editor William Dean Howells to believe that the government had used the eight citizens as scapegoats. The Homestead Strike in 1892 at the Carnegie Steel Company plant in Pennsylvania was met by management with hired Pinkerton forces and then the state militia. The Pullman Strike in 1894, the result of wages being cut 25 to 40 percent, ended with President Grover Cleveland ordering federal troops in to crush the American Railway Union. Eugene Debs, the union organizer, was jailed for six months. The Triangle Shirtwaist Factory fire in New York City in 1911, in which 146 women died because their bosses had locked them in their overcrowded workrooms, made undeniable the horrible working conditions of the sweatshops.

Against this backdrop of labor unrest, economic inequity, unprecedented immigration, and increasing internal migration, racial oppression and violence accelerated at the end of the nineteenth and beginning of the twentieth century. In 1896 the Supreme Court decision of *Plessy v. Ferguson* sanctioned segregation by ruling in favor of separate but equal public facilities for African Americans. Lynchings, particularly of black men on fabricated charges of raping white women, increased with impunity; and the Ku Klux Klan was praised in the best-selling 1902 novel *The Leopard's Spots* (subtitled *The White Man's Burden*) by Thomas Dixon, which became the basis for the famous 1915 racist film *The Birth of a Nation*. Growing in numbers, the Klan marched openly in their white hoods and gowns and conducted a nationally tolerated campaign of terror, specifically against blacks but also against Jews and Catholics. At great peril to themselves, courageous citizens such as the African American writer and activist Ida B. Wells spoke out against this terrorism; and a coalition of blacks and whites formed the NAACP in 1909 to combat the increase of race hatred. As the stories in this volume by Chesnutt, Dunbar-Nelson, Brown, Hopkins, and Du Bois demonstrate, local color fiction by African American writers addressed this assault on black America in many ways, ranging from overt counterattack to representations of African American experience and culture that ignored white America.

Racism in the United States was not limited to discrimination against African Americans; Native Americans, Asians, Mexicans, Irish, and Jews were also targeted. In 1890 the U.S. Army shot and killed more than 250 unarmed Sioux women, men, and children at the Massacre at Wounded Knee in South Dakota. Earlier the Dawes Act (1887) had dissolved the communal land rights of Indians, except for Pueblo groups; and government-mandated boarding schools for Indian children systematically set about breaking up families and eradicating traditional cultures. In 1882 the Chinese Exclusion Act, renewed in 1892 and 1902, ended immigration from China, which had effectively been limited to men from the beginning. Now, because of the Exclusion Act plus antimiscegenation laws, large communities of Chinese

American men lived in urban Chinese ghettos, dubbed China-towns. Throughout the late nineteenth century, Anglo-dominated courts in the Southwest consistently ruled against Mexican American land claims; in New Mexico, for example, four fifths of the land originally held by Mexicans was in the hands of whites by the opening of the twentieth century. Among the new Americans discriminated against were the Irish, who were racialized in the hate rhetoric of the time as "yellow," lazy, bestial, and oversexed; they were barred from employment by signs stating "No Irish Need Apply." Anti-Semitic discrimination in hiring and housing was no less virulent; Jews were excluded from hotels, private schools, and elite social clubs and were the subjects of xenophobic rhetoric in the popular press.

Supporting this widespread national structure of racial bigotry and terrorism was an elaborate foundation of theory. Given African American and Mexican American migration, Indian resistance to colonization, the unassimilated presence of Chinese workers, and substantial eastern European, Italian, and Irish immigration, efforts to maintain the United States as an Anglo-Saxon-dominant country—and to expand that dominance beyond existing national borders—became the obsession of the entrenched Protestant elite. To argue for white dominance in an age in which science was displacing religion as the ultimate source of "truth," scientific theories justifying Anglo-Saxon superiority were invoked, especially from the new social sciences of anthropology and sociology.

Writing for *Century Magazine* in 1913, Edward Alsworth Ross, identified on the title page as a professor of sociology at the University of Wisconsin, maintains in "American and Immigrant Blood: A Study of the Effects of Immigration" that the United States is heading into decline. As the headnote written by the magazine's editor explained, Professor Ross "shows how the sturdy blood of northern Europe once poured its red riches into American arteries to strengthen and to quicken, and he exhibits by contrast the vitiated and diseased and enfeebling mixtures making in recent years." The editor declared: "This paper constitutes one of the gravest and most important considerations ever laid before the American people" (225). According to Ross, Slavic, Italian, and Asiatic (mainly Turkish) immigrants were lowering the literacy rate of the United States and therefore "the plane of popular intelligence" (226). Ross said that those immigrants who could read devoured yellow journalism, so "the arts that win the immigrant deprave the taste of native readers and lower the intelligence of the community" (227). These new-comers were dirty, as was revealed by even a glimpse at the tidy houses of Germans compared with the "huddled," "dilapi-dated," "noisome and repulsive" quarters of Slavs (228); and nine out of ten of their children were delinquents. The women in eastern European, Polish, Portuguese, southern Italian, and Greek communities were said by Ross to be treated brutally. He said alcohol consumption ran ungoverned; sexual vice was ram-pant; and insanity was common, with immigrants often becom-ing public charges. Ross argues: "Of the asylum population they appear to constitute about a third" (230).

Ross's representation of undesirable new Americans reflected a clear set of racial and ethnic stereotypes, which are at times reproduced and at other times challenged in the stories in this volume. Swarthy of complexion, not from the North, and not Protestant, the people he despised were said to be dirty, licen-tious, lawless, stupid, brutal, and undisciplined. All of this, as the title of his article indicates, was a matter of blood. Con-versely, in Ross's typically dominant culture view, Anglo-Saxon and Saxon people (English, Scotch, Welsh, and German) were clean, orderly, intelligent, self-disciplined, and industrious. Oth-ers, no matter how diverse (or what their skin color)—eastern and southern Europeans, African Americans, Latinos, Asians, European Jews, Middle Easterners, and Irish—constituted a co-herent and inferior group which was racialized as not white.

Ross's argument illustrates the truism that race is a political concept. As Michael W. Apple explains in the introduction to *Racial Formation in the United States* (1986) by Michael Omi and Howard Winant, "Race is not an essence. It is not 'some-thing fixed, concrete and objective.' Rather, race needs to be seen 'as an unstable and "decentered" complex of social mean-ings constantly being transformed by political struggle.' The stress . . . on race not as a thing but as a set of social meanings is key here" (x). To comprehend the set of social meanings at play in the late nineteenth and early twentieth century—meanings that are obvious or implied in the fiction that follows, such as that of Jack London or Joel Chandler Harris—it is important to understand that race theorists used Darwin's concept of survival of the fittest to rank and categorize human groups. The most famous among these biologistic Social Darwinists was Herbert Spencer, who, as Thomas Gossett explains in *Race: The History of an Idea in America* (1963), argued that natural selection was "nature's indispensable method for producing superior men, superior nations, and superior races" (145). With scientific inquiry attempting to establish reliable, objective, physical evidence of "race," social scientists and biologists conducted elaborate studies that ranged from measuring heads (craniometry) to scrutinizing hair. Although all such attempts failed, theorists continued to maintain that "race" was primary, innate, and objectively demonstrable.

In the absence of scientific data to make the case, historical events were all the more important in corroborating racial difference and white superiority. At the end of the nineteenth century, the presumed right—indeed, duty—of Anglo-Saxons to conquer and "civilize" racialized others was used to justify U.S. imperialist expansion into Mexico, the Philippines, Native American lands, Puerto Rico, Hawaii, and Samoa. As Gossett explains, "By the time of the Spanish-American War [1898], the idea of race superiority had deeply penetrated nearly every field—biology, sociology, history, literature, and political science. Then there was no doubt whatever concerning the name of the race . . . Anglo-Saxon" (311).

Some Americans challenged this systematic and pervasive racist thinking. For example, Frederick Douglass, the famous ex-slave, abolitionist, and women's rights advocate, criticized the spectacular 1893 Chicago World's Columbian Exposition, created to commemorate the 400th anniversary of Columbus's "discovery" of America. Attending the fair's opening as a commissioner from Haiti because his own government ignored him, Douglass praised the wonders of the exposition, but later wrote for *Campbell's Illustrated History of the World's Columbian Exposition* (1894): "Yet, I saw, or thought I saw, an intentional slight to that part of the American population with which I am identified. Although there are eight millions of men of African descent in this country, not one of them seems to have been worthy of a place on the platform of these inaugural ceremonies." He calls this an "intentional humiliation of the race" or an attempt to conciliate racist southern whites. In either case, the exclusion was wrong, particularly since the United States was built by slave labor. "The leisure that exempted the Washingtons, the Jeffersons and Madisons from physical toil and enabled them to give their study to the constructive principles of our republic, was bought by enforced African labor" (250). Douglass ends by observing that all the magnificent turrets and domes of the exposition do not make up for the exclusion of blacks from the U.S. delegation on the inaugural platform.

If, as Douglass was well aware, one effect of the Chicago Fair (known because of its architecture as the White City) was to promote whiteness by excluding people of color from positions of power, another was to enforce racialized thinking by collecting, ordering, authenticating, and mapping difference. Comprised of hundreds of displays from around the nation and the world, the exposition attempted literally to master and control heterogeneity—to force global and national diversity into one organized, hierarchical interpretation, the resulting vision of which was a dazzling white. Authorized and funded by the U.S. Congress, the fair perfectly displayed dominant culture perspectives on ethnicity and race, which are also reflected in certain local color writing. All kinds of interesting, often exoticized, diverse local colors, fascinating to gaze upon, could be displayed as long as in the end they were carefully contained and disciplined by the white master plan. Whether at the Columbian Exposition or in the fiction of the period, this meaning of local color is preservationist and reactionary. It is touristic, and like turn-of-the-century anthropology, its equivalent in the social sciences, obsessed with cataloging and control.

But as both the fair and much of the fiction in this volume show, important resistant possibilities also inhere in local color. Whether ethnography or autoethnography, to return to Pratt's terms, local color has the ability to challenge and deconstruct monolithic national, imperial, and racial agendas. The sheer display of diversity offered by local color, for all the attempts to control and hierarchize it, speaks to a multicultural reality that defies homogenization and erasure. Alternative ways of thinking, being, and feeling exist. There are spaces beyond the control and sometimes the comprehension of the dominant culture. The tensions, ironies, and glimpses of other worlds, including other power relations, that local color often yields, as the stories in this volume demonstrate, are perceptible and significant. In terms of race, local color does not simply assert that the local is masterable, knowable, controllable. It also frequently suggests that the local is resistant and alternative.

GENDER AND SEXUALITY

If the era in which local color writing came to prominence was one of tremendous change, one full of anxiety concerning race, immigration, territorial expansion, and urbanization in the United States, it was also a time of crucial shifts in notions of gender and sexuality. As women moved into the public sphere in search of education and careers, as an attempt was made to understand and regulate women's sexuality, and as the woman suffrage movement gathered strength, the "Woman Question" became a subject of public debate. The regionalist literature that appeared between 1880 and 1920 reflects many of these concerns.

In the feminist criticism of the 1970s and 1980s, local color writing was hailed as a "woman's genre"; local color, according to such readings, was produced predominantly by women writers, centrally concerned with gender issues, and historically perceived as a "feminine" genre. Certainly the best-known writers of New England regionalism—Sarah Orne Jewett, Mary Wilkins Freeman, Harriet Beecher Stowe, Rose Terry Cooke—were women. And the association of local color writing with miniaturism, descriptiveness, and domesticity bears the hallmarks of the dominant nineteenth-century gender ideology, specifically the notion of separate spheres and the dismissal of most women's writing as merely ornamental. In the American canon, local color writing often emphasized description, not linear narrative; the private sphere, not the public; domestic matters, not affairs of state; and ordinary material reality, not the transcendent realm of "masculine" ideas. The fact that the short story was the most common expression of regionalism further linked the genre with "minor" literature and miniaturism. Despite its popularity among late nineteenth- and early twentieth-century readers, therefore, local color has occupied a marginal, feminized place in the literary canon.

Yet the gendering of regionalism is still more complex: U.S. local color was written by as many men as women: in addition to Chesnutt, Harris, London, Harte, Garland, Posey, and Anderson, whose writing appears in this volume, there were Lafcadio Hearn, George Washington Cable, Owen Wister, Frank Norris, Joaquin Miller, Sinclair Lewis, Edward Eggleston, Paul Laurence Dunbar, H. H. Boyesen, and Mark Twain. Male authors and questions of masculinity were influential in much regional literature and preeminent in frontier writing. Moreover, the place of femininity in local color is itself not monolithic but strongly inflected by differences of region, class, race, and sexuality.

The rise of local color writing coincided with the woman suffrage movement, which began in the United States with the Seneca Falls Convention in 1848 and reached its peak between 1900 and 1920. In 1892 Elizabeth Cady Stanton delivered a speech titled "The Solitude of Self" to the Judiciary Committee of the United States Congress, advocating woman suffrage. Citing cultural change and the opportunities provided by the "machinery" of industrial society, she urged the members of Congress not "to hold the developed woman of this day within the narrow political limits as the dame with the spinning wheel and knitting needle occupied in the past" (DuBois, 253). Although the suffrage movement eventually involved women from many racial, class, and regional backgrounds, it did not succeed in building coalitions until its last decade. After the Civil War, the movement was divided; some women felt that woman suffrage should be included in the Fourteenth Amendment along with voting rights for African American men, while others saw woman suffrage as a separate issue that could only jeopardize that amendment. Although Stanton, Susan B. Anthony, and Frances E. W. Harper attempted an alliance between African American and white feminist activists with the formation of the American Equal Rights Association in 1866, in the decades that followed some arguments for suffrage stooped to racism, presenting white women's suffrage as a way to counteract the votes of African American and immigrant men. Yet, despite these divisions, the commitment to suffrage was shared by women across race and ethnic lines. After gaining strength through the 1910s, the suffrage movement achieved its goal with the enactment of the Nineteenth Amendment in 1920; in the process, it had made women's issues a major public concern and had become an emblem of women's changing roles.

After the Civil War, American women for the first time had begun to attend college in significant numbers. Women's education was aided by the expansion of university facilities in western states after the 1862 Morrow Land Grant bill, the gradual admission of women to previously all-male institutions, the creation of black coeducational institutions such as Howard University, and the founding of prestigious women's colleges such as Vassar and Smith in the last half of the century. While higher education was by no means available to all women, it allowed some middle-class women to move into the public sphere, train for formerly male-dominated professions, and establish bonds with other women based on shared educational experience. Other middle-class women, their domestic duties lightened by industrialization, became involved in the women's club movement, expanding their "domestic" sphere of influence into the public realm through local organizations devoted to education, civic improvements, social welfare, and reforms such as temperance. In 1896 the General Federation of Women's Clubs was established, comprising over 500 white women's clubs with 150,000 members. That same year the National Association of Colored Women, led by Mary Church Terrell, was formed to work for racial "uplift," to fight lynching and discrimination, and to promote health and education in black communities. The temperance movement, which resulted in Prohibition in 1919, was also supported by middle-class women's organizations and led by the national Woman's Christian Temperance Union, founded in 1874. Working-class women organized the International Ladies Garment Workers Union in 1900 and the Women's Trade Union League in 1903 to advance unionization, education, and women's rights.

Changes in gender roles at the turn of the century were popularly represented by the figure of the "New Woman," one of several generations of middle-class, usually white, women who sought higher education, entered the labor force, and often postponed or rejected marriage and motherhood. The marked decline in birthrates among white middle- and upper-class women—due to the ideology of "voluntary motherhood" and newly available birth control methods, as well as expanding opportunities for women—produced enormous cultural anxiety around the turn of the century. Between 1905 and 1910, this anxiety took shape in the antifeminist and racist rhetoric of "race suicide," which cited the growing numbers of nonwhite and immigrant Americans as reason for privileged white women not to shirk their reproductive duties, lest they commit, as President Theodore Roosevelt wrote in 1911, the "racial crime" of "willful sterility" (DiNunzio, 340). Concerns about the New Woman and reproduction also intertwined with changing notions of sexuality in American culture. In the late nineteenth century, romantic friendships between women, which earlier in the century had been considered normal, were redefined as pathological. Prompted by Victorian sexologists' recent definition of homosexuality and by the social changes embodied in the New Woman, lay writers and scientists around the turn of the century produced a new distinction between normative femininity, understood in terms of "heterosexuality," itself a very recent idea, and "lesbianism," which entered the medical vocabulary in the 1880s.

The sexual theories and ideologies of the first decades of the twentieth century had significant effects on American women, as the notion of lesbianism, newly available to the American public, became a weapon against women's education, careers, and public life. The New Woman and the suffragist were subjected to accusations of lesbianism as well as "masculinization." From the turn of the century into the 1920s, the notion of companionate marriage, in which husband and wife were more equal, was promoted both as a response to women's changing roles and as a way to promote heterosexuality and marriage at a time when these institutions seemed threatened by female independence.

As notions of femininity changed around the turn of the century, so too did the American ideology of masculinity. Not only did women's pursuit of formerly male privileges threaten to collapse the distinction between the sexes and women reformers seek to "feminize" the public sphere, but urbanization and the rise of corporate culture also meant more bureaucratic roles for middle-class men in the workforce. These changes, combined with new ideas of male homosexuality as a "feminine" sexual identity, impelled Americans to subscribe to new ideas of masculinity, distinguishing the true man from the "sissy," the warrior from the aristocrat. President Theodore Roosevelt, whose adventures as a "Rough Rider" in the Spanish-American War (1898) became legendary, both served as an emblem of and promoted this new masculine ideal, advocating the "strenuous life" for American men and the nation alike:

> The timid man, the lazy man, the man who distrusts his country, the overcivilized man, who has lost the great fighting masterful virtues . . . these are the men who fear the strenuous life, who fear the only national life which is really worth leading. They believe in that cloistered life which saps the hardy virtues in a nation, as it saps them in the individual. (7–8)

Against the threat of an "overcivilized," aestheticized, feminized culture, Roosevelt presented a fantasy of frontier life, the military, and "primitive" societies as sites of an ideal masculinity. Preindustrial existence was remembered nostalgically as a virile realm in which "effete scions of civilization," like Jack London's doomed miners of "In a Far Country," had no place.

Women writers were for the most part significantly less nostalgic. While white women regionalists often addressed the conflict between marriage and self-realization, suggesting that even the best marriage may be confining for women, African American women writers found the meaning of marriage complicated by the legacy of slavery. Looking back at the Civil War and the slave economy of the antebellum South, they described the historical intersections of misogyny and racism, the problem of miscegenation, and slavery's assault on black families. As Hortense Spillers has argued in her essay "Mama's Baby, Papa's Maybe," the experience of motherhood was denied to slave women, who brought forth children under an economic structure which denied all claims but those of white patriarchal ownership (74–76). And because slaves had been prohibited from legally marrying, at the turn of the century African Americans considered marriage a civil right, like suffrage, whose exercise marked a commitment to racial progress. In *Domestic Allegories of Political Desire*, Claudia Tate notes that after Emancipation, African American women writers often linked racial equality and their rights as women to marriage, motherhood, and the restoration of stable families within the black community (91–92). Thus local color stories about marriage by African American women reflect the importance of marriage as a cultural institution in middle-class African American communities. Other women regionalists address the social forces that bear upon marriage—for example, economic need or the lack of other options—or present the institution of marriage as a metaphor for cultural assimilation.

At the turn of the century, regionalist writing was portrayed by its detractors as an unhealthy genre in specifically gendered terms. As Caroline Gebhard notes in "The Spinster in the House of American Criticism," the feminization of local color writing in American literary criticism took shape around the figure of the spinster, linking regionalist writing with repression and neurosis, arrested development and sterility (79). Although this idea focuses on particular stories that address women's concerns and on female local colorists, like Jewett, Murfree, and Woolson, who did not marry, it extends to the texts themselves, positing local color, as a genre, as the "dead end" of a literary tradition (Gebhard, 84). Writing in the *Century Magazine* in 1883, James Herbert Morse noted with regret an emphasis on "the reproduction of eccentricities, oddities, peculiarities" in recent American literature (374). Morse's "reproduction" is no doubt meant to signify "representation," but in American literature the two are often inseparable. Indeed, at the turn of the century, the New Woman was seen as sexually deviant or lesbian because she seemed to have forsaken motherhood; and this cultural anxiety about proper reproduction also extended to literature, shaping a concern about the healthy growth and propagation of the American canon. Discussing the marginalization of local color writing in *Provisions*, Judith Fetterley notes that local color often "appears as a minor or secondary strain, an interesting path off the main road of development" (104–105). Like Morse's notion of a literature that reproduces only "oddities" and "peculiarities," this view of local color as a digression from "the main road of development" links it with the arrested (economic) development of the rural communities it often describes and a regressive, nonreproductive female sexuality.

Although local color may treat the eccentricities of its subject gently, it may also attempt to control them. While the differences central to local color writing can work to resist patriarchal ideologies of gender and sexuality, they can also support them. Regionalist writing is in this sense a double genre, at once normal and perverse, central and marginal. Because it tends to fetishize the differences—sexual and gendered as well as racial and cultural—that define "the local," questions of particularity and of the *overly* particular haunt regionalist writing. How can one distinguish a conscientious attention to detail from an obsession with it? When does the observer's investment in differences, in the accouterments of local color, betray her or his own desire? In "Local Color in Art," Hamlin Garland writes, "It is the differences which interest us; the similarities do not please, do not forever stimulate and feed as do the differences" (49). And indeed, at the turn of the century, American dominant culture showed an almost insatiable appetite for others'—and its own—differences, recording peculiarities to support mechanisms of social discipline and celebrating diversity in the service of a coherent American tradition.

READING "LOCAL COLOR"

Local color writing is perhaps most interesting, then, in its articulation of certain contradictions in American ideology: conflicts between the general and the particular, the normative and the peculiar, the local and the national. Since its rise to prominence in the late nineteenth century, regionalist writing has played an ambivalent role in the construction of an American literary canon and of a fantasy of national identity in the United States. Between 1880 and 1920, U.S. dominant culture was concerned with the narratives of its own meaning and origins, and

regionalist writing was placed in relation to that nationalist project in part through discussions of literary realism and progressive politics. Proponents of local color from around the turn of
the century stressed its affiliation with realism, a genre regarded
as aesthetically superior to the romances or sentimental novels
of the nineteenth century, as well as more masculine and more
politically progressive. As such, realism enabled what Howells
termed the "democratic" impulse and the "appreciation of the
common" in regionalist writing (66–67). Disdaining artifice as
feminine, local colorists sought language that was "natural and
unstrained," "*not* picturesque" or "imitative"; it was, Garland
writes, "not the literature of scholars" but of "men who love
the modern and who have not been educated to despise common
things" (50–54).

Yet the notion of local color as an essentially realist genre by
no means covers the full range of regional writing. Attempts to
define the boundaries of "true" regionalism—or, as Austin
writes, "to discriminate between genuine regionalism and mistaken presentiments of it" (98)—work, whatever their intent, as
exclusionary mechanisms, for such attempts obscure other
modes of regional writing and the cultural and gender differences
they reflect. Feminist critics have noted women regionalists'
combination of realism with nineteenth-century genres in which
women writers had been successful, specifically the romance and
the sentimental novel. Other important alternatives to realism
include supernatural themes in African American writing,
whether shaped by "conjure" or by gothic conventions; tales or
fables based in African American or Native American folk
traditions; and newspaper columns whose political commentary
or dialect humor was aimed for a broad popular audience. The
richness of these nonrealist styles in local color writing not only
makes problematic the notion of regionalism *as* realism, but also
suggests the limitations of accuracy and authenticity in local
color writing.

Regionalist literature offers a part of the United States *as to-
ken of* the nation, hinting at the relation between state and nation articulated in the rhetoric of states' rights during the Civil
War and Reconstruction. This substitution of the part for the
whole—named, in rhetoric, *synecdoche*—is exemplified in Me-

na's story "The Vine-Leaf" by the relations between a vine-leaf birthmark and the woman herself, and between Mexico as a colony and the Spanish empire as a whole. The synecdochical relation implies a certain assimilation; like local color itself, it involves not only the recognition of difference but also the incorporation of the other, not only the celebration of regional difference but also the promotion of a nationalist fantasy.

Between 1880 and 1920, regionalist writing served the country's idealized self-image *and* reflected tensions of sectional, racial, linguistic, gender, and sexual difference. This doubleness was reflected in early criticism: while some readers faulted local color for divisiveness, others claimed that it bolstered American literature and national coherence precisely *because* it represented particularity and difference, not unity and homogeneity. Although the question of a distinct American literature had been debated for at least a century, it became more urgent amid the tensions of the late nineteenth century. In a 1901 essay titled "An American School of Fiction?" Frank Norris claimed that "the United States of America has never been able to boast of a school of fiction distinctively its own" (193) and echoed Garland's call for a "national literature" unlike the existing American writing—which had, Garland complained, "very little national color" (51). These writers saw the promise of "national color" in regional differences; as Garland bluntly put it, "local color means national character" (53). Edward Eggleston, in his 1892 preface to *The Hoosier Schoolmaster*, concurred: "The taking up of life in this regional way has made our literature really national by the only process possible. . . . The 'great American novel,' for which prophetic critics yearned so fondly twenty years ago, is appearing in sections" (Perosa, 165). At the same time, what Howells called "our literary decentralization" (64) raised the specter of national fragmentation. Noting that "the United States are not yet, in the European sense, united . . . there is no homogeneousness among us as yet," Norris called for a unified school of American fiction, "a rallying of many elements under one standard" (199). And in 1892 an anonymous critic argued in the *Nation* that local color had betrayed the cause of national literature: "American fiction has distinctly forsaken the expansive and the illimitable to run after the contracted and the limited. Instead of a national novel, we now have a rapidly accumulating series of regional novels—or, rather, so far has the subdividing and minimizing process gone, of local tales, neighborhood sketches, short stories confined to the author's backyard" (Perosa, 167).

But if fragmentation was one danger of local color literature, its homogenizing tendency was another, perhaps more serious threat. In American regionalism the desire for a correlation between the part and the whole could become coercive, pressing "the local" into the service of national meaning. Mary Noailles Murfree's view of rural life as a "microcosm" of the larger world, for example, leads her to assert that "human nature is the same everywhere" and to subordinate differences of class and culture to her idealized portrait of male friendship. Moreover, the notion of local color *as* national character cannot account for regions or cultures of the United States that are not analogous with but signally different from the dominant fantasy of the national "whole"—including African American culture and "conjure," Native American legends, immigrants' concerns about cultural assimilation, and even the persistent separatism of the white South.

While this volume is organized geographically, with writers from each region—the South, Midwest, Northeast, and West—grouped together in order to illustrate how different authors have widely varied takes on the same region, this is not the only possible organization. As we have suggested, there are also themes that traverse regionalist writing as a whole, shaping the meaning of local color. If Joel Chandler Harris's Uncle Remus stories offer a nostalgic view of race relations in the Old South, for example, Gertrude Dorsey Brown[e]'s story "Scrambled Eggs" suggests that slavery's disastrous effects touch both master and slave. Contemporary issues facing African Americans are examined in W. E. B. Du Bois's parable of racism, "On Being Crazy"; Pauline Hopkins's satirical look at a middle-class urban black community in "Bro'r Abr'm Jimson's Wedding"; and Alice Dunbar-Nelson's meditation on "passing" in "The Stones of the Village." Similar links among authors across geographical boundaries can be sketched using gender, sexuality, and class as organizing principles.

Hardly insular or escapist literature, local color writing addresses complex turn-of-the-century social issues: immigration and cultural assimilation in Abraham Cahan's story "The Apostate of Chego-Chegg" and Finley Peter Dunne's more ironic column on "Immigration"; the allotment act and other federal Indian policies in Alexander Posey's "Fus Fixico Letters"; and anti-Chinese sentiment in Sui Sin Far's "Its Wavering Image." Gender is also a central concern in the texts collected here: if Jack London's tales of Alaska and Hamlin Garland's "Up the Coolly" idealize male bonding and equate "the artistic" with effeminacy, Sherwood Anderson's portrait of a gay man in "Hands" shows local color at its most fetishistic. And while Sarah Orne Jewett's "The Queen's Twin" examines national and sexual nostalgia, women writers including Kate Chopin, Mary Wilkins Freeman, María Cristina Mena, and Mary Catherwood consider the limitations of marriage for women.

Local color remains a paradoxical genre, an example of both the marginal and the central, deviance and social discipline, diversity and the imperative to nationalistic unity. But despite, or perhaps because of, the difficulties that attend regionalism's treatment of difference, it offers, as a genre, a powerful literary allegory of what is now called multiculturalism. It shares many of the concerns of the various contemporary approaches to American literature that recognize as centrally important the experiences and literatures of not one but many U.S. cultures. While some readers still take the region in regionalism at its most literal, comparing regionalist literature with environmentalism and nature writing, the texts collected here suggest that local color or region is more accurately a metaphor that describes differences of culture as well as geography. In her essay on regionalism Austin offers a vision of local color, less nationalistic than Garland's, which hints at these multicultural implications. Describing regionalism as writing that provides "something less than the proverbial bird's eye view of the American scene" (107), Austin calls for writers to take up "the task of completely knowing, not one vast, pale figure of America, but several Americas, in many subtle and significant characterizations" (98). We hope that this volume will contribute to that task.

WORKS CITED

Austin, Mary. "Regionalism in American Fiction." *The English Journal* 21 (1932): 97–107.

Campbell, James B., ed. *Campbell's Illustrated History of the World's Columbian Exposition*, 2 vols. Chicago: J. B. Campbell, 1894.

The Columbian Gallery: A Portfolio of Photographs from the World's Fair. Chicago: The Werner Company, 1894.

DiNunzio, Mario R., ed. *Theodore Roosevelt: An American Mind*. New York: St. Martin's, 1994.

DuBois, Ellen Carol, ed. *Elizabeth Cady Stanton/Susan B. Anthony: Correspondence, Writings, Speeches*. New York: Schocken Books, 1981.

Elliott, Emory, ed. *The Columbia Literary History of the United States*. New York: Columbia University Press, 1988.

Fetterley, Judith, ed. *Provisions: A Reader from Nineteenth-Century American Women*. Bloomington: Indiana University Press, 1985.

Garland, Hamlin. *Crumbling Idols*. Cambridge: The Belknap Press of Harvard University, 1960.

Gebhard, Caroline. "The Spinster in the House of American Criticism." *Tulsa Studies in Women's Literature* 10 (1991): 79–91.

Gossett, Thomas F. *Race: the History of an Idea in America*. Dallas: Southern Methodist University Press, 1963.

Howells, William Dean. *Criticism and Fiction*. Clara Marburg Kirk and Rudolf Kirk, eds. New York: New York University Press, 1959.

Morse, James Herbert. "The Native Element in American Fiction." *The Century Magazine* 26 (1883): 362–75.

Norris, Frank. *The Responsibilities of the Novelist* [1901]. Rpt. New York: Greenwood, 1968.

Omi, Michael, and Howard Winant. *Racial Formation in the United States from the 1960s to the 1980s*. New York: Routledge, 1986.

Perosa, Sergio. *American Theories of the Novel, 1793–1903*. New York: New York University Press, 1985.

Pratt, Mary Louise. *Imperial Eyes: Travel Writing and Transculturation*. New York: Routledge, 1992.

Roosevelt, Theodore. *The Strenuous Life: Essay and Addresses*. New York, 1902.

Ross, Edward Alsworth. "American and Immigrant Blood: A Study of the Effects of Immigration." *The Century Magazine* 65 (December 1913): 225–32.

Spillers, Hortense. "Mama's Baby, Papa's Maybe: An American Grammar Book." *diacritics* 17 (1987): 65–81.

Takaki, Ronald. *A Different Mirror: A History of Multicultural America*. Boston: Little, Brown, 1993.

Tate, Claudia. *Domestic Allegories of Political Desire: The Black Heroine's Text at the Turn of the Century*. New York: Oxford University Press, 1992.

ACKNOWLEDGMENTS

The editors would like to thank Judith Brown, Amy Doherty, Virginia Drachman, Annamaria Formichella, Ruth Hsiao, Alexia Kosmider, Yuko Matsukawa, and Margot Sempreora for helping in various ways as we prepared this volume.

SOUTH

JOEL CHANDLER HARRIS

1848–1908

BEST KNOWN for his popular Uncle Remus stories, Joel Chandler Harris was born in a small town in Georgia to white working-class parents. After writing for newspapers in Macon, Georgia, New Orleans, and Savannah, he spent nearly thirty years on the staff of the *Atlanta Constitution*. In 1873 he married Esther LaRose, with whom he had nine children. His first Uncle Remus story, published in the *Constitution* in 1879, was followed by a series of Uncle Remus tales, collected in *Uncle Remus: His Songs and Sayings* (1880) and other volumes. These tales, based on African American oral traditions, center on the adventures of the trickster figure Brer Rabbit. Writing in dialect and using an African American narrator in an antebellum plantation setting, Harris advanced a nostalgic view of the Old South that appealed to white readers in both the North and the South during the era of Reconstruction; indeed, Harris was particularly admired by Theodore Roosevelt for his Uncle Remus stories. Like other southern white writers of the time, Harris created an idealized vision of race relations meant to demonstrate the validity of southern white self-rule. As more recent readers have noted, however, the duplicity and cleverness of figures like Brer Rabbit also suggest the resistance of African American culture to white authority.

In addition to the Uncle Remus tales, Harris published children's books, several novels and novellas, and volumes of more traditional local color stories set in Georgia, such as *Mingo, and Other Sketches in Black and White* (1884) and *Free Joe and Other Georgian Sketches* (1887).

[To give a cue to the imagination of the reader, it may be necessary to state that the stories related in this paper are supposed
to be told to a little boy on a Southern plantation, before the
war, by an old family servant.]

I.

THE MOON IN THE MILL POND.

One night when the little boy made his usual visit to Uncle
Remus, he found the old man sitting up in his chair fast asleep.
The child said nothing. He was prepared to exercise a good deal
of patience upon occasion, and the occasion was when he wanted
to hear a story. But in making himself comfortable, he aroused
Uncle Remus from his nap.

"I let you know, honey," said the old man, adjusting his spectacles, and laughing rather sheepishly, "I let you know, honey,
w'en I git's my head r'ar'd back dat away, en my eyeleds shot,
en my mouf open, en my chin p'intin' at de rafters, den dey's
some mighty quare gwines on in my min'. Dey is dat, des ez
sho ez youer settin' dar. W'en I fuss year you comin' down de
paf," Uncle Remus continued, rubbing his beard thoughtfully,
"I 'uz sorter fear'd you mought 'spicion dat I done gone off on
my journeys fer ter see old man Nod."[1]

This was accompanied by a glance of inquiry, to which the
little boy thought it best to respond.

"Well, Uncle Remus," he said, "I did think I heard you snoring when I came in."

"Now you see dat!" exclaimed Uncle Remus in a tone of
grieved astonishment; "you see dat! Man can't lean hisse'f 'pun
his 'membunce, 'ceppin' dey's some un fer ter come high-
primin'[2] roun' en 'lowin' dat he done gone ter sleep. *Shoo!* W'en
you stept in dat do' dar I 'uz right in 'mungs some mighty quare
notions—mighty quare notions. Dey aint no two ways; ef I 'uz
ter up en let on 'bout all de notions w'at I gits in mungs, folks

4

'ud hatter come en kyar me off ter de place whar dey puts 'stracted people."

"Atter I sop up my supper," Uncle Remus went on, "I tuck'n year some flutterments up dar 'mungs de rafters, en I look up, en dar wuz a bat sailin' 'roun'. 'Roun' en 'roun', en 'roun' she go—und' de rafters, 'bove de rafters—en ez she sail she make noise lak she grittin' 'er toofies. Now, w'at dat bat atter, I be bless ef I kin tell you, but dar she wuz; 'roun' en 'roun', over en under. I ax 'er w'at do she want up dar, but she aint got no time fer ter tell; 'roun' en 'roun', en over en under. En bimeby, out she flip, en I boun' she grittin' 'er toofies en gwine 'roun' en 'roun' out dar, en dodgin' en flippin' des lak de elements wuz full er rafters en cobwebs.

"W'en she flip out I le'nt my head back, I did, en 'twa'nt no time 'fo' I git mix up wid my notions. Dat bat wings so limber en 'er will so good dat she done done 'er day's work dar 'fo' you could 'er run ter de big house[3] en back. De bat put me in min' er folks," continued Uncle Remus, settling himself back in his chair, "en folks put me in min' er de creeturs."

Immediately the little boy was all attention.

"Dey wuz times," said the old man, with something like a sigh, "w'en de creeturs 'ud segashuate tergedder des like dey aint had no fallin' out. Dem wuz de times w'en ole Brer Rabbit 'ud 'ten' lak he gwine quit he 'havishness, en dey'd all go 'roun' same lak dey b'long ter de same fambly connexion.

"One time atter dey bin gwine in cohoots dis away, Brer Rabbit 'gun ter feel his fat,[4] he did, en dis make 'im git projecky terreckly. De mo' peace w'at dey had, de mo' wuss Brer Rabbit feel, twel bimeby he git restless in de min'. W'en de sun shine he'd go en lay off in de grass en kick at de gnats; he nibble at de mullen stalk en waller in de san'. One night atter supper, w'iles he 'uz romancin' 'roun', he run up wid ole Brer Tarrypin, en atter dey shuck han's dey sot down on de side er de road en run on 'bout ole times. Dey talk en dey talk, dey did, en bimeby Brer Rabbit say it done come ter dat pass whar he bleedz ter have some fun, en Brer Tarrypin 'low dat Brer Rabbit des de ve'y man he bin lookin' fer.

" 'Well, den,' says Brer Rabbit, sezee, 'we'll des put Brer Fox, en Brer Wolf, en Brer B'ar on notice, en ter-morrer night we'll meet down by de mill-pon' en have a little fishin' frolic. I'll do de talkin',' says Brer Rabbit, sezee, 'en you kin set back en say *yea*,' sezee.

"Brer Tarrypin laugh.

"'Ef I aint dar,' sezee, 'den you may know de grasshopper done fly 'way wid me,' sezee.

"'En you neenter bring no fiddle, n'er,' sez Brer Rabbit, sezee, 'kaze dey aint gwineter be no dancin' dar,' sezee.

"Wid dat," continued Uncle Remus, "Brer Rabbit put out fer home, en went ter bed, en Brer Tarrypin bruise 'roun' en make his way tords de place so he kin be dar 'gin 'de 'p'inted time.

"Nex' day Brer Rabbit sont wud ter de yuther creeturs, en dey all make great 'miration, kaze dey aint think 'bout dis dey-se'f. Brer Fox, he 'low, he did, dat he gwine atter Miss Meadows en Miss Motts, en de yuther gals.

"Sho nuff, w'en de time come dey wuz all dar. Brer B'ar, he fotch a hook en line; Brer Wolf, he fotch a hook en line; Brer Fox, he fotch a dip-net, en Brer Tarrypin, not ter be out-done, he fotch de bait."

"What did Miss Meadows and Miss Motts bring?" the little boy asked.

Uncle Remus dropped his head slightly to one side, and looked over his spectacles at the little boy.

"Miss Meadows en Miss Motts," he continued, "dey tuck'n stan' way back fum de aidge er de pon' en squeal eve'y time Brer Tarrypin shuck de box er bait at um. Brer B'ar 'low he gwine ter fish fer mud-cats; Brer Wolf 'low he gwine ter fish fer horny-heads; Brer Fox 'low he gwine ter fish fer peerch fer de ladies; Brer Tarrypin 'low he gwine ter fish fer minners, en Brer Rabbit wink at Brer Tarrypin' en 'low he gwine ter fish fer suckers.

"Dey all git ready, dey did, en Brer Rabbit march up ter de pon' en make fer ter th'ow he hook in de water, but des 'bout dat time, hit seem lak he see sump'n. De t'er creeturs, dey stop en watch his motions. Brer Rabbit, he drap he pole, he did, en he stan' dar scratchin' he head en lookin' down in de water.

"De gals dey 'gun ter git oneasy w'en dey see dis, en Miss Meadows, she up en holler out, she did:

"'Law, Brer Rabbit, w'at de name er goodness de marter in dar?'

"Brer Rabbit scratch he head en look in de water. Miss Motts, she hilt up 'er petticoats, she did, en 'low she monstus fear'd er snakes. Brer Rabbit keep on scratchin' en lookin'.

"Bimeby he fetch a long bref, he did, en he 'low:

" 'Ladies en gentermuns all, we des might ez well make tracks fum dish yer place, kaze dey aint no fishin' in dat pon' for none er dis crowd.'

"Wid dat, Brer Tarrypin, he scramble up ter de aidge en look over, en shake he head, en 'low:

" 'Tooby sho'—tooby sho! Tut-tut-tut!' en den he crawl back, he did, en do lak he wukkin' he min'.

" 'Don't be skeert, ladies, kaze we er boun' ter take keer un you, let come w'at will, let go w'at mus',' sez Brer Rabbit, sezee. 'Accidents got ter happen unter we all, des same ez dey is unter yuther folks; en dey aint nothin' much de marter, 'ceppin' dat de Moon done drap in de water. Ef you don't b'leeve me you kin look fer yo'se'f,' sezee.

"Wid dat dey all went ter de bank en lookt in; en, sho nuff, dar lay de moon, a-swingin' an' a-swayin' at de bottom er de pon'."

The little boy laughed. He had often seen the reflection of the sky in shallow pools of water, and the startling depths that seemed to lie at his feet had caused him to draw back with a shudder.

"Brer Fox, he look in, he did, en he 'low, 'Well, well, well.' Brer Wolf, he look in, en he 'low, 'Mighty bad, mighty bad!' Brer B'ar, he look in, en he 'low, 'Tum, tum, tum!' De ladies dey look in, en Miss Meadows, she squall out, 'Aint dat too much?' Brer Rabbit, he look in ag'in, en he up en 'low, he did:

" 'Ladies en gentermuns, you all kin hum en haw, but less'n we gits dat Moon out er de pon', dey aint no fish kin be ketch 'roun' yer dis night; en ef you'll ax Brer Tarrypin, he'll tell you de same.'

"Den dey ax how kin dey git de Moon out er dar, en Brer Tarrypin 'low dey better lef' dat wid Brer Rabbit. Brer Rabbit he shot he eyes, he did, en make lak he wukkin he min'. Bimeby, he up'n 'low:

" 'De nighes' way out'n dish yer diffikil is fer ter sen' roun' yer too ole Mr. Mud-Turkle en borry his sane,[5] en drag dat Moon up fum dar,' sezee.

" 'I 'clar' ter gracious I mighty glad you mention dat,' says Brer Tarrypin, sezee. 'Mr. Mud-Turkle is setch clos't kin ter me dat I calls 'im Unk Muck, en I lay ef you sen' dar atter dat sane you wont fine Unk Muck so mighty disaccomerdatin'.'

"Well," continued Uncle Remus, after one of his tantalizing pauses, "dey sont atter de sane, en wiles Brer Rabbit wuz gone, Brer Tarrypin, he 'low dat he done year tell time en time ag'in dat dem w'at fine de Moon in de water en fetch 'im out, lakwise dey ull fetch out a pot er money. Dis make Brer Fox, en Brer Wolf, en Brer B'ar feel mighty good, en dey 'low, dey did, dat long ez Brer Rabbit been so good ez ter run atter de sane, dey ull do de sanein'.

"Time Brer Rabbit git back, he see how de lan' lay, en he make lak he wanter go in atter de Moon. He pull off his coat, en he 'uz fixin' fer ter shuck his wescut,[6] but de yuther creeturs dey 'low dey wan't gwine ter let dry-foot man lak Brer Rabbit go in de water. So Brer Fox, he tuck holt er one staff er de sane, Brer Wolf he tuck holt er de yuther staff, en Brer B'ar he wade 'long behime fer ter lif' de sane 'cross logs en snags.

"Dey make one haul—no Moon; n'er haul, no Moon; n'er haul, no Moon. Den bimeby, dey git out furder fum de bank. Water run in Brer Fox year, he shake he head; water run in Brer Wolf year, he shake he head; water run in Brer B'ar year, he shake he head. En de fus news you know, w'iles dey wuz a-shakin', dey come to whar de bottom shelfed off. Brer Fox he step off en duck hisse'f; den Brer Wolf duck hisse'f; en Brer B'ar he make a splunge en duck hisse'f; en, bless gracious, dey kick en splatter twel it look lak dey 'uz gwine ter slosh all de water outer de mill pon'.

"W'en dey come out, de gals 'uz all a-snickerin' en a-gigglin', en well dey mought, 'kase, go whar you would, dey want no wuss lookin' creeturs dan dem; en Brer Rabbit, he holler, sezee:

" 'I speck you all, gents, better go home en git some dry duds, en n'er time we'll be in better luck,' sezee. 'I year talk dat de Moon'll bite at a hook ef you take fools fer baits, en I lay dat's de onliest way fer ter ketch 'er,' sezee.

"Brer Fox en Brer Wolf en Brer B'ar went drippin' off, en Brer Rabbit en Brer Tarrypin dey went home wid de gals."

* * *

III.
WHY BROTHER BEAR HAS NO TAIL.

"I 'clar' ter gracious, honey," Uncle Remus exclaimed one night, as the little boy ran in, "you sholy aint chaw'd yo' vittles. Hit aint bin no time, skacely, sence de supperbell rung, en ef you go on dis away, you'll des nat'ally pe'sh yo'se'f out."

"Oh, I wasn't hungry," said the little boy. "I had something before supper, and I wasn't hungry anyway."

The old man looked keenly at the child, and presently he said:

"De ins en de outs er dat kinder talk all come ter de same p'int in my min'. Youer bin a-cuttin' up at de table, en Mars. John, he tuck'n sont you 'way fum dar, en w'iles he think youer off some'rs a-snifflin' en a-feelin' bad, yer you is a-high-primin' 'roun' des lak you done had mo' supper dan de king er Philanders."

Before the little boy could inquire about the king of Philanders he heard his father calling him. He started to go out, but Uncle Remus motioned him back.

"Des set right whar you is, honey—des set right still."

Then Uncle Remus went to the door and answered for the child; and a very queer answer it was—one that could be heard half over the plantation:

"Mars. John, I wish you en Miss Sally be so good ez ter let dat chile 'lone. He down yer cryin' he eyes out, en he aint bodderin' 'long er nobody in de roun' worl'."

Uncle Remus stood in the door a moment to see what the reply would be, but he heard none. Thereupon he continued, in the same loud tone:

"I aint bin use ter no sich gwines on in Ole Miss time, en I aint gwine git use ter it now. Dat I aint."

Presently Tildy, the house-girl, carried the little boy his supper, and the girl was no sooner out of hearing than the child swapped it with Uncle Remus for a roasted yam, and the enjoyment of both seemed to be complete.

"Uncle Remus," said the little boy, after a while, "you know I wasn't crying just now."

"Dat's so, honey," the old man replied, "but 'twouldn't er bin long 'fo' you would er bin, kaze Mars. John bawl out lak a man w'at got a strop in he han', so w'at de diffunce?"

When they had finished eating, Uncle Remus busied himself in cutting and trimming some sole-leather for future use. His knife was so keen, and the leather fell away from it so smoothly and easily, that the little boy wanted to trim some himself. But to this Uncle Remus would not listen.

" 'Taint on'y chilluns w'at got de consate⁷ er doin' eve'ything dey see yuther folks do. Hit's grown folks w'at oughter know better," said the old man. "Dat's des de way Brer B'ar git his tail broke off smick-smack-smoove, en down ter dis day he de funniest-lookin' creetur w'at wobble on top er dry groun'."

Instantly the little boy forgot all about Uncle Remus's sharp knife.

"Hit seem lak dat in dem days Brer Rabbit en Brer Tarrypin done gone in kerhoots fer ter out-do de t'er creeturs. One time Brer Rabbit tuck'n make a call on Brer Tarrypin, but w'en he git ter Brer Tarrypin house, he year talk fum Miss Tarrypin dat her ole man done gone fer ter spen' de day wid Mr. Mud-Turkle, w'ich dey wuz blood kin. Brer Rabbit he put out atter Brer Tarrypin, en w'en he got ter Mr. Mud-Turkle house, dey all sot up, dey did, en tole tales, en den w'en twelf er'clock come dey had crawfish fer dinner, en dey 'joy deyse'f right erlong. Atter dinner dey went down ter Mr. Mud-Turkle mill-pon', en w'en dey git dar, Mr. Mud-Turkle en Brer Tarrypin dey 'muse deyse'f, dey did, wid slidin' fum de top uv a big slantin' rock down inter de water.

"I speck you moughter seen rocks in de water, 'fo' now, whar dey git green en slippy," said Uncle Remus.

The little boy had not only seen them, but had found them to be very dangerous to walk upon, and the old man continued:

"Well, den, dish yer rock wuz mighty slick en mighty slantin'. Mr. Mud-Turkle, he'd crawl ter de top, en tu'n loose, en go a-sailin' down inter de water—*kersplash!* Ole Brer Tarrypin, he'd foller atter, en slide down inter de water—*kersplash!* Ole Brer Rabbit, he sot off, he did, en praise um up.

"W'iles dey wuz a-gwine on dis away, a-havin' der fun, en 'joyin' deyse'f, yer come ole Brer B'ar. He year um 'laffin' en holl'in', en he hail 'um.

" 'Heyo, folks! W'at all dis? Ef my eye aint 'ceive me, dish yer's Brer Rabbit, en Brer Tarrypin, en old Unk' Tommy Mud-Turkle,' sez Brer B'ar, sezee.

" 'De same,' sez Brer Rabbit, sezee, 'en yer we is 'joyin' de day dat passes des lak dey wan't no hard times.'

" 'Well, well, well!' sez ole Brer B'ar, sezee, 'a-slippin' en a-slidin' en makin' free! En w'at de matter wid Brer Rabbit dat he aint j'inin' in?' sezee.

"Ole Brer Rabbit he wink at Brer Tarrypin, en Brer Tarrypin he hunch Mr. Mud-Turkle, en den Brer Rabbit he up'n 'low, he did:

" 'My goodness, Brer B'ar! you can't 'speck a man fer ter slip en slide de whole blessid day, kin you? I done had my fun, en now I'm a-settin' out yer lettin' my cloze dry. Hit's tu'n en tu'n about wid me en deze gents w'en dey's any fun gwine on,' sezee.

" 'Maybe Brer B'ar might jine in wid us,' sez Brer Tarrypin, sezee.

"Brer Rabbit he des holler en laff.

" 'Shoo!' sezee, 'Brer B'ar foot too big en he tail too long fer ter slide down dat rock,' sezee.

"Dis kinder put Brer B'ar on he mettle, en he up'n 'spon', he did:

" 'Maybe dey is, en maybe dey aint, yit I aint afeard ter try.'

"Wid dat, de yuthers tuck'n make way fer 'im, en ole Brer B'ar he git up on de rock, he did, en squat down on he hunkers, en quile he tail und' 'im, en start down. Fus' he go sorter slow, en he grin lak he feel good; den he go sorter peart, en he grin lak he feel bad; den he go mo' pearter, en he grin lak he skeerd; den he strack de slick part, en, gentermens! he swaller de grin en fetch a howl dat moughter bin yeard a mile, en he hit de water lak a chimbly a-fallin'.

"You kin gimme denial," Uncle Remus continued after a little pause, "but des ez sho' ez you er settin' dar, w'en Brer B'ar slick'd up en flew down dat rock, he break off he tail right

smick-smack-smoove, en mo'n dat, w'en he make his disappear'nce up de big road, Brer Rabbit holler out:

"'Brer B'ar!—Oh, Brer B'ar! I year tell dat flax-seed
poultices is mighty good fer so' places!'

"Yit Brer B'ar aint look back."

CHARLES CHESNUTT

1858–1932

NOW REGARDED as one of the most prominent African American authors of the nineteenth century, Charles Chesnutt was born in Cleveland, Ohio, where his parents had moved to escape slavery. He returned with his parents to Fayetteville, North Carolina, when the Civil War ended, in 1866. He had eight years of formal education, and became a teacher and administrator for schools established by the Freedmen's Bureau in North Carolina. After a brief stay in New York in 1883, he moved back to Cleveland, worked as a clerk and stenographer in a lawyer's office, and passed the Ohio bar examination in 1887. Chesnutt's first major story was published in 1885 by the McClure newspapers, and his story "The Goophered Grapevine" appeared in 1887 in the *Atlantic Monthly*, followed by many articles and short stories. His first book, *The Conjure Woman* (1899), is a collection of stories rendered in dialect and framed by antebellum plantation life, but unlike Joel Chandler Harris's Uncle Remus tales, Chesnutt's book stresses the brutality of slavery and the power of the act of storytelling.

After *The Conjure Woman* Chesnutt published *The Wife of His Youth and Other Stories of the Color Line* (1899); a biography of Frederick Douglass (1899); and three novels, *The House Behind the Cedars* (1900), *The Marrow of Tradition* (1901), and *The Colonel's Dream* (1905). His novels were for the most part financially unsuccessful, and Chesnutt returned to essays and short stories, and to making his living as a lawyer. In 1928 he received the Spingarn Award from the NAACP for his writing about African Americans.

"Have some dinner, Uncle Julius?" said my wife.

It was a Sunday afternoon in early autumn. Our two women-servants had gone to a camp-meeting[1] some miles away, and would not return until evening. My wife had served the dinner, and we were just rising from the table when Julius came up the lane, and, taking off his hat, seated himself on the piazza.

The old man glanced through the open door at the dinner-table, and his eyes rested lovingly upon a large sugar-cured ham, from which several slices had been cut, exposing a rich pink expanse that would have appealed strongly to the appetite of any hungry Christian.

"Thanky, Miss Annie," he said, after a momentary hesitation. "I dunno ez I keers ef I does tas'e a piece er dat ham, ef yer 'll cut me off a slice un it."

"No," said Annie, "I won't. Just sit down to the table and help yourself; eat all you want, and don't be bashful."

Julius drew a chair up to the table, while my wife and I went out on the piazza. Julius was in my employment; he took his meals with his own family, but when he happened to be about our house at mealtimes, my wife never let him go away hungry.

I threw myself into a hammock, from which I could see Julius through an open window. He ate with evident relish, devoting his attention chiefly to the ham, slice after slice of which disappeared in the spacious cavity of his mouth. At first the old man ate rapidly, but after the edge of his appetite had been taken off he proceeded in a more leisurely manner. When he had cut the sixth slice of ham (I kept count of them from a lazy curiosity to see how much he *could* eat) I saw him lay it on his plate; as he adjusted the knife and fork to cut it into smaller pieces, he paused, as if struck by a sudden thought, and a tear rolled down his rugged cheek and fell upon the slice of ham before him. But the emotion, whatever the thought that caused it, was transitory, and in a moment he continued his dinner. When he was through eating, he came out on the porch, and resumed his seat with the satisfied expression of countenance that usually follows a good dinner.

"Julius," I said, "you seemed to be affected by something a moment ago. Was the mustard so strong that it moved you to tears?"

"No, suh, it wa'n't de mustard; I wuz studyin' 'bout Dave."

"Who was Dave, and what about him?" I asked.

The conditions were all favorable to storytelling. There was an autumnal languor in the air, and a dreamy haze softened the dark green of the distant pines and the deep blue of the Southern sky. The generous meal he had made had put the old man in a very good humor. He was not always so, for his curiously undeveloped nature was subject to moods which were almost childish in their variableness. It was only now and then that we were able to study, through the medium of his recollection, the simple but intensely human inner life of slavery. His way of looking at the past seemed very strange to us; his view of certain sides of life was essentially different from ours. He never indulged in any regrets for the Arcadian² joyousness and irresponsibility which was a somewhat popular conception of slavery; his had not been the lot of the petted houseservant, but that of the toiling field-hand. While he mentioned with a warm appreciation the acts of kindness which those in authority had shown to him and his people, he would speak of a cruel deed, not with the indignation of one accustomed to quick feeling and spontaneous expression, but with a furtive disapproval which suggested to us a doubt in his own mind as to whether he had a right to think or to feel, and presented to us the curious psychological spectacle of a mind enslaved long after the shackles had been struck off from the limbs of its possessor. Whether the sacred name of liberty ever set his soul aglow with a generous fire; whether he had more than the most elementary ideas of love, friendship, patriotism, religion—things which are half, and the better half, of life to us; whether he even realized, except in a vague, uncertain way, his own degradation, I do not know. I fear not; and if not, then centuries of repression had borne their legitimate fruit. But in the simple human feeling, and still more in the undertone of sadness which pervaded his stories, I thought I could see a spark

which, fanned by favoring breezes and fed by the memories of
the past, might become in his children's children a glowing flame
of sensibility, alive to every thrill of human happiness or human
woe.

"Dave use' ter b'long ter my old marster," said Julius; "he
wuz raise' on dis yer plantation, en I kin 'member all erbout 'im,
fer I wuz old 'nuff ter chop cotton w'en it all happen'. Dave
wuz a tall man, en monst'us strong: he could do mo' wuk in a
day dan any yuther two niggers on de plantation. He wuz one
er dese yer solemn kine er men, en nebber run on wid much
foolishness, like de yuther darkies. He use' ter go out in de
woods en pray; en w'en he hear de han's on de plantation cussin'
en gwine on wid dere dancin' en foolishness, he use' ter tell 'em
'bout religion en jedgmen'-day, w'en dey would haf ter gin account fer eve'y idle word en all dey yuther sinful kyarin's-on.

"Dave had l'arn' how ter read de Bible. Dey wuz a free nigger
boy in de settlement w'at wuz monst'us smart, en could write
en cipher, en wuz alluz readin' books er papers. En Dave had
hi'ed dis free boy fer ter l'arn 'im how ter read. Hit wuz 'g'in'
de law,[3] but co'se none er de niggers did n' say nuffin ter de
w'ite folks 'bout it. Howsomedever, one day Mars Walker—he
wuz de oberseah—foun' out Dave could read. Mars Walker
wa'n't nuffin but a po' bockrah,[4] en folks said he could n' read
ner write hisse'f, en co'se he did n' lack ter see a nigger w'at
knowed mo' d'n he did; so he went en tole Mars Dugal'. Mars
Dugal' sont fer Dave, en ax' 'im 'bout it.

"Dave did n't hardly knowed w'at ter do; but he could n' tell
no lie, so he 'fessed he could read de Bible a little by spellin' out
de words. Mars Dugal' look' mighty solemn.

" 'Dis yer is a se'ious matter,' sezee; 'it 's 'g'in' de law ter
l'arn niggers how ter read, er 'low 'em ter hab books. But w'at
yer l'arn out'n dat Bible, Dave?'

"Dave wa'n't no fool, ef he wuz a nigger, en sezee:

" 'Marster, I l'arns dat it's a sin fer ter steal, er ter lie, er fer
ter want w'at doan b'long ter yer; en I l'arns fer ter love de Lawd
en ter 'bey my marster.'

"Mars Dugal' sorter smile' en laf' ter hisse'f, like he 'uz
might'ly tickle' 'bout sump'n, en sezee:

" 'Doan 'pear ter me lack readin' de Bible done yer much

harm, Dave. Dat 's w'at I wants all my niggers fer ter know. Yer keep right on readin', en tell de yuther han's w'at yer be'n tellin' me. How would yer lack fer ter preach ter de niggers on Sunday?'

"Dave say he'd be glad fer ter do w'at he could. So Mars Dugal' tole de oberseah fer ter let Dave preach ter de niggers, en tell 'em w'at wuz in de Bible, en it would he'p ter keep 'em fum stealin' er runnin' erway.

"So Dave 'mence' ter preach, en done de han's on de plantation a heap er good, en most un 'em lef' off dey wicked ways, en 'mence' ter love ter hear 'bout God, en religion, en de Bible; en dey done dey wuk better, en did n' gib de oberseah but mighty little trouble fer ter manage 'em.

"Dave wuz one er dese yer men w'at did n' keer much fer de gals—leastways he did n' 'tel Dilsey come ter de plantation. Dilsey wuz a monst'us peart,[5] good-lookin', gingybread-colored gal—one er dese yer high-steppin' gals w'at hol's dey heads up, en won' stan' no foolishness fum no man. She had b'long' ter a gemman over on Rockfish,[6] w'at died, en whose 'state ha' ter be sol' fer ter pay his debts. En Mars Dugal' had be'n ter de oction, en w'en he seed dis gal a-cryin' en gwine on 'bout bein' sol' erway fum her ole mammy, Aun' Mahaly, Mars Dugal' bid 'em bofe in, en fotch 'em ober ter our plantation.

"De young nigger men on de plantation wuz des wil' atter Dilsey, but it did n' do no good, en none un 'em could n' git Dilsey fer dey junesey,[7] 'tel Dave 'mence' fer ter go roun' Aun' Mahaly's cabin. Dey wuz a fine-lookin' couple, Dave en Dilsey wuz, bofe tall, en well-shape', en soopl'. En dey sot a heap by one ernudder. Mars Dugal' seed 'em tergedder one Sunday, en de nex' time he seed Dave atter dat, sezee:

" 'Dave, w'en yer en Dilsey gits ready fer ter git married, I ain' got no rejections. Dey 's a poun' er so er chawin'-terbacker up at de house, en I reckon yo' mist'iss kin fine a frock en a ribbin er two fer Dilsey. Youer bofe good niggers, en yer neenter be feared er bein' sol' 'way fum one ernudder long ez I owns dis plantation; en I 'spec's ter own it fer a long time yit.'

"But dere wuz one man on de plantation w'at did n' lack ter see Dave en Dilsey tergedder ez much ez ole marster did. W'en Mars Dugal' went ter de sale whar he got Dilsey en Mahaly, he

bought ernudder han', by de name er Wiley. Wiley wuz one er
dese yer shiny-eyed, double-headed[8] little niggers, sha'p ez a
steel trap, en sly ez de fox w'at keep out'n it. Dis yer Wiley had
be'n pesterin' Dilsey 'fo' she come ter our plantation, en had
nigh 'bout worried de life out'n her. She did n' keer nuffin fer
'im, but he pestered her so she ha' ter th'eaten ter tell her marster
fer ter make Wiley let her 'lone. W'en he come ober to our place
it wuz des ez bad, 'tel bimeby Wiley seed dat Dilsey had got ter
thinkin' a heap 'bout Dave, en den he sorter hilt off aw'ile, en
purten' lack he gin Dilsey up. But he wuz one er dese yer 'ceitful
niggers, en w'ile he wuz laffin' en jokin' wid de yuther han's
'bout Dave en Dilsey, he wuz settin' a trap fer ter ketch Dave
en git Dilsey back fer hisse'f.

"Dave en Dilsey made up dere min's fer ter git married long
'bout Christmas time, w'en dey 'd hab mo' time fer a weddin'.
But 'long 'bout two weeks befo' dat time ole mars 'mence' ter
lose a heap er bacon. Eve'y night er so somebody 'ud steal a side
er bacon, er a ham, er a shoulder, er sump'n, fum one er de
smoke'ouses. De smoke'ouses wuz lock', but somebody had a
key, en manage' ter git in some way er 'nudder. Dey 's mo' ways
'n one ter skin a cat, en dey 's mo' d'n one way ter git in a
smoke'ouse—leastways dat 's w'at I hearn say. Folks w'at had
bacon fer ter sell did n' hab no trouble 'bout gittin' rid un it.
Hit wuz 'g'in de law fer ter buy things fum slabes; but Lawd!
dat law did n' 'mount ter a hill er peas. Eve'y week er so one er
dese yer big covered waggins would come 'long de road, peddlin'
terbacker en w'iskey. Dey wuz a sight er room in one er dem
big waggins, en it wuz monst'us easy fer ter swop off bacon fer
sump'n ter chaw er ter wa'm yer up in de wintertime. I s'pose
de peddlers did n' knowed dey wuz breakin' de law, caze de
niggers alluz went at night, en stayed on de dark side er de
waggin; en it wuz mighty hard fer ter tell *w'at* kine er folks dey
wuz.

"Atter two er th'ee hund'ed er meat had be'n stole', Mars
Walker call all de niggers up one ebenin', en tol' 'em dat de fus'
nigger he cot stealin' bacon on dat plantation would git sump'n
fer ter 'member it by long ez he lib'. En he say he'd gin fi' dollars
ter de nigger w'at 'skiver' de rogue. Mars Walker say he s'picion'

one er two er de niggers, but he could n' tell fer sho, en co'se
dey all 'nied it w'en he 'cuse em un it.

"Dey wa'n't no bacon stole' fer a week er so, 'tel one dark
night w'en somebody tuk a ham fum one er de smoke'ouses.
Mars Walker des cusst awful w'en he foun' out de ham wuz
gone, en say he gwine ter sarch all de niggers' cabins; w'en dis
yer Wiley I wuz tellin' yer 'bout up'n say he s'picion' who tuk
de ham, fer he seed Dave comin' 'cross de plantation fum to'ds
de smoke'ouse de night befo'. W'en Mars Walker hearn dis fum
Wiley, he went en sarch' Dave's cabin, en foun' de ham hid
under de flo'.

"Eve'ybody wuz 'stonish'; but dere wuz de ham. Co'se Dave
'nied it ter de las', but dere wuz de ham. Mars Walker say it
wuz des ez he 'spected: he did n' b'lieve in dese yer readin' en
prayin' niggers; it wuz all 'pocrisy, en sarve' Mars Dugal' right
fer 'lowin' Dave ter be readin' books w'en it wuz 'g'in' de law.

"W'en Mars Dugal' hearn 'bout de ham, he say he wuz
might'ly 'ceived en dissapp'inted in Dave. He say he would n'
nebber hab no mo' conferdence in no nigger, en Mars Walker
could do des ez he wuz a mineter wid Dave er any er de res' er
de niggers. So Mars Walker tuk'n tied Dave up en gin 'im forty;
en den he got some er dis yer wire clof w'at dey uses fer ter
make sifters out'n, en tuk'n wrap' it roun' de ham en fasten it
tergedder at de little een'. Den he tuk Dave down ter de blacksmif shop, en had Unker Silas, de plantation blacksmif, fasten a
chain ter de ham, en den fasten de yuther een' er de chain roun'
Dave's neck. En den he says ter Dave, sezee:

" 'Now, suh, yer 'll wear dat neckliss fer de nex' six mont's;
en I 'spec's yer ner none er de yuther niggers on dis plantation
won' steal no mo' bacon dyoin' er dat time.'

"Well, it des 'peared ez if fum dat time Dave did n' hab nuffin
but trouble. De niggers all turnt ag'in' 'im, caze he be'n de 'ca-
sion er Mars Dugal' turnin' 'em all ober ter Mars Walker. Mars
Dugal' wa'n't a bad marster hisse'f, but Mars Walker wuz hard
ez a rock. Dave kep' on sayin' he did n' take de ham, but none
un 'em did n' b'lieve 'im.

"Dilsey wa'n't on de plantation w'en Dave wuz 'cused er
stealin' de bacon. Ole mist'iss had sont her ter town fer a week

er so fer ter wait on one er her darters w'at had a young baby, en she did n' fine out nuffin 'bout Dave's trouble 'tel she got back ter de plantation. Dave had patien'ly endyoed de finger er scawn, en all de hard words w'at de niggers pile' on 'im, caze he wuz sho' Dilsey would stan' by 'im, en would n' b'lieve he wuz a rogue, ner none er de yuther tales de darkies wuz tellin' 'bout 'im.

"W'en Dilsey come back fum town, en got down fum behine de buggy whar she b'en ridin' wid ole mars, de fus' nigger 'oo-man she met says ter her—

" 'Is yer seed Dave, Dilsey?'

" 'No, I ain' seed Dave,' says Dilsey.

" 'Yer des oughter look at dat nigger; reckon yer would n' want 'im fer yo' junesey no mo'. Mars Walker cotch 'im stealin' bacon, en gone en fasten' a ham roun' his neck, so he can't git it off'n hisse'f. He sut'nly do look quare.' En den de 'ooman bus' out laffin' fit ter kill herse'f. W'en she got thoo laffin' she up'n tole Dilsey all 'bout de ham, en all de yuther lies w'at de niggers be'n tellin' on Dave.

"W'en Dilsey started down ter de quarters, who should she meet but Dave, comin' in fum de cotton-fiel'. She turnt her head ter one side, en purten' lack she did n' seed Dave.

" 'Dilsey!' sezee.

"Dilsey walk' right on, en did n' notice 'im.

" '*Oh*, Dilsey!'

"Dilsey did n' paid no 'tention ter 'im, en den Dave knowed some er de niggers be'n tellin' her 'bout de ham. He felt mon-st'us bad, but he 'lowed ef he could des git Dilsey fer ter listen ter 'im for a minute er so, he could make her b'lieve he did n' stole de bacon. It wuz a week er two befo' he could git a chance ter speak ter her ag'in; but fine'ly he cotch her down by de spring one day, en sezee:

" 'Dilsey, w'at fer yer won' speak ter me, en purten' lack yer doan see me? Dilsey, yer knows me too well fer ter b'lieve I'd steal, er do dis yuther wick'ness de niggers is all layin' ter me— yer *knows* I would n' do dat, Dilsey. Yer ain' gwine back on yo' Dave, is yer?'

"But w'at Dave say did n' hab no 'fec' on Dilsey. Dem lies folks b'en tellin' her had p'isen' her min' 'g'in' Dave.

" 'I doan wanter talk ter no nigger,' says she, 'w'at be'n whip'
fer stealin', en w'at gwine roun' wid sich a lookin' thing ez dat
hung roun' his neck. I's a 'spectable gal, *I* is. W'at yer call dat,
Dave? Is dat a cha'm fer to keep off witches, er is it a noo kine
er neckliss yer got?'

"Po' Dave did n' knowed w'at ter do. De las' one he had
'pended on fer ter stan' by 'im had gone back on 'im, en dey
did n' 'pear ter be nuffin mo' wuf libbin' fer. He could n' hol'
no mo' pra'r-meetin's, fer Mars Walker would n' 'low 'im ter
preach, en de darkies would n' 'a' listen' ter 'im ef he had preach.'
He did n' eben hab his Bible fer ter comfort hisse'f wid, fer Mars
Walker had tuk it erway fum 'im en burnt it up, en say ef he
ketch any mo' niggers wid Bibles on de plantation he 'd do 'em
wuss'n he done Dave.

"En ter make it still harder fer Dave, Dilsey tuk up wid Wiley. Dave could see him gwine up ter Aun' Mahaly's cabin, en
settin' out on de bench in de moonlight wid Dilsey, en singin'
sinful songs en playin' de banjer. Dave use' ter scrouch down
behine de bushes, en wonder w'at de Lawd sen' 'im all dem
tribberlations fer.

"But all er Dave's yuther troubles wa'n't nuffin side er dat
ham. He had wrap' de chain roun' wid a rag, so it did n' hurt
his neck; but w'eneber he went ter wuk, dat ham would be
in his way; he had ter do his task, howsomedever, des de
sam ez ef he did n' hab de ham. W'eneber he went ter lay
down, dat ham would be in de way. Ef he turn ober in his
sleep, dat ham would be tuggin' at his neck. It wuz de las' thing
he seed at night, en de fus' thing he seed in de mawnin'.
W'eneber he met a stranger, de ham would be de fus' thing de
stranger would see. Most un 'em would 'mence' ter laf, en whar-
eber Dave went he could see folks p'intin' at him, en year 'em
sayin':

" 'W'at kine er collar dat nigger got roun' his neck?' er, ef
dey knowed 'im, 'Is yer stole any mo' hams lately?' er 'W'at yer
take fer yo' neckliss, Dave?' er some joke er 'nuther 'bout dat
ham.

"Fus' Dave did n' mine it so much, caze he knowed he had
n' done nuffin. But bimeby he got so he could n' stan' it no
longer, en he'd hide hisse'f in de bushes w'eneber he seed any-

body comin', en alluz kep' hisse'f shet up in his cabin atter he come in fum wuk.

"It wuz monst'us hard on Dave, en bimeby, w'at wid dat ham eberlastin' en etarnally draggin' roun' his neck, he 'mence' fer ter do en say quare things, en make de niggers wonder ef he wa'n't gittin' out'n his mine. He got ter gwine roun' talkin' ter hisse'f, en singin' cornshuckin' songs, en laffin' fit ter kill 'bout nuffin. En one day he tole one er de niggers he had 'skivered a noo way fer ter raise hams—gwine ter pick 'em off'n trees, en save de expense er smoke'ouses by kyoin' 'em in de sun. En one day he up'n tole Mars Walker he got sump'n pertickler fer ter say ter 'im; en he tuk Mars Walker off ter one side, en tole 'im he wuz gwine ter show 'im a place in de swamp whar dey wuz a whole trac' er lan' covered wid ham trees.

"W'en Mars Walker hearn Dave talkin' dis kine er fooltalk, en w'en he seed how Dave wuz 'mencin' ter git behine in his wuk, en w'en he ax' de niggers en dey tole 'im how Dave be'n gwine on, he 'lowed he reckon' he 'd punish' Dave ernuff, en it mou't do mo' harm dan good fer ter keep de ham on his neck any longer. So he sont Dave down ter de blacksmif shop en had de ham tuk off. Dey wa'n't much er de ham lef' by dat time, fer de sun had melt all de fat, en de lean had all swivel' up, so dey wa'n't but th'ee er fo' poun's lef'.

"W'en de ham had be'n tuk off'n Dave, folks kinder stopped talkin' 'bout 'im so much. But de ham had be'n on his neck so long dat Dave had sorter got use' ter it. He look des lack he 'd los' sump'n fer a day er so atter de ham wuz tuk off, en did n' 'pear ter know w'at ter do wid hisse'f; en fine'ly he up'n tuk'n tied a lighterd-knot[9] ter a string, en hid it under de flo' er his cabin, en w'en nobody wuz n' lookin' he'd take it out en hang it roun' his neck, en go off in de woods en holler en sing; en he allus tied it roun' his neck w'en he went ter sleep. Fac', it 'peared lack Dave done gone clean out'n his mine. En atter a w'ile he got one er de quarest notions you eber hearn tell un. It wuz 'bout dat time dat I come back ter de plantation fer ter wuk— I had be'n out ter Mars Dugal's yuther place on Beaver Crick for a mont' er so. I had hearn 'bout Dave en de bacon, en 'bout w'at wuz gwine on on de plantation; but I did n' b'lieve w'at dey all say 'bout Dave, fer I knowed Dave w'n't dat kine er

sezee

man. One day atter I come back, me'n Dave wuz choppin' cotton tergedder, w'en Dave lean' on his hoe, en motion' fer me ter come ober close ter 'im; en den he retch ober en w'ispered ter me.

" 'Julius,' sezee, 'did yer knowed yer wuz wukkin' long yer wid a ham?'

"I could n' 'magine w'at he meant. 'G'way fum yer, Dave,' says I. 'Yer ain' wearin' no ham no mo'; try en fergit 'bout dat; 't ain' gwine ter do yer no good fer ter 'member it.'

" 'Look a-yer, Julius,' sezee, 'kin yer keep a secret?'

" 'Co'se I kin, Dave,' says I. 'I doan go roun' tellin' people w'at yuther folks says ter me.'

" 'Kin I trus' yer, Julius? Will yer cross yo' heart?'

"I cross' my heart. 'Wush I may die ef I tells a soul,' says I.

"Dave look' at me des lack he wuz lookin' thoo me en 'way on de yuther side er me, en sezee:

" 'Did yer knowed I wuz turnin' ter a ham, Julius?'

"I tried ter 'suade Dave dat dat wuz all foolishness, en dat he ought n't ter be talkin' dat-a-way—hit wa'n't right. En I tole 'im ef he'd des be patien', de time would sho'ly come w'en eve'ything would be straighten' out, en folks would fine out who de rale rogue wuz w'at stole de bacon. Dave 'peared ter listen ter w'at I say, en promise' ter do better, en stop gwine on dat-a-way; en it seem lack he pick' up a bit w'en he seed dey wuz one pusson did n' b'lieve dem tales 'bout 'im.

"Hit wa'n't long atter dat befo' Mars Archie McIntyre, ober on de Wimbleton road, 'mence' ter complain 'bout somebody stealin' chickens fum his hen'ouse. De chickens kep' on gwine, en at las' Mars Archie tole de han's on his plantation dat he gwine ter shoot de fus' man he ketch in his hen'ouse. In less'n a week atter he gin dis warnin', he cotch a nigger in de hen'ouse, en fill' 'im full er squir'l-shot. W'en he got a light, he 'skivered it wuz a strange nigger; en w'en he call' one er his own sarven's, de nigger tole 'im it wuz our Wiley. W'en Mars Archie foun' dat out, he sont ober ter our plantation fer ter tell Mars Dugal' he had shot one er his niggers, en dat he could sen' ober dere en git w'at wuz lef' un 'im.

"Mars Dugal' wuz mad at fus'; but w'en he got ober dere en hearn how it all happen', he did n' hab much ter say. Wiley wuz

shot so bad he wuz sho' he wuz gwine ter die, so he up'n says
ter ole marster:

" 'Mars Dugal',' sezee, 'I knows I's be'n a monst'us bad nigger, but befo' I go I wanter git sump'n off'n my mine. Dave did
n' steal dat bacon w'at wuz tuk out'n de smoke'ouse. *I* stole it
all, en I hid de ham under Dave's cabin fer ter th'ow de blame
on him—en may de good Lawd fergib me fer it.'

"Mars Dugal' had Wiley tuk back ter de plantation, en sont
fer a doctor fer ter pick de shot out'n 'im. En de ve'y nex'
mawnin' Mars Dugal' sont fer Dave ter come up ter de big
house; he felt kinder sorry fer de way Dave had be'n treated.
Co'se it wa'n't no fault er Mars Dugal's, but he wuz gwine ter
do w'at he could fer ter make up fer it. So he sont word down
ter de quarters fer Dave en all de yuther han's ter 'semble up in
de yard befo' de big house at sunup nex' mawnin'.

"Yearly in de mawnin' de niggers all swarm' up in de yard.
Mars Dugal' wuz feelin' so kine dat he had brung up a bairl er
cider, en tole de niggers all fer ter he'p deyselves.

"All de han's on de plantation come but Dave; en bimeby,
w'en it seem lack he wa'n't comin', Mars Dugal' sont a nigger
down ter de quarters ter look fer 'im. De sun wuz gittin' up, en
dey wuz a heap er wuk ter be done, en Mars Dugal' sorter got
ti'ed waitin'; so he up'n says:

" 'Well, boys en gals, I sont fer yer all up yer fer ter tell yer
dat all dat 'bout Dave's stealin' er de bacon wuz a mistake, ez I
s'pose yer all done hearn befo' now, en I 's mighty sorry it
happen'. I wants ter treat all my niggers right, en I wants yer all
ter know dat I sets a heap by all er my han's w'at is hones' en
smart. En I want yer all ter treat Dave des lack yer did befo' dis
thing happen', en mine w'at he preach ter yer; fer Dave is a good
nigger, en has had a hard row ter hoe. En de fus' one I ketch
sayin' anythin' 'g'in' Dave, I'll tell Mister Walker ter gin 'im
forty. Now take ernudder drink er cider all roun', en den git at
dat cotton, fer I wanter git dat Persimmon Hill trac' all pick'
ober terday.'

"W'en de niggers wuz gwine 'way, Mars Dugal' tole me fer
ter go en hunt up Dave, en bring 'im up ter de house. I went
down ter Dave's cabin, but could n' fine 'im dere. Den I look'
roun' de plantation, en in de aidge er de woods, en 'long de road;

but I could n' fine no sign er Dave. I wuz 'bout ter gin up de sarch, w'en I happen' fer ter run 'cross a foot-track w'at look' lack Dave's. I had wukked 'long wid Dave so much dat I knowed his tracks: he had a monst'us long foot, wid a holler instep, w'ich wuz sump'n skase 'mongs' black folks. So I follered dat track 'cross de fiel' fum de quarters 'tel I get ter de smoke-'ouse. De fus' thing I notice' wuz smoke comin' out'n de cracks: it wuz cu'ous, caze dey had n' be'n no hogs kill' on de plantation fer six mont' er so, en all de bacon in de smoke'ouse wuz done kyoed. I could n' 'magine fer ter sabe my life w'at Dave wuz doin' in dat smoke'ouse. I went up ter de do' en hollered:

" 'Dave!'

"Dey did n' nobody answer. I did n' wanter open de do', fer w'ite folks is monst'us perttickler 'bout dey smoke'ouses; en ef de oberseah had a-come up en cotch me in dere, he mou't not wanter b'lieve I wuz des lookin' fer Dave. So I sorter knock at de do' en call' out ag'in:

" 'O Dave, hit's me—Julius! Doan be skeered. Mars Dugal' wants yer ter come up ter de big house—he done 'skivered who stole de ham.'

"But Dave did n' answer. En w'en I look' roun' ag'in en did n' seed none er his tracks gwine way fum de smoke'ouse, I knowed he wuz in dere yit, en I wuz 'termine' fer ter fetch 'im out; so I push de do' open en look in.

"Dey wuz a pile er bark burnin' in de middle er de flo', en right ober de fier, hangin' fum one er de rafters, wuz Dave; dey wuz a rope roun' his neck, en I did n' haf ter look at his face mo' d'n once fer ter see he wuz dead.

"Den I knowed how it all happen'. Dave had kep' on gittin' wusser en wusser in his mine, 'tel he des got ter b'lievin' he wuz all done turnt ter a ham; en den he had gone en built a fier, en tied a rope roun' his neck, des lack de hams wuz tied, en had hung hisse'f up in de smoke'ouse fer ter kyo.

"Dave wuz buried down by the swamp, in de plantation buryin' groun'. Wiley did n' died fum de woun' he got in Mars McIntyre's hen'ouse; he got well atter a w'ile, but Dilsey would n' hab nuffin mo' ter do wid 'im, en 't wa'n't long 'fo' Mars Dugal' sol' 'im ter a spekilater on his way souf—he say he did n' want no sich a nigger on de plantation, ner in de county, ef he could he'p it. En w'en de een' er de year come, Mars Dugal' turnt Mars Walker off, en run de plantation hisse'f atter dat.

"Eber sence den," said Julius in conclusion, "w'eneber I eats ham, it min's me er Dave. I lacks ham, but I nebber kin eat mo' d'n two er th'ee poun's befo' I gits ter studyin' 'bout Dave, en den I has ter stop en leab de res' fer ernudder time."

There was a short silence after the old man had finished his story, and then my wife began to talk to him about the weather, on which subject he was an authority. I went into the house. When I came out, half an hour later, I saw Julius disappearing down the lane, with a basket on his arm.

At breakfast, next morning, it occurred to me that I should like a slice of ham. I said as much to my wife.

"Oh, no, John," she responded, "you shouldn't eat anything so heavy for breakfast."

I insisted.

"The fact is," she said, pensively, "I couldn't have eaten any more of that ham, so I gave it to Julius."

Did the wife hear the story?

THE SHERIFF'S CHILDREN

Branson County, North Carolina, is in a sequestered district of one of the staidest and most conservative States of the Union. Society in Branson County is almost primitive in its simplicity. Most of the white people own the farms they till, and even before the war there were no very wealthy families to force their neighbors, by comparison, into the category of "poor whites."

To Branson County, as to most rural communities in the South, the war is the one historical event that overshadows all others. It is the era from which all local chronicles are dated,— births, deaths, marriages, storms, freshets.[1] No description of the life of any Southern community would be perfect that failed to emphasize the all pervading influence of the great conflict.

Yet the fierce tide of war that had rushed through the cities and along the great highways of the country had comparatively speaking but slightly disturbed the sluggish current of life in this region, remote from railroads and navigable streams. To the north in Virginia, to the west in Tennessee, and all along the seaboard the war had raged; but the thunder of its cannon had not disturbed the echoes of Branson County, where the loudest sounds heard were the crack of some hunter's rifle, the baying of some deep-mouthed hound, or the yodel of some tuneful negro on his way through the pine forest. To the east, Sherman's army[2] had passed on its march to the sea; but no straggling band of "bummers"[3] had penetrated the confines of Branson County. The war, it is true, had robbed the county of the flower of its young manhood; but the burden of taxation, the doubt and uncertainty of the conflict, and the sting of ultimate defeat, had been borne by the people with an apathy that robbed misfortune of half its sharpness.

The nearest approach to town life afforded by Branson County is found in the little village of Troy,[4] the county seat, a hamlet with a population of four or five hundred.

Ten years make little difference in the appearance of these remote Southern towns. If a railroad is built through one of them, it infuses some enterprise; the social corpse is galvanized by the fresh blood of civilization that pulses along the farthest ramifications of our great system of commercial highways. At the period of which I write, no railroad had come to Troy. If a traveler, accustomed to the bustling life of cities, could have ridden through Troy on a summer day, he might easily have fancied himself in a deserted village. Around him he would have seen weather-beaten houses, innocent of paint, the shingled roofs in many instances covered with a rich growth of moss. Here and there he would have met a razor-backed hog lazily rooting his way along the principal thoroughfare; and more than once he would probably have had to disturb the slumbers of some yellow dog, dozing away the hours in ardent sunshine, and reluctantly yielding up his place in the middle of the dusty road.

On Saturdays the village presented a somewhat livelier appearance, and the shade trees around the court-house square and along Front Street served as hitching-posts for a goodly number of horses and mules and stunted oxen, belonging to the farmerfolk who had come in to trade at the two or three local stores.

A murder was a rare event in Branson County. Every well-informed citizen could tell the number of homicides committed in the county for fifty years back, and whether the slayer, in any given instance, had escaped, either by flight or acquittal, or had suffered the penalty of the law. So, when it became known in Troy early one Friday morning in summer, about ten years after the war, that old Captain Walker, who had served in Mexico[5] under Scott, and had left an arm on the field of Gettysburg,[6] had been foully murdered during the night, there was intense excitement in the village. Business was practically suspended, and the citizens gathered in little groups to discuss the murder, and speculate upon the identity of the murderer. It transpired from testimony at the coroner's inquest, held during the morning, that a strange mulatto[7] had been seen going in the direction of Captain Walker's house the night before, and had been met going away from Troy early Friday morning, by a farmer on his way to town. Other circumstances seemed to connect the stranger with the crime. The sheriff organized a posse to search for him, and early in the evening, when most of the citizens of Troy were at supper, the suspected man was brought in and lodged in the county jail.

By the following morning the news of the capture had spread to the farthest limits of the county. A much larger number of people than usual came to town that Saturday—bearded men in straw hats and blue homespun shirts, and butternut trousers[8] of great amplitude of material and vagueness of outline; women in homespun frocks and slat-bonnets, with faces as expressionless as the dreary sandhills which gave them a meagre sustenance.

The murder was almost the sole topic of conversation. A steady stream of curious observers visited the house of mourning, and gazed upon the rugged face of the old veteran, now stiff and cold in death; and more than one eye dropped a tear at the remembrance of the cheery smile, and the joke—sometimes superannuated, generally feeble, but always good-natured—with which the captain had been wont to greet his acquaintances. There was a growing sentiment of anger among these stern men, toward the murderer who had thus cut down their friend, and a strong feeling that ordinary justice was too slight a punishment for such a crime.

Toward noon there was an informal gathering of citizens in Dan Tyson's store.

"I hear it 'lowed that Square Kyahtah's too sick ter hol' co'te this evenin'," said one, "an' that the purlim'nary hearin' 'll haf ter go over 'tel nex' week."

A look of disappointment went round the crowd.

"Hit 's the durndes', meanes' murder ever committed in this caounty," said another, with moody emphasis.

"I s'pose the nigger 'lowed the Cap'n had some greenbacks," observed a third speaker.

"The Cap'n," said another, with an air of superior information, "has left two bairls of Confedrit money, which he 'spected 'ud be good some day er nuther."

This statement gave rise to a discussion of the speculative value of Confederate money; but in a little while the conversation returned to the murder.

"Hangin' air too good fer the murderer," said one; "he oughter be burnt, stidier bein' hung."

There was an impressive pause at this point, during which a jug of moonlight whiskey went the round of the crowd.

"Well," said a round-shouldered farmer, who, in spite of his peaceable expression and faded gray eye, was known to have been one of the most daring followers of a rebel guerrilla chieftain, "what air yer gwine ter do about it? Ef you fellers air gwine ter set down an' let a wuthless nigger kill the bes' white man in Branson, an' not say nuthin' ner do nuthin', *I'll* move outen the caounty."

This speech gave tone and direction to the rest of the conversation. Whether the fear of losing the round-shouldered farmer operated to bring about the result or not is immaterial to this narrative; but, at all events, the crowd decided to lynch[9] the negro. They agreed that this was the least that could be done to avenge the death of their murdered friend, and that it was a becoming way in which to honor his memory. They had some vague notions of the majesty of the law and the rights of the citizen, but in the passion of the moment these sunk into oblivion; a white man had been killed by a negro.

"The Cap'n was an ole sodger," said one of his friends solemnly. "He'll sleep better when he knows that a co'te-martial has be'n hilt an' jestice done."

By agreement the lynchers were to meet at Tyson's store at five o'clock in the afternoon, and proceed thence to the jail, which was situated down the Lumberton Dirt Road (as the old turnpike antedating the plank-road was called), about half a mile south of the court-house. When the preliminaries of the lynching had been arranged, and a committee appointed to manage the affair, the crowd dispersed, some to go to their dinners, and some to secure recruits for the lynching party.

It was twenty minutes to five o'clock, when an excited negro, panting and perspiring, rushed up to the back door of Sheriff Campbell's dwelling, which stood at a little distance from the jail and somewhat farther than the latter building from the court-house. A turbaned colored woman came to the door in response to the negro's knock.

"Hoddy, Sis' Nance."

"Hoddy, Brer Sam."

"Is de shurff in," inquired the negro.

"Yas, Brer Sam, he's eatin' his dinner," was the answer.

"Will yer ax 'im ter step ter de do' a minute, Sis' Nance?"

The woman went into the dining-room, and a moment later the sheriff came to the door. He was a tall, muscular man, of a ruddier complexion than is usual among Southerners. A pair of keen, deep-set gray eyes looked out from under bushy eyebrows, and about his mouth was a masterful expression, which a full beard, once sandy in color, but now profusely sprinkled with gray, could not entirely conceal. The day was hot; the sheriff had discarded his coat and vest, and had his white shirt open at the throat.

"What do you want, Sam?" he inquired of the negro, who stood hat in hand, wiping the moisture from his face with a ragged shirt-sleeve.

"Shurff, dey gwine ter hang de pris'ner w'at's lock' up in de jail. Dey're comin' dis a-way now. I wuz layin' down on a sack er corn down at de sto', behine a pile er flour-bairls, w'en I hearn Doc' Cain en Kunnel Wright talkin' erbout it. I slip' outen de back do', en run here as fas' as I could. I hearn you say down

ter de sto' once't dat you would n't let nobody take a pris'ner
'way fum you widout walkin' over yo' dead body, en I thought
I'd let you know 'fo' dey come, so yer could pertec' de pris'ner."

The sheriff listened calmly, but his face grew firmer, and a
determined gleam lit up his gray eyes. His frame grew more
erect, and he unconsciously assumed the attitude of a soldier
who momentarily expects to meet the enemy face to face.

"Much obliged, Sam," he answered. "I'll protect the prisoner.
Who's coming?"

"I dunno who-all *is* comin'," replied the negro. "Dere's Mis-
tah McSwayne, en Doc' Cain, en Maje' McDonal', en Kunnel
Wright, en a heap er yuthers. I wuz so skeered I done furgot
mo' d'n half un em. I spec' dey mus' be mos' here by dis time,
so I'll git outen de way, fer I don' want nobody fer ter think I
wuz mix' up in dis business." The negro glanced nervously
down the road toward the town, and made a movement as if to
go away.

"Won't you have some dinner first?" asked the sheriff.

The negro looked longingly in at the open door, and sniffed
the appetizing odor of boiled pork and collards.

"I ain't got no time fer ter tarry, Shurff," he said, "but Sis'
Nance mought gin me sump'n I could kyar in my han' en eat
on de way."

A moment later Nancy brought him a huge sandwich of split
corn-pone, with a thick slice of fat bacon inserted between the
halves, and a couple of baked yams. The negro hastily replaced
his ragged hat on his head, dropped the yams in the pocket of
his capacious trousers, and, taking the sandwich in his hand,
hurried across the road and disappeared in the woods beyond.

The sheriff reëntered the house, and put on his coat and hat.
He then took down a double-barreled shotgun and loaded it
with buckshot. Filling the chambers of a revolver with fresh car-
tridges, he slipped it into the pocket of the sack-coat which he
wore.

A comely young woman in a calico dress watched these pro-
ceedings with anxious surprise.

"Where are you going, father?" she asked. She had not heard
the conversation with the negro.

"I am goin' over to the jail," responded the sheriff. "There's a mob comin' this way to lynch the nigger we've got locked up. But they won't do it," he added, with emphasis.

"Oh, father! don't go!" pleaded the girl, clinging to his arm; "they'll shoot you if you don't give him up."

"You never mind me, Polly," said her father reassuringly, as he gently unclasped her hands from his arm. "I'll take care of myself and the prisoner, too. There ain't a man in Branson County that would shoot me. Besides, I have faced fire too often to be scared away from my duty. You keep close in the house," he continued, "and if any one disturbs you just use the old horse-pistol in the top bureau drawer. It's a little old-fashioned, but it did good work a few years ago."

The young girl shuddered at this sanguinary allusion, but made no further objection to her father's departure.

The sheriff of Branson was a man far above the average of the community in wealth, education, and social position. His had been one of the few families in the county that before the war had owned large estates and numerous slaves. He had graduated at the State University at Chapel Hill,[10] and had kept up some acquaintance with current literature and advanced thought. He had traveled some in his youth, and was looked up to in the county as an authority on all subjects connected with the outer world. At first an ardent supporter of the Union, he had opposed the secession movement in his native State as long as opposition availed to stem the tide of public opinion. Yielding at last to the force of circumstances, he had entered the Confederate service rather late in the war, and served with distinction through several campaigns, rising in time to the rank of colonel. After the war he had taken the oath of allegiance,[11] and had been chosen by the people as the most available candidate for the office of sheriff, to which he had been elected without opposition. He had filled the office for several terms, and was universally popular with his constituents.

Colonel or Sheriff Campbell, as he was indifferently called, as the military or civil title happened to be most important in the opinion of the person addressing him, had a high sense of the responsibility attaching to his office. He had sworn to do his duty faithfully, and he knew what his duty was, as sheriff, perhaps more clearly than he had apprehended it in other passages of his life. It was, therefore, with no uncertainty in regard to his course that he prepared his weapons and went over to the jail. He had no fears for Polly's safety.

The sheriff had just locked the heavy front door of the jail behind him when a half dozen horsemen, followed by a crowd of men on foot, came round a bend in the road and drew near the jail. They halted in front of the picket fence that surrounded the building, while several of the committee of arrangements rode on a few rods farther to the sheriff's house. One of them dismounted and rapped on the door with his riding-whip.

"Is the sheriff at home?" he inquired.

"No, he has just gone out," replied Polly, who had come to the door.

"We want the jail keys," he continued.

"They are not here," said Polly. "The sheriff has them himself." Then she added, with assumed indifference, "He is at the jail now."

The man turned away, and Polly went into the front room, from which she peered anxiously between the slats of the green blinds of a window that looked toward the jail. Meanwhile the messenger returned to his companions and announced his discovery. It looked as though the sheriff had learned of their design and was preparing to resist it.

One of them stepped forward and rapped on the jail door.

"Well, what is it?" said the sheriff, from within.

"We want to talk to you, Sheriff," replied the spokesman.

There was a little wicket[12] in the door; this the sheriff opened, and answered through it.

"All right, boys, talk away. You are all strangers to me, and I don't know what business you can have." The sheriff did not think it necessary to recognize anybody in particular on such an occasion; the question of identity sometimes comes up in the investigation of these extra-judicial executions.

"We're a committee of citizens and we want to get into the jail."

"What for? It ain't much trouble to get into jail. Most people want to keep out."

The mob was in no humor to appreciate a joke, and the sheriff's witticism fell dead upon an unresponsive audience.

"We want to have a talk with the nigger that killed Cap'n Walker."

"You can talk to that nigger in the court-house, when he's brought out for trial. Court will be in session here next week. I know what you fellows want, but you can't get my prisoner today. Do you want to take the bread out of a poor man's mouth? I get seventy-five cents a day for keeping this prisoner, and he's the only one in jail. I can't have my family suffer just to please you fellows."

One or two young men in the crowd laughed at the idea of Sheriff Campbell's suffering for want of seventy-five cents a day; but they were frowned into silence by those who stood near them.

"Ef yer don't let us in," cried a voice, "we'll bu's' the do' open."

"Bust away," answered the sheriff, raising his voice so that all could hear. "But I give you fair warning. The first man that tries it will be filled with buckshot. I'm sheriff of this county; I know my duty, and I mean to do it."

"What's the use of kicking, Sheriff?" argued one of the leaders of the mob. "The nigger is sure to hang anyhow; he richly deserves it; and we've got to do something to teach the niggers their places, or white people won't be able to live in the county."

"There's no use talking, boys," responded the sheriff. "I'm a white man outside, but in this jail I'm sheriff; and if this nigger's to be hung in this county, I propose to do the hanging. So you fellows might as well right-about-face, and march back to Troy. You've had a pleasant trip, and the exercise will be good for you. You know *me*. I've got powder and ball, and I've faced fire before now, with nothing between me and the enemy, and I don't mean to surrender this jail while I'm able to shoot." Having thus announced his determination, the sheriff closed and fastened the wicket, and looked around for the best position from which to defend the building.

The crowd drew off a little, and the leaders conversed together in low tones.

The Branson County jail was a small, two-story brick build-

ing, strongly constructed, with no attempt at architectural ornamentation. Each story was divided into two large cells by a
passage running from front to rear. A grated iron door gave
entrance from the passage to each of the four cells. The jail seldom had many prisoners in it, and the lower windows had been
boarded up. When the sheriff had closed the wicket, he ascended
the steep wooden stairs to the upper floor. There was no window
at the front of the upper passage, and the most available position
from which to watch the movements of the crowd below was
the front window of the cell occupied by the solitary prisoner.

The sheriff unlocked the door and entered the cell. The prisoner was crouched in a corner, his yellow face, blanched with
terror, looking ghastly in the semi-darkness of the room. A cold
perspiration had gathered on his forehead, and his teeth were
chattering with affright.

"For God's sake, Sheriff," he murmured hoarsely, "don't let
'em lynch me; I did n't kill the old man."

The sheriff glanced at the cowering wretch with a look of
mingled contempt and loathing.

"Get up," he said sharply. "You will probably be hung
sooner or later, but it shall not be to-day, if I can help it. I'll
unlock your fetters, and if I can't hold the jail, you'll have to
make the best fight you can. If I'm shot, I'll consider my responsibility at an end."

There were iron fetters on the prisoner's ankles, and hand-
cuffs on his wrists. These the sheriff unlocked, and they fell
clanking to the floor.

"Keep back from the window," said the sheriff. "They might
shoot if they saw you."

The sheriff drew toward the window a pine bench which
formed a part of the scanty furniture of the cell, and laid his
revolver upon it. Then he took his gun in hand, and took his
stand at the side of the window where he could with least exposure of himself watch the movements of the crowd below.

The lynchers had not anticipated any determined resistance.
Of course they had looked for a formal protest, and perhaps a
sufficient show of opposition to excuse the sheriff in the eye of
any stickler for legal formalities. They had not, however, come
prepared to fight a battle, and no one of them seemed willing to

lead an attack upon the jail. The leaders of the party conferred together with a good deal of animated gesticulation, which was visible to the sheriff from his outlook, though the distance was too great for him to hear what was said. At length one of them broke away from the group, and rode back to the main body of the lynchers, who were restlessly awaiting orders.

"Well, boys," said the messenger, "we'll have to let it go for the present. The sheriff says he'll shoot, and he's got the drop on us this time. There ain't any of us that want to follow Cap'n Walker jest yet. Besides, the sheriff is a good fellow, and we don't want to hurt 'im. But," he added, as if to reassure the crowd, which began to show signs of disappointment, "the nigger might as well say his prayers, for he ain't got long to live."

There was a murmur of dissent from the mob, and several voices insisted that an attack be made on the jail. But pacific counsels finally prevailed, and the mob sullenly withdrew.

The sheriff stood at the window until they had disappeared around the bend in the road. He did not relax his watchfulness when the last one was out of sight. Their withdrawal might be a mere feint, to be followed by a further attempt. So closely, indeed, was his attention drawn to the outside, that he neither saw nor heard the prisoner creep stealthily across the floor, reach out his hand and secure the revolver which lay on the bench behind the sheriff, and creep as noiselessly back to his place in the corner of the room.

A moment after the last of the lynching party had disappeared there was a shot fired from the woods across the road; a bullet whistled by the window and buried itself in the wooden casing a few inches from where the sheriff was standing. Quick as thought, with the instinct borne of a semi-guerrilla army experience, he raised his gun and fired twice at the point from which a faint puff of smoke showed the hostile bullet to have been sent. He stood a moment watching, and then rested his gun against the window, and reached behind him mechanically for the other weapon. It was not on the bench. As the sheriff realized this fact, he turned his head and looked into the muzzle of the revolver.

"Stay where you are, Sheriff," said the prisoner, his eyes glistening, his face almost ruddy with excitement.

The sheriff mentally cursed his own carelessness for allowing him to be caught in such a predicament. He had not expected anything of the kind. He had relied on the negro's cowardice and subordination in the presence of an armed white man as a matter of course. The sheriff was a brave man, but realized that the prisoner had him at an immense disadvantage. The two men stood thus for a moment, fighting a harmless duel with their eyes.

"Well, what do you mean to do?" asked the sheriff with apparent calmness.

"To get away, of course," said the prisoner, in a tone which caused the sheriff to look at him more closely, and with an involuntary feeling of apprehension; if the man was not mad, he was in a state of mind akin to madness, and quite as dangerous. The sheriff felt that he must speak the prisoner fair, and watch for a chance to turn the tables on him. The keen-eyed, desperate man before him was a different being altogether from the groveling wretch who had begged so piteously for life a few minutes before.

At length the sheriff spoke:—

"Is this your gratitude to me for saving your life at the risk of my own? If I had not done so, you would now be swinging from the limb of some neighboring tree."

"True," said the prisoner, "you saved my life, but for how long? When you came in, you said Court would sit next week. When the crowd went away they said I had not long to live. It is merely a choice of two ropes."

"While there's life there's hope." replied the sheriff. He uttered this commonplace mechanically, while his brain was busy in trying to think out some way of escape. "If you are innocent you can prove it."

The mulatto kept his eye upon the sheriff. "I did n't kill the old man," he replied; "but I shall never be able to clear myself. I was at his house at nine o'clock. I stole from it the coat that was on my back when I was taken. I would be convicted, even with a fair trial, unless the real murderer were discovered beforehand."

The sheriff knew this only too well. While he was thinking what argument next to use, the prisoner continued:—

"Throw me the keys—no, unlock the door."

The sheriff stood a moment irresolute. The mulatto's eye glittered ominously. The sheriff crossed the room and unlocked the door leading into the passage.

"Now go down and unlock the outside door."

The heart of the sheriff leaped within him. Perhaps he might make a dash for liberty, and gain the outside. He descended the narrow stairs, the prisoner keeping close behind him.

The sheriff inserted the huge iron key into the lock. The rusty bolt yielded slowly. It still remained for him to pull the door open.

"Stop!" thundered the mulatto, who seemed to divine the sheriff's purpose. "Move a muscle, and I'll blow your brains out."

The sheriff obeyed; he realized that his chance had not yet come.

"Now keep on that side of the passage, and go back upstairs."

Keeping the sheriff under cover of the revolver, the mulatto followed him up the stairs. The sheriff expected the prisoner to lock him into the cell and make his own escape. He had about come to the conclusion that the best thing he could do under the circumstances was to submit quietly, and take his chances of recapturing the prisoner after the alarm had been given. The sheriff had faced death more than once upon the battlefield. A few minutes before, well armed, and with a brick wall between him and them, he had dared a hundred men to fight; but he felt instinctively that the desperate man confronting him was not to be trifled with, and he was too prudent a man to risk his life against such heavy odds. He had Polly to look after, and there was a limit beyond which devotion to duty would be quixotic and even foolish.

"I want to get away," said the prisoner, "and I don't want to be captured; for if I am I know I will be hung on the spot. I am afraid," he added somewhat reflectively, "that in order to save myself I shall have to kill you."

"Good God!" exclaimed the sheriff in involuntary terror; "you would not kill the man to whom you owe your own life."

"You speak more truly than you know," replied the mulatto. "I indeed owe my life to you."

The sheriff started. He was capable of surprise, even in that moment of extreme peril. "Who are you?" he asked in amazement.

"Tom, Cicely's son," returned the other. He had closed the door and stood talking to the sheriff through the grated opening. "Don't you remember Cicely—Cicely whom you sold, with her child, to the speculator on his way to Alabama?"

The sheriff did remember. He had been sorry for it many a time since. It had been the old story of debts, mortgages, and bad crops. He had quarreled with the mother. The price offered for her and her child had been unusually large, and he had yielded to the combination of anger and pecuniary stress.

"Good God!" he gasped, "you would not murder your own father?"

"My father?" replied the mulatto. "It were well enough for me to claim the relationship, but it comes with poor grace from you to ask anything by reason of it. What father's duty have you ever performed for me? Did you give me your name, or even your protection? Other white men gave their colored sons freedom and money, and sent them to the free States. *You* sold *me* to the rice swamps."

"I at least gave you the life you cling to," murmured the sheriff.

"Life?" said the prisoner, with a sarcastic laugh. "What kind of a life? You gave me your own blood, your own features,—no man need look at us together twice to see that,—and you gave me a black mother. Poor wretch! She died under the lash, because she had enough womanhood to call her soul her own. You gave me a white man's spirit, and you made me a slave, and crushed it out."

"But you are free now," said the sheriff. He had not doubted, could not doubt, the mulatto's word. He knew whose passions coursed beneath that swarthy skin and burned in the black eyes opposite his own. He saw in this mulatto what he himself might have become had not the safeguards of parental restraint and public opinion been thrown around him.

"Free to do what?" replied the mulatto. "Free in name, but despised and scorned and set aside by the people to whose race I belong far more than to my mother's."

"There are schools," said the sheriff. "You have been to school." He had noticed that the mulatto spoke more eloquently and used better language than most Branson County people.

"I have been to school, and dreamed when I went that it would work some marvelous change in my condition. But what did I learn? I learned to feel that no degree of learning or wisdom will change the color of my skin and that I shall always wear what in my own country is a badge of degradation. When I think about it seriously I do not care particularly for such a life. It is the animal in me, not the man, that flees the gallows. I owe you nothing," he went on, "and expect nothing of you; and it would be no more than justice if I should avenge upon you my mother's wrongs and my own. But still I hate to shoot you; I have never yet taken human life—for I did *not* kill the old captain. Will you promise to give no alarm and make no attempt to capture me until morning, if I do not shoot?"

So absorbed were the two men in their colloquy and their own tumultuous thoughts that neither of them had heard the door below move upon its hinges. Neither of them had heard a light step come stealthily up the stairs, nor seen a slender form creep along the darkening passage toward the mulatto.

The sheriff hesitated. The struggle between his love of life and his sense of duty was a terrific one. It may seem strange that a man who could sell his own child into slavery should hesitate at such a moment, when his life was trembling in the balance. But the baleful influence of human slavery poisoned the very fountains of life, and created new standards of right. The sheriff was conscientious; his conscience had merely been warped by his environment. Let no one ask what his answer would have been; he was spared the necessity of a decision.

"Stop," said the mulatto, "you need not promise. I could not trust you if you did. It is your life for mine; there is but one safe way for me; you must die."

He raised his arm to fire, when there was a flash—a report from the passage behind him. His arm fell heavily at his side, and the pistol dropped at his feet.

The sheriff recovered first from his surprise, and throwing open the door secured the fallen weapon. Then seizing the prisoner he thrust him into the cell and locked the door upon him;

after which he turned to Polly, who leaned half-fainting against the wall, her hands clasped over her heart.

"Oh, father, I was just in time!" she cried hysterically, and, wildly sobbing, threw herself into her father's arms.

"I watched until they all went away," she said. "I heard the shot from the woods and I saw you shoot. Then when you did not come out I feared something had happened, that perhaps you had been wounded. I got out the other pistol and ran over here. When I found the door open, I knew something was wrong, and when I heard voices I crept upstairs, and reached the top just in time to hear him say he would kill you. Oh, it was a narrow escape!"

When she had grown somewhat calmer, the sheriff left her standing there and went back into the cell. The prisoner's arm was bleeding from a flesh wound. His bravado had given place to a stony apathy. There was no sign in his face of fear or disappointment or feeling of any kind. The sheriff sent Polly to the house for cloth, and bound up the prisoner's wound with a rude skill acquired during his army life.

"I'll have a doctor come and dress the wound in the morning," he said to the prisoner. "It will do very well until then, if you will keep quiet. If the doctor asks you how the wound was caused, you can say that you were struck by the bullet fired from the woods. It would do you no good to have it known that you were shot while attempting to escape."

The prisoner uttered no word of thanks or apology, but sat in sullen silence. When the wounded arm had been bandaged, Polly and her father returned to the house.

The sheriff was in an unusually thoughtful mood that evening. He put salt in his coffee at supper, and poured vinegar over his pancakes. To many of Polly's questions he returned random answers. When he had gone to bed he lay awake for several hours.

In the silent watches of the night, when he was alone with God, there came into his mind a flood of unaccustomed thoughts. An hour or two before, standing face to face with death, he had experienced a sensation similar to that which drowning men are said to feel—a kind of clarifying of the moral faculty, in which the veil of the flesh, with its obscuring passions and prejudices, is pushed aside for a moment, and all the acts of one's life stand out, in the clear light of truth, in their correct proportions and relations,—a state of mind in which one sees himself as God may be supposed to see him. In the reaction following his rescue, this feeling had given place for a time to far different emotions. But now, in the silence of midnight, something of this clearness of spirit returned to the sheriff. He saw that he had owed some duty to this son of his,—that neither law nor custom could destroy a responsibility inherent in the nature of mankind. He could not thus, in the eyes of God at least, shake off the consequences of his sin. Had he never sinned, this wayward spirit would never have come back from the vanished past to haunt him. As these thoughts came, his anger against the mulatto died away, and in its place there sprang up a great pity. The hand of parental authority might have restrained the passions he had seen burning in the prisoner's eyes when the desperate man spoke the words which had seemed to doom his father to death. The sheriff felt that he might have saved this fiery spirit from the slough of slavery; that he might have sent him to the free North, and given him there, or in some other land, an opportunity to turn to usefulness and honorable pursuits the talents that had run to crime, perhaps to madness; he might, still less, have given this son of his the poor simulacrum of liberty which men of his caste could possess in a slaveholding community; or least of all, but still something, he might have kept the boy on the plantation, where the burdens of slavery would have fallen lightly upon him.

The sheriff recalled his own youth. He had inherited an honored name to keep untarnished; he had had a future to make; the picture of a fair young bride had beckoned him on to happiness. The poor wretch now stretched upon a pallet of straw between the brick walls of the jail had had none of these things,—no name, no father, no mother—in the true meaning of motherhood,—and until the past few years no possible future, and then one vague and shadowy in its outline, and dependent for form and substance upon the slow solution of a problem in which there were many unknown quantities.

From what he might have done to what he might yet do was an easy transition for the awakened conscience of the sheriff. It occurred to him, purely as a hypothesis, that he might permit his prisoner to escape; but his oath of office, his duty as sheriff, stood in the way of such a course, and the sheriff dismissed the idea from his mind. He could, however, investigate the circumstances of the murder, and move Heaven and earth to discover the real criminal, for he no longer doubted the prisoner's innocence; he could employ counsel for the accused, and perhaps influence public opinion in his favor. An acquittal once secured, some plan could be devised by which the sheriff might in some degree atone for his crime against this son of his—against society—against God.

When the sheriff had reached this conclusion he fell into an unquiet slumber, from which he awoke late the next morning.

He went over to the jail before breakfast and found the prisoner lying on his pallet, his face turned to the wall; he did not move when the sheriff rattled the door.

"Good-morning," said the latter, in a tone intended to waken the prisoner.

There was no response. The sheriff looked more keenly at the recumbent figure; there was an unnatural rigidity about its attitude.

He hastily unlocked the door and, entering the cell, bent over the prostrate form. There was no sound of breathing; he turned the body over—it was cold and stiff. The prisoner had torn the bandage from his wound and bled to death during the night. He had evidently been dead several hours.

ALICE DUNBAR-NELSON

1875–1935

ALTHOUGH she published only two volumes of short stories, Alice Moore Dunbar-Nelson is acclaimed as one of the finest African American short story writers of the turn of the century. Born in New Orleans to middle-class working parents, she studied at Straight College in New Orleans, Pennsylvania School of Industrial Arts, and the University of Pennsylvania, and she earned an M.A. at Cornell University. She began a career teaching kindergarten in New Orleans and at public schools in Brooklyn and Harlem, during which time she submitted poetry to the Boston *Monthly Review*. In 1889 she married Paul Laurence Dunbar but separated from him in 1902; though she married twice more, evidence suggests she also had lesbian relationships during the 1920s. Dunbar-Nelson continued teaching, first at Howard High School in Delaware and then at the State College for Colored Students (now Delaware State College).

Active in journalism throughout her life, she was associate editor of the *Wilmington Advocate*, a newspaper devoted to equal rights for African Americans; wrote for the Washington *Eagle*; and helped to edit the *A.M.E. Church Review*. Some of her writing was also syndicated by the Associated Negro Press. In the 1890s she was secretary of the National Association of Colored Women, and later was active in the struggle for woman suffrage, the campaign against lynching, and various organizations addressing women's rights, politics, African American issues, and social reform. Her first volume of poems and stories, *Violets and Other Tales*, was published in 1895; her second, a collection of New Orleans local color stories titled *The Goodness of St. Rocque and Other Stories*, appeared in 1899. Her personal journal was also published in 1984 under the title *Give Us Each Day*.

The praline woman sits by the side of the Archbishop's quaint little old chapel on Royal Street, and slowly waves her latanier fan over the pink and brown wares.

"Pralines, pralines. Ah, ma'amzelle, you buy? S'il vous plaît,[1] ma'amzelle, ces pralines, dey be fine, ver' fresh.

"Mais non, maman,[2] you are not sure?

"Sho', chile, ma bébé, ma petite,[3] she put dese up hissef. He's han's so small, ma'amzelle, lak you's, mais brune.[4] She put dese up dis morn'. You tak' none? No husban' fo' you den!

"Ah, ma petite, you tak'? Cinq sous, bébé, may le bon Dieu[5] keep you good!

"Mais oui, madame, I know you étrangér. You don' look lak dese New Orleans peop'. You lak' dose Yankee dat come down 'fo' de war."

Ding-dong, ding-dong, ding-dong, chimes the Cathedral bell across Jackson Square, and the praline woman crosses herself.

"Hail, Mary, full of grace—

"Pralines, madame? You buy lak' dat? Dix sous,[6] madame, an' one lil' piece fo' lagniappe[7] fo' madame's lil' bébé. Ah, c'est bon![8]

"Pralines, pralines, so fresh, so fine! M'sieu would lak' some fo' he's lil' gal' at home? Mais non, what's dat you say? She's daid! Ah, m'sieu, 't is my lil' gal what died long year ago. Misère, misère![9]

"Here come dat lazy Indien squaw. What she good fo', any-how? She jes' sit lak dat in de French Market an' sell her filé,[10] an' sleep, sleep, sleep, lak' so in he's blanket. Hey, dere, you, Tonita, how goes you' beezness?

"Pralines, pralines! Holy Father, you give me dat blessin' sho'? Tak' one, I know you lak dat w'ite one. It tas' good, I know, bien.

"Pralines, madame? I lak' you' face. What fo' you wear black? You' lil' boy daid? You tak' one, jes' see how it tas'. I had one lil' boy once, he jes' grow 'twell he's big lak' dis, den one day he tak' sick an' die. Oh, madame, it mos' brek my po' heart. I burn candle in St. Rocque,[11] I say my beads, I sprinkle holy water roun' he's bed; he jes' lay so, he's eyes turn up, he say 'Maman, maman,' den he die! Madame, you tak' one. Non, non, no l'argent,[12] you tak' one fo' my lil' boy's sake.

"Pralines, pralines, m'sieu? Who mak' dese? My lil' gal, Didele, of co'se. Non, non, I don't mak' no mo'. Po' Tante Marie get too ol'. Didele? She's one lil' gal I 'dopt. I see her one day in de strit. He walk so; hit col' she shiver, an' I say, 'Where you gone, lil' gal?' and he can' tell. He jes' crip close to me, an' cry so! Den I tak' her home wid me, and she say he's name Didele. You see dey wa'nt nobody dere. My lil' gal, she's daid of de yellow fever; my lil' boy, he's daid, po' Tante Marie all alone. Didele, she grow fine, she keep house an' mek' pralines. Den, when night come, she sit wid he's guitar an' sing,

" 'Tu l'aime ces trois jours,
Tu l'aime ces trois jours,
Ma coeur à toi,
Ma coeur à toi,
Tu l'aime ces trois jours!'

"Ah, he's fine gal, is Didele!

"Pralines, pralines! Dat lil' cloud, h'it look lak' rain, I hope no.

"Here come dat lazy I'ishman down de strit. I don't lak' I'ishman, me, non, dey so funny. One day one I'ishman, he say to me, 'Auntie, what fo' you talk so?' and I jes' say back, 'What fo' you say "Faith an' be jabers"?' Non, I don' lak I'ishman, me!

"Here come de rain! Now I got fo' to go. Didele, she be wait fo' me. Down h'it come! H'it fall in de Meesseesip, an' fill up —up—so, clean to de levee, den we have big crivasse,[13] an' po' Tante Marie float away. Bon jour, madame, you come again? Pralines! Pralines!"

Victor Grabért strode down the one, wide, tree-shaded street of the village, his heart throbbing with a bitterness and anger that seemed too great to bear. So often had he gone home in the same spirit, however, that it had grown nearly second nature to him —this dull, sullen resentment, flaming out now and then into almost murderous vindictiveness. Behind him there floated derisive laughs and shouts, the taunts of little brutes, boys of his own age.

He reached the tumble down cottage at the farther end of the street and flung himself on the battered step. Grandmére Grabért sat rocking herself to and fro, crooning a bit of song brought over from the West Indies years ago; but when the boy sat silent, his head bowed in his hands she paused in the midst of a line and regarded him with keen, piercing eyes.

"Eh, Victor?" she asked. That was all, but he understood. He raised his head and waved a hand angrily down the street towards the lighted square that marked the village center.

"Dose boy," he gulped.

Grandmére Grabért laid a sympathetic hand on his black curls, but withdrew it the next instant.

"Bien," she said angrily, "Fo' what you go by dem, eh? W'y not keep to yo'self? Dey don' want you, dey don' care fo' you. H'ain' you got no sense?"

"Oh, but Grandmére," he wailed piteously, "I wan' fo' to play."

The old woman stood up in the doorway, her tall, spare form towering menacingly over him.

"You wan' fo' to play, eh? Fo' w'y? You don' need no play. Dose boy," she swept a magnificent gesture down the street, "Dey fools!"

"Eef I could play wid—" began Victor, but his grandmother caught him by the wrist, and held him as in a vise.

"Hush," she cried, "You mus' be goin' crazy," and still holding him by the wrist, she pulled him indoors.

It was a two room house, bare and poor and miserable but

never had it seemed so meagre before to Victor as it did this night. The supper was frugal almost to the starvation point. They ate in silence, and afterwards Victor threw himself on his cot in the corner of the kitchen and closed his eyes. Grandmére Grabért thought him asleep, and closed the door noiselessly as she went into her own room. But he was awake, and his mind was like a shifting kaleidoscope of miserable incidents and heartaches. He had lived fourteen years, and he could remember most of them as years of misery. He had never known a mother's love, for his mother had died, so he was told, when he was but a few months old. No one ever spoke to him of a father, and Grandmére Grabért had been all to him. She was kind, after a stern, unloving fashion, and she provided for him as best she could. He had picked up some sort of an education at the parish school. It was a good one after its way, but his life there had been such a succession of miseries, that he rebelled one day and refused to go any more.

His earliest memories were clustered about this poor little cottage. He could see himself toddling about its broken steps, playing alone with a few broken pieces of china which his fancy magnified into glorious toys. He remembered his first whipping too. Tired one day of the loneliness which even the broken china could not mitigate, he had toddled out the side gate after a merry group of little black and yellow boys of his own age. When Grandmére Grabért, missing him from his accustomed garden corner, came to look for him, she found him sitting contentedly in the center of the group in the dusty street, all of them gravely scooping up handsful of the gravelly dirt and trickling it down their chubby bare legs. Grandmére snatched at him fiercely, and he whimpered, for he was learning for the first time what fear was.

"What you mean?" she hissed at him, "What you mean playin' in de strit wid dose niggers?" And she struck at him wildly with her open hand.

He looked up into her brown face surmounted by a wealth of curly black hair faintly streaked with gray, but he was too frightened to question.

It had been loneliness ever since. For the parents of the little black and yellow boys resenting the insult Grandmére had offered their offspring, sternly bade them have nothing more to do with Victor. Then when he toddled after some other little boys, whose faces were white like his own, they ran him away with derisive hoots of "Nigger! Nigger!" And again, he could not understand.

Hardest of all, though, was when Grandmére sternly bade him cease speaking the soft, Creole patois that they chattered together, and forced him to learn English. The result was a confused jumble which was no language at all; that when he spoke it in the streets or in the school, all the boys, white and black and yellow hooted at him and called him "White nigger! White nigger!"

He writhed on his cot that night and lived over all the anguish of his years until hot tears scalded their way down a burning face, and he fell into a troubled sleep wherein he sobbed over some dreamland miseries.

The next morning, Grandmére eyed his heavy swollen eyes sharply, and a momentary thrill of compassion passed over her and found expression in a new tenderness of manner toward him as she served his breakfast. She too, had thought over the matter in the night, and it bore fruit in an unexpected way.

Some few weeks after, Victor found himself timidly ringing the door-bell of a house on Hospital Street in New Orleans. His heart throbbed in painful unison to the jangle of the bell. How was he to know that old Madame Guichard, Grandmére's one friend in the city, to whom she had confided him, would be kind? He had walked from the river landing to the house, timidly inquiring the way of busy pedestrians. He was hungry and frightened. Never in all his life had he seen so many people before, and in all the busy streets there was not one eye which would light up with recognition when it met his own. Moreover, it had been a weary journey down the Red River,[2] thence into the Mississippi, and finally here. Perhaps it had not been devoid of interest, after its fashion, but Victor did not know. He was too heartsick at leaving home.

However, Mme. Guichard was kind. She welcomed him with a volubility and overflow of tenderness that acted like balm to the boy's sore spirit. Thence they were firm friends, even confidants.

Victor must find work to do. Grandmére Grabért's idea in sending him to New Orleans was that he might "mek one man of himse'f" as she phrased it. And Victor, grown suddenly old in the sense that he had a responsibility to bear, set about his search valiantly.

It chanced one day that he saw a sign in an old bookstore on Royal Street that stated in both French and English the need of a boy. Almost before he knew it, he had entered the shop and was gasping out some choked words to the little old man who sat behind the counter.

The old man looked keenly over his glasses at the boy and rubbed his bald head reflectively. In order to do this, he had to take off an old black silk cap which he looked at with apparent regret.

"Eh, what you say?" he asked sharply, when Victor had finished.

"I—I—want a place to work," stammered the boy again.

"Eh, you do? Well, can you read?"

"Yes sir," replied Victor.

The old man got down from his stool, came from behind the counter, and putting his finger under the boy's chin, stared hard into his eyes. They met his own unflinchingly, though there was the suspicion of pathos and timidity in their brown depths.

"Do you know where you live, eh?"

"On Hospital Street," said Victor. It did not occur to him to give the number, and the old man did not ask.

"Trés bien,"³ grunted the book-seller, and his interest relaxed. He gave a few curt directions about the manner of work Victor was to do, and settled himself again upon his stool, poring into his dingy book with renewed ardor.

Thus began Victor's commercial life. It was an easy one. At seven, he opened the shutters of the little shop and swept and dusted. At eight, the book-seller came down stairs, and passed out to get his coffee at the restaurant across the street. At eight in the evening, the shop was closed again. That was all.

Occasionally, there came a customer, but not often, for there were only odd books and rare ones in the shop, and those who came were usually old, yellow, querulous bookworms, who nosed about for hours, and went away leaving many bank notes behind them. Sometimes there was an errand to do, and sometimes there came a customer when the proprietor was out. It was an easy matter to wait on them. He had but to point to the shelves and say, "Monsieur will be in directly," and all was settled, for those who came here to buy had plenty of leisure and did not mind waiting.

So a year went by, then two and three, and the stream of Victor's life flowed smoothly on its uneventful way. He had grown tall and thin, and often Mme. Guichard would look at him and chuckle to herself, "Ha, he is lak one bean-pole, yaas, *mais*—" and there would be a world of unfinished reflection in that last word.

Victor had grown pale from much reading. Like a shadow of the old book-seller he sat day after day poring into some dusty yellow-paged book, and his mind was a queer jumble of ideas. History and philosophy and old-fashioned social economy were tangled with French romance and classic mythology and astrology and mysticism. He had made few friends, for his experience in the village had made him chary of strangers. Every week, he wrote to Grandmére Grabért and sent her part of his earnings. In his way he was happy, and if he was lonely, he had ceased to care about it, for his world was peopled with images of his own fancying.

Then all at once, the world he had built about him tumbled down, and he was left, staring helplessly at its ruins. The little book-seller died one day, and his shop and its books were sold by an unscrupulous nephew who cared not for bindings nor precious yellowed pages, but only for the grossly material things that money can buy. Victor ground his teeth as the auctioneer's strident voice sounded through the shop where all once had been hushed quiet, and wept as he saw some of his favorite books carried away by men and women, whom he was sure could not appreciate their value.

He dried his tears however, the next day when a grave faced lawyer came to the little house on Hospital Street, and informed him that he had been left a sum of money by the book-seller.

Victor sat staring at him helplessly. Money meant little to

him. He never needed it, never used it. After he had sent Grand-mére her sum each week, Mme. Guichard kept the rest and doled it out to him as he needed it for carfare and clothes.

"The interest of the money," continued the lawyer clearing his throat, "is sufficient to keep you very handsomely without touching the principal. It was my client's wish that you should enter Tulane College,[4] and there fit yourself for your profession. He had great confidence in your ability."

"Tulane College!" cried Victor. "Why—why—why—" then he stopped suddenly, and the hot blood mounted to his face. He glanced furtively about the room. Mme. Guichard was not near; the lawyer had seen no one but him. Then why tell him? His heart leaped wildly at the thought. Well, Grandmére would have willed it so.

The lawyer was waiting politely for him to finish his sentence.

"Why—why—I should have to study in order to enter there," finished Victor lamely.

"Exactly so," said Mr. Buckley, "and as I have, in a way, been appointed your guardian, I will see to that."

Victor found himself murmuring confused thanks and good-byes to Mr. Buckley. After he had gone, the boy sat down and gazed blankly at the wall. Then he wrote a long letter to Grandmére.

A week later, he changed boarding places at Mr. Buckley's advice, and entered a preparatory school for Tulane. And still, Mme. Guichard and Mr. Buckley had not met.

*   *   *

It was a handsomely furnished office on Carondelet Street in which Lawyer Grabért sat some years later. His day's work done, he was leaning back in his chair and smiling pleasantly out of the window. Within, was warmth and light and cheer; with-out, the wind howled and gusty rains beat against the window pane. Lawyer Grabért smiled again as he looked about at the comfort, and found himself half pitying those without who were forced to buffet the storm afoot. He rose finally, and donning his overcoat, called a cab and was driven to his rooms in the most fashionable part of the city. There he found his old-time college friend, awaiting him with some impatience.

"Thought you never were coming, old man," was his greeting.

Grabért smiled pleasantly, "Well, I was a bit tired, you know," he answered, "and I have been sitting idle for an hour or more, just relaxing, as it were."

Vannier laid his hand affectionately on the other's shoulder. "That was a mighty effort you made to-day," he said earnestly, "I, for one, am proud of you."

"Thank you," replied Grabért simply, and the two sat silent for a minute.

"Going to the Charles' dance to-night?" asked Vannier finally.

"I don't believe I am. I am tired and lazy."

"It will do you good. Come on."

"No, I want to read and ruminate."

"Ruminate over your good fortune of to-day?"

"If you will have it so, yes."

But it must not simply over his good fortune of that day over which Grabért pondered. It was over the good fortune of the past fifteen years. From school to college, and from college to law school he had gone, and thence into practice, and he was now accredited a successful young lawyer. His small fortune, which Mr. Buckley, with generous kindness, had invested wisely, had almost doubled, and his school career, while not of the brilliant, meteoric kind, had been pleasant and profitable. He had made friends, at first, with the boys he met and they in turn, had taken him into their homes. Now and then, the Buckleys asked him to dinner, and he was seen occasionally in their box at the opera. He was rapidly becoming a social favorite, and girls vied with each other to dance with him. No one had asked any questions, and he had volunteered no information concerning himself. Vannier, who had known him in preparatory school days, had said that he was a young country fellow with some money, no connections, and a ward of Mr. Buckley's, and somehow, contrary to the usual social custom of the South, this meagre account had passed muster. But Vannier's family had been a social arbiter for many years, and Grabért's personality was pleasing, without being aggressive, so he had passed through the portals of the social world and was in the inner circle.

One year, when he and Vannier were in Switzerland, pretending to climb impossible mountains and in reality smoking many cigars a day on hotel porches, a letter came to Grabért from the priest of his old-time town, telling him that Grandmére Grabért had been laid away in the parish church-yard. There was no more to tell. The little old hut had been sold to pay funeral expenses.

"Poor Grandmére," sighed Victor, "She did care for me after her fashion. I'll go take a look at her grave when I go back."

But he did not go, for when he returned to Louisiana, he was too busy, then he decided that it would be useless, sentimental folly. Moreover, he had no love for the old village. Its very name suggested things that made him turn and look about him nervously. He had long since eliminated Mme. Guichard from his list of acquaintances.

And yet, as he sat there in his cozy study that night, and smiled as he went over in his mind triumph after triumph which he had made since the old bookstore days in Royal Street, he was conscious of a subtle undercurrent of annoyance; a sort of mental reservation that placed itself on every pleasant memory.

"I wonder what's the matter with me?" he asked himself as he rose and paced the floor impatiently. Then he tried to recall his other triumph, the one of the day. The case of Tate vs. Tate, a famous will contest, had been dragging through the courts for seven years and his speech had decided it that day. He could hear the applause of the courtroom as he sat down, but it rang hollow in his ears, for he remembered another scene. The day before he had been in another court, and found himself interested in the prisoner before the bar. The offence was a slight one, a mere technicality. Grabért was conscious of a something pleasant in the man's face; a scrupulous neatness in his dress, an unostentatious conforming to the prevailing style. The Recorder, however, was short and brusque.

"Wilson—Wilson—" he growled, "Oh, yes, I know you, always kicking up some sort of a row about theatre seats and cars.[5] Hum-um. What do you mean by coming before me with a flower in your buttonhole?"

The prisoner looked down indifferently at the bud on his coat, and made no reply.

"Hey?" growled the Recorder. "You niggers are putting yourselves up too much for me."

At the forbidden word, the blood rushed to Grabért's face, and he started from his seat angrily. The next instant, he had recovered himself and buried his face in a paper. After Wilson had paid his fine, Grabért looked at him furtively as he passed out. His face was perfectly impassive, but his eyes flashed defiantly. The lawyer was tingling with rage and indignation, although the affront had not been given him.

"If Recorder Grant had any reason to think that I was in any way like Wilson, I would stand no better show," he mused bitterly.

However, as he thought it over to-night, he decided that he was a sentimental fool. "What have I to do with them?" he asked himself, "I must be careful."

The next week, he discharged the man who cared for his office. He was a Negro, and Grabért had no fault to find with him generally, but he found himself with a growing sympathy toward the man, and since the episode in the courtroom, he was morbidly nervous lest a something in his manner would betray him. Thereafter, a round-eyed Irish boy cared for his rooms.

The Vanniers were wont to smile indulgently at his every move. Elise Vannier particularly, was more than interested in his work. He had a way of dropping in of evenings and talking over his cases and speeches with her in a cosy corner of the library. She had a gracious sympathetic manner that was soothing and a cheery fund of repartee to whet her conversation. Victor found himself drifting into sentimental bits of talk now and then. He found himself carrying around in his pocketbook,[6] a faded rose which she had once worn, and when he laughed at it one day and started to throw it in the wastebasket, he suddenly kissed it instead, and replaced it in the pocketbook. That Elise was not indifferent to him he could easily see. She had not learned yet how to veil her eyes and mask her face under a cool assumption of superiority. She would give him her hand when they met with a girlish impulsiveness, and her color came and went under his gaze. Sometimes, when he held her hand a bit longer than necessary, he could feel it flutter in his own, and she would sigh a quick little gasp that made his heart leap and choked his utterance.

They were tucked away in their usual cosy corner one evening, and the conversation had drifted to the problem of where they would spend the summer.

"Papa wants to go to the country house," pouted Elise, "and mama and I don't want to go. It isn't fair, of course, because when we go so far away, Papa can be with us only for a few weeks when he can get away from his office, while if we go to the country place, he can run up every few days. But it is so dull there, don't you think so?"

Victor recalled some pleasant vacation days at the plantation home and laughed, "Not if you are there."

"Yes, but you see, I can't take myself for a companion. Now if you'll promise to come up sometimes, it will be better."

"If I may, I shall be delighted to come."

Elise laughed intimately, "If you may—" she replied, "as if such a word had to enter into our plans. Oh, but Victor, haven't you some sort of plantation somewhere? It seems to me that I heard Steven years ago speak of your home in the country, and I wondered sometimes that you never spoke of it, or ever mentioned having visited it."

The girl's artless words were bringing cold sweat to Victor's brow, his tongue felt heavy and useless, but he managed to answer quietly, "I have no home in the country."

"Well, didn't you ever own one, or your family?"

"It was old quite a good many years ago," he replied, and a vision of the little old hut with its tumble down steps and weed-grown garden came into his mind.

"Where was it?" pursued Elise innocently.

"Oh, away up in St. Landry parish,[7] too far away from civilization to mention." He tried to laugh, but it was a hollow forced attempt that rang false. But Elise was too absorbed in her own thoughts of the summer to notice.

"And you haven't a relative living?" she continued.

"Not one."

"How strange. Why it seems to me if I did not have a half a hundred cousins and uncles and aunts that I should feel somehow out of touch with the world."

He did not reply, and she chattered away on another topic.

When he was alone in his room that night, he paced the floor again, chewing wildly at a cigar that he had forgotten to light.

"What did she mean? What did she mean?" he asked himself over and over. Could she have heard or suspected anything that she was trying to find out about? Could any action, any unguarded expression of his have set the family thinking? But he soon dismissed the thought as unworthy of him. Elise was too frank and transparent a girl to stoop to subterfuge. If she wished to know anything, she was wont to ask out at once, and if she had once thought anyone was sailing under false colors, she would say so frankly, and dismiss them from her presence.

Well, he must be prepared to answer questions if he were going to marry her. The family would want to know all about him, and Elise, herself, would be curious for more than her brother, Steve Vannier's meagre account. But was he going to marry Elise? That was the question.

He sat down and buried his head in his hands. Would it be right for him to take a wife, especially such a woman as Elise, and from such a family as the Vanniers? Would it be fair? Would it be just? If they knew and were willing, it would be different. But they did not know, and they would not consent if they did. In fancy, he saw the dainty girl whom he loved, shrinking from him as he told her of Grandmére Grabért and the village boys. This last thought made him set his teeth hard, and the hot blood rushed to his face.

Well, why not, after all, why not? What was the difference between him and the hosts of other suitors who hovered about Elise? They had money; so had he. They had education, polite training, culture, social position; so had he. But they had family traditions, and he had none. Most of them could point to a long line of family portraits with justifiable pride; while if he had had a picture of Grandmére Grabért, he would have destroyed it fearfully, lest it fall into the hands of some too curious person. This was the subtle barrier that separated them. He recalled with a sting how often he had had to sit silent and constrained when the conversation turned to ancestors and family traditions. He might be one with his companions and friends in everything but this. He must ever be on the outside, hovering at the gates, as it were. Into the inner life of his social world, he might never enter. The charming impoliteness of an intercourse begun by their fathers and grandfathers, was not for him. There must always be a certain formality with him, even though they were his most intimate friends. He had not fifty cousins, therefore, as Elise phrased it, he was "out of touch with the world."

"If ever I have a son or a daughter," he found himself saying unconsciously, "I would try to save him from this."

Then he laughed bitterly as he realized the irony of the thought. Well, anyway, Elise loved him. There was a sweet consolation in that. He had but to look into her frank eyes and read her soul. Perhaps she wondered why he had not spoken. Should he speak? There he was back at the old question again.

"According to the standard of the world," he mused reflectively, "my blood is tainted in two ways. Who knows it? No one but myself, and I shall not tell. Otherwise, I am quite as good as the rest, and Elise loves me."

But even this thought failed of its sweetness in a moment. Elise loved him because she did not know. He found a sickening anger and disgust rising in himself at a people whose prejudices made him live a life of deception. He would cater to their traditions no longer; he would be honest. Then he found himself shrinking from the alternative with a dread that made him wonder. It was the old problem of his life in the village; and the boys, both white and black and yellow, stood as before, with stones in their hands to hurl at him.

He went to bed worn out with the struggle, but still with no definite idea what to do. Sleep was impossible. He rolled and tossed miserably, and cursed the fate that had thrown him in such a position. He had never thought very seriously over the subject before. He had rather drifted with the tide and accepted what came to him as a sort of recompense the world owed him for his unhappy childhood. He had known fear, yes, and qualms now and then, and a hot resentment occasionally when the outsideness of his situation was inborne to him; but that was all. Elise had awakened a disagreeable conscientiousness within him, which he decided was as unpleasant as it was unnecessary.

He could not sleep, so he arose, and dressing, walked out and stood on the banquette.[8] The low hum of the city came to him like the droning of some sleepy insect, and ever and anon, the quick flash and fire of the gas houses[9] like a huge winking fiery eye lit up the south of the city. It was inexpressingly soothing to Victor; the great unknowing city, teeming with life and with lives whose sadness mocked his own teacup tempest. He smiled and shook himself as a dog shakes off the water from his coat.

"I think a walk will help me out," he said absently, and presently he was striding down St. Charles Avenue, around Lee Circle and down to Canal Street, where the lights and glare absorbed him for a while. He walked out the wide boulevard towards Claiborne Street, hardly thinking, hardly realizing that he was walking. When he was thoroughly worn out, he retraced his steps and dropped wearily into a restaurant near Bourbon Street.

"Hullo!" said a familiar voice from a table as he entered. Victor turned and recognized Frank Ward, a little oculist, whose office was in the same building as his own.

"Another night owl besides myself," laughed Ward, making room for him at his table. "Can't you sleep too, old fellow?"

"Not very well," said Victor taking the proferred seat, "I believe I'm getting nerves. Think I need toning up."

"Well, you'd have been toned up if you had been in here a few minutes ago. Why—why—" and Ward went off into peals of laughter at the memory of the scene.

"What was it?" asked Victor.

"Why—a fellow came in here, nice sort of fellow, apparently, and wanted to have supper. Well, would you believe it, when they wouldn't serve him, he wanted to fight everything in sight. It was positively exciting for a time."

"Why wouldn't the waiter serve him?" Victor tried to make his tone indifferent, but he felt the quaver in his voice.

"Why? Why, he was a darkey, you know."

"Well, what of it?" demanded Grabért fiercely, "Wasn't he quiet, well-dressed, polite? Didn't he have money?"

"My dear fellow," began Ward mockingly, "Upon my word, I believe you are losing your mind. You do need toning up or something. Would you—could you—?"

"Oh, pshaw," broke in Grabért, "I—I—believe I am losing my mind. Really, Ward, I need something to make me sleep. My head aches."

Ward was at once all sympathy and advice, and chiding to the waiter for his slowness in filling their order. Victor toyed with his food, and made an excuse to leave the restaurant as soon as he could decently.

"Good heavens," he said when he was alone, "What will I do next?" His outburst of indignation at Ward's narrative had come from his lips almost before he knew it, and he was frightened, frightened at his own unguardedness. He did not know what had come over him.

"I must be careful, I must be careful," he muttered to himself. "I must go to the other extreme, if necessary." He was pacing his rooms again, and suddenly, he faced the mirror.

"You wouldn't fare any better than the rest, if they knew," he told the reflection, "You poor wretch, what are you?"

When he thought of Elise, he smiled. He loved her, but he hated the traditions which she represented. He was conscious of a blind fury which bade him wreak vengeance on those traditions, and of a cowardly fear which cried out to him to retain his position in the world's and Elise's eyes at any cost.

*   *   *

Mrs. Grabért was delighted to have visiting her her old school friend from Virginia, and the two spent hours laughing over their girlish escapades, and comparing notes about their little ones. Each was confident that her darling had said the cutest things, and their polite deference to each other's opinions on the matter was a sham through which each saw without resentment.

"But Elise," remonstrated Mrs. Allen, "I think it so strange you don't have a mammy for Baby Vannier. He would be so much better cared for than by that harum-scarum young white girl you have."

"I think so too, Adelaide," sighed Mrs. Grabért, "It seems strange for me not to have a darkey maid about, but Victor can't bear them. I cried and cried for my old mammy, but he was stern. He doesn't like darkies, you know, and he says old mammies just frighten children, and ruin their childhood. I don't see how he could say that, do you?" She looked wistfully to Mrs. Allen for sympathy.

"I don't know," mused that lady, "We were all looked after by our mammies, and I think they are the best kind of nurses."

"And Victor won't have any kind of darkey servant either here or at the office. He says they're shiftless and worthless and generally no-account. Of course, he knows, he's had lots of experience with them in his business."

Mrs. Allen folded her hands behind her head and stared hard at the ceiling. "Oh, well, men don't know everything," she said, "and Victor may come around to our way of thinking after all."

It was late that evening when the lawyer came in for dinner. His eyes had acquired a habit of veiling themselves under their lashes as if they were constantly concealing something which they feared might be wrenched from them by a stare. He was nervous and restless, with a habit of glancing about him furtively, and a twitching compressing of his lips when he had finished a sentence, which somehow reminded you of a kindhearted judge, who is forced to give a death sentence.

Elise met him at the door as was her wont, and she knew from the first glance into his eyes that something had disturbed him more than usual that day, but she forbore asking questions, for she knew he would tell her when the time had come.

They were in their room that night when the rest of the household lay in slumber. He sat for a long while gazing at the open fire, then he passed his hand over his forehead wearily.

"I have had a rather unpleasant experience to-day," he began.

"Yes."

"Pavageau, again."

His wife was brushing her hair before the mirror. At the name she turned hastily with the brush in her uplifted hand.

"I can't understand, Victor, why you must have dealings with that man. He is constantly irritating you. I simply wouldn't associate with him."

"I don't," and he laughed at her feminine argument. "It isn't a question of association, cherie, it's a purely business and unsocial relation, if relation it may be called, that throws us together."

She threw down the brush petulantly, and came to his side,

"Victor," she began hesitatingly, her arms about his neck, her face close to his, "Won't you—won't you give up politics for me? It was ever so much nicer when you were just a lawyer and wanted only to be the best lawyer in the state, without all this worry about corruption and votes and such things. You've changed, oh, Victor, you've changed so. Baby and I won't know you after a while."

He put her gently on his knee. "You mustn't blame the poor politics, darling. Don't you think, perhaps, it's the inevitable hardening and embittering that must come to us all as we grow older?"

"No, I don't," she replied emphatically, "Why do you go into this struggle, anyhow? You have nothing to gain but an empty honor. It won't bring you more money, or make you more loved or respected. Why must you be mixed up with such—such—awful people?"

"I don't know," he said wearily.

And in truth, he did not know. He had gone on after his marriage with Elise making one success after another. It seemed that a beneficent Providence had singled him out as the one man in the state upon whom to heap the most lavish attentions. He was popular after the fashion of those who are high in the esteem of the world; and this very fact made him tremble the more, for he feared that should some disclosure come, he could not stand the shock of public opinion that must overwhelm him.

"What disclosure?" he would say impatiently when such a thought would come to him, "Where could it come from, and then, what is there to disclose?"

Thus he would deceive himself for as much as a month at a time.

He was surprised to find awaiting him in his office one day the man Wilson, whom he remembered in the courtroom before Recorder Grant. He was surprised and annoyed. Why had the man come to his office? Had he seen the telltale flush on his face that day?

But it was soon evident that Wilson did not even remember having seen him before.

"I came to see if I could retain you in a case of mine," he began, after the usual formalities of greeting were over.

"I am afraid, my good man," said Grabért brusquely, "that you have mistaken the office."

Wilson's face flushed at the appellation, but he went on bravely, "I have not mistaken the office. I know you are the best civil lawyer in the city, and I want your services."

"An impossible thing."

"Why? Are you too busy? My case is a simple thing, a mere point in law, but I want the best authority and the best opinion brought to bear on it."

"I could not give you any help—and—I fear, we do not understand each other—I do not wish to." He turned to his desk abruptly.

"What could he have meant by coming to me?" he questioned himself fearfully, as Wilson left the office. "Do I look like a man likely to take up his impossible contentions?"

He did not look like it, nor was he. When it came to a question involving the Negro, Victor Grabért was noted for his stern, unrelenting attitude; it was simply impossible to convince him that there was anything but sheerest incapacity in that race. For him, no good could come out of this Nazareth.[10] He was liked and respected by men of his political belief, because, even when he was a candidate for a judgeship, neither money nor the possible chance of a deluge of votes from the First and Fourth Wards could cause him to swerve one hair's breadth from his opinion of the black inhabitants of those wards.

Pavageau, however, was his *bête noir.*[11] Pavageau was a lawyer, a coolheaded, calculating man with steely eyes set in a grim brown face. They had first met in the courtroom in a case which involved the question whether a man may set aside the will of his father, who disregarding the legal offspring of another race than himself, chooses to leave his property to educational institutions which would not have granted admission to that son. Pavageau represented the son. He lost, of course. The judge, the jury, the people and Grabért were against him; but he fought his fight with a grim determination which commanded Victor's admiration and respect.

"Fools," he said between his teeth to himself, when they were crowding about him with congratulations, "Fools, can't they see who is the abler man of the two?"

He wanted to go up to Pavageau and give him his hand; to tell him that he was proud of him and that he had really won the case, but public opinion was against him; but he dared not. Another one of his colleagues might; but he was afraid. Pavageau and the world might misunderstand, or would it be understanding?

Thereafter they met often. Either by some freak of nature, or because there was a shrewd sense of the possibilities in his position, Pavageau was of the same political side of the fence as Grabért. Secretly, he admired the man; he respected him; he liked him, and because of this he was always ready with sneer and invective for him. He fought him bitterly when there was no occasion for fighting, and Pavageau became his enemy, and his name a very synonym of horror to Elise, who learned to trace her husband's fits of moodiness and depression to the one source.

Meanwhile, Vannier Grabért was growing up, a handsome lad, with his father's and mother's physical beauty, and a strength and force of character that belonged to neither. In him, Grabért saw the reparation of all his childhood's wrongs and sufferings. The boy realized all his own longings. He had family traditions, and a social position which was his from birth and an inalienable right to hold up his head without an unknown fear gripping at his heart. Grabért felt that he could forgive all; the village boys of long ago, and the imaginary village boys of to-day when he looked at his son. He had bought and paid for Vannier's freedom and happiness. The coins may have been each a drop of his heart's blood, but he had reckoned the cost before he had given it.

It was a source of great pride for him to take the boy to court with him, and one Saturday morning when he was starting out, Vannier asked if he might go.

"There is nothing that would interest you to-day, mon fils," he said tenderly, "but you may go."

In fact, there was nothing interesting that day; merely a troublesome old woman, who instead of taking her fair-skinned grandchild out of the school where it had been found it did not belong, had preferred to bring the matter to court. She was represented by Pavageau. Of course, there was not the ghost of a show for her. Pavageau had told her that. The law was very explicit about the matter. The only question lay in proving the child's affinity to the Negro race, which was not such a difficult matter to do, so the case was quickly settled, since the child's grandmother accompanied him. The judge, however, was irritated. It was a hot day and he was provoked that such a trivial matter should have taken up his time. He lost his temper as he looked at his watch.

"I don't see why these people want to force their children into the white schools," he declared, "There should be a rigid inspection to prevent it, and all the suspected children put out and made to go where they belong."

Pavageau, too, was irritated that day. He looked up from some papers which he was folding, and his gaze met Grabért's with a keen, cold, penetrating flash.

"Perhaps Your Honor would like to set the example by taking your son from the schools."

There was an instant silence in the courtroom, a hush intense and eager. Every eye turned upon the judge who sat still, a figure carven in stone with livid face and fear-stricken eyes. After the first flash of his eyes, Pavageau had gone on cooly sorting the papers.

The courtroom waited, waited, for the judge to rise and thunder forth a fine against the daring Negro lawyer for contempt. A minute passed, which seemed like an hour. Why did not Grabért speak? Pavageau's implied accusation was too absurd for denial; but he should be punished. Was His Honor ill, or did he merely hold the man in too much contempt to notice him or his remark?

Finally Grabért spoke; he moistened his lips, for they were dry and parched, and his voice was weak and sounded far away in his own ears. "My son—does—not—attend the public schools."

Someone in the rear of the room laughed, and the atmosphere lightened at once. Plainly Pavageau was an idiot, and His Honor too far above him; too much of a gentleman to notice him. Grabért continued calmly; "The gentleman," there was an unmistakable sneer in this word, habit if nothing else, and not even fear could restrain him, "The gentleman doubtless intended a little pleasantry, but I shall have to fine him for contempt of court."

"As you will," replied Pavageau, and he flashed another look at Grabért. It was a look of insolent triumph and derision. His Honor's eyes dropped beneath it.

"What did that man mean, father, by saying you should take me out of school?" asked Vannier on his way home.

"He was provoked, my son, because he had lost his case, and when a man is provoked he is likely to say silly things. By the way, Vannier, I hope you won't say anything to your mother about the incident. It would only annoy her."

For the public, the incident was forgotten as soon as it had closed, but for Grabért, it was indelibly stamped on his memory; a scene that shrieked in his mind and stood out before him at every footstep he took. Again and again as he tossed on a sleepless bed did he see the cold flash of Pavageau's eyes, and hear his quiet accusation. How did he know? Where had he gotten his information? For he spoke, not as one who makes a random shot in anger; but as one who knows, who has known a long while, and who is betrayed by irritation into playing his trump card too early in the game.

He passed a wretched week, wherein it seemed that his every footstep was dogged, his every gesture watched and recorded. He fancied that Elise, even, was suspecting him. When he took his judicial seat each morning, it seemed that every eye in the courtroom was fastened upon him in derision; every one who spoke, it seemed were but biding their time to shout the old village street refrain which had haunted him all his life, "Nigger!—Nigger!—White nigger!"

Finally, he could stand it no longer, and with leaden feet and furtive glances to the right and left for fear he might be seen; he went up a flight of dusty stairs in an Exchange Alley building, which led to Pavageau's office.

The latter was frankly surprised to see him. He made a polite attempt to conceal it, however. It was the first time in his legal life that Grabért had ever sought out a Negro; the first time that he had ever voluntarily opened conversation with one.

He mopped his forehead nervously as he took the chair Pavageau offered him; he stared about the room for an instant; then with a sudden, almost brutal directness, he turned on the lawyer.

"See here, what did you mean by that remark you made in court the other day?"

"I meant just what I said," was the cool reply.

Grabért paused, "Why did you say it?" he asked slowly.

"Because I was a fool. I should have kept my mouth shut until another time, should I not?"

"Pavageau," said Grabért softly, "let's not fence. Where did you get your information?"

Pavageau paused for an instant. He put his fingertips together and closed his eyes as one who meditates. Then he said with provoking calmness,

"You seem anxious—well, I don't mind letting you know. It doesn't really matter."

"Yes, yes," broke in Grabért impatiently.

"Did you ever hear of a Mme. Guichard of Hospital Street?"

The sweat broke out on the judge's brow as he replied weakly, "Yes."

"Well, I am her nephew."

"And she?"

"Is dead. She told me about you once—with pride, let me say. No one else knows."

Grabért sat dazed. He had forgotten about Mme. Guichard. She had never entered into his calculations at all. Pavageau turned to his desk with a sigh as if he wished the interview were ended. Grabért rose.

"If—if—this were known—to—to—my—my wife," he said thickly, "it would hurt her very much."

His head was swimming. He had had to appeal to this man, and to appeal in his wife's name. His wife, whose name he scarcely spoke to men whom he considered his social equals.

Pavageau looked up quickly. "It happens that I often have cases in your court," he spoke deliberately, "I am willing, if I lose fairly, to give up; but I do not like to have a decision made against me because my opponent is of a different complexion from mine, or because the decision against me would please a certain class of people. I only ask what I have never had from you—fair play."

"I understand," said Grabért.

He admired Pavageau more than ever as he went out of his office, yet this admiration was tempered by the knowledge that this man was the only person in the whole world who possessed positive knowledge of his secret. He groveled in a self-abasement at his position; and yet he could not but feel a certain relief that the vague formless fear which had hitherto dogged his life and haunted it, had taken on a definite shape. He knew where it was now; he could lay his hands on it, and fight it.

But with what weapons? There were none offered him save a substantial backing down from his position on certain questions; the position that had been his for so long that he was almost known by it. For in the quiet deliberate sentence of Pavageau's, he read that he must cease all the oppression, all the little injustices which he had offered Pavageau's clientele. He must act now as his convictions and secret sympathies and affiliations had bidden him act; not as prudence and fear and cowardice had made him act.

Then what would be the result? he asked himself. Would not the suspicions of the people be aroused by this sudden change in his manner? Would not they begin to question and to wonder? Would not someone remember Pavageau's remark that morning, and putting two and two together, start some rumor flying? His heart sickened again at the thought.

There was a banquet that night. It was in his honor, and he was to speak, and the thought was distasteful to him beyond measure. He knew how it all would be. He would be hailed with shouts and acclamations, as the finest flower of civilization. He would be listened to deferentially, and younger men would go away holding him in their hearts as a truly worthy model. When all the while—

He threw back his head and laughed. Oh, what a glorious revenge he had on those little white village boys! How he had made a race atone for Wilson's insult in the courtroom; for the man in the restaurant at whom Ward had laughed so uproariously; for all the affronts seen and unseen given these people of his own whom he had denied. He had taken a diploma from their most exclusive college; he had broken down the barriers of their social world; he had taken the highest possible position among them; and aping their own ways, had shown them that he too, could despise this inferior race they despised. Nay, he had taken for his wife the best woman among them all, and she had borne him a son. Ha, ha! What a joke on them all!

And he had not forgotten the black and yellow boys either. They had stoned him too, and he had lived to spurn them; to look down upon them, and to crush them at every possible turn from his seat on the bench. Truly, his life had not been wasted.

He had lived forty-nine years now, and the zenith of his power was not yet reached. There was much more to do, much more, and he was going to do it. He owed it to Elise and the boy. For their sake he must go on and on and keep his tongue still, and truckle to Pavageau and suffer alone. Some day, perhaps, he would have a grandson, who would point with pride to "My grandfather, the famous Judge Grabért!" Ah, that in itself, was a reward. To have founded a dynasty; to bequeath to others that which he had never possessed himself, and the lack of which had made his life a misery.

It was a banquet with a political significance; one that meant a virtual triumph for Judge Grabért in the next contest for the District Judge. He smiled around at the eager faces which were turned up to his as he arose to speak. The tumult of applause which had greeted his rising had died away, and an expectant hush fell on the room.

"What a sensation I could make now," he thought. He had but to open his mouth and cry out, "Fools! Fools! I whom you are honoring, I am one of the despised ones. Yes, I'm a nigger —do you hear, a nigger!" What a temptation it was to end the whole miserable farce. If he were alone in the world, if it were not for Elise and the boy; he would, just to see their horror and wonder. How they would shrink from him! But what could they do? They could take away his office; but his wealth, and his former successes, and his learning, they could not touch. Well, he must speak, and he must remember Elise and the boy.

Every eye was fastened on him in eager expectancy. Judge Grabért's speech was expected to outline the policy of their faction in the coming campaign. He turned to the chairman at the head of the table.

"Mr. Chairman," he began, and paused again. How peculiar it was that in the place of the chairman there sat Grandmére

Grabért as she had been wont to sit on the steps of the tumble down cottage in the village. She was looking at him sternly and bidding him give an account of his life since she had kissed him good-bye ere he had sailed down the river to New Orleans. He was surprised, and not a little annoyed. He had expected to address the chairman; not Grandmére Grabért. He cleared his throat and frowned.

"Mr. Chairman," he said again. Well, what was the use of addressing her that way? She would not understand him. He would call her Grandmére, of course. Were they not alone again on the cottage steps at twilight with the cries of the little brutish boys ringing derisively from the distant village square?

"Grandmére," he said softly, "you don't understand—" and then he was sitting down in his seat pointing one finger angrily at her because the other words would not come. They stuck in his throat, and he choked and beat the air with his hands. When the men crowded around him with water and hastily improvised fans, he fought them away wildly and desperately with furious curses that came from his blackened lips. For were they not all boys with stones to pelt him because he wanted to play with them? He would run away to Grandmére who would soothe him and comfort him. So he arose, and stumbling, shrieking and beating them back from him, ran the length of the hall, and fell across the threshold of the door.

The secret died with him, for Pavageau's lips were ever sealed.

KATE CHOPIN

1851–1904

THOUGH BEST KNOWN for her stories of Creole communities in Louisiana, Kate O'Flaherty Chopin was born into an affluent Irish American family in St. Louis and attended the St. Louis Academy of the Sacred Heart. In 1870 she married Oscar Chopin, a Louisiana businessman of white Creole heritage, and moved with him to New Orleans, where she lived until his death in 1882. There she devoted her time to her six children, beginning to write only after she was widowed and had returned to St. Louis in 1884. In 1889 she published a poem in *America*, a Chicago magazine, and that same year the *Philadelphia Musical Journal* published her first story, "Wiser Than a God." Other stories followed, among them the tales of Louisiana Creole life collected in *Bayou Folk* (1894) and *A Night in Acadie* (1897). In 1890 she published a novel, *At Fault*, and in 1899 another novel, *The Awakening. The Awakening* was so unfavorably received that it is thought that Chopin chose to stop writing for publication as a result. Although it was considered scandalous at the time for its portrayal of a married woman's resistance to conventional norms of sexuality and female propriety, the novel is now regarded as an American classic.

THE STORY OF AN HOUR

Knowing that Mrs. Mallard was afflicted with a heart trouble, great care was taken to break to her as gently as possible the news of her husband's death.

It was her sister Josephine who told her, in broken sentences; veiled hints that revealed in half concealing. Her husband's friend Richards was there, too, near her. It was he who had been in the newspaper office when intelligence of the railroad disaster was received, with Brently Mallard's name leading the list of "killed." He had only taken the time to assure himself of its truth by a second telegram, and had hastened to forestall any less careful, less tender friend in bearing the sad message.

She did not hear the story as many women have heard the same, with a paralyzed inability to accept its significance. She wept at once, with sudden, wild abandonment, in her sister's arms. When the storm of grief had spent itself she went away to her room alone. She would have no one follow her.

There stood, facing the open window, a comfortable, roomy armchair. Into this she sank, pressed down by a physical exhaustion that haunted her body and seemed to reach into her soul.

She could see in the open square before her house the tops of trees that were all aquiver with the new spring life. The delicious breath of rain was in the air. In the street below a peddler was crying his wares. The notes of a distant song which some one was singing reached her faintly, and countless sparrows were twittering in the eaves.

There were patches of blue sky showing here and there through the clouds that had met and piled one above the other in the west facing her window.

She sat with her head thrown back upon the cushion of the chair, quite motionless, except when a sob came up into her throat and shook her, as a child who has cried itself to sleep continues to sob in its dreams.

She was young, with a fair, calm face, whose lines bespoke repression and even a certain strength. But now there was a dull stare in her eyes, whose gaze was fixed away off yonder on one of those patches of blue sky. It was not a glance of reflection, but rather indicated a suspension of intelligent thought.

There was something coming to her and she was waiting for it, fearfully. What was it? She did not know; it was too subtle and elusive to name. But she felt it, creeping out of the sky, reaching toward her through the sounds, the scents, the color that filled the air.

Now her bosom rose and fell tumultuously. She was beginning to recognize this thing that was approaching to possess her, and she was striving to beat it back with her will—as powerless as her two white slender hands would have been.

When she abandoned herself a little whispered word escaped her slightly parted lips. She said it over and over under her breath: "free, free, free!" The vacant stare and the look of terror that had followed it went from her eyes. They stayed keen and bright. Her pulses beat fast, and the coursing blood warmed and relaxed every inch of her body.

She did not stop to ask if it were or were not a monstrous joy that held her. A clear and exalted perception enabled her to dismiss the suggestion as trivial.

She knew that she would weep again when she saw the kind, tender hands folded in death; the face that had never looked save with love upon her, fixed and gray and dead. But she saw beyond that bitter moment a long procession of years to come that would belong to her absolutely. And she opened and spread her arms out to them in welcome.

There would be no one to live for her during those coming years; she would live for herself. There would be no powerful will bending hers in that blind persistence with which men and women believe they have a right to impose a private will upon a fellow-creature. A kind intention or a cruel intention made the act seem no less a crime as she looked upon it in that brief moment of illumination.

And yet she had loved him—sometimes. Often she had not. What did it matter! What could love, the unsolved mystery, count for in face of this possession of self-assertion which she suddenly recognized as the strongest impulse of her being!

"Free! Body and soul free!" she kept whispering.

Josephine was kneeling before the closed door with her lips to the keyhole, imploring for admission. "Louise, open the door! I beg; open the door—you will make yourself ill. What are you doing, Louise? For heaven's sake open the door."

"Go away. I am not making myself ill." No; she was drinking in a very elixir of life through that open window.

Her fancy was running riot along those days ahead of her. Spring days, and summer days, and all sorts of days that would be her own. She breathed a quick prayer that life might be long. It was only yesterday she had thought with a shudder that life might be long.

She arose at length and opened the door to her sister's importunities. There was a feverish triumph in her eyes, and she carried herself unwittingly like a goddess of Victory.[1] She clasped her sister's waist, and together they descended the stairs. Richards stood waiting for them at the bottom.

Some one was opening the front door with a latchkey. It was Brently Mallard who entered, a little travel-stained, composedly carrying his grip-sack and umbrella. He had been far from the scene of accident, and did not even know there had been one. He stood amazed at Josephine's piercing cry; at Richards' quick motion to screen him from the view of his wife.

But Richards was too late.

When the doctors came they said she had died of heart disease—of joy that kills.

THE STORM

A SEQUEL TO "AT THE 'CADIAN BALL"

I

The leaves were so still that even Bibi thought it was going to rain. Bobinôt, who was accustomed to converse on terms of perfect equality with his little son, called the child's attention to certain sombre clouds that were rolling with sinister intention from the west, accompanied by a sullen, threatening roar. They were at Friedheimer's store and decided to remain there till the storm had passed. They sat within the door on two empty kegs. Bibi was four years old and looked very wise.

"Mama'll be 'fraid, yes," he suggested with blinking eyes.

"She'll shut the house. Maybe she got Sylvie helpin' her this evenin'," Bobinôt responded reassuringly.

"No; she ent got Sylvie. Sylvie was helpin' her yistiday," piped Bibi.

Bobinôt arose and going across to the counter purchased a

can of shrimps, of which Calixta was very fond. Then he returned to his perch on the keg and sat stolidly holding the can
of shrimps while the storm burst. It shook the wooden store and
seemed to be ripping great furrows in the distant field. Bibi laid
his little hand on his father's knee and was not afraid.

II

Calixta, at home, felt no uneasiness for their safety. She sat at a
side window sewing furiously on a sewing machine. She was
greatly occupied and did not notice the approaching storm. But
she felt very warm and often stopped to mop her face on which
the perspiration gathered in beads. She unfastened her white
sacque[1] at the throat. It began to grow dark, and suddenly realizing the situation she got up hurriedly and went about closing
windows and doors.

Out on the small front gallery she had hung Bobinôt's Sunday
clothes to air and she hastened out to gather them before the
rain fell. As she stepped outside, Alcée Laballière rode in at the
gate. She had not seen him very often since her marriage, and
never alone. She stood there with Bobinôt's coat in her hands,
and the big rain drops began to fall. Alcée rode his horse under
the shelter of a side projection where the chickens had huddled
and there were plows and a harrow[2] piled up in the corner.

"May I come and wait on your gallery till the storm is over,
Calixta?" he asked.

"Come 'long in, M'sieur Alcée."

His voice and her own startled her as if from a trance, and
she seized Bobinôt's vest. Alcée, mounting to the porch, grabbed
the trousers and snatched Bibi's braided jacket that was about
to be carried away by a sudden gust of wind. He expressed an
intention to remain outside, but it was soon apparent that he
might as well have been out in the open: the water beat in upon
the boards in driving sheets, and he went inside, closing the door
after him. It was even necessary to put something beneath the
door to keep the water out.

"My! what a rain! It's good two years sence it rain' like that,"
exclaimed Calixta as she rolled up a piece of bagging and Alcée
helped her to thrust it beneath the crack.

She was a little fuller of figure than five years before when she married; but she had lost nothing of her vivacity. Her blue eyes still retained their melting quality; and her yellow hair, dishevelled by the wind and rain, kinked more stubbornly than ever about her ears and temples.

The rain beat upon the low, shingled roof with a force and clatter that threatened to break an entrance and deluge them there. They were in the dining room—the sitting room—the general utility room. Adjoining was her bed room, with Bibi's couch along side her own. The door stood open, and the room with its white, monumental bed, its closed shutters, looked dim and mysterious.

Alcée flung himself into a rocker and Calixta nervously began to gather up from the floor the lengths of a cotton sheet which she had been sewing.

"If this keeps up, *Dieu sait*[3] if the levees goin' to stan' it!" she exclaimed.

"What have you got to do with the levees?"

"I got enough to do! An' there's Bobinôt with Bibi out in that storm—if he only didn' left Friedheimer's!"

"Let us hope, Calixta, that Bobinôt's got sense enough to come in out of a cyclone."

She went and stood at the window with a greatly disturbed look on her face. She wiped the frame that was clouded with moisture. It was stiflingly hot. Alcée got up and joined her at the window, looking over her shoulder. The rain was coming down in sheets obscuring the view of far-off cabins and enveloping the distant wood in a gray mist. The playing of the lightning was incessant. A bolt struck a tall chinaberry tree at the edge of the field. It filled all visible space with a blinding glare and the crash seemed to invade the very boards they stood upon.

Calixta put her hands to her eyes, and with a cry, staggered backward. Alcée's arm encircled her, and for an instant he drew her close and spasmodically to him.

"*Bonté!*"[4] she cried, releasing herself from his encircling arm and retreating from the window, "the house'll go next! If I only knew w'ere Bibi was!" She would not compose herself; she would not be seated. Alcée clasped her shoulders and looked into her face. The contact of her warm, palpitating body when he had unthinkingly drawn her into his arms, had aroused all the old-time infatuation and desire for her flesh.

"Calixta," he said, "don't be frightened. Nothing can happen. The house is too low to be struck, with so many tall trees standing about. There! aren't you going to be quiet? say, aren't you?" He pushed her hair back from her face that was warm and steaming. Her lips were as red and moist as pomegranate seed. Her white neck and a glimpse of her full, firm bosom disturbed him powerfully. As she glanced up at him the fear in her liquid blue eyes had given place to a drowsy gleam that unconsciously betrayed a sensuous desire. He looked down into her eyes and there was nothing for him to do but to gather her lips in a kiss. It reminded him of Assumption.[5]

"Do you remember—in Assumption, Calixta?" he asked in a low voice broken by passion. Oh! she remembered; for in Assumption he had kissed her and kissed and kissed her; until his senses would well nigh fail, and to save her he would resort to a desperate flight. If she was not an immaculate dove in those days, she was still inviolate; a passionate creature whose very defenselessness had made her defense, against which his honor forbade him to prevail. Now—well, now—her lips seemed in a manner free to be tasted, as well as her round, white throat and her whiter breasts.

They did not heed the crashing torrents, and the roar of the elements made her laugh as she lay in his arms. She was a revelation in that dim, mysterious chamber; as white as the couch she lay upon. Her firm, elastic flesh that was knowing for the first time its birthright, was like a creamy lily that the sun invites to contribute its breath and perfume to the undying life of the world.

The generous abundance of her passion, without guile or trickery, was like a white flame which penetrated and found response in depths of his own sensuous nature that had never yet been reached.

When he touched her breasts they gave themselves up in quivering ecstasy, inviting his lips. Her mouth was a fountain of delight. And when he possessed her, they seemed to swoon together at the very borderland of life's mystery.

He stayed cushioned upon her, breathless, dazed, enervated,

with his heart beating like a hammer upon her. With one hand she clasped his head, her lips lightly touching his forehead. The other hand stroked with a soothing rhythm his muscular shoulders.

The growl of the thunder was distant and passing away. The rain beat softly upon the shingles, inviting them to drowsiness and sleep. But they dared not yield.

The rain was over; and the sun was turning the glistening green world into a palace of gems. Calixta, on the gallery, watched Alcée ride away. He turned and smiled at her with a beaming face; and she lifted her pretty chin in the air and laughed aloud.

III

Bobinôt and Bibi, trudging home, stopped without at the cistern to make themselves presentable.

"My! Bibi, w'at will yo' mama say! You ought to be ashame'. You oughtn' put on those good pants. Look at 'em! An' that mud on yo' collar! How you got that mud on yo' collar, Bibi? I never saw such a boy!" Bibi was the picture of pathetic resignation. Bobinôt was the embodiment of serious solicitude as he strove to remove from his own person and his son's the signs of their tramp over heavy roads and through wet fields. He scraped the mud off Bibi's bare legs and feet with a stick and carefully removed all traces from his heavy brogans. Then, prepared for the worst—the meeting with an over-scrupulous housewife, they entered cautiously at the back door.

Calixta was preparing supper. She had set the table and was dripping coffee at the hearth. She sprang up as they came in.

"Oh, Bobinôt! You back! My! but I was uneasy. W'ere you been during the rain? An' Bibi? he ain't wet? he ain't hurt?" She had clasped Bibi and was kissing him effusively. Bobinôt's explanations and apologies which he had been composing all along the way, died on his lips as Calixta felt him to see if he were dry, and seemed to express nothing but satisfaction at their safe return.

"I brought you some shrimps, Calixta," offered Bobinôt,

hauling the can from his ample side pocket and laying it on the table.

"Shrimps! Oh, Bobinôt! you too good fo' anything! and she gave him a smacking kiss on the cheek that resounded. "*J'vous réponds,*[6] we'll have a feas' to night! umph-umph!"

Bobinôt and Bibi began to relax and enjoy themselves, and when the three seated themselves at table they laughed much and so loud that anyone might have heard them as far away as Laballière's.

IV

Alcée Laballière wrote to his wife, Clarisse, that night. It was a loving letter, full of tender solicitude. He told her not to hurry back, but if she and the babies liked it at Biloxi,[7] to stay a month longer. He was getting on nicely; and though he missed them, he was willing to bear the separation a while longer—realizing that their health and pleasure were the first things to be considered.

V

As for Clarisse, she was charmed upon receiving her husband's letter. She and the babies were doing well. The society was agreeable; many of her old friends and acquaintances were at the bay. And the first free breath since her marriage seemed to restore the pleasant liberty of her maiden days. Devoted as she was to her husband, their intimate conjugal life was something which she was more than willing to forego for a while.

So the storm passed and every one was happy.

MARY NOAILLES MURFREE

1850–1922

IF REGIONALIST WRITING was distinctly seen as a "woman's genre" in New England, this was not the case in the South, as Mary Noailles Murfree's career suggests. When Murfree published her first story "The Dancin' Party at Harrison's Cove" in the *Atlantic Monthly* in 1878, she used the pen name Charles Egbert Craddock, in part because publishing fiction was thought unsuitable for a white southern lady. She retained her male pseudonym until 1885, when her revelation of her identity to *Atlantic* publisher Thomas Bailey Aldrich brought her national publicity; the style of Murfree's fiction had been considered "masculine."

Born on the family plantation in Murfreesboro, Tennessee, Murfree attended school in Nashville and Philadelphia, then read law with her father, a successful lawyer and author. Her first stories appeared in *Lippincott's Magazine* in 1874, and were collected in a volume, *In the Tennessee Mountains*, published in 1884. A number of novels and short story collections followed, including *The Prophet of the Great Smoky Mountains* (1885), *The "Stranger People's" Country* (1892), and *The Phantoms of the Foot-Bridge and Other Stories* (1895). Murfree's regionalist writing was noted for its romance elements and its attention to class differences. The Civil War had brought regional differences to the attention of U.S. readers, and Murfree's local color stories, consistently featuring the setting and dialect of the southern mountains, were admired for their minute description and regional detail. After the turn of the century her popularity diminished, and Murfree turned to historical themes. She never married, living throughout her life with her family, and making her closest companion her older sister Fanny.

The Dancin' Party at Harrison's Cove

"Fur ye see, Mis' Darley, them Harrison folks over yander ter the Cove hev determined on a dancin' party."

The drawling tones fell unheeded on old Mr. Kenyon's ear, as he sat on the broad hotel piazza of the New Helvetia Springs, and gazed with meditative eyes at the fair August sky. An early moon was riding, clear and full, over this wild spur of the Alleghanies;[1] the stars were few and very faint; even the great Scorpio[2] lurked, vaguely outlined, above the wooded ranges; and the white mist, that filled the long, deep, narrow valley between the parallel lines of mountains, shimmered with opalescent gleams.

All the world of the watering-place[3] had converged to that focus, the ball-room, and the cool, moonlit piazzas were nearly deserted. The fell determination of the "Harrison folks" to give a dancing party made no impression on the preoccupied old gentleman. Another voice broke his reverie,—a soft, clear, well-modulated voice,—and he started and turned his head as his own name was called, and his niece, Mrs. Darley, came to the window.

"Uncle Ambrose,—are you there? So glad! I was afraid you were down at the summer-house, where I hear the children singing. Do come here a moment, please. This is Mrs. Johns, who brings the Indian peaches to sell,—you know the Indian peaches?"

Mr. Kenyon knew the Indian peaches, the dark crimson fruit streaked with still darker lines, and full of blood-red juice, which he had meditatively munched that very afternoon. Mr. Kenyon knew the Indian peaches right well. He wondered, however, what had brought Mrs. Johns back in so short a time, for although the principal industry of the mountain people about the New Helvetia Springs is selling fruit to the summer sojourners, it is not customary to come twice on the same day, nor to appear at all after nightfall.

Mrs. Darley proceeded to explain.

"Mrs. Johns's husband is ill and wants us to send him some medicine."

Mr. Kenyon rose, threw away the stump of his cigar, and entered the room. "How long has he been ill, Mrs. Johns?" he asked, dismally.

Mr. Kenyon always spoke lugubriously, and he was a dismal-looking old man. Not more cheerful was Mrs. Johns; she was tall and lank, and with such a face as one never sees except in these mountains,—elongated, sallow, thin, with pathetic, deeply sunken eyes, and high cheek-bones, and so settled an expression of hopeless melancholy that it must be that naught but care and suffering had been her lot; holding out wasted hands to the years as they pass,—holding them out always, and always empty. She wore a shabby, faded calico, and spoke with the peculiar expressionless drawl of the mountaineer. She was a wonderful contrast to Mrs. Darley, all furbelows[4] and flounces, with her fresh, smooth face and soft hair, and plump, round arms half-revealed by the flowing sleeves of her thin, black dress. Mrs. Darley was in mourning, and therefore did not affect the ball-room. At this moment, on benevolent thoughts intent, she was engaged in uncorking sundry small phials, gazing inquiringly at their labels, and shaking their contents.

In reply to Mr. Kenyon's question, Mrs. Johns, sitting on the extreme edge of a chair and fanning herself with a pink calico sun-bonnet, talked about her husband, and a misery in his side and in his back, and how he felt it "a-comin' on nigh on ter a week ago." Mr. Kenyon expressed sympathy, and was surprised by the announcement that Mrs. Johns considered her husband's illness "a blessin', 'kase ef he war able ter git out'n his bed, he 'lowed ter go down ter Harrison's Cove ter the dancin' party, 'kase Rick Pearson war a-goin' ter be thar, an' he'd said ez how none o' the Johnses should come."

"What, Rick Pearson, that terrible outlaw!" exclaimed Mrs. Darley, with wide open blue eyes. She had read in the newspapers sundry thrilling accounts of a noted horse thief and outlaw, who with a gang of kindred spirits defied justice and roamed certain sparsely-populated mountainous counties at his own wild will, and she was not altogether without a feeling of fear as she heard of his proximity to the New Helvetia Springs,—not fear for life or limb, because she was practical-minded enough to reflect that the sojourners and employés of the watering-place would far outnumber the outlaw's troop, but fear that a pair of shiny bay ponies, Castor and Pollux,[5] would fall victims to the crafty wiles of the expert horse thief.

"I think I have heard something of a difficulty between your people and Rick Pearson," said old Mr. Kenyon. "Has a peace never been patched up between them?"

"No-o," drawled Mrs. Johns; "same as it always war. My old man'll never believe but what Rick Pearson stole that thar bay filly we lost 'bout five year ago. But I don't believe he done it; plenty other folks around is ez mean ez Rick, leastways mos' ez mean; plenty mean enough ter steal a horse, ennyhow. Rick *say* he never tuk the filly; say he war a-goin' ter shoot off the nex' man's head ez say so. Rick say he'd ruther give two bay fillies than hev a man say he tuk a horse ez he never tuk. Rick say ez how he kin stand up ter what he does do, but it's these hyar lies on him what kills him out. But ye know, Mis' Darley, ye know yerself, he never give nobody two bay fillies in this world, an' what's more he's never goin' ter. My old man an' my boy Kossute talks on 'bout that thar bay filly like she war stole yestiddy, an' 't war five year ago an' better; an' when they hearn ez how Rick Pearson hed showed that red head o' his'n on this hyar mounting las' week, they war fightin' mad, an' would hev lit out fur the gang sure, 'ceptin' they hed been gone down the mounting fur two days. An' my son Kossute, he sent Rick word that he had better keep out'n gunshot o' these hyar woods; that he did n't want no better mark than that red head o' his'n, an' he could hit it two mile off. An' Rick Pearson, he sent Kossute word that he would kill him fur his sass the very nex' time he see him, an' ef he don't want a bullet in that pumpkin head o' his'n he hed better keep away from that dancin' party what the Harrisons hev laid off ter give, 'kase Rick say he 's a-goin' ter it hisself, an' is a-goin' ter dance too; he ain't been invited, Mis' Darley, but Rick don't keer fur that. He is a-goin' enny-how, an' he say ez how he ain't a-goin' ter let Kossute come, 'count o' Kossute's sass an' the fuss they 've all made 'bout that bay filly that war stole five year ago,—'t war five year an' better. But Rick say ez how he is goin', fur all he ain't got no invite, an' is a-goin' ter dance too, 'kase you know, Mis' Darley, it 's a-goin' ter be a dancin' party; the Harrisons hev determinated on that. Them gals of theirn air mos' crazed 'bout a dancin' party. They ain't been a bit of account sence they went ter Cheatham's Cross-Roads ter see thar gran'mother, an' picked up all them queer new notions. So the Harrisons hev determined on a dancin' party; an' Rick say ez how he is goin' ter dance too; but Jule, *she* say ez how she know thar ain't a gal on the mounting ez would dance with him; but I ain't so sure 'bout that, Mis' Darley; gals air cur'ous critters, ye know yerself; thar's no sort o' countin' on 'em; they'll do one thing one time, an' another thing nex' time; ye can't put no dependence in 'em. But Jule say ef he kin git Mandy Tyler ter dance with him, it 's the mos' he kin do, an' the gang 'll be no whar. Mebbe he kin git Mandy ter dance with him, 'kase the other boys say ez how none o' them is a-goin' ter ax her ter dance, 'count of the trick she played on 'em down ter the Wilkins settlemint—las' month, war it? no, 't war two month ago, an' better; but the boys ain't forgot how scandalous she done 'em, an' none of 'em is a-goin' ter ax her ter dance."

"Why, what did she do?" exclaimed Mrs. Darley, surprised. "She came here to sell peaches one day, and I thought her such a nice, pretty, well-behaved girl."

"Waal, she hev got mighty quiet say-nuthin' sort 'n ways, Mis' Darley, but that thar gal do behave *rediculous*. Down thar ter the Wilkins settlemint,—ye know it 's 'bout two mile or two mile 'n a half from hyar,—waal, all the gals walked down thar ter the party an hour by sun, but when the boys went down they tuk thar horses, ter give the gals a ride home behind 'em. Waal, every boy axed his gal ter ride while the party war goin' on, an' when 't war all over they all set out fur ter come home. Waal, this hyar Mandy Tyler is a mighty *favorite* 'mongst the boys,—they ain't got no sense, ye know, Mis' Darley,—an' stid-dier one of 'em axin' her ter ride home, thar war five of 'em axed her ter ride, ef ye 'll believe me, an' what do ye think she done, Mis' Darley? She tole all five of 'em yes; an' when the party war over, she war the last ter go, an' when she started out 'n the door, thar war all five of them boys a-standin' thar waitin' fur her, an' every one a-holdin' his horse by the bridle, an' none of 'em knowed who the others war a-waitin' fur. An' this hyar

Mandy Tyler, when she got ter the door an' seen 'em all a-standin' thar, never said one word, jest walked right through 'mongst 'em, an' set out fur the mounting on foot with all them five boys a-followin' an' a-leadin' thar horses an' a-quarrelin' enough ter take off each others' heads 'bout which one war a-goin' ter ride with her; which none of 'em did, Mis' Darley, fur I hearn ez how the whole lay-out footed it all the way ter New Helveshy. An' thar would hev been a fight 'mongst 'em, 'ceptin' her brother, Jacob Tyler, went along with 'em, an' tried ter keep the peace atwixt 'em. An' Mis' Darley, all them married folks down thar at the party—them folks in the Wilkins settlemint is the biggest fools, sure—when all them married folks come out ter the door, an' see the way Mandy Tyler hed treated them boys, they jest hollered and laffed an' thought it war mighty smart an' funny in Mandy; but she never say a word till she kem up the mounting, an' I never hearn ez how she say ennything then. An' now the boys all say none of 'em is a-goin' ter ax her ter dance, ter pay her back fur them fool airs of hern. But Kossute say he'll dance with her ef none the rest will. Kossute he thought 't war all mighty funny too,—he's sech a fool 'bout gals, Kossute is,—but Jule, she thought ez how 't war scandalous."

Mrs. Darley listened in amused surprise; that these mountain wilds could sustain a first-class coquette was an idea that had not hitherto entered her mind; however, "that thar Mandy" seemed, in Mrs. Johns's opinion at least, to merit the unenviable distinction, and the party at Wilkins settlement and the pro-spective gayety of Harrison's Cove awakened the same senti-ments in her heart and mind as do the more ambitious germans and kettledrums[6] of the lowland cities in the heart and mind of Mrs. Grundy. Human nature is the same everywhere, and the Wilkins settlement is a microcosm. The metropolitan centres, stripped of the civilization of wealth, fashion, and culture, would present only the bare skeleton of humanity outlined in Mrs. Johns's talk of Harrison's Cove, the Wilkins settlement, the en-mities and scandals and sorrows and misfortunes of the moun-tain ridge. As the absurd resemblance developed, Mrs. Darley could not forbear a smile. Mrs. Johns looked up with a momen-tary expression of surprise; the story presented no humorous phase to her perceptions, but she too smiled a little as she repeated, "Scandalous, ain't it?" and proceeded in the same lacklustre tone as before.

"Yes,—Kossute say ez how he 'll dance with her ef none the rest will, fur Kossute say ez how he hev laid off ter dance, Mis' Darley; an' when I ax him what he thinks will become of his soul ef he dances, he say the devil may crack away at it, an' ef he kin hit it he's welcome. Fur soul or no soul he 's a-goin' ter dance. Kossute is a-fixin' of hisself this very minit ter go; but I am verily afeard the boy'll be slaughtered, Mis' Darley, 'kase thar is goin' ter be a fight, an' ye never in all yer life hearn sech sass ez Kossute and Rick Pearson done sent word ter each other."

Mr. Kenyon expressed some surprise that she should fear for so young a fellow as Kossuth. "Surely," he said, "the man is not brute enough to injure a mere boy; your son is a mere boy."

"That's so," Mrs. Johns drawled. "Kossute ain't more 'n twenty year old, an' Rick Pearson is double that ef he is a day; but ye see it's the fire-arms ez makes Kossute more 'n a match fur him, 'kase Kossute is the best shot on the mounting, an' Rick knows that in a shootin' fight Kossute's better able ter take keer of hisself an' hurt somebody else nor ennybody. Kossute's more likely ter hurt Rick nor Rick is ter hurt him in a shootin' fight; but ef Rick did n't hurt him, an' he war ter shoot Rick, the gang would tear him ter pieces in a minit; and 'mongst 'em I 'm actially afeard they 'll slaughter the boy."

Mr. Kenyon looked even graver than was his wont upon receiving this information, but said no more; and after giving Mrs. Johns the febrifuge[7] she wished for her husband, he returned to his seat on the piazza.

Mrs. Darley watched him with some little indignation as he proceeded to light a fresh cigar. "How cold and unsympathetic uncle Ambrose is," she said to herself. And after condoling effusively with Mrs. Johns on her apprehensions for her son's safety, she returned to the gossips in the hotel parlor, and Mrs. Johns, with her pink calico sun-bonnet on her head, went her way in the brilliant summer moon light.

The clear lustre shone white upon all the dark woods and chasms and flashing waters that lay between the New Helvetia Springs and the wide, deep ravine called Harrison's Cove, where from a rude log hut the vibrations of a violin, and the quick throb of dancing feet, already mingled with the impetuous rush of a mountain stream close by and the weird night-sounds of the hills,—the cry of birds among the tall trees, the stir of the wind, the monotonous chanting of frogs at the water side, the long, drowsy drone of the nocturnal insects, the sudden faint blast of a distant hunter's horn, and the far baying of hounds.

Mr. Harrison had four marriageable daughters, and had arrived at the conclusion that something must be done for the girls; for, strange as it may seem, the prudent father exists even among the "mounting folks." Men there realize the importance of providing suitable homes for their daughters as men do elsewhere, and the eligible youth is as highly esteemed in those wilds as is the much scarcer animal at a fashionable watering-place. Thus it was that Mr. Harrison had "determined on a dancin' party." True, he stood in bodily fear of the judgment day and the circuit-rider;[8] but the dancing party was a rarity eminently calculated to please the young hunters of the settlements round about, so he swallowed his qualms, to be indulged at a more convenient season, and threw himself into the vortex of preparation with an ardor very gratifying to the four young ladies, who had become imbued with sophistication at Cheatham's Cross-Roads.

Not so Mrs. Harrison; she almost expected the house to fall and crush them, as a judgment on the wickedness of a dancing party; for so heinous a sin, in the estimation of the greater part of the mountain people, had not been committed among them for many a day. Such trifles as killing a man in a quarrel, or on suspicion of stealing a horse, or wash-tub, or anything that came handy, of course, does not count; but a dancing party! Mrs. Harrison could only hold her idle hands, and dread the heavy penalty that must surely follow so terrible a crime.

It certainly had not the gay and lightsome aspect supposed to be characteristic of such a scene of sin: the awkward young mountaineers clogged heavily about in their uncouth clothes and rough shoes, with the stolid-looking, lacklustre maids of the hill, to the violin's monotonous iteration of The Chicken in the Bread-Trough, or The Rabbit in the Pea-Patch,—all their grave faces as grave as ever. The music now and then changed suddenly to one of those wild, melancholy strains sometimes heard in old-fashioned dancing tunes, and the strange pathetic cadences seemed more attuned to the rhythmical dash of the waters rushing over their stone barricades out in the moonlight yonder, or to the plaintive sighs of the winds among the great dark arches of the primeval forests, than to the movement of the heavy, coarse feet dancing a solemn measure in the little log cabin in Harrison's Cove. The elders, sitting in rush-bottomed chairs close to the walls, and looking on at the merriment, well-pleased despite their religious doubts, were somewhat more lively; every now and then a guffaw mingled with the violin's resonant strains and the dancers' well-marked pace; the women talked to each other with somewhat more animation than was their wont, under the stress of the unusual excitement of a dancing party, and from out the shed-room adjoining came an anticipative odor of more substantial sin than the fiddle or the grave jiggling up and down the rough floor. A little more cider too, and a very bad article of illegally-distilled whiskey, were ever and anon circulated among the pious abstainers from the dance; but the sinful votaries of Terpsichore[9] could brook no pause nor delay, and jogged up and down quite intoxicated with the mirthfulness of the plaintive old airs and the pleasure of other motion than following the plow or hoeing the corn.

And the moon smiled right royally on her dominion: on the long, dark ranges of mountains and mist-filled valleys between; on the woods and streams, and on all the half-dormant creatures either amongst the shadow-flecked foliage or under the crystal waters; on the long, white, sandy road winding in and out through the forest; on the frowning crags of the wild ravine; on the little bridge at the entrance of the gorge, across which a party of eight men, heavily armed and gallantly mounted, rode swiftly and disappeared amid the gloom of the shadows.

The sound of the galloping of horses broke suddenly on the music and the noise of the dancing; a moment's interval, and the door gently opened and the gigantic form of Rick Pearson appeared in the aperture. He was dressed, like the other mountaineers, in a coarse suit of brown jeans[10] somewhat the worse for wear, the trowsers stuffed in the legs of his heavy boots; he wore an old soft felt hat, which he did not remove immediately

on entering, and a pair of formidable pistols at his belt conspic-
uously challenged attention. He had auburn hair, and a long full
beard of a lighter tint reaching almost to his waist; his complexion was much tanned by the sun, and roughened by exposure
to the inclement mountain weather; his eyes were brown, deep-
set, and from under his heavy brows they looked out with quick,
sharp glances, and occasionally with a roguish twinkle; the expression of his countenance was rather good-humored,—a sort
of imperious good-humor, however,—the expression of a man
accustomed to have his own way and not to be trifled with, but
able to afford some amiability since his power is undisputed.

He stepped slowly into the apartment, placed his gun against
the wall, turned, and solemnly gazed at the dancing, while his
followers trooped in and obeyed his example. As the eight guns,
one by one, rattled against the wall, there was a startled silence
among the pious elders of the assemblage, and a sudden disappearance of the animation that had characterized their intercourse during the evening. Mrs. Harrison, who by reason of
flurry and a housewifely pride in the still unrevealed treasures
of the shed-room had well-nigh forgotten her fears, felt that the
anticipated judgment had even now descended, and in what terrible and unexpected guise! The men turned the quids of tobacco
in their cheeks and looked at each other in uncertainty; but the
dancers bestowed not a glance upon the newcomers, and the
musician in the corner, with his eyes half-closed, his head bent
low upon the instrument, his hard, horny hand moving the bow
back and forth over the strings of the crazy old fiddle, was utterly rapt by his own melody. At the supreme moment when
the great red beard had appeared portentously in the doorway
and fear had frozen the heart of Mrs. Harrison within her at the
ill-omened apparition, the host was in the shed-room filling a
broken-nosed pitcher from the cider-barrel. When he reentered,
and caught sight of the grave sunburned face with its long red
beard and sharp brown eyes, he too was dismayed for an instant,
and stood silent at the opposite door with the pitcher in his
hand. The pleasure and the possible profit of the dancing party,
for which he had expended so much of his scanty store of this
world's goods and risked the eternal treasures laid up in heaven,
were a mere phantasm; for, with Rick Pearson among them, in

an ill frame of mind and at odds with half the men in the room,
there would certainly be a fight, and in all probability one would
be killed, and the dancing party at Harrison's Cove would be a
text for the bloody-minded sermons of the circuit-rider for all
time to come. However, the father of four marriageable daughters is apt to become crafty and worldly-wise; only for a moment
did he stand in indecision; then, catching suddenly the small
brown eyes, he held up the pitcher with a grin of invitation.
"Rick!" he called out above the scraping of the violin and the
clatter of the dancing feet, "slip round hyar ef ye kin, I've got
somethin' for ye;" and he shook the pitcher significantly.

Not that Mr. Harrison would for a moment have thought of
Rick Pearson in a matrimonial point of view, for even the sophistication of the Cross-Roads had not yet brought him to the
state of mind to consider such a half loaf as this better than no
bread, but he felt it imperative from every point of view to keep
that set of young mountaineers dancing in peace and quiet, and
their guns idle and out of mischief against the wall. The great
red beard disappeared and reappeared at intervals, as Rick Pearson slipped along the gun-lined wall to join his host and the
cider-pitcher, and after he had disposed of the refreshment, in
which the gang shared, he relapsed into silently watching the
dancing and meditating a participation in that festivity.

Now, it so happened that the only young girl unprovided
with a partner was "that thar Mandy Tyler," of Wilkins settlement renown; the young men had rigidly adhered to their resolution to ignore her in their invitations to dance, and she had
been sitting since the beginning of the festivities, quite neglected,
among the married people, looking on at the amusement which
she had been debarred sharing by that unpopular bit of coquetry
at Wilkins settlement. Nothing of disappointment or mortification was expressed in her countenance; she felt the slight of
course,—even a "mounting" woman is susceptible of the sting
of wounded pride; all her long-anticipated enjoyment had come
to naught by this infliction of penance for her ill-timed jest at
the expense of those five young fellows dancing with their triumphant partners and bestowing upon her not even a glance;
but she looked the express image of immobility as she sat in her
clean pink calico, so carefully gotten up for the occasion, her

short black hair curling about her ears, and watched the unend-
ing reel with slow, dark eyes. Rick's glance fell upon her, and
without further hesitation he strode over to where she was sitting and proffered his hand for the dance. She did not reply
immediately, but looked timidly about her at the shocked pious
ones on either side, who were ready but for mortal fear to aver
that "dancin' enny-how air bad enough, the Lord knows, but
dancin' with a horse thief air jest scandalous!" Then, for there
is something of defiance to established law and prejudice in the
born flirt everywhere, with a sudden daring spirit shining in her
brightening eyes, she responded, "Don't keer ef I do," with a
dimpling half-laugh; and the next minute the two outlaws were
flying down the middle together.

While Rick was according grave attention to the intricacies of
the mazy dance and keeping punctilious time to the scraping of
the old fiddle, finding it all a much more difficult feat than galloping from the Cross Roads to the "Snake's Mouth" on some
other man's horse with the sheriff hard at his heels, the solitary
figure of a tall gaunt man had followed the long winding path
leading deep into the woods, and now began the steep descent
to Harrison's Cove. Of what was old Mr. Kenyon thinking, as
he walked on in the mingled shadow and sheen? Of St. Augustin
and his Forty Monks,[11] probably, and what they found in Britain. The young men of his acquaintance would gladly have laid
you any odds that he could think of nothing but his antique
hobby, the ancient church. Mr. Kenyon was the most prominent
man in St. Martin's church in the city of B——, not excepting
the rector. He was a lay-reader,[12] and officiated upon occasions
of "clerical sore-throat," as the profane denominate the minis-
terial summer exodus from heated cities. This summer, however,
Mr. Kenyon's own health had succumbed, and he was having a
little "sore-throat" in the mountains on his own account. Very
devout was Mr. Kenyon. Many people wondered that he had
never taken orders. Many people warmly congratulated themselves that he never had; for drier sermons than those he selected
were surely never heard, and a shuddering imagination shrinks
appalled from the problematic mental drought of his ideal original discourse. But he was an integrant part of St. Martin's; much
of his piety, materialized into contributions, was built up in its

walls and shone before men in the costliness of its decorations. Indeed, the ancient name had been conferred upon the building as a sort of tribute to Mr. Kenyon's well-known enthusiasm concerning apostolic succession and kindred doctrines.

Dull and dismal was Mr. Kenyon, and therefore it may be considered a little strange that he should be a notable favorite with men. They were of many different types, but with one invariable bond of union: they had all at one time served as soldiers; for the war,[13] now ten years passed by, its bitterness almost forgotten, had left some traces that time can never obliterate. What a friend was the droning old churchman in those days of battle and bloodshed and suffering and death! Not a man sat within the walls of St. Martin's who had not received some signal benefit from the hand stretched forth to impress the claims of certain ante-Augustin British clergy to consideration and credibility; not a man who did not remember stricken fields where a good Samaritan[14] went about under shot and shell, succoring the wounded and comforting the dying; not a man who did not applaud the indomitable spirit and courage that cut his way from surrender and safety, through solid barriers of enemies, to deliver the orders on which the fate of an army depended; not a man whose memory did not harbor fatiguing recollections of long, dull sermons read for the souls' health of the soldiery. And through it all,—by the camp-fires at night, on the long white country-roads in the sunshiny mornings; in the mountains and the morasses; in hilarious advance and in cheerless retreat; in the heats of summer and by the side of frozen rivers, the ancient British clergy went through it all. And, whether the old churchman's premises and reasoning were false, whether his tracings of the succession were faulty, whether he dropped a link here or took in one there, he had caught the spirit of those staunch old martyrs, if not their falling churchly mantle.

The mountaineers about the New Helvetia Springs supposed that Mr. Kenyon was a regularly ordained preacher, and that the sermons which they had heard him read were, to use the vernacular, out of his own head. For many of them were accustomed on Sunday mornings to occupy humble back benches in the ball-room, where on week-day evenings the butterflies sojourning at New Helvetia danced, and on the Sabbath metaphorically beat their breasts, and literally avowed that they were "miserable sinners," following Mr. Kenyon's lugubrious lead.

The conclusion of the mountaineers was not unnatural, therefore, and when the door of Mr. Harrison's house opened and another uninvited guest entered, the music suddenly ceased. The half-closed eyes of the fiddler had fallen upon Mr. Kenyon at the threshold, and, supposing him a clergyman, he immediately imagined that the man of God had come all the way from New Helvetia Springs to stop the dancing and snatch the revelers from the jaws of hell. The rapturous bow paused shuddering on the string, the dancing feet were palsied, the pious about the walls were racking their slow brains to excuse their apparent conniving at sin and bargaining with Satan, and Mr. Harrison felt that this was indeed an unlucky party and it would undoubtedly be dispersed by the direct interposition of Providence before the shed-room was opened and the supper eaten. As to his soul—poor man! these constantly recurring social anxieties were making him callous to immortality; this life was about to prove too much for him, for the fortitude and tact even of a father of four marriageable young ladies has a limit. Mr. Kenyon, too, seemed dumb as he hesitated in the door-way, but when the host, partially recovering himself, came forward and offered a chair, he said with one of his dismal smiles that he hoped Mr. Harrison had no objection to his coming in and looking at the dancing for a while. "Don't let me interrupt the young people, I beg," he added, as he seated himself. The astounded silence was unbroken for a few moments. To be sure he was not a circuit-rider, but even the sophistication of Cheatham's Cross-Roads had never heard of a preacher who did not object to dancing. Mr. Harrison could not believe his ears, and asked for a more explicit expression of opinion.

"Ye say ye don't keer ef the boys an' gals dance?" he inquired. "Ye don't think it's sinful?"

And after Mr. Kenyon's reply, in which the astonished "mounting folks" caught only the surprising statement that dancing if properly conducted was an innocent, cheerful, and healthful amusement, supplemented by something about dancing in the fear of the Lord,[15] and that in all charity he was disposed to consider objections to such harmless recreations a tithing of

mint and anise and cummin,[16] whereby might ensue a neglect of
weightier matters of the law; that clean hands and clean hearts
—hands clean of blood and ill-gotten goods, and hearts free
from falsehood and cruel intention—these were the things well-
pleasing to God,—after his somewhat prolix reply, the gayety
recommenced. The fiddle quavered tremulously at first, but soon
resounded with its former vigorous tones, and the joy of the
dance was again exemplified in the grave joggling back and forth.

Meanwhile Mr. Harrison sat beside this strange new guest and
asked him questions concerning his church, being instantly, it is
needless to say, informed of its great antiquity, of the journeying
of St. Augustin and his Forty Monks to Britain, of the church
they found already planted there, of its retreat to the hills of
Wales under its oppressors' tyranny, of many cognate themes,
side issues of the main branch of the subject, into which the talk
naturally drifted, the like of which Mr. Harrison had never heard
in all his days. And as he watched the figures dancing to the
violin's strains, and beheld as in a mental vision the solemn gy-
rations of those renowned Forty Monks to the monotone of old
Mr. Kenyon's voice, he abstractedly hoped that the double dance
would continue without interference till a peaceable dawn.

His hopes were vain. It so chanced that Kossuth Johns, who
had by no means relinquished all idea of dancing at Harrison's
Cove and defying Rick Pearson, had hitherto been detained by
his mother's persistent entreaties, some necessary attentions to
his father, and the many trials which beset a man dressing for a
party who has very few clothes, and those very old and worn.
Jule, his sister-in-law, had been most kind and complaisant, putting on a button here, sewing up a slit there, darning a refractory
elbow, and lending him the one bright ribbon she possessed as
a neck-tie. But all these things take time, and the moon did not
light Kossuth down the gorge until she was shining almost ver-
tically from the sky, and the Harrison Cove people and the
Forty Monks were dancing together in high feather. The eccle-
siastic dance halted suddenly, and a watchful light gleamed in
old Mr. Kenyon's eyes as he became silent and the boy stepped
into the room. The moonlight and the lamp-light fell mingled
on the calm, inexpressive features and tall, slender form of the
young mountaineer. "Hy're, Kossute!" A cheerful greeting from

many voices met him. The next moment the music ceased once
again, and the dancing came to a standstill, for as the name fell
on Pearson's ear he turned, glanced sharply toward the door,
and drawing one of his pistols from his belt advanced to the
middle of the room. The men fell back; so did the frightened
women, without screaming, however, for that indication of feminine sensibility had not yet penetrated to Cheatham's Cross-
Roads, to say nothing of the mountains.

"I told ye that ye war n't ter come hyar," said Rick Pearson
imperiously; "and ye 've got ter go home ter yer mammy, right
off, or ye 'll never git thar no more, youngster."

"I've come hyar ter put *you* out, ye cussed red-headed horse
thief!" retorted Kossuth, angrily; "ye hed better tell me whar
that thar bay filly is, or light out, one."

It is not the habit in the mountains to parley long on these
occasions. Kossuth had raised his gun to his shoulder as Rick,
with his pistol cocked, advanced a step nearer. The outlaw's
weapon was struck upward by a quick, strong hand, the little
log cabin was filled with flash, roar, and smoke, and the stars
looked in through a hole in the roof from which Rick's bullet
had sent the shingles flying. He turned in mortal terror and
caught the hand that had struck his pistol,—in mortal terror, for
Kossuth was the crack shot of the mountains and he felt he was
a dead man. The room was somewhat obscured by smoke, but
as he turned upon the man who had disarmed him, for the force
of the blow had thrown the pistol to the floor, he saw that the
other hand was over the muzzle of young Johns's gun, and Kossuth was swearing loudly that by the Lord Almighty if he did
n't take it off he would shoot it off.

"My young friend," Mr. Kenyon began, with the calmness
appropriate to a devout member of the one catholic and apostolic
church;[17] but then, the old Adam[18] suddenly getting the upper-
hand, he shouted out in irate tones, "If you don't stop that noise,
I 'll break your head! Well, Mr. Pearson," he continued, as he
stood between the combatants, one hand still over the muzzle
of young Johns's gun, the other, lean and sinewy, holding Pearson's powerful right arm with a vise-like grip, "well, Mr. Pearson, you are not so good a soldier as you used to be; you
did n't fight boys in the old times."

Rick Pearson's enraged expression suddenly gave way to a surprised recognition. "Ye may drag me through hell an' beat me with a soot-bag ef hyar ain't the old fightin' preacher agin!" he cried.

"I have only one thing to say to you," said Mr. Kenyon. "You must go. I will not have you here shooting boys and breaking up a party."

Rick demurred. "See hyar, now," he said, "ye 've got no business meddlin'."

"You must go," Mr. Kenyon reiterated.

"Preachin 's yer business," Rick continued; " 'pears like ye don't 'tend to it, though."

"You must go."

"S'pose I say I won't," said Rick, good-humoredly; "I s'pose ye 'd say ye 'd make me."

"You must go," repeated Mr. Kenyon. "I am going to take the boy home with me, but I intend to see you off first."

Mr. Kenyon had prevented the hot-headed Kossuth from firing by keeping his hand persistently over the muzzle of the gun; and young Johns had feared to try to wrench it away lest it should discharge in the effort. Had it done so, Mr. Kenyon would have been in sweet converse with the Forty Monks in about a minute and a quarter. Kossuth had finally let go the gun, and made frantic attempts to borrow a weapon from some of his friends, but the stern authoritative mandate of the belligerent peace-maker had prevented them from gratifying him, and he now stood empty-handed beside Mr. Kenyon, who had shouldered the old rifle in an absent-minded manner, although still retaining his powerful grasp on the arm of the outlaw.

"Waal, parson," said Rick at length, "I 'll go, jest ter pleasure you-uns. Ye see, I ain't forgot Shiloh."[19]

"I am not talking about Shiloh now," said the old man. "You must get off at once,—all of you," indicating the gang, who had been so whelmed in astonishment that they had not lifted a finger to aid their chief.

"Ye say ye 'll take that—that"—Rick looked hard at Kossuth while he racked his brains for an injurious epithet—"that sassy child home ter his mammy?"

"Come, I am tired of this talk," said Mr. Kenyon; "you must go."

Rick walked heavily to the door and out into the moonlight. "Them was good old times," he said to Mr. Kenyon, with a regretful cadence in his peculiar drawl; "good old times, them War days. I wish they was back agin,—I wish they was back agin. I ain't forgot Shiloh yit, though, and I ain't a-goin' ter. But I 'll tell ye one thing, parson," he added, his mind reverting from ten years ago to the scene just past, as he unhitched his horse and carefully examined the saddle-girth and stirrups, "ye 're a mighty queer preacher, ye air, a-sittin' up an' lookin' at sinners dance an' then gittin' in a fight that don't consarn ye,—ye 're a mighty queer preacher! Ye ought ter be in my gang, that's whar *ye* ought ter be," he exclaimed with a guffaw, as he put his foot in the stirrup; "ye 've got a damned deal too much grit fur a preacher. But I ain't forgot Shiloh yit, an' I don't mean ter, nuther."

A shout of laughter from the gang, an oath or two, the quick tread of horses' hoofs pressing into a gallop, and the outlaw's troop were speeding along the narrow paths that led deep into the vistas of the moonlit summer woods.

As the old churchman, with the boy at his side and the gun still on his shoulder, ascended the rocky, precipitous slope on the opposite side of the ravine above the foaming waters of the wild mountain stream, he said but little of admonition to his companion; with the disappearance of the flame and smoke and the dangerous ruffian his martial spirit had cooled; the last words of the outlaw, the highest praise Rick Pearson could accord to the highest qualities Rick Pearson could imagine—he had grit enough to belong to the gang—had smitten a tender conscience. He, at his age, using none of the means rightfully at his command, the gentle suasion of religion, must needs rush between armed men, wrench their weapons from their hands, threatening with such violence that an outlaw and desperado, recognizing a parallel of his own belligerent and lawless spirit, should say that he ought to belong to the gang! And the heaviest scourge of the sin-laden conscience was the perception that, so far as the unsubdued old Adam went, he ought indeed.

He was not so tortured, though, that he did not think of others. He paused on reaching the summit of the ascent, and looked back at the little house nestling in the ravine, the lamp-light streaming through its open doors and windows across the path among the laurel bushes, where Rick's gang had hitched their horses.

"I wonder," said the old man, "if they are quiet and peaceable again; can you hear the music and dancing?"

"Not now," said Kossuth. Then, after a moment, "Now, I kin," he added, as the wind brought to their ears the oft-told tale of the rabbit's gallopade[20] in the pea-patch. "They 're a-dancin' now, and all right agin."

As they walked along, Mr. Kenyon's racked conscience might have been in a slight degree comforted had he known that he was in some sort a revelation to the impressible lad at his side, that Kossuth had begun dimly to comprehend that a Christian may be a man of spirit also, and that bravado does not constitute bravery. Now that the heat of anger was over, the young fellow was glad that the fearless interposition of the warlike peace-maker had prevented any killing, " 'kase ef the old man hed n't hung on ter my gun like he done, I'd have been a murderer like he said, an' Rick would hev been dead. An' the bay filly ain't sech a killin' matter nohow; ef it war the roan three-year-old now, 't would be different."

MIDWEST

About Gertrude Dorsey Brown[e] little is known except her stories, published in the *Colored American Magazine* between 1902 and 1907. She lived in Newark, Ohio, where she was a sales and distribution agent, as well as a contributing writer, for the *Colored American Magazine*. Besides "Scrambled Eggs" (January 1905) and "The Voice of the Rich Pudding" (October 1907), collected here, Brown[e]'s published work includes the short stories "An Equation" (August 1902) and "The Better Looking" (March 1903), and a novelette titled "A Case of Measure for Measure" (April–October 1906). Her stories were not collected in a book during her lifetime, but are included in the Schomburg Library volume *Short Fiction by Black Women, 1900–1920*.

SCRAMBLED EGGS

I

It was Easter morning. Each room in the big house was in characteristic and suggestive attire. In the dining room and parlors large bouquets of Easter lilies and early violets were in evidence. The library had been temporarily converted into a kind of still life poultry show, for on the mantel and shelves sundry stuffed ducks and candy chickens shared common quarters with rabbits of doubtful origin and eggs of many sizes and all colors. In the dressing rooms, tidy house-maids were spreading out divers and costly arrays of feminine finery,—laces, bonnets and dresses. In the kitchen large baskets of fresh eggs hinted at the possibility of delicious omelets and muffins.

At seven o'clock the family and guests began to assemble in

the sitting room, each in turn with bright happy faces and pleasant greetings, but the host, Mr. Grayson, was hungry. He wanted his breakfast; he was conscious that something was wrong, and his sensitive nature seemed to divine by intuition that the domestic economy of his establishment was in immediate danger of dissolution. Accordingly, he walked to the kitchen door and looked in. Everything was in scrupulous order, but no where to be seen was cook or serving maid. The fire was not yet lighted in the range, and alas! no signs of breakfast did he see.

"What can this mean,—where the deuce is Mandy and Bess?" soliloquized the bewildered Mr. Grayson. He rang the servants' bell several times but without response, save from his wife who now came rushing into the entry to inquire into the cause of such delay. Her husband explained, and then added, "It just seems that if we want any breakfast to-day we must prepare it ourselves or wait for the Lord to work a miracle, for there isn't a servant in sight."

"Well I do declare!" and Mrs. Grayson seated herself on the meal bin and for the twentieth time in as many hours, she made a diligent search through her store of resources for some solution to this new problem. Finally she arose and bidding her husband return to their guests she gathered up the train of her elegant gown and hurried from the house. In fifteen minutes she returned, accompanied by an old colored lady and a young girl.

"Now Aunt Caddy, I want you and Lulu to—"

"Look here Mrs. Grayson! Before the war when I belonged to you'uns I was 'Aunt Caddy,' but now I'm 'Mrs. Caroline Somebody' and please, you jes' call me that hereafter." The quiet dignity with which the old lady gave this gentle rebuke awakened both pity and respect.

"Well you must excuse me—I—I didn't know your name in full—At any rate please get us up some breakfast as soon as possible. Thank goodness there are plenty of fresh rolls and butter and cream. Just fry some ham and some potatoes, and cook some eggs, yes, boil some, and fry some, and poach a few and scramble some for the children, and make an omelet or two, and some coffee and—"

—"Run along honey' I know how to get an Easter Breakfast and that mighty quick, so don't you worry."

An hour later at 8:30 the family were summoned to the dining room, where true to her promise and profession, Mrs. Caroline Somebody had not only provided the prescribed articles, but a tempting tray of hot muffins and fried chicken.

Mr. Grayson exchanged satisfied glances with the lady who presided so gracefully at his board and mentally congratulated himself upon such a valuable possession.

"My wife," he was prone to say, "is equal to any emergency in the domestic government of the house. She is so graceful and competent in discharging her social duties, and on the whole as handsome a woman as there is in Georgia."

It was seven o'clock that evening before husband and wife were free to discuss together the proceeding of a most unusual day. Fortunately the guests and Miss Dora were "invited out" for the evening—Aunt Effie and Malcolm had gone to church and the twins were safely stored away for the night, each with a stomach full of hard boiled eggs and a mind filled with wonderful recollections of the Easter tide.

"Now Elizabeth, do sit in this easy chair with me for an hour or so. Poor little wife, you look so tired,—and Oh, that ugly frown that sits so comfortably on your pretty brow. Tell me dear of what you are thinking?" and Mr. Grayson took a seat beside his adored Elizabeth, and gently smoothed out the frown on her face.

"Really Merrit, it is hard to explain, but the sum of matter is—I'm worried and perplexed about Aunt Caddy. She actually frightens me sometimes and some how she makes me feel so uncomfortable. When the cook and Bessie left us so unceremoniously, my only resource was a call upon the services of Aunt Caddy.—Now do you know she refuses to be called Aunt Caddy any more? To-day she told me to call her Mrs. Caroline Somebody."

"Mrs. Caroline Fiddlesticks! nonsense! And you have allowed that foolishness to worry you all day?—You see Lizzie it is but another phase of the subject that is agitating not only the individual, the family and the community, but it is stirring up the whole state. What must be done for these ex-slaves who are too poor to live independently of us and who must yet dictate terms of moral and social propriety that would raise the hair of an imperialist?—I say, 'crush them.' I have no patience with such mistaken ideas of citizenship, as are advanced in the legislature by such fellows as Slaughter and Owens. I shall never consent for my daughter Dora, to make an alliance with young Slaughter while he advocates the principles of a doctrine so foreign to the education and so distasteful to the nature of all Southern gentlemen. Do you not see in this foolish revolt of Aunt Caddy a spirit of—'I—am—as—good—as—you, Sir?' Lewis struck the keynote when he presented his bill providing for separate traveling apartments and for certain restrictions in the suffrage of these people. Now I shall go a step further and shall bring before the municipal council a petition to grant the whites either separate street cars or the reservation of a distinct section of a car, and absolute control of the theatres, concert halls and public parks. Social equality will never do. One drop of the African blood is, in my estimation, sufficient cause for ostracism. Education and all the adornment of music, art, literature and travel can never fully eradicate from our minds the thought that but one drop of blood can make a Negro, and 'Once a Negro, always a Negro.' There! my dear, I have finished," and Mr. Grayson looked expectantly at his wife as if he had rather anticipated a round of applause or at least some favorable comment.

"Well Merrit, your ideas and mine usually coincide, but in this instance I am bound to disagree, at least I am not in harmony with your proposed method of dealing with these true but simple minded creatures. Aunt Caddy is a type of one class of Negroes who certainly has proved its legitimate title to our respect and confidence. She has been well raised and for honesty and faithful service was rewarded with treachery. My greatest regret is that my own father wronged her as he did."

"Lizzie you are supersensitive."

"Why do you say so?"

"For the reason that you imagine your father did wrong when he disposed of his own property as he thought best. Aunt Caddy's daughter, although a quadroon[1] and a very beautiful child, deserved no exemption from the lot or condition of the blackest

African slave, and in selling her he simply exercised the right of every slave holding gentleman in the South. It but brings us back to the original hypothesis—'Once a Negro, always a Negro.'— But let us not discuss the subject any further, and do not let the whims of a half-witted old woman worry or in any way annoy my dear little wife. Not for every Negro in the world would I willingly spare one of your sweet smiles, or see a frown upon this handsomest of all faces," and bending over, the fond husband kissed his wife and bade her good-night.

One month later, the entire state was talking over the wonderful victory of the youngest member of the legislature. How did Slaughter manage it? What right had he, what right had any one, to rule the vote, to induce men to defeat the very bill that they were bound by their constituents to support? But Slaughter did it, and the "keynote" struck by Lewis, received such an astounding shock that after wandering disconsolately over the heads of quandom admirers it suddenly suffered a complete loss of identity.

Flushed with a triumph of a hard earned victory, yet modest in claiming the reward that he felt awaited him, the young giant, Slaughter, presented himself at the Grayson mansion and inquired for Miss Dora. Merrit Grayson, dignified and stern-faced, met the young man who had dared much that he might gain more, and in unqualified terms forbade him the premises and any future communication with his daughter, and by way of further admonition, he added, "Young man, be careful hereafter how you use for your own glory and selfish ambition, the talent you have derived from an honorable Southern ancestry. Your father whom we respected and loved, and your mother who gave all of her vast fortune to the cause that we loved but lost, are thrice blessed in that they do not live to see their son a bigot in a false position."

"Respect for myself, and for those who like yourself differ with me politically—forbids that I say to what extent this same heresy of which I am accused, exists in your own family. Some day, God only knows when, I firmly believe that you will reap the benefits that will result to us, as a people, from the defeat of Mr. Lewis' bill. As for your daughter, I love her—yes quite as much as you loved her mother when you were my age, but I refuse to sacrifice principle and every true conviction, for the boon of a sweet help mate who must ever afterward regard me as a coward and one unworthy of her confidence. You need fear no future intrusion on my part, for as a gentleman I expect you to acquaint your family of our interview. Good afternoon," and Mr. Slaughter, late of Atlanta, returned on the evening train to his city office.

Next afternoon two little girls were jumping rope on the lawn in front of a neat little cottage, and as a carriage rolled by, both children stopped their play and stared in opened-mouth wonder.

"Why that were Miss Dora, or I done seen a spirit," said one.

"It were Miss Dora, or this chile has done swallowed a gopher sure"—replied the other.

"How you reckon it feels to be took like she is? Sam say las' night that she were all broken up and they have to get a 'pasition'[2] to come and take the spell off'en her."

"Sam don't know; he only hear say—I knows, cause my Aunt Caddy were over there when it happened. She aint got no spell and she ain't got the janders,[3] nor the measles nor nothing like us cullud folks gets. It's somethin' 'fectin' on the heart and the stomach, Aunt Caddy say," responded the proud possessor of the correct diagnosis of the case.

The other little girl eyed her companion knowingly and then said simply—"How do it ail her?"

"Why she jes cry all the time and won't go no where, and can't eat nothing," said Miss Importance.

"Lordy! is it ketchin?"

"Not with cullud folks."

"I'm mighty glad, fer I'd hate like all get out, to have to cry all the time and not eat any grub, and stay in bed all day—that's worse'n our baby, for if it do cry a heap and can't walk, it got a bottle milk to chew on every time it wants it. T'aint so bad after all to be cullud, least it aint so resky, but there! our baby's crying and course I got to go in and sing it back to sleep." Soon the rich voice of a little girl was heard singing:

"Bringing in the sheeps,
Bringing in the sheeps,

We shall come rejoicing,
Bringing in the sheeps."[4]

At an open window in an office in the ware-house opposite,
sat Merrit Grayson, holding in his hand a petition conceived,
composed and circulated by himself. It was to be presented to
the city council at its next meeting and was signed by hundreds
of influential citizens. The sudden illness of Dora Grayson had
made it impossible for him to present it the night before as he
had intended. The conversation of the little girls had been distinctly heard by himself and his three clerks, and it awakened in
the father a train of new thoughts. Had he been cruel in his
attempt to be just? Was Dora's illness really serious? Did his
wife fully sympathize with his method of righting a fancied
wrong? Was his a position ethical, or ethnical? For some time
he sat very still and mused over the situation while he tapped
the petition monotonously against his forehead. He was aroused
by the unceremonious banging of the door and the sudden appearance of Sam—the man of all work.

"Mister Grayson your wife sent me to say that you are
wanted at home, and to stop by the drug store and get some oil
of olives grease, and to come straight home and don't stop no
where."

"What's the trouble Sam?"

"Your two twin children, sir."

"My God Sam, can't you tell me what is wrong, what has
happened to the twins?"

"They was botherin' around where 'Liza was boilin' the soft
soap and natchelly they took on fire"—but the excited father
had rushed from the building and Sam, unexpectedly deprived
of the privilege of inflicting further torture, sauntered out of the
office.

A scene of confusion presented itself at the home of the Gray-
sons. Aunt Effie with her best Holland apron tied hind part
before, across her generous proportions, met her brother at the
door with a look of "I-alone-have-escaped-to-tell-you."

Malcolm was hitching the doctor's horse to a prop that helped
to support a clothes line. Dora was making linen bandages from
a whole bolt of unbleached muslin, and no where did the un-

happy man see the light of sanity but in the eyes of his faithful wife who very quietly, very calmly, drew him into the cool sitting room and explained the case. The twins had been burned, and with what serious results they would know after the doctor had completed his examination. Thanks to God and Mrs. Caroline Somebody that the little dears were not then disfigured and unrecognizable corpses. Aunt Caddy had saved their lives at the risk of her own, and was now lying unconscious in the room over head, attended by Lulu, her granddaughter, and Aunt Effie's maid. The doctor had done all in his power to relieve the pain and to make the dying woman as comfortable as possible; and then the parents, hand in hand, went softly into the darkened nursery where two little sufferers were groaning in the restless sleep that an opiate produces. The medical man with the brief statement—"painful but not serious"—passed out of the room and sought the bed of the old colored lady. Tears of gratitude mingled with tears of sorrow flowed, as Mr. and Mrs. Grayson sat beside those little iron beds and thought of the noble sacrifice that had been made to keep from their hearts the bitter experience of a fireside containing two vacant chairs.

Supper time came and went and gradually the house became quiet and its inmates composed. The summon which all were expecting, did not come until almost midnight, and then the maid softly opened the door of the sitting room, and motioning to Mr. and Mrs. Grayson—"Come," and silently they followed her into the presence of death. The seal of the "Great Beyond" was stamped upon the wrinkled yellow face, but intelligence and perfect composure shone in the keen grey eyes, and when she began to speak, the truth of all she said was impressed upon her hearers. The maid was dismissed and the doctor left the room, while in a solemn voice, Mrs. Caroline Somebody began her remarkable testimony.

"I have so much to say to you, and though my time is short, I know the good Lord is goin' to let me tell you all of it. Never mind honey, about my pillow—the burn don't hurt now, I've gone clear past all aches and pains and have stepped into the healing, cooling stream of the River of Life. Forty years ago when I lived on the large plantation with Master and Missus I laid aside the robes of the righteous and not until this very day

have I called upon the name of the Lord. Now I see all of my
wickedness, and now I know I done scrambled more eggs than
I ever intended.

"You see it was like this. Missus was took sick one Easter
morning and it was at the town house and nobody was handy
to wait on her but me. When Miss 'Lisbeth was born old Doctor
Slaughter hand her to me and say—'Caddy you take keer of the
baby and keep it in your room for awhile until your mistress is
better. She's too nervous to have it around her just yet.' Well I
was nervous too, but I took the little thing and I done for it all
that I could do. That very night my own child was born—a
pretty plump little girl, as much like missus' babe as could be
'ceptin' mine had darker hair and much more of it. Old Hannah
waited on me and both the children, as much as she could until
master bring three or four of the slaves in from the plantation.
He come in to see me directly he come back, and he was in
powerful bad humor. He say: 'Look here, Caddy, I done left
you to take care of my wife while I gone for more servants and
what you mean by gettin' sick now and leavin' my wife all alone?
I tell you I won't stand no sech airs. Soon as you git up I reckon
you'll want to have your brat take all your 'tention and that'll
be a excuse for not looking after your young mistress. But my
chile comes first, and I reckon the first trader comes along can
have yours and take the keer of it offen your shoulders.' At first
I was too surprised to say anything, then my Spanish come to
the top. I reckon you don't know that my father was Spanish—
well he was. Then I up and says to master:

" 'Kernel Claybourn, you wouldn't dar'st to sell my child,
for you know that both these children are your own flesh and
blood and you know you wouldn't sell the one any sooner than
you would the other.' He looked at me kind a hard like and
then he come up to the little crib where both babies lay and say,
kind a' soft like: 'Caddy, which of these children belong to your
mistress?'

"Now, Hannah had just had time to dress one of them before
she was obliged to go get breakfast, and that one was mine,
because it happened to be awake. I wanted to see how it would
look in the fine clothes that belonged to 'Lisbeth, and Hannah
had dressed it up so cunning, while poor little 'Lisbeth was still

asleep in a plain little muslin slip. Well, I could see there was mischief in master's eye and I reckon I got some of the same stuff in mine, for I reached over, past my own baby and picked up little 'Lisbeth and I said to him: 'Now, jest look here, Mast' Claybourn, if my poor little girl had on a fine dress like your'n and was all fixed up, wouldn't she be jest as white, jest as pretty as that chile? Aint my baby as good as missus' baby?' Then he grab up the other baby and say: 'No, not by a damn sight, is your young'un as good as this,' and he walked out of the room with it and gave it to Molly, who had just come, and tole her to take good care of it and as soon as the doctor come to carry it to its mother. Hannah was kept in the kitchen after that and little black Betty looked after me, so no body but me knew of the exchange. A few days after this master sent for me to come to the liberry. I was pretty weak but I went, and when I got there he said: 'Caddy, you been sick long enough now, so I want you to get breakfast, for Hannah has to go away to help out over at Jedge Whites' during Miss Jessie's wedding. You seem to think because we always been good to you that you are a great somebody, but it's a mistake. You ain't nobody more'n the rest of your kind. I might as well tell you first as last that I done sold your baby up-river to a speculator[5] in Memphis. Don't do any bad actin' over this affair for it won't count, and jist you turn around in the kitchen and make yourself as useful as you ken; and mind you scramble my eggs for my breakfast. I like them scrambled best.'

"When I left that room I seem to see everything I saw when I had the swamp fever. I knew I was almost as sinful as master, but I was so glad that I had done jest the sort of sinning that I had."

"Good God," broke from the lips of Mr. Grayson, who in the midst of this confession looked longingly and hungrily at his wife, who in turn had drawn her chair nearer to the bed and in a moment had clasped the almost lifeless hand, and whispered "Mother—my own poor mother."

"It does not matter," continued the dying woman, "how long I was getting that breakfast, nor how often I kept saying over and over, 'I certainly done scrambled your eggs.' I cried over dear little 'Lisbeth, when they took her away next day, and then

I took mighty sick in my head and Hannah said I didn't know beans from a cock-roach for five weeks. From the day that I began to get better until now, I don't seem to see anything or hear anything but scrambled eggs. Everything around me is mixed with yellow and white. When the war broke out and word came to us that master was sick with yellow fever, up in Tennessee, I jest said to myself, 'Serves him right, he always would have scrambled eggs, and now let the yellow fever mix itself all through and through that white-livered coward,—yellow and white still makes yellow. Just a little bit of yellow and a lot of white, and bless you it ain't white no more.' When mistress began to droop and pine away, I reckon I saw that same yellow mixin' up with the white in her eyes, and though the doctor said it was janders, I knew it was scrambled eggs.

"My time is almost up, but I want to ask you, Mr. Grayson, what you going to do for my daughter? Is she still your wife; is her children your children? I ain't claimin' no relation to yours, but your family is bound to be relations of mine. Now when I'm gone will you leave my daughter and her family to go to the dogs? Will you have your wife ride in a dirty car with the very lowest of 'cullud' people while you sit back in a first class coach and smoke a cigar? Will you take her to an opera, or one of them song concerts and let her sit in the peanut ring,[6] while you are in a fine box? When you enter a hotel or one of them fine eating rooms, will you call the manager aside and say: 'Take this Negro woman back behind the screen to a side table, while I sit with my friends at the first table by the door'?

"When your sons, the twins, become men, will you follow them to the voting place and say: 'You shall vote for this man,' or 'you shan't vote for that man, because you have no right to choose for yourself. You must vote as I think best'?

"When an honest white man comes and asks you for your daughter, Dora, are you going to say: 'She is a Negro and any one can have her,' or will you say, 'She is my only daughter and no man is quite worthy of her'?

"If your son, Malcolm, is accused of some awful crime, will you join in the cry of 'Lynch him, string him up, he is only a Negro and he don't need a trial'? Tell me, Merrit Grayson, how do you intend to use your share of scrambled eggs?"

With suffering and intense pain written upon every feature, and with a trembling voice, the miserable man answered:

"Before God, I will do all for my family that man can do. I shall continue to love and protect my dear wife and my children, and I shall try to be more just to my fellow men. 'Tis a hard lesson you have taught me but I believe I have learned it well. My wife and my family are, regardless of Negro blood, as good, as pure, and as capable as any family on God's green earth."

He stopped, giving his wife a nod, pointed toward the east window. It was dawn,—and yellow streaks from the rising sun were mingling with the first white lights. A soul was passing away, and the feeble voice, before it was forever silent, softly said: "Yellow and white—scrambled eggs."

II

"Tis thy wedding morning
   Shining in the skies
      Bridal bells are ringing
      Bridal songs arise
   Opening the portals
   Of thy Paradise
      Arise, sweet maid, arise."

The windows of the bed chambers on the second floor were soon filled with eager faces and each delighted listener inquired of the other from whence came this bridal chorus so early in the morning.

Dora Grayson stood on the balcony over-looking the garden, and from that vine-covered nook she discovered that several white robed creatures had taken possession of the little arbor that faced the balcony and stood directly under the window of her own bed chamber. But to her, the chorus meant nothing and with an abstracted half sigh, she turned to re-enter the large French window of her dressing room, but that space was occupied by the ample figure of her aunt Effie.

"Why Dora Grayson, what are you doing up and dressed so early: and in this solemn looking black gown? Why child, this is your wedding morning and even now the bridesmaids and flower girls are singing your bridal. Come quick, throw this opera cape over your shoulders and while I bring the rose bowl you must make your courtesy and for mercy sake look happy. 'Mr. Choppang' couldn't help writing another funeral march if he could see you now. It's enough to make an American weep, much less a heathen Chinaman," and with a gentle but resolute push, Aunt Effie parted the vines and drew Dora forward.

"The bride! the bride! how lovely," and laughing and dancing gayly below the jolly serenaders threw kisses at Dora while she, with a graceful movement, from the handsome rose jar showered bridal roses upon them. Whether from the effort required to do this, or for some other reason, the beautiful white opera cape became disengaged from its fastenings and slipped to the floor, leaving a pale faced girl in a simple blace[7]—alone on the balcony,—superstitious people might have said it was an evil omen, but of course no superstitious people were there. Carl Slaughter entering the yard at that moment saw his betrothed and breathing a fervent "God bless her" started for the house, but was met by Merrit Grayson and the two stopped to exchange greetings. The latter did not look like the same man who had one year before forbade him the premises and denied him all future association or communication with his daughter. That Merrit Grayson had long ceased to exist. It had been a trying year and by no means was it an easy task to make the change and reformation in thought, word and action that he had done.

Any coward can avoid unpleasant issues by professing to adopt popular ideas; by saying green is pink because public sentiment says so. But it requires a real hero to yield stubborn prejudices and preference to a conviction inspired by the unsubstantiated testimony of one whom he considers in every way his inferior.

True to his promise to Mrs. Caroline Somebody, Mr. Grayson had tried to undo the wrong he had started, for he realized that to pursue the course he had undertaken he must give up all that was nearest and dearest—a sacrifice upon the very altar he had erected whereon he had designed that other men's liberties should perish. After talking it over with his wife, he decided to go to Atlanta, call upon Mr. Slaughter and apologize for his actions. The young lawyer received him politely if not cordially and after listening in wonder to the retraction of statements most emphatically advocated such a short time before, he thanked Merrit Grayson for his offer of renewed friendship and boldly asked permission to see Miss Dora.

A great wave of crimson suffused the face of the strong man, and his emotions overcoming him he burst into tears, "O Slaughter for God's sake, as you live, as you prize your manhood, do not betray this sacred confidence, and were it not that my daughter loves you—No, by the eternal God—no—I would not tell you this secret," exclaimed the excited father.

"Your confidence is safe with me, although I do not know for what reason you should distress yourself thus—" replied the lawyer.

Merrit Grayson briefly told the story he had heard from the lips of the dying woman, and with a look half of sorrow half of defiance, faced the man who wished above all else to become his son-in-law. "Now Slaughter you professed to love Dora, before this, what do you think of it since you know her to be a—I can't say the word? Excuse me but I never made a practice of saying colored people, and Negress hardly seems appropriate, it is so much like tigress. But since you know, that things are not what they have seemed, tell me truly if your love is as unchanged and as sincere, as is the character of my oldest-born? I am her father, and I wish above all else to protect her and the rest of my family, who are, mind you, as good as any and better than most people under the heavens above."

For a few minutes the room was as silent as a tomb, then Carl Slaughter with a peculiar expression on his face arose—and taking a key from his pocket unlocked the door to a private drawer in his desk and took therefrom a small book which he proceeded to open and finally placed before the other, with the remark— "This was my father's diary and among other things concerning his professional career I found the statements I place before you. I have known of this for some time, and in that fact alone you may be better convinced of my love for Dora. Read for yourself."

It was an old style memoranda with a substantial morocco

case and although the writing was yellow, yet it was perfectly legible and easily read.

Under date of Easter Sunday, April 18—was written.—"Attendance upon Mrs. Clayborne, etc—Strange experience with a servant called Hannah. She stopped me in the hall one evening as I was leaving the Clayborne house and told me she wanted to tell me something no one else must hear. I stepped into the library and closed the door for I saw by the excited features that the poor creature was in great distress.

" 'Mars Slaughter, Missus done sent for me to come and show the gal Molly how to dress de baby, and shore as I'm alive that ain't missus' baby a' tall. Hit's Caddie's baby for I done dressed it my self yestidy in dem very close and moresoever, I knows them babies apart. This'in is sure cullored and ain't missus' baby, but she done seen it now and say hit got eyes like hits pap', and mouf like hits granny and she done put a little ring on its finger and say hit must stay there till the finger out grow it, for she say she put it on with a wish.'

"I tried to persuade Hannah that she must be mistaken but she would not have it so, and as nothing else would satisfy her I promised to speak to the Col. about it the next day. That night I was called to Montgomery[8] and it was some days later before I again visited the Claybornes. The horror I saw in the eyes of Hannah and the manner in which she watched my movements convinced me that she had something to say. I made an excuse for sending her for my case, and as she returned I met her in the dressing room.

" 'Oh Mars Slaughter! Mars Clayborne done gone and sold his own baby and left this here'n for missus. He and Caddie must a got things mixed for he sure done sold the wrong child and its gone up river to the Lord-don't-know-where.'

"The earnestness of the poor creature, and a thorough knowledge of the caprices of a mother about to be robbed of her child, led me to make an investigation, first cautioning Hannah to say nothing to any one of her discovery. I sought out Col. Clayborne and stated the case to him. He flatly refused to credit it and declared he believed this so-called discovery, but a put-up-job to cause him trouble. Hot words followed and then and there

I severed my connections with Clayborne. He made no effort
so far as I know to follow up, or locate the child he had sold,
and as a physician my position was little better than that of
father confessor, for I dared not push matters without better
testimony than that of a slave,—a slave's mere suspicion. Heaven
will reveal all things, but God knows I believe that somewhere
in this Southland—a slave—a pure white child is in bondage,
and that child is the daughter of Col. Ellwood Clayborne."

Merrit Grayson, his face white, and his features strained, yet
with a certain dignity, closed the little book and returned it to
Carl Slaughter. "Well my boy, if my daughter's happiness depends upon you, then make her happy, and if ever you feel that
you cannot do so, I"—but he did not finish for the men had
been so engrossed in their mutual sorrow that they had not
heard the opening of the door of the outer office some fifteen
minutes before, and now when it closed with a bang, both gentlemen sprang to their feet and hurried to the hall. A discharged
office clerk was just stepping into the elevator. Slaughter turned
a trifle pale, and then said—"If agreeable to your daughter I will
call to-morrow evening."

This interview and others that followed were soon productive
of definite arrangements for an early marriage, and a consequent
trip to Europe. The time was fixed for June 1st, and now that
day had arrived. After the celebration of the old custom of awakening the bride with the singing of the bridal, the different members of the family prepared in their own way for the festivities
of the day.

The twins—Raymond and Marcellus—were bringing glad-
ness to the hearts and sweet-meats to the stomachs of a crowd
of urchins who had solicited "errand work" at the kitchen door.
Small corners of cake, and pans of icing with stray pieces of ham
and chicken wings, were rapidly disappearing, while Ray and
Marc entertained the children with accounts of the inner work-
ings of the great event. "I reckon you'uns won't allow we'uns
to git a look at the bright grooms," and one little fellow looked
wistfully at Ray as he munched the cookie in his dirty little hand,
but Ray unheeding the warning look from Marc, stoutly declared "O yes we will. Its to be at the big church and every one

who comes and brings one of our tickets is sure to get in, cause my aunt Effie told me so." Then a bright idea occurring to him, he called his brother aside and unfolded his plan, which meeting the instant approval of the practical Marc, away ran the twins while the urchins, their number augmented by the arrival of a strange, hungry looking young man, wondered how and by what means the tickets spoken of could be obtained. They had not long to wait, for the boys soon returned with a box containing twenty engraved cards which bore this simple statement:

"Please present this card at the church."

In some manner the idea was soon understood and the tickets began to sell like hot cakes, for from three to ten cents, according to the reputed wealth of the purchaser.

Little Edna Clayborne, who with the year-and-a-half-old baby, had joined the crowd, was anxiously watching the sale, and trying to decide upon some plan whereby she too, might witness Miss Dora's marriage. Then remembering her own valued possession—an Angora kitten—she bounded away leaving Isaac Orlando to the tender mercies of his fellow scamps.

When Edna returned she marched boldly up to the twins and demanded: "A kitten's worth of tickets." This demand was met with a shout of derision from the spectators, while the youthful merchants, cast into doubt by the problem of a satisfactory adjustment of such a purchase, examined the cat, and as it was a beautiful creature and promised new diversion they decided it was worth three tickets. The tickets thus disposed of, the children separated, and little Edna was wearily "luggin" the baby home to the favorite strains of "Bringing in the sheeps" when she was accosted by the stranger who had watched the sale a few minutes before.

"I say sissy, I'll give you a quarter for one of them tickets you just got" and the piece of silver was temptingly held out to the ex-owner of the Angora. Edna eyed him suspiciously and then said loftily, "Who is you, and is you 'spectable?"

"Never mind about me—I'm his royal Nibs of Nibbsville. Just you hand over one of them cards before I cut yer ears off"—replied the man.

Thus appealed to and seeing no way of escape, the card was

given in exchange for the quarter and the baby was gently admonished to hurry along, cause the beans would sure burn, if he didn't.

It was five o'clock in the afternoon, and the large crowd gathered at the church bore evidence of the popularity of the couple about to be married.

To be sure, some surprise was evinced when the ushers seated two rows of little black girls and boys and when Edna and the baby, duly arrayed in their Sunday best, were seated beside the fashionable Mrs. Norman Rossin, that worthy dame, in the name of her departed ancestry—requested the usher to please find other accommodations for the "persons" who sat beside her.

The bridal party finally arrived and with the usual pomp and ceremony of such occasions, each participant took his place and the minister began the sacred service.

In the midst of that silence which follows the words "Speak now," a young man arose from no one knew where, and distinctly said, "I forbid the bans. It is an illegal act in this state for any minister of any religious denomination to marry a colored or Negro woman to a white man. Dora Grayson has Negro blood in her veins and you dare not perform this ceremony."

The effect was all that could have been desired from such a malicious source. Merrit Grayson had arisen and faced the accuser, and then white and shaking in every limb, he had sunk back into the seat. Slaughter and his best man, had involuntarily reached for the hip pocket, and then helplessly dropped their arms. The minister, with blazing eyes, and threatening attitude in stern words, commanded the young man to come forward and produce proof of his assertion. But proof came from another source.

Dora Grayson, dignified, sweet, composed, turned to the minister and in clear tones said—"It is true, let us not listen to the story of the past, now. If this ceremony cannot proceed under the conditions we may at least withdraw in peace."

Slaughter, the lion[9] of the senate, the pet of the club, the wit of the banquet, led from the church, past the pews of the proudest and wealthiest the girl whom he loved but whom the laws of his state forbade him to marry. Crushed yet resolute, defeated yet defiant, the groom-elect handed the girl into the waiting car-

riage and was driven back to the Grayson home. The family soon
followed, and in which face was the most misery, the most suffering, would be hard to decide. The guests went to their own
homes and no one save the minister and the strange young man
remained. The latter explained very glibly that at one time he
was a clerk in the office of Carl Slaughter, and after being dismissed he had returned one day for a talk with his former employer and hearing him in conversation with another gentleman
in his private office, he had seated himself and thus heard the
story of that skeleton which occupied the spare closet at the
Grayson home.

He had taken a run up from Atlanta the day before, hoping
to see Slaughter and exact quieting money from him, but finding
an easier way of humiliating Mr. Slaughter and the rest of them
big-bugs he had abandoned the former plan and procured an
entrance card to the church and now he guessed their cake was
all dough.[10] In disgust the minister turned abruptly from the
informer and was about to leave the church when one of the
trustees approached and desired an interview.

"If all this stuff is true, we might as well get through with
the unpleasant part at once. This church does not fellowship
Negroes, and as senior trustee I shall call a meeting and have
this settled before we lose our best members."

"My God! my God! and has the church no place in it for
such as we have just seen denied the privileges of the most sacred
of its ordinances? God forbid that I wear the holy garments only
to deny the faith that I am trying to instil in others. I see the
whole thing now. We are the servants of the world, we are the
most abject slaves of mammon,[11] we are crucifying our Lord
daily, and I for one, shall begin now to ask God's mercy upon
me, chief of sinners, that I know myself to be." The minister
knelt at the deserted railing of the altar and poured out his soul
before the God of Sabaoth. The trustee, bored and uncomfortable, took his hat and went out.

For three weeks after the sensational revelation at the fash-
ionable church very little was seen of any of the members of the
Grayson family. It was known that Slaughter had returned to
Atlanta, but for how long and for what purpose, none could say.
In fact society canvassed and gossiped the affair in a guarded

way, for openly it avoided any direct investigation. It felt that its own foundations were of such a nature that it must handle with care any stones which came within its way.

Mrs. Norman Rossin, upon her return from the church walked straight to the library, took from its shelf the large family Bible and carried it to her room and never again was it seen by any member of her household.

Mrs. Grayson and Dora seemed strangely self possessed. Malcolm spent most of his time with his favorite pony, the twins tried to adapt themselves to the new order of affairs by acquiring a knowledge of the life of little colored boys. When no one was near they took turns in calling each other "nigger" just to see how it felt. To Aunt Effie the blow was mortal. She had been kept in ignorance of everything until disclosure was made at the church and then she had done what she usually did at a crisis—fainted. Afterward when her brother told her the facts she became hysterical and blamed Aunt Caddy for all their misery, and now at the end of three weeks she was reduced to a mere nonentity.

The family was seated at the table and the fish was being served when a servant entered and handed a letter to Mr. Grayson. He glanced over it and laid it by his plate, then picking it up and reading it a second time the full significance of it burst upon him and in a frenzy he tore the sheet into bits.

"The Rev. Mr. Voorhees regrets his inability to accommodate my sons at his private school, for the next term," and he abruptly left the room. His wife did not tell him that upon her dresser lay three envelopes, each containing some such insult. The first was from Capt. and Mrs. Benjamin, recalling their invitation to dinner, but assigning no reason. Another was from Madame Carée, announcing her regrets that she could no longer accommodate the ladies at her dressmaking establishment; the last, and worst of all, was from the man-of-all-work, Sam.

He wished her to know that they had treated him well, but it was a matter of "principle" with him, and he would not work for "cullord folks. As long as you was white it was all right, and if you'en is ever white again, just send for me and I'm your man, but I won't work for no niggers if I knows it," and thus Sam's resignation was filed.

The minister called and although the call was not a pleasant one, yet his unspoken sympathy and love went far towards the soothing of the ruffled sea.

Judge White's son, Ben, came often and stayed late with Malcolm, and several ladies made it known in various ways that they were friends of the family in spite of reverses.

One morning Dora came into the sitting room with such a radiant face that every one asked what good news she bore.

"It is a message I received from Carl, in the first place. He says, he has arranged everything and we may all start for Europe next week if we can get ready in time. He has put papa's business in the hands of a capable agent and there is nothing left to do, but to get ready for our vacation.

"My second cause for joy is this: I think we all have been very silly to spend so much time weeping and mourning over the fact that we are of Negro extraction. Are we not as good as we were before we found this out? If not it is our own fault. Have we changed in our love for each other? Have our feet become larger or our lips thicker or have horns begun to grow on our heads? If we have endured insults and calumny, it has been only for three or four weeks. Think what it has been to those around us, who have endured these things not three weeks only, but all their lives. We have ourselves heaped upon them some of the very burdens which now threaten to overcome us. If I am a Negro, from this day forward I mean to be just as persevering, just as ambitious, just as successful, as the white Dora Grayson of a year ago. After our marriage, Carl and I shall return to this same place and live before these people the lives of two honest God-fearing citizens, and the right people will recognize and encourage us too."

Ten days later when the family left for New York, a little colored girl stood on the deserted porch holding to her breast an Angora kitten. She watched the carriage as it drove out of sight and taking a corner of her gingham apron she wiped the tears from her eyes and then turned to Isaac Orlando with the philosophic remark:

"If poor Miss Dora and them boys is not white, then they is the most respectable colored folks in the world, and if they finds they can't pass for white where they is going, maybe they kin fix it so as Mr. Grayson an' Mr. Carl can pass for colored."

The Voice of the Rich Pudding

The door bell rang furiously, and Mr. Willis, who was in the act of blowing out the light, hastily retraced his steps down the hall, and stopped at the front door.

"Who's there?"

"Father's dead," came the answer, in an excited, childish voice.

Mr. Willis lost no time in drawing the bolts and unlocking the door, but the messenger had vanished and further questioning was impossible.

"Who the deuce was that kid, and why did he come to tell me about it at eleven o'clock?" and as he walked slowly back to his bed chamber he reviewed his limited list of acquaintances and wondered who could possibly consider his friendship and sympathy of sufficient moment that he should be notified at this hour of their loss.

"Now, let's see, there's Tyler, I've known him longer than any one else here, but since when did he become a father? and O—pshaw! I might as well dress and get myself collected. Jones has a family and is tolerably fond of me, but it's a long walk for one of his kids at this time of night. Guess I'll call up and find out the particulars. Yes, I'm afraid it is Jones. Poor old fellow, of course they'd send for me to look after things until his folks can be communicated with. I'll go right down and call up. These telephones are a great thing. Thank God! he didn't say Estella is dead."

Mr. and Mrs. Sarter were roaming about in the sweet land of Nod[1] when they were recalled to things present and terrestrial by loud knocking at their door.

"Go down Jim, for mercy's sake, and find out what's the matter," Mrs. Sarter advised.

The sleepy man very ungraciously stumbled down the stairs,

through the sitting room into the parlor and peered through the window at a small white figure on the porch.

"Hey, sonny, what's the row?" he yelled through the window.

"Mother's dead!"

"Whose mother? Mine or Annie's?" screamed Mr. Sarter as he dashed to the door and threw it open.

No one answered him for the porch was empty. In the sitting room, as he returned, he found his wife seated on the floor rocking to and fro moaning and groaning in a most distressing manner.

"Did you hear him Annie? It's so sudden and we're so unprepared for it."

"Oh, Jim, is it my mother?"

"I don't know, but its somebody's mother."

"There now, don't be foolish. If it ain't my mother why would any one come and wake us up in the middle of the night?" responded Mrs. Jim.

"There's just a possibility that should my own mother die, the folks would remember to notify her only son," sarcastically from Jim.

"We won't quarrel Jim, dear, don't be a bear, but if it should be poor, dear, devoted Mama, O——" and the crying began afresh.

"Now, see here, Annie, you might as well calm yourself, for we don't know whether it's proper to laugh or cry."

"We don't, hey? Well maybe you don't. If it's your mother you'll know it's proper to cry, and if it's mine, you'll laugh ——O, you beast," wailed Mrs. Sarter.

"I'm going out to Hunters' to see if there's anything wrong, and on the way back I'll stop at your mother's," with which announcement Mr. Sarter slammed the front door.

"He needn't been so grumpy, I guess I stumped my toe against that old rocker hard enough to make a stone image cry," and Mrs. Sarter limped painfully to the switch and turned on the light.

At eleven P.M. Miss Stella Warner had left her sister Alice and brother-in-law Horace and retired to her room, not to sleep, but to "think it all out."

"I don't see why we can't. I'm no infant, and I don't care a snap whether he's high church or low church[2] or any church at all, he suits me, so there! Calls us sinners, just as if he is accusing angel of the judgment." Thus ran the tearful meditations of Stella.

"Horace, I think it is perfectly ridiculous to stand in their way just on account of the slight difference in their church service. For the love of goodness let them alone, and let us get back home. I know little Marie wants to see us. I shouldn't wonder if, because of the stand you take in this matter, something should happen to Marie in our absence, which will always cause us to associate the two affairs."

Pretty Alice Thordeau was half angry with her resolute husband, but far from allowing her indignation to get the better of her prudence, she diplomatically brought into the subject the name and possible welfare of their three-year-old daughter Marie.

"Alice, I am resolved to do my duty by my ward. If Mr. Willis cannot consent to conform with the requirements of the high church, I can not consider his proposal for the hand of Estella. If they are so unwise as to do this thing without my consent, Estella loses a fortune and need expect nothing from me." Mr. Thordeau spoke with the earnest decision of a conscientious man.

"Of course, Horace, you have the say so, but just suppose Marie should ever be left to the care of a guardian and that guardian was a—was a—a Mormon or a—a—"

"Impossible!" impatiently replied Horace. "Utterly impossible, why do you suppose I would ever commit Marie into the hands of any person of whose character I was not certain? Really, Alice, you flatter my judgment by conceiving of such impossible conditions."

"Well, at any rate, father didn't make our church and mode of worship a handicap for Estella, and I'm sure he would hardly appreciate the wisdom of keeping them apart on that issue. If I thought that Marie would be compelled to eat fish on Friday[3] or burn incense to an ebony god, why I should cry my eyes out, I know."

"Very likely," was the dry return. Then with kindness, "Alice, don't confuse our personal affairs with the question we are considering, Marie is not an orphan and God knows—What was that?"

Some one tapping on the window. A faint, but persistent tap. As Mr. Thordeau opened the hall door a voice in the darkness greeted him with the words:

"Baby is dead."

"What is it, Horace?" asked Alice, coming into the hall.

"Baby is dead," he answered in a hoarse whisper. "Come— let us go—If we hurry we can catch the midnight express. Why, in the name of all that is holy, are we here, anyhow?"

But Alice, the emotional, the hysterical, was running out after the messenger.

"Here, stop! whose baby is dead? My Marie isn't dead, stop," she cried as she ran and stumbled over the shrubbery, down the avenue and out upon the street.

"Absurd—simply impossible. Oh, it must have been one of Myrtle's children—the baby—why of course—little Elizabeth. What a pity, but then the Lord knows best." She stopped at the end of the street and considered whether it was best to go on or to return to Mr. Thordeau, who by this time was thoroughly excited. Finally deciding upon the latter course, she hurried back to the house.

"Listen, Horace, have some reason. That was a child who spoke to you, and it couldn't be our Marie, she is with mother in Dayton, and telegrams don't yell at a man in the dark. They are always written or typewritten on paper. Why, it must be one of your cousin's children, the baby—little Elizabeth, no doubt. We might go over there and see what we can do, for Myrtle is utterly prostrated, I know." All the time she was talking, Alice had been making hurried preparations to visit the stricken home, and, as they entered the hall, they were joined by Stella, who insisted upon accompanying them.

"I don't know why that call should upset me as it did, I might have known it wasn't Marie, but all the same I—well—I want to get back home. I'm convinced that converting sinners from the errors of their ways isn't my forte, but mind, Miss Estella, I'm exempt from all reproach if it doesn't result harmoniously," remarked Mr. Thordeau.

Alice and Estella were both unprepared for such a concession from such a stubborn source, and the remainder of the walk was made in complete silence.

When they reached the Smith residence they found it enveloped in darkness. In response to a light rap Otis Smith's head appeared at an upstairs window and his sleepy voice inquired:

"Who's there?"

"Why, it's us," inelegantly replied Horace. "We thought we'd come over and see—and I mean ask—that, is—Say how's your baby? She ain't dead or nothing, is she?"

"For God's sake! hold on a minute and I'll be down."

The head was withdrawn and a few minutes later Otis walked out on the veranda.

"Say, what's the fun? I don't seem to understand this death notice racket. About ten minutes ago Myrt went over to her mother's to see if Helen is dead. Some one came here and made noise enough to wake up the kids, and that's going some—and when Myrt asked what was the trouble, he said her sister or my sister or some sister was dead, and Myrt just threw her rain coat over her shoulders and ran, and left me to look after Elizabeth."

The quartet sank on the steps, overcome by the mystery, and compared notes as they were able.

"Listen, there comes some one now, maybe its the bird of evil omen," cautioned Stella. But when the solitary figure of a man was about to pass them by she called after it, "O, Mr. Willis is that you?"

"It certainly is I, but why this select gathering at the witching hour of night?" he asked as he greeted the other occupants of the veranda steps.

"Who's dead?" abruptly asked Horace. "Have you heard of any deaths to-night, Mr. Willis?"

"Quite a number, I should say, but I can't tell you who."

"For instance," persisted the imaginative Horace.

"Well, for instance, I am informed that father is dead, and I just met Jim Sarter and he is trying to locate a dead mother, having satisfactorily accounted for his own and his wife's mother," was the good natured reply of Willis.

While he was talking, the telephone in the hall began to ring, and Otis answered it.

"That you, Myrt? Come on home, get one of the boys to come with you. Yes—yes—I know. Whose sister? O, is that so? No! Who! Me? You bet I ain't dead. O, rot. It's a shame—why it's the rumest⁴ game I ever heard or saw played. Yes. Good-bye."

When he rejoined the company on the steps Otis mopped his perspiring brow.

"O, Lord, my mother is on her way over here to put pennies on my waxen eyelids, and I'm afraid I don't make a very successful corpse just now. At least I can't be one of the silent kind."

"Say, let's all go home and go to bed," advised Alice, to whom each new development was a separate and distinct shock.

"Kind a reminds a fellow of the passover or the ten virgins or the Johnstown flood or something—don't it?" asked Otis as he bade his guests good night and soothed the fretful crying of little Elizabeth.

*   *   *

The supper bell had rung the second time and the tea was in danger of cooling, before the Rev. Harvey Reynolds and wife entered the dining room. Their son Max—a lad of thirteen—was impatiently awaiting them, and amusing himself in the meantime by deftly balancing a dessert spoon on the edge of a cut glass candlestick.

Rev. Reynolds led his wife to the head of the table, placed her chair, and rang the bell, requesting the maid to serve.

"That was a singular experience I must say—very singular, but quite a pretty little ceremony, Willa, did you not think so?"

"Very pretty, indeed, dear, and O, wasn't she happy?"

"The gentleman, Mr. Thordeau, rather impressed me as being a somewhat zealous person. He didn't seem to hesitate about giving her away, like they sometimes do," remarked the minister.

"After all, the dream of life is happiness and if the reality is more than the dream how very happy they ought to be," Mrs. Reynolds responded.

"Dream? What dream, Mama?" Max inquired.

"Why, dear, the dream that we are speaking of is the dream of two happy hearts made one," laughed his mother.

"O, shucks, I wouldn't give my dream for a dozen old hearts as happy as a bunch of tops."[5]

"Well son, if you've had such a pleasant dream relate it to us. I'm sure we always find pleasure in your dreams."

"I think they supply the lack of printed fiction to which I am not a generous subscriber," added his father.

"Well, sir, last night I dremp—"

"Dreamed, you mean, dear," corrected Rev. Reynolds.

"Well, then, I dreamed that Mr. Morehead took me into the Western Union, where I've always wanted to be, and he made a messenger boy out of me.

"O, shucks, if you could of seen me hustling.

"The telegrams, it seems, were written out on a blackboard and I had to learn ten or more at a time. They was all about people dying. Mr. Morehead would let me study 'em for a while and then he'd say, 'Run to So and So's and tell 'em their father's dead or sister's dead, and stop at What's his Name on your way back and tell 'em the baby's dead.' O, shucks, I almost ran myself to death. When I got up this morning I was so sore and tired I could hardly dress."

"Please excuse me," weakly interposed Mrs. Reynolds.

She left the room, but was gone only a few minutes—with horror she gasped:

"Look, Harvey! see this boy's gown, it's muddy and grass stained and the sheets of his bed—there, there, father, don't give him another bit of that rich pudding."

HAMLIN GARLAND

1860–1940

PERHAPS the best-known local colorist of the Midwest, Hamlin Garland did much to popularize the genre and define theories of realism and regionalism in literature. Born on a farm in Wisconsin, Garland left his family when they joined other homesteaders in the Dakota Territory. After working in various parts of the Midwest, in 1884 he went to Boston, where he worked to educate himself by reading at the Boston Public Library, then became a teacher at the Boston School of Oratory. In Boston he also met William Dean Howells and other prominent writers and became interested in social and economic reform.

After a trip west, Garland returned to Boston and began to write stories describing the hardships of white rural life, which would become the volume *Main-Travelled Roads* (1891). In addition to later collections of regional stories such as *Prairie Folks* (1892), Garland published many novels, including *A Spoil of Office* (1892); *Rose of Dutcher's Coolly* (1895); and a series of more romantic popular novels about Indians and the West, such as *The Captain of the Gray Horse Troop* (1902). In 1894 he published a book of essays on literature, *Crumbling Idols*, which discussed contemporary American writing and promoted his theory of "veritism"—a literary approach that sought to combine realism with psychological depth. Always concerned with social and political issues, as in stories like "Under the Lion's Paw," Garland was also active in campaigning for the Populist Party.

The ride from Milwaukee to the Mississippi is a fine ride at any time, superb in summer. To lean back in a reclining-chair and whirl away in a breezy July day, past lakes, groves of oak, past fields of barley being reaped, past hay-fields, where the heavy grass is toppling before the swift sickle, is a panorama of delight, a road full of delicious surprises, where down a sudden vista lakes open, or a distant wooded hill looms darkly blue, or swift streams, foaming deep down the solid rock, send whiffs of cool breezes in at the window.

It has majesty, breadth. The farming has nothing apparently petty about it. All seems vigorous, youthful, and prosperous. Mr. Howard McLane in his chair let his newspaper fall on his lap, and gazed out upon it with dreaming eyes. It had a certain mysterious glamour to him; the lakes were cooler and brighter to his eye, the greens fresher, and the grain more golden than to any one else, for he was coming back to it all after an absence of ten years. It was, besides, *his* West. He still took pride in being a Western man.

His mind all day flew ahead of the train to the little town, far on toward the Mississippi,[1] where he had spent his boyhood and youth. As the train passed the Wisconsin River,[2] with its curiously carved cliffs, its cold, dark, swift-swirling water eating slowly under cedar-clothed banks, Howard began to feel curious little movements of the heart, like those of a lover nearing his sweetheart.

The hills changed in character, growing more intimately recognizable. They rose higher as the train left the ridge and passed down into the Black River[3] valley, and specifically into the La Crosse[4] valley. They ceased to have any hint of upheavals of rock, and became simply parts of the ancient level left standing after the water had practically given up its post-glacial scooping action.

It was about six o'clock as he caught sight of the splendid broken line of hills on which his baby eyes had looked thirty-five years ago. A few minutes later, and the train drew up at the grimy little station set into the hillside, and, giving him just time to leap off, plunged on again toward the West. Howard felt a ridiculous weakness in his legs as he stepped out upon the broiling-hot, splintery planks of the station and faced the few idlers lounging about. He simply stood and gazed with the same intensity and absorption one of the idlers might show standing before the Brooklyn Bridge.[5]

The town caught and held his eyes first. How poor and dull and sleepy and squalid it seemed! The one main street ended at the hillside at his left, and stretched away to the north, between two rows of the usual village stores, unrelieved by a tree or a touch of beauty. An unpaved street, with walled, drab-colored, miserable, rotting wooden buildings, with the inevitable battlements;[6] the same—only worse and more squalid—was the town.

The same, only more beautiful still, was the majestic amphitheater of green wooded hills that circled the horizon, and toward which he lifted his eyes. He thrilled at the sight.

"Glorious!" he cried involuntarily.

Accustomed to the White Mountains,[7] to the Alleghenies, he had wondered if these hills would retain their old-time charm. They did. He took off his hat to them as he stood there. Richly wooded, with gently sloping green sides, rising to massive square or rounded tops with dim vistas, they glowed down upon the squat little town, gracious, lofty in their greeting, immortal in their vivid and delicate beauty.

He was a goodly figure of a man as he stood there beside his valise. Portly, erect, handsomely dressed, and with something unusually winning in his brown mustache and blue eyes, something scholarly suggested by the pinch-nose glasses, something strong in the repose of the head. He smiled as he saw how unchanged was the grouping of the old loafers on the salt-barrels and nail-kegs. He recognized most of them—a little dirtier, a little more bent, and a little grayer.

They sat in the same attitudes, spat tobacco with the same calm delight, and joked each other, breaking into short and sudden fits of laughter, and pounded each other on the back, just as when he was a student at the La Crosse Seminary and going to and fro daily on the train.

They ruminated on him as he passed, speculating in a perfectly audible way upon his business.

"Looks like a drummer."[8]

"No, he ain't no drummer. See them Boston glasses?"

"That's so. Guess he's a teacher."

"Looks like a moneyed cuss."

"Bos'n, I *guess*."

He knew the one who spoke last—Freeme Cole, a man who was the fighting wonder of Howard's boyhood, now degenerated into a stoop-shouldered, faded, garrulous, and quarrelsome old man. Yet there was something epic in the old man's stories, something enthralling in the dramatic power of recital.

Over by the blacksmith shop the usual game of "quaits"[9] was in progress, and the drug-clerk on the corner was chasing a crony with the squirt-pump with which he was about to wash the windows. A few teams stood ankle-deep in the mud, tied to the fantastically gnawed pine pillars of the wooden awnings. A man on a load of hay was "jawing" with the attendant of the platform scales, who stood below, pad and pencil in hand.

"Hit 'im! hit 'im! Jump off and knock 'im!" suggested a bystander, jovially.

Howard knew the voice.

"Talk's cheap. Takes money to buy whiskey," he said, when the man on the load repeated his threat of getting off and whipping the scales-man.

"You're William McTurg," Howard said, coming up to him.

"I am, sir," replied the soft-voiced giant, turning and looking down on the stranger, with an amused twinkle in his deep brown eyes. He stood as erect as an Indian, though his hair and beard were white.

"I'm Howard McLane."

"Ye begin t' look it," said McTurg, removing his right hand from his pocket. "How are ye?"

"I'm first-rate. How's mother and Grant?"

"Saw 'm ploughing corn as I came down. Guess he's all right. Want a boost?"

"Well, yes. Are you down with a team?"

"Yep. 'Bout goin' home. Climb right in. That's my rig, right there," nodding at a sleek bay colt hitched in a covered buggy. "Heave y'r grip under the seat."

They climbed into the seat after William had lowered the buggy-top and unhitched the horse from the post. The loafers were mildly curious. Guessed Bill had got hooked onto by a lightnin'-rod peddler, or somethin' o' that kind.

"Want to go by river, or 'round by the hills?"

"Hills, I guess."

The whole matter began to seem trivial, as if he had been away only for a month or two.

William McTurg was a man little given to talk. Even the coming back of a nephew did not cause any flow of questions or reminiscences. They rode in silence. He sat a little bent forward, the lines held carelessly in his hands, his great lion-like head swaying to and fro with the movement of the buggy.

As they passed familiar spots, the younger man broke the silence with a question.

"That's old man McElvaine's place, ain't it?"

"Yep."

"Old man living?"

"I *guess* he is. Husk more corn'n any man he c'n hire."

In the edge of the village they passed an open lot on the left, marked with circus-rings of different eras.

"There's the old ball-ground. Do they have circuses on it just the same as ever?"

"Just the same."

"What fun that field calls up! The games of ball we used to have! Do you play yet?"

"Sometimes. Can't stoop as well as I used to." He smiled a little. "Too much fat."

It all swept back upon Howard in a flood of names and faces and sights and sounds; something sweet and stirring somehow, though it had little of aesthetic charms at the time. They were passing along lanes now, between superb fields of corn, wherein ploughmen were at work. Kingbirds flew from post to post ahead of them; the insects called from the grass. The valley slowly outspread below them. The workmen in the fields were "turning out"[10] for the night. They all had a word of chaff[11] with McTurg.

Over the western wall of the circling amphitheatre the sun was setting. A few scattering clouds were drifting on the west wind, their shadows sliding down the green and purpled slopes. The dazzling sunlight flamed along the luscious velvety grass, and shot amid the rounded, distant purple peaks, and streamed in bars of gold and crimson across the blue mist of the narrower upper Coollies.[12]

The heart of the young man swelled with pleasure almost like pain, and the eyes of the silent older man took on a far-off, dreaming look, as he gazed at the scene which had repeated itself a thousand times in his life, but of whose beauty he never spoke.

Far down to the left was the break in the wall through which the river ran on its way to join the Mississippi. They climbed slowly among the hills, and the valley they had left grew still more beautiful as the squalor of the little town was hid by the dusk of distance. Both men were silent for a long time. Howard knew the peculiarities of his companion too well to make any remarks or ask any questions, and besides it was a genuine pleasure to ride with one who understood that silence was the only speech amid such splendors.

Once they passed a little brook singing in a mournfully sweet way its eternal song over its pebbles. It called back to Howard the days when he and Grant, his younger brother, had fished in this little brook for trout, with trousers rolled above the knee and wrecks of hats upon their heads.

"Any trout left?" he asked.

"Not many. Little fellers." Finding the silence broken, William asked the first question since he met Howard. "Le' 's see: you're a show feller now? B'long to a troupe?"

"Yes, yes; I'm an actor."

"Pay much?"

"Pretty well."

That seemed to end William's curiosity about the matter.

"Ah, there's our old house, ain't it?" Howard broke out, pointing to one of the houses farther up the Coolly. "It'll be a surprise to them, won't it?"

"Yep; only they don't live there."

"What! They don't!"

"No."

"Who does?"

"Dutchman."

Howard was silent for some moments. "Who lives on the Dunlap place?"

" 'Nother Dutchman."

"Where's Grant living, anyhow?"

"Farther up the Coolly."

"Well, then, I'd better get out here, hadn't I?"

"Oh, I'll drive ye up."

"No, I'd rather walk."

The sun had set, and the Coolly was getting dusk when Howard got out of McTurg's carriage and set off up the winding lane toward his brother's house. He walked slowly to absorb the coolness and fragrance and color of the hour. The katydids sang a rhythmic song of welcome to him. Fireflies were in the grass. A whippoorwill in the deep of the wood was calling weirdly, and an occasional night-hawk, flying high, gave his grating shriek, or hollow boom, suggestive and resounding.

He had been wonderfully successful, and yet had carried into his success as a dramatic author as well as actor a certain puritanism that made him a paradox to his fellows. He was one of those actors who are always in luck, and the best of it was he kept and made use of his luck. Jovial as he appeared, he was inflexible as granite against drink and tobacco. He retained through it all a certain freshness of enjoyment that made him one of the best companions in the profession; and now, as he walked on, the hour and the place appealed to him with great power. It seemed to sweep away the life that came between.

How close it all was to him, after all! In his restless life, surrounded by the glare of electric lights, painted canvas, hot colors, creak of machinery, mock trees, stones, and brooks, he had not lost, but gained, appreciation for the coolness, quiet, and low tones, the shyness of the wood and field.

In the farmhouse ahead of him a light was shining as he peered ahead, and his heart gave another painful movement. His brother was awaiting him there, and his mother, whom he had not seen for ten years and who had lost the power to write. And when Grant wrote, which had been more and more seldom of late, his letters had been cold and curt.

He began to feel that in the pleasure and excitement of his life he had grown away from his mother and brother. Each summer he had said, "Well, now, I'll go home *this* year, sure." But a new play to be produced, or a new yachting trip, or a tour of Europe, had put the home-coming off; and now it was with a distinct consciousness of neglect of duty that he walked up to the fence and looked into the yard, where William had told him his brother lived.

It was humble enough—a small white story-and-a-half structure, with a wing set in the midst of a few locust-trees; a small drab-colored barn with a sagging ridge-pole;[13] a barnyard full of mud, in which a few cows were standing, fighting the flies and waiting to be milked. An old man was pumping water at the well; the pigs were squealing from a pen near by; a child was crying.

Instantly the beautiful, peaceful valley was forgotten. A sickening chill struck into Howard's soul as he looked at it all. In the dim light he could see a figure milking a cow. Leaving his valise at the gate, he entered and walked up to the old man, who had finished pumping and was about to go to feed the hogs.

"Good-evening," Howard began. "Does Mr. Grant McLane live here?"

"Yes, sir, he does. He's right over there milkin'."

"I'll go over there an——"

"Don't b'lieve I would. It's darn muddy over there. It's been turrible rainy. He'll be done in a minute, anyway."

"Very well; I'll wait."

As he waited, he could hear a woman's fretful voice and the impatient jerk and jar of kitchen things, indicative of ill-temper or worry. The longer he stood absorbing this farm-scene, with all its sordidness, dullness, triviality, and its endless drudgeries, the lower his heart sank. All the joy of the home-coming was gone, when the figure arose from the cow and approached the gate, and put the pail of milk down on the platform by the pump.

"Good-evening," said Howard, out of the dusk.

Grant stared a moment. "Good-evening."

Howard knew the voice, though it was older and deeper and more sullen. "Don't you know me, Grant? I am Howard."

The man approached him, gazing intently at his face. "You are?" after a pause. "Well, I'm glad to see you, but I can't shake hands. That damned cow had laid down in the mud."

They stood and looked at each other. Howard's cuffs, collar, and shirt, alien in their elegance, showed through the dusk, and a glint of light shot out from the jewel of his necktie, as the light from the house caught it at the right angle. As they gazed in silence at each other, Howard divined something of the hard, bitter feeling that came into Grant's heart, as he stood there, ragged, ankle-deep in muck, his sleeves rolled up, a shapeless old straw hat on his head.

The gleam of Howard's white hands angered him. When he spoke, it was in a hard, gruff tone, full of rebellion.

"Well, go in the house and set down. I'll be in soon's I strain the milk and wash the dirt off my hands."

"But mother——"

"She's 'round somewhere. Just knock on the door under the porch round there."

Howard went slowly around the corner of the house, past a vilely smelling rain-barrel, toward the west. A gray-haired woman was sitting in a rocking-chair on the porch, her hands in her lap, her eyes fixed on the faintly yellow sky, against which the hills stood, dim purple silhouettes, and on which the locust trees were etched as fine as lace. There was sorrow, resignation, and a sort of dumb despair in her attitude.

Howard stood, his throat swelling till it seemed as if he would suffocate. This was his mother—the woman who bore him, the being who had taken her life in her hand for him; and he, in his excited and pleasurable life, had neglected her!

He stepped into the faint light before her. She turned and looked at him without fear. "Mother!" he said. She uttered one little, breathing, gasping cry, called his name, rose, and stood still. He bounded up the steps, and took her in his arms.

"Mother! Dear old mother!"

In the silence, almost painful, which followed, an angry woman's voice could be heard inside: "I don't care! I ain't goin' to wear myself out fer him. He c'n eat out here with us, or else——"

Mrs. McLane began speaking. "Oh, I've longed to see yeh, Howard. I was afraid you wouldn't come till—too late."

"What do you mean, mother? Ain't you well?"

"I don't seem to be able to do much now 'cept sit around and knit a little. I tried to pick some berries the other day, and I got so dizzy I had to give it up."

"You mustn't work. You *needn't* work. Why didn't you write to me how you were?" Howard asked, in an agony of remorse.

"Well, we felt as if you probably had all you could do to take care of yourself. Are you married, Howard?" she broke off to ask.

"No, mother; and there ain't any excuse for me—not a bit," he said, dropping back into her colloquialisms. "I'm ashamed when I think of how long it's been since I saw you. I could have come."

"It don't matter now," she interrupted gently. "It's the way things go. Our boys grow up and leave us."

"Well, come in to supper," said Grant's ungracious voice from the doorway. "Come, mother."

Mrs. McLane moved with difficulty. Howard sprang to her aid, and, leaning on his arm, she went through the little sitting room, which was unlighted, out into the kitchen, where the supper table stood near the cook-stove.

"How.—this is my wife," said Grant, in a cold, peculiar tone. Howard bowed toward a remarkably handsome young woman, on whose forehead was a scowl, which did not change as she looked at him and the old lady.

"Set down anywhere," was the young woman's cordial invitation.

Howard sat down next his mother, and facing the wife, who had a small, fretful child in her arms. At Howard's left was the old man, Lewis. The supper was spread upon a gay-colored oilcloth, and consisted of a pan of milk, set in the midst, with bowls at each plate. Beside the pan was a dipper and a large plate of bread, and at one end of the table was a dish of fine honey.

A boy of about fourteen leaned upon the table, his bent shoulders making him look like an old man. His hickory shirt,[14] like Grant's, was still wet with sweat, and discolored here and there with grease, or green from grass. His hair, freshly wet and combed, was smoothed away from his face, and shone in the light of the kerosene lamp. As he ate, he stared at Howard, as though he would make an inventory of each thread of the visitor's clothing.

"Did I look like that at his age?" thought Howard.

"You see we live just about the same as ever," said Grant, as they began eating, speaking with a grim, almost challenging, inflection.

The two brothers studied each other curiously, as they talked of neighborhood scenes. Howard seemed incredibly elegant and handsome to them all, with his rich, soft clothing, his spotless linen, and his exquisite enunciation and ease of speech. He had always been "smooth-spoken," and he had become "elegantly persuasive," as his friends said of him, and it was a large factor in his success.

Every detail of the kitchen, the heat, the flies buzzing aloft, the poor furniture, the dress of the people—all smote him like the lash of a wire whip. His brother was a man of great character. He could see that now. His deep-set, gray eyes and rugged face showed at thirty a man of great natural ability. He had more of the Scotch in his face than Howard, and he looked much older.

He was dressed, like the old man and the boy, in a checked shirt, without vest. His suspenders, once gay-colored, had given most of their color to his shirt, and had marked irregular broad bands of pink and brown and green over his shoulders. His hair was uncombed, merely pushed away from his face. He wore a mustache only, though his face was covered with a week's growth of beard. His face was rather gaunt, and was brown as leather.

Howard could not eat much. He was disturbed by his mother's strange silence and oppression, and sickened by the long-drawn gasps with which the old man ate his bread and milk, and by the way the boy ate. He had his knife gripped tightly in his fist, knuckles up, and was scooping honey upon his bread.

The baby, having ceased to be afraid, was curious, gazing silently at the stranger.

"Hello, little one! Come and see your uncle. Eh? Course 'e will," cooed Howard, in the attempt to escape the depressing atmosphere. The little one listened to his inflections as a kitten does, and at last lifted its arms in sign of surrender.

The mother's face cleared up a little. "I declare, she wants to go to you."

"Course she does. Dogs and kittens always come to me when I call 'em. Why shouldn't my own niece come?"

He took the little one and began walking up and down the kitchen with her, while she pulled at his beard and nose. "I ought to have you, my lady, in my new comedy. You'd bring down the house."

"You don't mean to say you put babies on the stage, Howard?" said his mother in surprise.

"Oh, yes. Domestic comedy must have a baby these days."

"Well, that's another way of makin' a livin', sure," said Grant. The baby had cleared the atmosphere a little. "I s'pose you fellers make a pile of money."

"Sometimes we make a thousand a week; oftener we don't."

"A thousand dollars!" They all stared.

"A thousand dollars sometimes, and then lose it all the next week in another town. The dramatic business is a good deal like gambling—you take your chances."

"I wish you weren't in it, Howard. I don't like to have my son——"

"I wish I was in somethin' that paid better than farmin'. Anything under God's heavens is better 'n farmin'," said Grant.

"No, I ain't laid up much," Howard went on, as if explaining why he hadn't helped them. "Costs me a good deal to live, and I need about ten thousand dollars leeway to work on. I've made a good living, but I—I ain't made any money."

Grant looked at him, darkly meditative.

Howard went on: "How'd ye come to sell the old farm? I was in hopes——"

"How'd we come to sell it?" said Grant with terrible bitterness. "We had something on it that didn't leave anything to sell. You probably don't remember anything about it, but there was a mortgage on it that eat us up in just four years by the almanac. 'Most killed mother to leave it. We wrote to you for money, but I don't suppose you remember *that*."

"No, you didn't."

"Yes, I did."

"When was it? I don't—why, it's—I never received it. It must have been that summer I went with Bob Manning to Europe." Howard put the baby down and faced his brother. "Why, Grant, you didn't think I refused to help?"

"Well, it looked that way. We never heard a word from yeh, all summer, and when y' did write, it was all about yerself 'n plays 'n things we didn't know anything about. I swore to God I'd never write to you again, and I won't."

"But, good heavens! I never got it."

"Suppose you didn't. You might have known we were poor as Job's off-ox.[15] Everybody is that earns a living. We fellers on the farm have to earn a livin' for ourselves and you fellers that don't work. I don't blame you. I'd do it if I could."

"Grant, don't talk so! Howard didn't realize——"

"I tell yeh I don't blame him! Only I don't want him to come the brotherly business over me, after livin' as he has—that's all." There was a bitter accusation in the man's voice.

Howard leaped to his feet, his face twitching.

"By God, I'll go back to-morrow morning!" he threatened.

"Go, an' be damned! I don't care what yeh do," Grant growled, rising and going out.

"Boys," called the mother, piteously, "it's terrible to see you quarrel."

"But I'm not to blame, mother," cried Howard, in a sickness that made him white as chalk. "The man is a savage. I came home to help you all, not to quarrel."

"Grant's got one o' his fits on," said the young wife, speaking for the first time. "Don't pay any attention to him. He'll be all right in the morning."

"If it wasn't for you, mother, I'd leave now, and never see that savage again."

He lashed himself up and down in the room, in horrible disgust and hate of his brother and of this home in his heart. He remembered his tender anticipations of the home-coming with a kind of self-pity and disgust. This was his greeting!

He went to bed, to toss about on the hard, straw-filled mattress in the stuffy little best room. Tossing, writhing under the bludgeoning of his brother's accusing inflections, a dozen times he said, with a half-articulate snarl:

"He can go to hell! I'll not try to do anything more for him. I don't care if he *is* my brother; he has no right to jump on me like that. On the night of my return, too. My God! he is a brute, a fool!"

He thought of the presents in his trunk and valise, which he couldn't show to him that night after what had been said. He had intended to have such a happy evening of it, such a tender reunion! It was to be so bright and cheery!

In the midst of his cursings—his hot indignation—would come visions of himself in his own modest rooms. He seemed to be yawning and stretching in his beautiful bed, the sun shining in, his books, foils, pictures, around him to say good-morning and tempt him to rise, while the squat little clock on the mantel struck eleven warningly.

He could see the olive walls, the unique copper-and-crimson arabesque frieze[16] (his own selection), and the delicate draperies; an open grate full of glowing coals, to temper the sea-winds; and in the midst of it, between a landscape by Enneking[17] and an Indian in a canoe in a cañon, by Brush, he saw a sombre landscape by a master greater than Millet, a melancholy subject, treated with pitiless fidelity.

A farm in the valley! Over the mountains swept jagged, gray, angry, sprawling clouds, sending a freezing, thin drizzle of rain, as they passed, upon a man following a plough. The horses had a sullen and weary look, and their manes and tails streamed sidewise in the blast. The ploughman, clad in a ragged gray coat, with uncouth, muddy boots upon his feet, walked with his head inclined toward the sleet, to shield his face from the cold and sting of it. The soil rolled away black and sticky and with a dull sheen upon it. Near by, a boy with tears on his cheeks was watching cattle; a dog seated near, his back to the gale.

As he looked at this picture, his heart softened. He looked down at the sleeve of his soft and fleecy night-shirt, at his white, rounded arm, muscular, yet fine as a woman's, and when he looked for the picture it was gone. Then came again the assertive odor of stagnant air, laden with camphor;[18] he felt the springless bed under him, and caught dimly a few soap-advertising litho-graphs[19] on the walls. He thought of his brother, in his still more inhospitable bedroom, disturbed by the child, condemned to rise at five o'clock and begin another day's pitiless labor. His heart shrank and quivered, and the tears started to his eyes.

"I forgive him, poor fellow! He's not to blame."

II

He woke, however, with a dull, languid pulse, and an oppressive melancholy on his heart. He looked around the little room, clean enough, but oh, how poor! how barren! Cold plaster walls, a cheap wash-stand, a wash-set of three pieces, with a blue band around each; the windows rectangular, and fitted with fantastic green shades.

Outside he could hear the bees humming. Chickens were merrily moving about. Cow-bells far up the road were sounding irregularly. A jay came by and yelled an insolent reveille,[20] and Howard sat up. He could hear nothing in the house but the rattle of pans on the back side of the kitchen. He looked at his watch, which indicated half-past seven. Grant was already in the field, after milking, currying the horses, and eating breakfast—had been at work two hours and a half.

He dressed himself hurriedly, in a negligé[21] shirt, with a Windsor scarf,[22] light-colored, serviceable trousers with a belt, russet shoes, and a tennis hat—a knockabout costume, he considered. His mother, good soul, thought it a special suit put on for her benefit, and admired it through her glasses.

He kissed her with a bright smile, nodded at Laura, the young wife, and tossed the baby, all in a breath, and with the manner, as he himself saw, of the returned captain in the war-dramas of the day.

"Been to breakfast?" He frowned reproachfully. "Why didn't you call me? I wanted to get up, just as I used to, at sunrise."

"We thought you was tired, and so we didn't——"

"Tired! Just wait till you see me help Grant pitch hay or something. Hasn't finished his haying yet, has he?"

"No, I guess not. He will to-day if it don't rain again."

"Well, breakfast is all ready—Howard," said Laura, hesitating a little on his name.

"Good! I am ready for it. Bacon and eggs, as I'm a jay![23] Just what I was wanting. I was saying to myself: 'Now if they'll only get bacon and eggs and hot biscuits and honey—' Oh, say, mother, I heard the bees humming this morning; same noise they used to make when I was a boy, exactly. Must be the same bees,—Hey, you young rascal! come here and have some breakfast with your uncle."

"I never saw her take to any one so quick," Laura said, emphasizing the baby's sex. She had on a clean calico dress and a gingham apron, and she looked strong and fresh and handsome. Her head was intellectual, her eyes full of power. She seemed anxious to remove the impression of her unpleasant looks and words the night before. Indeed it would have been hard to resist Howard's sunny good-nature.

The baby laughed and crowed. The old mother could not take her dim eyes off the face of her son, but sat smiling at him as he ate and rattled on. When he rose from the table at last, after eating heartily and praising it all, he said, with a smile:

"Well, now I'll just telephone down to the express and have my trunk brought up. I've got a few little things in there you'll enjoy seeing. But this fellow," indicating the baby, "I didn't take him into account. But never mind: Uncle How.'ll make that all right."

"You ain't going to lay it up agin Grant, be you, my son?" Mrs. McLane faltered, as they went out into the best room.

"Of course not! He didn't mean it. Now, can't you send word down and have my trunk brought up? Or shall I have to walk down?"

"I guess I'll see somebody goin' down," said Laura.

"All right. Now for the hay-field," he smiled, and went out into the glorious morning.

The circling hills were the same, yet not the same as at night, a cooler, tenderer, more subdued cloak of color lay upon them. Far down the valley a cool, deep, impalpable, blue mist hung, beneath which one divined the river ran, under its elms and basswoods and wild grapevines. On the shaven slopes of the hill cattle and sheep were feeding, their cries and bells coming to the

ear with a sweet suggestiveness. There was something imme-
morial in the sunny slopes dotted with red and brown and gray
cattle.

Walking toward the haymakers, Howard felt a twinge of pain
and distrust. Would Grant ignore it all and smile——

He stopped short. He had not seen Grant smile in so long—
he couldn't quite see him smiling. He had been cold and bitter
for years. When he came up to them, Grant was pitching on; the
old man was loading, and the boy was raking after.

"Good-morning," Howard cried cheerily; the old man nodded, the boy stared. Grant growled something, without looking
up. These "finical"[24] things of saying good-morning and good-
night are not much practised in such homes as Grant McLane's.

"Need some help? I'm ready to take a hand. Got on my regimentals[25] this morning."

Grant looked at him a moment. "You look it."

Howard smiled. "Gimme a hold on that fork, and I'll show
you. I'm not so soft as I look, now you bet."

He laid hold upon the fork in Grant's hands, who released it
sullenly and stood back sneering. Howard stuck the fork into
the pile in the old way, threw his left hand to the end of the
polished handle, brought it down into the hollow of his thigh,
and laid out his strength till the handle bent like a bow. "Oop
she rises!" he called laughingly, as the huge pile began slowly to
rise, and finally rolled upon the high load.

"Oh, I ain't forgot how to do it," he laughed, as he looked
around at the boy, who was eyeing the tennis suit with a de-
vouring gaze.

Grant was studying him, too, but not in admiration.

"I shouldn't say you had," said the old man, tugging at the
forkful.

"Mighty funny to come out here and do a little of this. But
if you had to come here and do it all the while, you wouldn't
look so white and soft in the hands," Grant said, as they moved
on to another pile. "Give me that fork. You'll be spoiling your
fine clothes."

"Oh, these don't matter. They're made for this kind of thing."

"Oh, are they? I guess I'll dress in that kind of a rig. What
did that shirt cost? I need one."

"Six dollars a pair; but then it's old."

"And them pants," he pursued; "they cost six dollars, too, didn't they?"

Howard's face darkened. He saw his brother's purpose. He resented it. "They cost fifteen dollars, if you want to know, and the shoes cost six-fifty. This ring on my cravat cost sixty dollars, and the suit I had on last night cost eighty-five. My suits are made by Breckstein, on Fifth Avenue, if you want to patronize him," he ended brutally, spurred on by the sneer in his brother's eyes. "I'll introduce you."

"Good idea," said Grant, with a forced, mocking smile.

"I need just such a get-up for haying and corn-ploughing. Singular I never thought of it. Now my pants cost eighty-five cents, s'spenders fifteen, hat twenty, shoes one-fifty; stockin's I don't bother about."

He had his brother at a disadvantage, and he grew fluent and caustic as he went on, almost changing places with Howard, who took the rake out of the boy's hand, and followed, raking up the scatterings.

"Singular we fellers here are discontented and mulish, ain't it? Singular we don't believe your letters when you write, sayin', 'I just about make a live of it'? Singular we think the country's goin' to hell, we fellers, in a two-dollar suit, wadin' around in the mud or sweatin' around in the hay-field, while you fellers lay around New York and smoke and wear good clothes and toady to millionaires?"

Howard threw down the rake and folded his arms. "My God! you're enough to make a man forget the same mother bore us!"

"I guess it wouldn't take much to make you forget that. You ain't put much thought on me nor her for ten years."

The old man cackled, the boy grinned, and Howard, sick and weak with anger and sorrow, turned away and walked down toward the brook. He had tried once more to get near his brother, and had failed. Oh, God! how miserably, pitiably! The hot blood gushed all over him as he thought of the shame and disgrace of it.

He, a man associating with poets, artists, sought after by brilliant women, accustomed to deference even from such people, to be sneered at, outfaced, shamed, shoved aside, by a man in a stained hickory shirt and patched overalls, and that man his brother! He lay down on the bright grass, with the sheep all around him, and writhed and groaned with the agony and despair of it.

And worst of all, underneath it was a consciousness that Grant was right in distrusting him. He *had* neglected him; he *had* said, "I guess they're getting along all right." He had put them behind him when the invitation to spend summer on the Mediterranean or in the Adirondacks, came.

"What can I do? What can I do?" he groaned.

The sheep nibbled the grass near him, the jays called pertly, "Shame, shame," a quail piped somewhere on the hillside, and the brook sung a soft, soothing melody that took away at last the sharp edge of his pain, and he sat up and gazed down the valley, bright with the sun and apparently filled with happy and prosperous people.

Suddenly a thought seized him. He stood up so suddenly that the sheep fled in affright. He leaped the brook, crossed the flat, and began searching in the bushes on the hillside. "Hurrah!" he said, with a smile.

He had found an old road which he used to travel when a boy—a road that skirted the edge of the valley, now grown up to brush, but still passable for footmen. As he ran lightly along down the beautiful path, under oaks and hickories, past masses of poison-ivy, under hanging grapevines, through clumps of splendid hazel-nut bushes loaded with great sticky, rough, green burs, his heart threw off part of its load.

How it all came back to him! How many days, when the autumn sun burned the frost of the bushes, had he gathered hazel-nuts here with his boy and girl friends—Hugh and Shelley McTurg, Rome Sawyer, Orrin McIlvaine, and the rest! What had become of them all? How he had forgotten them!

This thought stopped him again, and he fell into a deep muse, leaning against an oak tree, and gazing into the vast fleckless space above. The thrilling, inscrutable mystery of life fell upon him like a blinding light. Why was he living in the crush and thunder and mental unrest of a great city, while his companions, seemingly his equals in powers, were milking cows, making butter, and growing corn and wheat in the silence and drear monotony of the farm?

His boyish sweethearts! their names came back to his ear now, with a dull, sweet sound as of faint bells. He saw their faces, their pink sunbonnets tipped back upon their necks, their brown ankles flying with the swift action of the scurrying partridge. His eyes softened, he took off his hat. The sound of the wind and the leaves moved him almost to tears.

A woodpecker gave a shrill, high-keyed, sustained cry "Ki, ki, ki!" and he started from his revery, the dapples of the sun and shade falling upon his lithe figure as he hurried on down the path.

He came at last to a field of corn that ran to the very wall of a large weather-beaten house, the sight of which made his breathing quicker. It was the place where he was born. The mystery of his life began there. In the branches of those poplar and hickory trees he had swung and sung in the rushing breeze, fearless as a squirrel. Here was the brook where, like a larger kildee,[26] he with Grant had waded after crawfish, or had stolen upon some wary trout, rough-cut pole in hand.

Seeing someone in the garden, he went down along the corn-row through the rustling ranks of green leaves. An old woman was picking berries, a squat and shapeless figure.

"Good-morning," he called cheerily.

"Morgen," she said, looking up at him with a startled and very red face. She was German in every line of her body.

"Ich bin Herr McLane," he said, after a pause.

"So?" she replied, with a questioning inflection.

"Yah; ich bin Herr Grant's Bruder."

"Ach, so!" she said, with a downward inflection. "Ich no spick Inglish. No spick Inglis."

"Ich bin durstig,"[27] he said. Leaving her pans, she went with him to the house, which was what he really wanted to see.

"Ich bin hier geboren."[28]

"Ach, so!" She recognized the little bit of sentiment, and said some sentences in German whose general meaning was sympathy. She took him to the cool cellar where the spring had been trained to run into a tank containing pans of cream and milk; she gave him a cool draught from a large tin cup, and at his request went with him upstairs. The house was the same, but somehow seemed cold and empty. It was clean and sweet, but it showed so little evidence of being lived in. The old part, which was built of logs, was used as best room, and modelled after the best rooms of the neighboring "Yankee" homes, only it was emptier, without the cabinet organ[29] and the rag-carpet and the chromos.[30]

The old fireplace was bricked up and plastered—the fireplace beside which, in the far-off days, he had lain on winter nights, to hear his uncles tell tales of hunting, or to hear them play the violin, great dreaming giants that they were.

The old woman went out and left him sitting there, the centre of a swarm of memories, coming and going like so many ghostly birds and butterflies.

A curious heartache and listlessness, a nerveless mood came on him. What was it worth, anyhow—success? Struggle, strife, trampling on some one else. His play crowding out some other poor fellow's hope. The hawk eats the partridge, the partridge eats the flies and bugs, the bugs eat each other and the hawk, when he in his turn is shot by man. So in the world of business, the life of one man seemed to him to be drawn from the life of another man, each success to spring from other failures.

He was like a man from whom all motives had been withdrawn. He was sick, sick to the heart. Oh, to be a boy again! An ignorant baby, pleased with a block and string, with no knowledge and no care of the great unknown! To lay his head again on his mother's bosom and rest! To watch the flames on the hearth!——

Why not? Was not that the very thing to do? To buy back the old farm? It would cripple him a little for the next season, but he could do it. Think of it! To see his mother back in the old home, with the fireplace restored, the old furniture in the sitting room around her, and fine new things in the parlor!

His spirits rose again. Grant couldn't stand out when he brought to him a deed of the farm. Surely his debt would be cancelled when he had seen them all back in the wide old kitchen. He began to plan and to dream. He went to the windows, and looked out on the yard to see how much it had changed.

He'd build a new barn and buy them a new carriage. His heart glowed again, and his lips softened into their usual feminine grace—lips a little full and falling easily into curves.

The old German woman came in at length, bringing some cakes and a bowl of milk, smiling broadly and hospitably as she waddled forward.

"Acht! Goot!" he said, smacking his lips over the pleasant draught.

"Wo ist ihre goot mann?"[31] he inquired, ready for business.

III

When Grant came in at noon Mrs. McLane met him at the door with a tender smile on her face.

"Where's Howard, Grant?"

"I don't know," he replied, in a tone that implied "I don't care."

The dim eyes clouded with quick tears.

"Ain't you seen him?"

"Not since nine o'clock."

"Where do you think he is?"

"I tell yeh I don't know. He'll take care of himself; don't worry."

He flung off his hat and plunged into the wash-basin. His shirt was wet with sweat and covered with dust of the hay and fragments of leaves. He splashed his burning face with the water, paying no further attention to his mother. She spoke again, very gently, in reproof:

"Grant, why do you stand out against Howard so?"

"I don't stand out against him," he replied harshly, pausing with the towel in his hands. His eyes were hard and piercing. "But if he expects me to gush over his coming back, he's fooled, that's all. He's left us to paddle our own canoe all this while, and, so far as *I'm* concerned, he can leave us alone hereafter. He looked out for his precious hide mighty well, and now he comes

back here to play big gun and pat us on the head. I don't propose
to let him come that over me."

Mrs. McLane knew too well the temper of her son to say any
more, but she inquired about Howard of the old hired man.

"He went off down the valley. He 'n' Grant had s'm *words,*
and he pulled out down toward the old farm. That's the last I
see of 'im."

Laura took Howard's part at the table. "Pity you can't be
decent," she said, brutally direct as usual. "You treat Howard
as if he was a—a—I do' know what."

"Will you let me alone?"

"No, I won't. If you think I'm going to set by an' agree to
your bullyraggin' him, you're mistaken. It's a shame! You're
mad 'cause he's succeeded and you hain't. He ain't to blame for
his brains. If you and I'd had any, we'd 'a' succeeded too. It
ain't our fault, and it ain't his; so what's the use?"

A look came into Grant's face which the wife knew meant
bitter and terrible silence. He ate his dinner without another
word.

It was beginning to cloud up. A thin, whitish, all-pervasive
vapor which meant rain was dimming the sky, and Grant forced
his hands to their utmost during the afternoon, in order to get
most of the down hay in before the rain came. He was pitching
from the load into the barn when Howard came by, just before
one o'clock.

It was windless there. The sun fell through the white mist
with undiminished fury, and the fragrant hay sent up a breath
that was hot as an oven-draught. Grant was a powerful man, and
there was something majestic in his action as he rolled the huge
flakes of hay through the door. The sweat poured from his face
like rain, and he was forced to draw his drenched sleeve across
his face to clear away the blinding sweat that poured into his
eyes.

Howard stood and looked at him in silence, remembering
how often he had worked there in that furnaceheat, his muscles
quivering, cold chills running over his flesh, red shadows dancing before his eyes.

His mother met him at the door, anxiously, but smiled as she
saw his pleasant face and cheerful eyes.

"You're a little late, m' son."

Howard spent most of the afternoon sitting with his mother on the porch, or under the trees, lying sprawled out like a boy, resting at times with sweet forgetfulness of the whole world, but feeling a dull pain whenever he remembered the stern, silent man pitching hay in the hot sun on the torrid side of the barn.

His mother did not say anything about the quarrel; she feared to reopen it. She talked mainly of old times in a gentle monotone of reminiscence, while he listened, looking up into her patient face.

The heat slowly lessened as the sun sank down toward the dun clouds rising like a more distant and majestic line of mountains beyond the western hills. The sound of cow-bells came irregularly to the ear, and the voices and sounds of the haying-fields had a jocund, pleasant sound to the ear of the city-dweller.

He was very tender. Everything conspired to make him simple, direct, and honest.

"Mother, if you'll only forgive me for staying away so long, I'll surely come to see you every summer."

She had nothing to forgive. She was so glad to have him there at her feet—her great, handsome, successful boy! She could only love him and enjoy him every moment of the precious days. If Grant would only reconcile himself to Howard! That was the great thorn in her flesh.

Howard told her how he had succeeded.

"It was luck, mother. First I met Cook, and he introduced me to Jake Saulsman of Chicago. Jake asked me to go to New York with him, and—I don't know why—took a fancy to me some way. He introduced me to a lot of the fellows in New York, and they all helped me along. I did nothing to merit it. Everybody helps me. Anybody can succeed in that way."

The doting mother thought it not at all strange that they all helped him.

At the supper table Grant was gloomily silent, ignoring Howard completely. Mrs. McLane sat and grieved silently, not daring to say a word in protest. Laura and the baby tried to amuse Howard, and under cover of their talk the meal was eaten.

The boy fascinated Howard. He "sawed wood"[32] with a rapidity and uninterruptedness which gave alarm. He had the air of coaling up for a long voyage.

"At that age," Howard thought, "I must have gripped my knife in my right hand so, and poured my tea into my saucer so. I must have buttered and bit into a huge slice of bread just so, and chewed at it with a smacking sound in just that way. I must have gone to the length of scooping up honey with my knife-blade."

The sky was magically beautiful over all this squalor and toil and bitterness, from five till seven—a moving hour. Again the falling sun streamed in broad banners across the valleys; again the blue mist lay far down the Coolly over the river; the cattle called from the hills in the moistening, sonorous air; the bells came in a pleasant tangle of sound; the air pulsed with the deepening chorus of katydids and other nocturnal singers.

Sweet and deep as the very springs of his life was all this to the soul of the elder brother; but in the midst of it, the younger man, in ill-smelling clothes and great boots that chafed his feet, went out to milk the cows,—on whose legs the flies and mosquitoes swarmed, bloated with blood, to—sit by the hot side of a cow and be lashed with her tail as she tried frantically to keep the savage insects from eating her raw.

"The poet who writes of milking the cows does it from the hammock, looking on," Howard soliloquized, as he watched the old man Lewis racing around the filthy yard after one of the young heifers that had kicked over the pail in her agony with the flies, and was unwilling to stand still and be eaten alive.

"So, *so!* you beast!" roared the old man, as he finally cornered the shrinking, nearly frantic creature.

"Don't you want to look at the garden?" asked Mrs. McLane of Howard; and they went out among the vegetables and berries.

The bees were coming home heavily laden and crawling slowly into the hives. The level, red light streamed through the trees, blazed along the grass, and lighted a few old-fashioned flowers into red and gold flame. It was beautiful, and Howard looked at it through his half-shut eyes as the painters do, and turned away with a sigh at the sound of blows where the wet and grimy men were assailing the frantic cows.

"There's Wesley with your trunk," Mrs. McLane said, recalling him to himself.

Wesley helped him carry the trunk in, and waved off thanks. "Oh, that's all right," he said; and Howard knew the Western man too well to press the matter of pay.

As he went in an hour later and stood by the trunk, the dull ache came back to his heart. How he had failed! It seemed like a bitter mockery now to show his gifts.

Grant had come in from his work, and with his feet released from his chafing boots, in his wet shirt and milk-splashed overalls, sat at the kitchen table reading a newspaper which he held close to a small kerosene lamp. He paid no attention to any one. His attitude, curiously like his father's, was perfectly definite to Howard. It meant that from that time forward there were to be no words of any sort between them. It meant that they were no longer brothers, not even acquaintances. "How inexorable that face!" thought Howard.

He turned sick with disgust and despair, and would have closed his trunk without showing any of the presents, only for the childish expectancy of his mother and Laura.

"Here's something for you, mother," he said, assuming a cheerful voice, as he took a fold of fine silk from the trunk and held it up. "All the way from Paris." He laid it on his mother's lap and stooped and kissed her, and then turned hastily away to hide the tears that came to his own eyes as he saw her keen pleasure.

"And here's a parasol for Laura. I don't know how I came to have that in here. And here's General Grant's autobiography for his namesake," he said, with an effort at carelessness, and waited to hear Grant rise.

"Grant, won't you come in?" asked his mother, quaveringly.

Grant did not reply nor move. Laura took the handsome volumes out and laid them beside him on the table. He simply pushed them one side and went on with his reading.

Again that horrible anger swept hot as flame over Howard. He could have cursed him. His hands shook as he handed out other presents to his mother and Laura and the baby. He tried to joke.

"I didn't know how old the baby was, so she'll have to grow to some of these things."

But the pleasure was all gone for him and for the rest. His heart swelled almost to a feeling of pain as he looked at his mother. There she sat with the presents in her lap. The shining silk came too late for her. It threw into appalling relief her age, her poverty, her work-weary frame. "My God!" he almost cried aloud, "how little it would have taken to lighten her life!"

Upon this moment, when it seemed as if he could endure no more, came the smooth voice of William McTurg:

"Hello, folkses!"

"Hello, Uncle Bill! Come in."

"That's what we came for," laughed a woman's voice.

"Is that you, Rose?" asked Laura.

"It's me—Rose," replied the laughing girl, as she bounced into the room and greeted everybody in a breathless sort of way.

"You don't mean little Rosy?"

"Big Rosy now," said William.

Howard looked at the handsome girl and smiled, saying in a nasal sort of tone, "Wal, wal! Rosy, how you've growed since I saw yeh!"

"Oh, look at all this purple and fine linen! Am I left out?"

Rose was a large girl of twenty-five or thereabouts, and was called an old maid. She radiated good-nature from every line of her buxom self. Her black eyes were full of drollery, and she was on the best of terms with Howard at once. She had been a teacher, but that did not prevent her from assuming a homely directness of speech. Of course they talked about old friends.

"Where's Rachel?" Howard inquired. Her smile faded away.

"Shellie married Orrin McIlvaine. They're 'way out in Dakota. Shellie's havin' a hard row of stumps."[33]

There was a little silence.

"And Tommy?"

"Gone West. Most all the boys have gone West. That's the reason there's so many old maids."

"You don't mean to say——"

"I don't *need* to say—I'm an old maid. Lots of the girls are. It don't pay to marry these days. Are you married?"

"Not *yet.*" His eyes lighted up again in a humorous way.

"Not yet! That's good! That's the way old maids all talk."

"You don't mean to tell me that no young fellow comes prowling around——"

"Oh, a young Dutchman or Norwegian once in a while. Nobody that counts. Fact is, we're getting like Boston—four women to one man; and when you consider that we're getting more particular each year, the outlook is—well, it's dreadful!"

"It certainly is."

"Marriage is a failure these days for most of us. We can't live on a farm, and can't get a living in the city, and there we are." She laid her hand on his arm. "I declare, Howard, you're the same boy you used to be. I ain't a bit afraid of you, for all your success."

"And you're the same girl? No, I can't say that. It seems to me you've grown more than I have—I don't mean physically, I mean mentally," he explained, as he saw her smile in the defensive way a fleshy girl has, alert to ward off a joke.

They were in the midst of talk, Howard telling one of his funny stories, when a wagon clattered up to the door, and merry voices called loudly:

"Whoa, there, Sampson!"

"Hullo, the house!"

Rose looked at her father with a smile in her black eyes exactly like his. They went to the door.

"Hullo! What's wanted?"

"Grant McLane live here?"

"Yup. Right here."

A moment later there came a laughing, chattering squad of women to the door. Mrs. McLane and Laura stared at each other in amazement. Grant went outdoors.

Rose stood at the door as if she were hostess.

"Come in, Nettie. Glad to see yeh—glad to see yeh! Mrs. McIlvaine, come right in! Take a seat. Make yerself to home, *do!* And Mrs. Peavey! Wal, I never! This must be a surprise party. Wal, I swan! How many more o' ye air they?"

All was confusion, merriment, hand-shakings as Rose introduced them in her roguish way.

"Folks, this is Mr. Howard McLane of New York. He's an

actor, but it hain't spoiled him a bit as *I* can see. How., this is Nettie McIlvaine—Wilson that was."

Howard shook hands with Nettie, a tall, plain girl with prominent teeth.

"This is Ma McIlvaine."

"She looks just the same," said Howard, shaking her hand and feeling how hard and work-worn it was.

And so amid bustle, chatter, and invitations "to lay off y'r things an' stay awhile," the women got disposed about the room at last. Those that had rocking-chairs rocked vigorously to and fro to hide their embarrassment. They all talked in loud voices.

Howard felt nervous under this furtive scrutiny. He wished that his clothes didn't look so confoundedly dressy. Why didn't he have sense enough to go and buy a fifteen-dollar suit of diagonals[34] for everyday wear.

Rose was the life of the party. Her tongue rattled on in the most delightful way.

"It's all Rose and Bill's doin's," Mrs. McIlvaine explained. "They told us to come over and pick up anybody we see on the road. So we did."

Howard winced a little at her familiarity of tone. He couldn't help it for the life of him.

"Well, I wanted to come to-night because I'm going away next week, and I wanted to see how he'd act at a surprise-party again," Rose explained.

"Married, I s'pose?" said Mrs. McIlvaine, abruptly.

"No, not yet."

"Good land! Why, y' mus' be thirty-five, How. Must 'a' dis'-p'inted y'r mam not to have a young 'un to call 'er granny."

The men came clumping in, talking about haying and horses. Some of the older ones Howard knew and greeted, but the younger ones were mainly too much changed. They were all very ill at ease. Most of them were in compromise dress—something lying between working "rig"[35] and Sunday dress. Some of them had on clean shirts and paper collars, and wore their Sunday coats (thick woollen garments) over rough trousers. Most of them crossed their legs at once, and all of them sought the wall and leaned back perilously upon the hind legs of their chairs, eyeing Howard slowly.

For the first few minutes the presents were the subjects of conversation. The women especially spent a good deal of talk upon them.

Howard found himself forced to taking the initiative, so he inquired about the crops and about the farms.

"I see you don't plough the hills as we used to. And reap! *What* a job it used to be. It makes the hills more beautiful to have them covered with smooth grass and cattle."

There was only dead silence to this touching upon the idea of beauty.

"I s'pose it pays reasonably?"

"Not enough to kill," said one of the younger men. "You c'n see that by the houses we live in—that is, most of us. A few that came in early an' got land cheap, like McIlvaine, here—he got a lift that the rest of us can't get."

"I'm a free-trader, myself," said one young fellow, blushing and looking away as Howard turned and said cheerily:

"So 'm I."

The rest seemed to feel that this was a tabooed subject—a subject to be talked out of doors, where a man could prance about and yell and do justice to it.

Grant sat silently in the kitchen doorway, not saying a word, not looking at his brother.

"Well, I don't never use hot vinegar for mine," Mrs. McIlvaine was heard to say. "I jest use hot water, and I rinse 'em out good, and set 'em bottom-side up in the sun. I do' know but what hot vinegar *would* be more cleansin'."

Rose had the younger folks in a giggle with a droll telling of a joke on herself.

"How d' y' stop 'em from laffin'?"

"I let 'em laugh. Oh, my school is a disgrace—so one director says. But I like to see children laugh. It broadens their cheeks."

"Yes, that's all hand-work."[36] Laura was showing the baby's Sunday clothes.

"Goodness Peter! How do you find time to do so much?"

"I take time."

Howard, being the lion of the evening, tried his best to be agreeable. He kept near his mother, because it afforded her so much pride and satisfaction, and because he was obliged to keep away from Grant, who had begun to talk to the men. Howard talked mainly about their affairs, but still was forced more and more into telling of his life in the city. As he told of the theatre and the concerts, a sudden change fell upon them; they grew sober, and he felt deep down in the hearts of these people a melancholy which was expressed only illusively with little tones or sighs. Their gayety was fitful.

They were hungry for the world, for life—these young people. Discontented, and yet hardly daring to acknowledge it; indeed, few of them could have made definite statement of their dissatisfaction. The older people felt it less. They practically said, with a sigh of pathetic resignation:

"Well, I don't expect ever to see these things *now*."

A casual observer would have said, "What a pleasant bucolic[37]—this little surprise-party of welcome!" But Howard, with his native ear and eye, had no such pleasing illusion. He knew too well these suggestions of despair and bitterness. He knew that, like the smile of the slave, this cheerfulness was self-defence; deep down was another unsatisfied ego.

Seeing Grant talking with a group of men over by the kitchen door, he crossed over slowly and stood listening. Wesley Cosgrove—a tall, raw-boned young fellow with a grave, almost tragic face—was saying:

"Of course I ain't. Who is? A man that's satisfied to live as we do is a fool."

"The worst of it is," said Grant, without seeing Howard, "a man can't get out of it during his lifetime, and *I* don't know that he'll have any chance in the next—the speculator 'll[38] be there ahead of us."

The rest laughed, but Grant went on grimly:

"Ten years ago Wess, here, could have got land in Dakota pretty easy, but now it's about all a feller's life's worth to try it. I tell you things seem shuttin' down on us fellers."

"Plenty o' land to rent," suggested some one.

"Yes, in terms that skin a man alive. More than that, farmin' ain't so free a life as it used to be. This cattle-raisin' and butter-makin' makes a nigger of a man. Binds him right down to the grindstone and he gets nothin' out of it—that's what rubs it in. He simply wallers around in the manure for somebody else. I'd like to know what a man's life is worth who lives as we do? How much higher is it than the lives the niggers used to live?"

These brutally bald words made Howard thrill with emotion like the reading of some great tragic poem. A silence fell on the group.

"That's the God's truth, Grant," said young Cosgrove, after a pause.

"A man like me is helpless," Grant was saying. "Just like a fly in a pan of molasses. There's no escape for him. The more he tears around the more liable he is to rip his legs off."

"What can he do?"

"Nothin'."

The men listened in silence.

"Oh, come, don't talk politics all night!" cried Rose, breaking in. "Come, let's have a dance. Where's that fiddle?"

"Fiddle!" cried Howard, glad of a chance to laugh. "Well, now! Bring out that fiddle. Is it William's?"

"Yes, pap's old fiddle."

"O Gosh! he don't want to hear me play," protested William. "He's heard s' many fiddlers."

"Fiddlers! I've heard a thousand violinists, but not fiddlers. Come, give us 'Honest John.' "[39]

William took the fiddle in his work-calloused and crooked hands and began tuning it. The group at the kitchen door turned to listen, their faces lighting up a little. Rose tried to get a "set"[40] on the floor.

"Oh, good land!" said some. "We're all tuckered out. What makes you so anxious?"

"She wants a chance to dance with the New Yorker."

"That's it, exactly," Rose admitted.

"Wal, if you'd churned and mopped and cooked for hayin' hands as I have to-day, you wouldn't be so full o' nonsense."

"Oh, bother! Life's short. Come, quick, get Bettie out. Come, Wess, never mind your hobby-horse."

By incredible exertion she got a set on the floor, and William got the fiddle in tune. Howard looked across at Wesley, and thought the change in him splendidly dramatic. His face was lighted with a timid, deprecating, boyish smile. Rose could do anything with him.

William played some of the old tunes that had a thousand associated memories in Howard's brain, memories of harvest-moons, of melon-feasts, and of clear, cold winter nights. As he danced, his eyes filled with a tender light. He came closer to them all than he had been able to do before. Grant had gone out into the kitchen.

After two or three sets had been danced, the company took seats and could not be stirred again. So Laura and Rose disappeared for a few moments, and returning, served strawberries and cream, which Laura said she "just happened to have in the house."

And then William played again. His fingers, now grown more supple, brought out clearer, firmer tones. As he played, silence fell on these people. The magic of music sobered every face; the women looked older and more careworn, the men slouched sullenly in their chairs, or leaned back against the wall.

It seemed to Howard as if the spirit of tragedy had entered this house. Music had always been William's unconscious expression of his unsatisfied desires. He was never melancholy except when he played. Then his eyes grew sombre, his drooping face full of shadows.

He played on slowly, softly, wailing Scotch tunes and mournful Irish love songs. He seemed to find in these melodies, and especially in a wild, sweet, low-keyed negro song, some expression for his indefinable inner melancholy.

He played on, forgetful of everybody, his long beard sweeping the violin, his toil-worn hands marvellously obedient to his will.

At last he stopped, looked up with a faint, apologetic smile, and said with a sigh:

"Well, folkses, time to go home."

The going was quiet. Not much laughing. Howard stood at the door and said good-night to them all, his heart very tender.

"Come and see us," they said.

"I will," he replied cordially. "I'll try and get around to see everybody, and talk over old times, before I go back."

After the wagons had driven out of the yard, Howard turned and put his arm about his mother's neck.

"Tired?"

"A little."

"Well, now good night. I'm going for a little stroll."

His brain was too active to sleep. He kissed his mother good-night, and went out into the road, his hat in his hand, the cool moist wind on his hair.

It was very dark, the stars being partly hidden by a thin vapor. On each side the hills rose, every line familiar as the face of an old friend. A whippoorwill called occasionally from the hillside, and the spasmodic jangle of a bell now and then told of some cow's battle with the mosquitoes.

As he walked, he pondered upon the tragedy he had redis-covered in these people's lives. Out here under the inexorable spaces of the sky, a deep distaste of his own life took possession of him. He felt like giving it all up. He thought of the infinite tragedy of these lives which the world loves to call peaceful and pastoral. His mind went out in the aim to help them. What could he do to make life better worth living? Nothing.

They must live and die practically as he saw them to-night.

And yet he knew this was a mood, and that in a few hours the love and the habit of life would come back upon him and upon them; that he would go back to the city in a few days; that these people would live on and make the best of it.

"*I'll* make the best of it," he said at last, and his thought came back to his mother and Grant.

IV

The next day was a rainy day; not a shower, but a steady rain —an unusual thing in midsummer in the West. A cold, dismal day in the fireless, colorless farmhouses. It came to Howard in that peculiar reaction which surely comes during a visit of this character, when thought is a weariness, when the visitor longs for his own familiar walls and pictures and books, and longs to meet his friends, feeling at the same time the tragedy of life which makes friends nearer and more congenial than blood-relations.

Howard ate his breakfast alone, save Baby and Laura its mother going about the room. Baby and mother alike insisted on feeding him to death. Already dyspeptic[41] pangs were setting in.

"Now ain't there something more I can——"

"Good heavens! No!" he cried in dismay. "I'm likely to die of dyspepsia now. This honey and milk, and these delicious hot biscuits——"

"I'm afraid it ain't much like the breakfasts you have in the city."

"Well, no, it ain't," he confessed. "But this is the kind a man needs when he lives in the open air."

She sat down opposite him, with her elbows on the table, her chin in her palm, her eyes full of shadows.

"I'd like to go to a city once. I never saw a town bigger'n La Crosse. I've never seen a play, but I've read of 'em in the magazines. It must be wonderful; they say they have wharves and real ships coming up to the wharf, and people getting off and on. How do they do it?"

"Oh, that's too long a story to tell. It's a lot of machinery and paint and canvas. If I told you how it was done, you wouldn't enjoy it so well when you come on and see it."

"Do you ever expect to see *me* in New York?"

"Why, yes. Why not? I expect Grant to come on and bring you all some day, especially Tonikins here. Tonikins, you hear, sir? I expect you to come on you' forf birfday, sure." He tried thus to stop the woman's gloomy confidence.

"I hate farm-life," she went on with a bitter inflection. "It's nothing but fret, fret, and work the whole time, never going any place, never seeing anybody but a lot of neighbors just as big fools as you are. I spend my time fighting flies and washing dishes and churning. I'm sick of it all."

Howard was silent. What could he say to such an indictment? The ceiling swarmed with flies which the cold rain had driven to seek the warmth of the kitchen. The gray rain was falling with a dreary sound outside, and down the kitchen stove-pipe an occasional drop fell on the stove with a hissing, angry sound.

The young wife went on with a deeper note:

"I lived in La Crosse two years, going to school, and I know a little something of what city life is. If I was a man, I bet I wouldn't wear my life out on a farm, as Grant does. I'd get away and I'd do something. I wouldn't care what, but I'd get away."

There was a certain volcanic energy back of all the woman said, that made Howard feel she would make the attempt. She did not know that the struggle for a place to stand on this planet was eating the heart and soul out of men and women in the city, just as in the country. But he could say nothing. If he had said in conventional phrase, sitting there in his soft clothing, "We must make the best of it all," the woman could justly have thrown the dish-cloth in his face. He could say nothing.

"I was a fool for ever marrying," she went on, while the baby pushed a chair across the room. "I made a decent living teaching, I was free to come and go, my money was my own. Now I'm tied right down to a churn or a dish-pan, I never have a cent of my own. *He's* growlin' 'round half the time, and there's no chance of his ever being different."

She stopped with a bitter sob in her throat. She forgot she was talking to her husband's brother. She was conscious only of his sympathy.

As if a great black cloud had settled down upon him, Howard felt it all—the horror, hopelessness, imminent tragedy of it all. The glory of nature, the bounty and splendor of the sky, only made it the more benumbing. He thought of a sentence Millet once wrote:

"I see very well the aureole of the dandelions,[42] and the sun also, far down there behind the hills, flinging his glory upon the clouds. But not alone that—I see in the plains the smoke of the tired horses at the plough, or, on a stony-hearted spot of ground, a back-broken man trying to raise himself upright for a moment to breathe. The tragedy is surrounded by glories—that is no invention of mine."

Howard arose abruptly and went back to his little bedroom, where he walked up and down the floor till he was calm enough to write, and then he sat down and poured it all out to "Dearest Margaret," and his first sentence was this:

"If it were not for you (just to let you know the mood I'm in)—if it were not *for* you, and I had the world in my hands, I'd crush it like a puff-ball;[43] evil so predominates, suffering is so universal and persistent, happiness so fleeting and so infrequent."

He wrote on for two hours, and by the time he had sealed and directed several letters he felt calmer, but still terribly depressed. The rain was still falling, sweeping down from the half-seen hills, wreathing the wooded peaks with a gray garment of mist, and filling the valley with a whitish cloud.

It fell around the house drearily. It ran down into the tubs placed to catch it, dripped from the mossy pump, and drummed on the upturned milk-pails, and upon the brown and yellow bee-hives under the maple trees. The chickens seemed depressed, but the irrepressible bluejay screamed amid it all, with the same insolent spirit, his plumage untarnished by the wet. The barnyard showed a horrible mixture of mud and mire, through which Howard caught glimpses of the men, slumping to and fro without more additional protection than a ragged coat and a shapeless felt hat.

In the sitting room where his mother sat sewing there was not an ornament, save the etching he had brought. The clock stood on a small shelf, its dial so much defaced that one could not tell the time of day; and when it struck, it was with noticeably disproportionate deliberation, as if it wished to correct any mistake into which the family might have fallen by reason of its illegible dial.

The paper on the walls showed the first concession of the Puritans[44] to the Spirit of Beauty, and was made up of a heterogeneous mixture of flowers of unheard-of shapes and colors, arranged in four different ways along the wall. There were no books, no music, and only a few newspapers in sight—a bare, blank, cold, drab-colored shelter from the rain, not a home. Nothing cosy, nothing heart-warming; a grim and horrible shed.

"What are they doing? It can't be they're at work such a day as this," Howard said, standing at the window.

"They find plenty to do, even on rainy days," answered his mother. "Grant always has some job to set the men at. It's the only way to live."

"I'll go out and see them." He turned suddenly. "Mother, why should Grant treat me so? Have I deserved it?"

Mrs. McLane sighed in pathetic hopelessness. "I don't know, Howard. I'm worried about Grant. He gets more an' more downhearted an' gloomy every day. Seems if he'd go crazy. He don't care how he looks any more, won't dress up on Sunday. Days an' days he'll go aroun' not sayin' a word. I was in hopes you could help him, Howard."

"My coming seems to have had an opposite effect. He hasn't spoken a word to me, except when he had to, since I came. Mother, what do you say to going home with me to New York?"

"Oh, I couldn't do that!" she cried in terror. "I couldn't live in a big city—never!"

"There speaks the truly rural mind," smiled Howard at his mother, who was looking up at him through her glasses with a pathetic forlornness which sobered him again. "Why, mother, you could live in Orange, New Jersey, or out in Connecticut, and be just as lonesome as you are here. You wouldn't need to live in the city. I could see you then every day or two."

"Well, I couldn't leave Grant an' the baby, anyway," she replied, not realizing how one could live in New Jersey and do business daily in New York.

"Well, then, how would you like to go back into the old house?"

The patient hands fell to the lap, the dim eyes fixed in searching glance on his face. There was a wistful cry in the voice.

"Oh, Howard! Do you mean——"

He came and sat down by her, and put his arm about her and hugged her hard. "I mean, you dear, good, patient, work-weary old mother, I'm going to buy back the old farm and put you in it."

There was no refuge for her now except in tears, and she put up her thin, trembling old hands about his neck, and cried in that easy, placid, restful way age has.

Howard could not speak. His throat ached with remorse and pity. He saw his forgetfulness of them all once more without relief,—the black thing it was!

"There, there, mother, don't cry!" he said, torn with anguish by her tears. Measured by man's tearlessness, her weeping seemed terrible to him. "I didn't realize how things were going here. It was all my fault—or, at least, most of it. Grant's letter didn't reach me. I thought you were still on the old farm. But no matter; it's all over now. Come, don't cry any more, mother dear. I'm going to take care of you now."

It had been years since the poor, lonely woman had felt such warmth of love. Her sons had been like her husband, chary of expressing their affection; and like most Puritan families, there was little of caressing among them. Sitting there with the rain on the roof and driving through the trees, they planned getting back into the old house. Howard's plan seemed to her full of splendor and audacity. She began to understand his power and wealth now, as he put it into concrete form before her.

"I wish I could eat Thanksgiving dinner there with you," he said at last, "but it can't be thought of. However, I'll have you all in there before I go home. I'm going out now and tell Grant. Now don't worry any more; I'm going to fix it all up with him, sure." He gave her a parting hug.

Laura advised him not to attempt to get to the barn; but as he persisted in going, she hunted up an old rubber coat for him. "You'll mire down and spoil your shoes," she said, glancing at his neat calf gaiters.

"Darn the difference!" he laughed in his old way. "Besides, I've got rubbers."

"Better go round by the fence," she advised, as he stepped out into the pouring rain.

How wretchedly familiar it all was! The miry cowyard, with the hollow trampled out around the horse-trough, the disconsolate hens standing under the wagons and sheds, a pig wallowing across its sty, and for atmosphere the desolate, falling rain. It was so familiar he felt a pang of the old rebellious despair which seized him on such days in his boyhood.

Catching up courage, he stepped out on the grass, opened the gate and entered the barn-yard. A narrow ribbon of turf ran around the fence, on which he could walk by clinging with one hand to the rough boards. In this way he slowly made his way around the periphery, and came at last to the open barn-door without much harm.

It was a desolate interior. In the open floor-way Grant, seated upon a half-bushel, was mending a harness. The old man was holding the trace in his hard brown hands; the boy was lying on a wisp of hay. It was a small barn, and poor at that. There was a bad smell, as of dead rats, about it, and the rain fell through the shingles here and there. To the right, and below, the horses stood, looking up with their calm and beautiful eyes, in which the whole scene was idealized.

Grant looked up an instant, and then went on with his work.

"Did yeh wade through?" grinned Lewis, exposing his broken teeth.

"No, I kinder circumambiated the pond." He sat down on the little tool-box near Grant. "Your barn is a good deal like that in 'The Arkansaw Traveller.'⁴⁵ Needs a new roof, Grant." His voice had a pleasant sound, full of the tenderness of the scene through which he had just been. "In fact, you need a new barn."

"I need a good many things, more'n I'll ever get," Grant replied shortly.

"How long did you say you'd been on this farm?"

"Three years this fall."

"I don't s'pose you've been able to think of buying—Now hold on, Grant," he cried, as Grant threw his head back. "For God's sake, don't get mad again! Wait till you see what I'm driving at."

"I don't see what you're drivin' at, and I don't care. All I want you to do is to let us alone. That ought to be easy enough for you."

"I tell you, I didn't get your letter. I didn't know you'd lost the old farm." Howard was determined not to quarrel. "I didn't suppose——"

"You might 'a' come to see."

"Well, I'll admit that. All I can say in excuse is that since I got to managing plays I've kept looking ahead to making a big hit and getting a barrel of money—just as the old miners used to hope and watch. Besides, you don't understand how much pressure there is on me. A hundred different people pulling and hauling to have me go here or go there, or do this or do that. When it isn't yachting, it's canoeing, or——"

He stopped. His heart gave a painful throb, and a shiver ran through him. Again he saw his life, so rich, so bright, so free, set over against the routine life in the little low kitchen, the barren sitting room, and this still more horrible barn. Why should his brother sit there in wet and grimy clothing, mending a broken trace, while he enjoyed all the light and civilization of the age?

He looked at Grant's fine figure, his great, strong face; recalled his deep, stern, masterful voice. "Am I so much superior to him? Have not circumstances made me and destroyed him?"

"Grant, for God's sake, don't sit there like that! I'll admit I've been negligent and careless. I can't understand it all myself. But let me do something for you now. I've sent to New York for five thousand dollars. I've got terms on the old farm. Let me see you all back there once more before I return."

"I don't want any of your charity."

"It ain't charity. It's only justice to you." He rose. "Come, now, let's get at an understanding, Grant. I can't go on this way. I can't go back to New York and leave you here like this."

Grant rose too. "I tell you, I don't ask your help. You can't fix this thing up with money. If you've got more brains'n I have, why, it's all right. I ain't got any right to take anything that I don't earn."

"But you don't get what you do earn. It ain't your fault. I begin to see it now. Being the oldest, I had the best chance. I was going to town to school while you were ploughing and husking corn. Of course I thought you'd be going soon yourself. I had three years the start of you. If you'd been in my place, *you* might have met a man like Cook, *you* might have gone to New York and have been where I am."

"Well, it can't be helped now. So drop it."

"But it must be helped!" Howard said, pacing about, his hands in his coat-pockets. Grant had stopped work, and was gloomily looking out of the door at a pig nosing in the mud for stray grains of wheat at the granary door. The old man and the boy quietly withdrew.

"Good God! I see it all now," Howard burst out in an impassioned tone. "I went ahead with *my* education, got *my* start in life, then father died, and you took up his burdens. Circumstances made me and crushed you. That's all there is about that. Luck made me and cheated you. It ain't right."

His voice faltered. Both men were now oblivious of their

companions and of the scene. Both were thinking of the days when they both planned great things in the way of education, two ambitious, dreamful boys.

"I used to think of you, Grant, when I pulled out Monday morning in my best suit—cost fifteen dollars in those days." He smiled a little at the recollection. "While you in overalls and an old 'wammus'[46] were going out into the field to plough, or husk corn in the mud. It made me feel uneasy, but, as I said, I kept saying to myself, 'His turn'll come in a year or two.' But it didn't."

His voice choked. He walked to the door, stood a moment, came back. His eyes were full of tears.

"I tell you, old man, many a time in my boarding-house down to the city, when I thought of the jolly times I was having, my heart hurt me. But I said, 'It's no use to cry. Better go on and do the best you can, and then help them afterward. There'll only be one more miserable member of the family if you stay at home.' Besides, it seemed right to me to have first chance. But I never thought you'd be shut off, Grant. If I had, I never would have gone on. Come, old man, I want you to believe that." His voice was very tender now and almost humble.

"I don't know as I blame you for that, How.," said Grant, slowly. It was the first time he had called Howard by his boyish nickname. His voice was softer, too, and higher in key. But he looked steadily away.

"I went to New York. People liked my work. I was very successful, Grant; more successful than you realize. I could have helped you at any time. There's no use lying about it. And I ought to have done it; but some way—it's no excuse, I don't mean it for an excuse, only an explanation—some way I got in with the boys. I don't mean I was a drinker and all that. But I bought pictures and kept a horse and a yacht, and of course I had to pay my share of all expeditions, and—oh, what's the use!"

He broke off, turned, and threw his open palms out toward his brother, as if throwing aside the last attempt at an excuse.

"I *did* neglect you, and it's a damned shame! and I ask your forgiveness. Come, old man!"

He held out his hand, and Grant slowly approached and took

it. There was a little silence. Then Howard went on, his voice trembling, the tears on his face.

"I want you to let me help you, old man. That's the way to forgive me. Will you?"

"Yes, if you can help me."

Howard squeezed his hand. "That's all right, old man. Now you make me a boy again. Course I can help you. I've got ten—"

"I don't mean that, How." Grant's voice was very grave. "Money can't give me a chance now."

"What do you mean?"

"I mean life ain't worth very much to me. I'm too old to take a new start. I'm a dead failure. I've come to the conclusion that life's a failure for ninety-nine per cent of us. You can't help me now. It's too late."

The two men stood there, face to face, hands clasped, the one fair-skinned, full-lipped, handsome in his neat suit; the other tragic, sombre in his softened mood, his large, long, rugged Scotch face bronzed with sun and scarred with wrinkles that had histories, like sabre-cuts on a veteran, the record of his battles.

MARY HARTWELL CATHERWOOD

1847–1902

CELEBRATED as the first woman novelist born west of the Alleghenies, Mary Hartwell Catherwood began to write stories and serial novels for magazines such as *Lippincott's* and the *Atlantic Monthly*, eventually publishing novels such as *A Woman in Armor* (1857) and the historical romances *The Romance of Dollard* (1889) and *Lazarre* (1901). She was born in a small town in Ohio and graduated from Granville Female College in Ohio, then began her career teaching school in Ohio and Illinois. In her early writing Catherwood combined realism and regionalism with melodrama; the realist style is most prominent in her local color stories set in the white communities of midwestern towns and French-American settlements. After 1889 she rejected realism, famously arguing with Hamlin Garland at the World's Columbian Exposition in Chicago in 1893, where she championed "the aristocratic in literature."

PONTIAC'S LOOKOUT

Jenieve Lalotte came out of the back door of her little house on Mackinac[1] beach. The front door did not open upon either street of the village; and other domiciles were scattered with it along the strand, each little homestead having a front inclosure palisaded with oaken posts. Wooded heights sent a growth of bushes and young trees down to the pebble rim of the lake.

It had been raining, and the island was fresh as if new made. Boats and bateaux,[2] drawn up in a great semicircle about the crescent bay, had also been washed; but they kept the marks of their long voyages to the Illinois Territory,[3] or the Lake Superior region, or Canada. The very last of the winterers were in with their bales of furs, and some of these men were now roaring along the upper street in new clothes, exhilarated by spending on good cheer in one month the money it took them eleven months to earn. While in "hyvernements," or winter quarters, and on the long forest marches, the allowance of food per day, for a winterer, was one quart of corn and two ounces of tallow. On this fare the hardiest voyageurs ever known threaded a pathless continent and made a great traffic possible. But when they returned to the front of the world,—that distributing point in the straits,—they were fiercely importunate for what they considered the best the world afforded.

A segment of rainbow showed over one end of Round Island. The sky was dull rose, and a ship on the eastern horizon turned to a ship of fire, clean-cut and poised, a glistening object on a black bar of water. The lake was still, with blackness in its depths. The American flag on the fort rippled, a thing of living light, the stripes transparent. High pink clouds were riding down from the north, their flush dying as they piled aloft. There were shadings of peacock colors in the shoal water. Jenieve enjoyed this sunset beauty of the island, as she ran over the rolling pebbles, carrying some leather shoes by their leather strings. Her face was eager. She lifted the shoes to show them to three little boys playing on the edge of the lake.

"Come here. See what I have for you."

"What is it?" inquired the eldest, gazing betwixt the hairs scattered on his face; he stood with his back to the wind. His bare shins reddened in the wash of the lake, standing beyond its rim of shining gravel.

"Shoes," answered Jenieve, in a note triumphant over fate.

"What's shoes?" asked the smallest half-breed, tucking up his smock around his middle.

"They are things to wear on your feet," explained Jenieve; and her red-skinned half-brothers heard her with incredulity. She had told their mother, in their presence, that she intended to buy the children some shoes when she got pay for her spinning; and they thought it meant fashions from the Fur Company's store to wear to mass, but never suspected she had set her mind on dark-looking clamps for the feet.

"You must try them on," said Jenieve, and they all stepped

experimentally from the water, reluctant to submit. But Jenieve was mistress in the house. There is no appeal from a sister who is a father to you, and even a substitute for your living mother.

"You sit down first, François, and wipe your feet with this cloth."

The absurdity of wiping his feet before he turned in for the night tickled François, though he was of a strongly aboriginal cast, and he let himself grin. Jenieve helped him struggle to encompass his lithe feet with the clumsy brogans.

"You boys are living like Indians."

"We are Indians," asserted François.

"But you are French, too. You are my brothers. I want you to go to mass looking as well as anybody."

Hitherto their object in life had been to escape mass. They objected to increasing their chances of church-going. Moccasins were the natural wear of human beings, and nobody but women needed even moccasins until cold weather. The proud look of an Iroquois[4] taking spoils disappeared from the face of the youngest, giving way to uneasy anguish. The three boys sat down to tug, Jenieve going encouragingly from one to another. François lay on his back and pushed his heels skyward. Contempt and rebellion grew also in the faces of Gabriel and Toussaint. They were the true children of François Iroquois, her mother's second husband, who had been wont to lounge about Mackinac village in dirty buckskins and a calico shirt having one red and one blue sleeve. He had also bought a tall silk hat at the Fur Company's store, and he wore the hat under his blanket when it rained. If tobacco failed him, he scraped and dried willow peelings, and called them kinnickinnick. This worthy relation had worked no increase in Jenieve's home except an increase of children. He frequently yelled around the crescent bay, brandishing his silk hat in the exaltation of rum. And when he finally fell off the wharf into deep water, and was picked out to make another mound in the Indian burying-ground, Jenieve was so fiercely elated that she was afraid to confess it to the priest. Strange matches were made on the frontier, and Indian wives were commoner than any other kind; but through the whole mortifying existence of this Indian husband Jenieve avoided the sight of him, and called her mother steadily Mama Lalotte. The

girl had remained with her grandmother, while François Iroquois carried off his wife to the Indian village on a western
height of the island. Her grandmother had died, and Jenieve continued to keep house on the beach, having always with her one
or more of the half-breed babies, until the plunge of François
Iroquois allowed her to bring them all home with their mother.
There was but one farm on the island, and Jenieve had all the
spinning which the sheep afforded. She was the finest spinner in
that region. Her grandmother had taught her to spin with a little
wheel, as they still do about Quebec. Her pay was small. There
was not much money then in the country, but bills of credit on
the Fur Company's store were the same as cash, and she managed to feed her mother and the Indian's family. Fish were to
be had for the catching, and she could get corn-meal and vegetables for her soup pot in partial exchange for her labor. The
luxuries of life on the island were air and water, and the glories
of evening and morning. People who could buy them got such
gorgeous clothes as were brought by the Company. But usually
Jenieve felt happy enough when she put on her best red homespun bodice and petticoat for mass or to go to dances. She did
wish for shoes. The ladies at the fort had shoes, with heels which
clicked when they danced. Jenieve could dance better, but she
always felt their eyes on her moccasins, and came to regard shoes
as the chief article of one's attire.

Though the joy of shoeing her brothers was not to be put
off, she had not intended to let them keep on these precious
brogans of civilization while they played beside the water. But
she suddenly saw Mama Lalotte walking along the street near
the lake with old Michel Pensonneau. Beyond these moving figures were many others, of engagés[5] and Indians, swarming in
front of the Fur Company's great warehouse. Some were talking
and laughing; others were in a line, bearing bales of furs from
bateaux just arrived at the log-and-stone wharf stretched from
the centre of the bay. But all of them, and curious women peeping from their houses on the beach, particularly Jean Bati'
McClure's wife, could see that Michel Pensonneau was walking
with Mama Lalotte.

This sight struck cold down Jenieve's spine. Mama Lalotte
was really the heaviest charge she had. Not twenty minutes be-

fore had that flighty creature been set to watch the supper pot, and here she was, mincing along, and fixing her pale blue laughing eyes on Michel Pensonneau, and bobbing her curly flaxen head at every word he spoke. A daughter who has a marrying mother on her hands may become morbidly anxious; Jenieve felt she should have no peace of mind during the month the coureurs-de-bois[6] remained on the island. Whether they arrived early or late, they had soon to be off to the winter hunting-grounds; yet here was an emergency.

"Mama Lalotte!" called Jenieve. Her strong young fingers beckoned with authority. "Come here to me. I want you."

The giddy parent, startled and conscious, turned a conciliating smile that way. "Yes, Jenieve," she answered obediently, "I come." But she continued to pace by the side of Michel Pensonneau.

Jenieve desired to grasp her by the shoulder and walk her into the house; but when the world, especially Jean Bati' McClure's wife, is watching to see how you manage an unruly mother, it is necessary to use some adroitness.

"Will you please come here, dear Mama Lalotte? Toussaint wants you."

"No, I don't!" shouted Toussaint. "It is Michel Pensonneau I want, to make me some boats."

The girl did not hesitate. She intercepted the couple, and took her mother's arm in hers. The desperation of her act appeared to her while she was walking Mama Lalotte home; still, if nothing but force will restrain a parent, you must use force.

Michel Pensonneau stood squarely in his moccasins, turning redder and redder at the laugh of his cronies before the warehouse. He was dressed in new buckskins, and their tawny brightness made his florid cheeks more evident. Michel Pensonneau had been brought up by the Cadottes of Sault Ste. Marie, and he had rich relations at Cahokia, in the Illinois Territory. If he was not as good as the family of François Iroquois, he wanted to know the reason why. It is true, he was past forty and a bachelor. To be a bachelor, in that region, where Indian wives were so plenty and so easily got rid of, might bring some reproach on a man. Michel had begun to see that it did. He was

an easy, gormandizing, good fellow, shapelessly fat, and he never
had stirred himself during his month of freedom to do any
courting. But Frenchmen of his class considered fifty the limit
of an active life. It behooved him now to begin looking around;
to prepare a fireside for himself. Michel was a good clerk to his
employers. Cumbrous though his body might be, when he was
in the woods he never shirked any hardship to secure a specially
fine bale of furs.

Mama Lalotte, propelled against her will, sat down, trembling,
in the house. Jenieve, trembling also, took the wooden bowls
and spoons from a shelf and ladled out soup for the evening
meal. Mama Lalotte was always willing to have the work done
without trouble to herself, and she sat on a three-legged stool,
like a guest. The supper pot boiled in the centre of the house,
hanging on the crane which was fastened to a beam overhead.
Smoke from the clear fire passed that richly darkened transverse
of timber as it ascended, and escaped through a hole in the bark
roof. The Fur Company had a great building with chimneys; but
poor folks were glad to have a cedar hut of one room, covered
with bark all around and on top. A fire-pit, or earthen hearth,
was left in the centre, and the nearer the floor could be brought
to this hole, without danger, the better the house was. On winter
nights, fat French and half-breed children sat with heels to this
sunken altar, and heard tales of massacre or privation which
made the family bunks along the wall seem couches of luxury.
It was the aboriginal hut patterned after his Indian brother's by
the Frenchman; and the succession of British and American
powers had not yet improved it. To Jenieve herself, the crisis
before her, so insignificant against the background of that his-
toric island, was more important than massacre or conquest.

"Mama,"—she spoke tremulously,—"I was obliged to bring
you in. It is not proper to be seen on the street with an engagé.
The town is now full of these bush-lopers."[7]

"Bush-lopers, mademoiselle!" The little flaxen-haired woman
had a shrill voice. "What was your own father?"

"He was a clerk, madame," maintained the girl's softer treble,
"and always kept good credit for his family at the Company's
store."

"I see no difference. They are all the same."

"François Iroquois was not the same." As the girl said this she felt a powder-like flash from her own eyes.

Mama Lalotte was herself a little ashamed of the François Iroquois alliance, but she answered, "He let me walk outside the house, at least. You allow me no amusement at all. I cannot even talk over the fence to Jean Bati' McClure's wife."

"Mama, you do not understand the danger of all these things, and I do. Jean Bati' McClure's wife will be certain to get you into trouble. She is not a proper woman for you to associate with. Her mind runs on nothing but match-making."

"Speak to her, then, for yourself. I wish you would get married."

"I never shall," declared Jenieve. "I have seen the folly of it."

"You never have been young," complained Mama Lalotte. "You don't know how a young person feels."

"I let you go to the dances," argued Jenieve. "You have as good a time as any woman on the island. But old Michel Pensonneau," she added sternly, "is not settling down to smoke his pipe for the remainder of his life on this doorstep."

"Monsieur Pensonneau is not old."

"Do you take up for him, Mama Lalotte, in spite of me?" In the girl's rich brunette face the scarlet of the cheeks deepened. "Am I not more to you than Michel Pensonneau or any other engagé? He is old; he is past forty. Would I call him old if he were no more than twenty?"

"Every one cannot be only twenty and a young agent," retorted her elder; and Jenieve's ears and throat reddened, also.

"Have I not done my best for you and the boys? Do you think it does not hurt me to be severe with you?"

Mama Lalotte flounced around on her stool, but made no reply. She saw peeping and smiling at the edge of the door a neighbor's face, that encouraged her insubordinations. Its broad, good-natured upper lip thinly veiled with hairs, its fleshy eyelids and thick brows, expressed a strength which she had not, yet would gladly imitate.

"Jenieve Lalotte," spoke the neighbor, "before you finish whipping your mother you had better run and whip the boys. They are throwing their shoes in the lake."

"Their shoes!" Jenieve cried, and she scarcely looked at Jean Bati' McClure's wife, but darted outdoors along the beach.

"Oh, children, have you lost your shoes?"

"No," answered Toussaint, looking up with a countenance full of enjoyment.

"Where are they?"

"In the lake."

"You didn't throw your new shoes in the lake?"

"We took them for boats," said Gabriel freely. "But they are not even fit for boats."

"I threw mine as far as I could," observed François. "You can't make anything float in them."

She could see one of them stranded on the lake bottom, loaded with stones, its strings playing back and forth in the clear water. The others were gone out to the straits. Jenieve remembered all her toil for them, and her denial of her own wants that she might give to these half-savage boys, who considered nothing lost that they threw into the lake.

She turned around to run to the house. But there stood Jean Bati' McClure's wife, talking through the door, and encouraging her mother to walk with coureurs-de-bois. The girl's heart broke. She took to the bushes to hide her weeping, and ran through them towards the path she had followed so many times when her only living kindred were at the Indian village. The pine woods received her into their ascending heights, and she mounted towards sunset.

Panting from her long walk, Jenieve came out of the woods upon a grassy open cliff, called by the islanders Pontiac's Lookout, because the great war chief used to stand on that spot, forty years before, and gaze southward, as if he never could give up his hope of the union of his people. Jenieve knew the story. She had built playhouses here, when a child, without being afraid of the old chief's lingering influence; for she seemed to understand his trouble, and this night she was more in sympathy with Pontiac[8] than ever before in her life. She sat down on the grass, wiping the tears from her hot cheeks, her dark eyes brooding on the lovely straits. There might be more beautiful sights in the world, but Jenieve doubted it; and a white gull drifted across her vision like a moving star.

Pontiac's Lookout had been the spot from which she watched her father's bateau disappear behind Round Island. He used to go by way of Detroit to the Canadian woods. Here she wept out her first grief for his death; and here she stopped, coming and going between her mother and grandmother. The cliff down to the beach was clothed with a thick growth which took away the terror of falling, and many a time Jenieve had thrust her bare legs over the edge to sit and enjoy the outlook.

There were old women on the island who could remember seeing Pontiac. Her grandmother had told her how he looked. She had heard that, though his bones had been buried forty years beside the Mississippi, he yet came back to the Lookout every night during that summer month when all the tribes assembled at the island to receive money from a new government. He could not lie still while they took a little metal and ammunition in their hands in exchange for their country. As for the tribes, they enjoyed it. Jenieve could see their night fires begin to twinkle on Round Island and Bois Blanc,⁹ and the rising hubbub of their carnival came to her like echoes across the strait. There was one growing star on the long hooked reef which reached out from Round Island, and figures of Indians were silhouetted against the lake, running back and forth along that high stone ridge. Evening coolness stole up to Jenieve, for the whole water world was purpling; and sweet pine and cedar breaths, humid and invisible, were all around her. Her trouble grew small, laid against the granite breast of the island, and the woods darkened and sighed behind her. Jenieve could hear the shout of some Indian boy at the distant village. She was not afraid, but her shoulders contracted with a shiver. The place began to smell rankly of sweetbrier. There was no sweetbrier on the cliff or in the woods, though many bushes grew on alluvial slopes around the bay. Jenieve loved the plant, and often stuck a piece of it in her bosom. But this was a cold smell, striking chill to the bones. Her flesh and hair and clothes absorbed the scent, and it cooled her nostrils with its strange ether, the breath of sweetbrier, which always before seemed tinctured by the sun. She had a sensation of moving sidewise out of her own person; and then she saw the chief Pontiac standing on the edge of the cliff. Jenieve knew his back, and the feathers in his hair which the wind did not move.

His head turned on a pivot, sweeping the horizon from St. Ignace,[10] where the white man first set foot, to Round Island, where the shameful fires burned. His hard, set features were silver color rather than copper, as she saw his profile against the sky. His arms were folded in his blanket. Jenieve was as sure that she saw Pontiac as she was sure of the rock on which she sat. She poked one finger through the sward to the hardness underneath. The rock was below her, and Pontiac stood before her. He turned his head back from Round Island to St. Ignace. The wind blew against him, and the brier odor, sickening sweet, poured over Jenieve.

She heard the dogs bark in Mackinac village, and leaves moving behind her, and the wash of water at the base of the island which always sounded like a small rain. Instead of feeling afraid, she was in a nightmare of sorrow. Pontiac had loved the French almost as well as he loved his own people. She breathed the sweetbrier scent, her neck stretched forward and her dark eyes fixed on him; and as his head turned back from St. Ignace his whole body moved with it, and he looked at Jenieve.

His eyes were like a cat's in the purple darkness, or like that heatless fire which shines on rotting bark. The hoar-frosted countenance was noble even in its most brutal lines. Jenieve, without knowing she was saying a word, spoke out:—

"Monsieur the chief Pontiac, what ails the French and Indians?"

"Malatat," answered Pontiac. The word came at her with force.

"Monsieur the chief Pontiac," repeated Jenieve, struggling to understand, "I say, what ails the French and Indians?"

"Malatat!" His guttural cry rang through the bushes. Jenieve was so startled that she sprung back, catching herself on her hands. But without the least motion of walking he was far westward, showing like a phosphorescent bar through the trees, and still moving on, until the pallor was lost from sight.

Jenieve at once began to cross herself. She had forgotten to do it before. The rankness of sweetbrier followed her some distance down the path, and she said prayers all the way home.

You cannot talk with great spirits and continue to chafe about little things. The boys' shoes and Mama Lalotte's lightness were the same as forgotten. Jenieve entered her house with dew in her hair, and an unterrified freshness of body for whatever might happen. She was certain she had seen Pontiac, but she would never tell anybody to have it laughed at. There was no candle burning, and the fire had almost died under the supper pot. She put a couple of sticks on the coals, more for their blaze than to heat her food. But the Mackinac night was chill, and it was pleasant to see the interior of her little home flickering to view. Candles were lighted in many houses along the beach, and amongst them Mama Lalotte was probably roaming,—for she had left the door open towards the lake,—and the boys' voices could be heard with others in the direction of the log wharf.

Jenieve took her supper bowl and sat down on the doorstep. The light cloud of smoke, drawn up to the roof-hole, ascended behind her, forming an azure gray curtain against which her figure showed, round-wristed and full-throated. The starlike camp fires on Round Island were before her, and the incessant wash of the water on its pebbles was company to her. Somebody knocked on the front door.

"It is that insolent Michel Pensonneau," thought Jenieve. "When he is tired he will go away." Yet she was not greatly surprised when the visitor ceased knocking and came around the palisades.

"Good-evening, Monsieur Crooks," said Jenieve.

"Good-evening, mademoiselle," responded Monsieur Crooks, and he leaned against the hut side, cap in hand, where he could look at her. He had never yet been asked to enter the house. Jenieve continued to eat her supper.

"I hope monsieur your uncle is well?"

"My uncle is well. It isn't necessary for me to inquire about madame your mother, for I have just seen her sitting on McClure's doorstep."

"Oh," said Jenieve.

The young man shook his cap in a restless hand. Though he spoke French easily, he was not dressed like an engagé, and he showed through the dark the white skin of the Saxon.

"Mademoiselle Jenieve,"—he spoke suddenly,—"you know my uncle is well established as agent of the Fur Company, and as his assistant I expect to stay here."

"Yes, monsieur. Did you take in some fine bales of furs to-day?"

"That is not what I was going to say."

"Monsieur Crooks, you speak all languages, don't you?"

"Not all. A few. I know a little of nearly every one of our Indian dialects."

'Monsieur, what does 'malatat' mean?"

" 'Malatat'? That's a Chippewa[11] word. You will often hear that. It means 'good for nothing.' "

"But I have heard that the chief Pontiac was an Ottawa."[12]

The young man was not interested in Pontiac.

"A chief would know a great many dialects," he replied. "Chippewa was the tongue of this island. But what I wanted to say is that I have had a serious talk with the agent. He is entirely willing to have me settle down. And he says, what is the truth, that you are the best and prettiest girl at the straits. I have spoken my mind often enough. Why shouldn't we get married right away?"

Jenieve set her bowl and spoon inside the house, and folded her arms.

"Monsieur, have I not told you many times? I cannot marry. I have a family already."

The young agent struck his cap impatiently against the bark weather-boarding. "You are the most offish[13] girl I ever saw. A man cannot get near enough to you to talk reason."

"It would be better if you did not come down here at all, Monsieur Crooks," said Jenieve. "The neighbors will be saying I am setting a bad example to my mother."

"Bring your mother up to the Fur Company's quarters with you, and the neighbors will no longer have a chance to put mischief into her head."

Jenieve took him seriously, though she had often suspected, from what she could see at the fort, that Americans had not the custom of marrying an entire family.

"It is really too fine a place for us."

Young Crooks laughed. Squaws[14] had lived in the Fur Company's quarters, but he would not mention this fact to the girl.

His eyes dwelt fondly on her in the darkness, for though the fire behind her had again sunk to embers, it cast up a little glow;

and he stood entirely in the star-embossed outside world. It is not safe to talk in the dark: you tell too much. The primitive instinct of truth-speaking revives in force, and the restraints of another's presence are gone. You speak from the unseen to the unseen over leveled barriers of reserve. Young Crooks had scarcely said that place was nothing, and he would rather live in that little house with Jenieve than in the Fur Company's quarters without her, when she exclaimed openly, "And have old Michel Pensonneau put over you!"

The idea of Michel Pensonneau taking precedence of him as master of the cedar hut was delicious to the American, as he recalled the engagé's respectful slouch while receiving the usual bill of credit.

"One may laugh, monsieur. I laugh myself; it is better than crying. But it is the truth that Mama Lalotte is more care to me than all the boys. I have no peace except when she is asleep in bed."

"There is no harm in Madame Lalotte."

"You are right, monsieur. Jean Bati' McClure's wife puts all the mischief in her head. She would even learn to spin, if that woman would let her alone."

"And I never heard any harm of Michel Pensonneau. He is a good enough fellow, and he has more to his credit on the Company's books than any other engagé now on the island."

"I suppose you would like to have him sit and smoke his pipe the rest of his days on your doorstep?"

"No, I wouldn't," confessed the young agent. "Michel is a saving man, and he uses very mean tobacco, the cheapest in the house."

"You see how I am situated, monsieur. It is no use to talk to me."

"But Michel Pensonneau is not going to trouble you long. He has relations at Cahokia, in the Illinois Territory, and he is fitting himself out to go there to settle."

"Are you sure of this, monsieur?"

"Certainly I am, for we have already made him a bill of credit to our correspondent at Cahokia. He wants very few goods to carry across the Chicago portage."[15]

"Monsieur, how soon does he intend to go?"

"On the first schooner that sails to the head of the lake; so
he may set out any day. Michel is anxious to try life on the
Mississippi, and his three years' engagement with the Company
is just ended."

"I also am anxious to have him try life on the Mississippi,"
said Jenieve, and she drew a deep breath of relief. "Why did you
not tell me this before?"

"How could I know you were interested in him?"

"He is not a bad man," she admitted kindly. "I can see that
he means very well. If the McClures would go to the Illinois
Territory with him—But, Monsieur Crooks," Jenieve asked
sharply, "do people sometimes make sudden marriages?"

"In my case they have not," sighed the young man. "But I
think well of sudden marriages myself. The priest comes to the
island this week."

"Yes, and I must take the children to confession."

"What are you going to do with me, Jenieve?"

"I am going to say good-night to you, and shut my door."
She stepped into the house.

"Not yet. It is only a little while since they fired the sunset
gun at the fort. You are not kind to shut me out the moment I
come."

She gave him her hand, as she always did when she said good-
night, and he prolonged his hold of it.

"You are full of sweetbrier. I didn't know it grew down here
on the beach."

"It never did grow here, Monsieur Crooks."

"You shall have plenty of it in your garden, when you come
home with me."

"Oh, go away, and let me shut my door, monsieur. It seems
no use to tell you I cannot come."

"No use at all. Until you come, then, good-night."

Seldom are two days alike on the island. Before sunrise the
lost dews of paradise always sweeten those scented woods, and
the birds begin to remind you of something you heard in another
life, but have forgotten. Jenieve loved to open her door and surprise the east. She stepped out the next morning to fill her pail.
There was a lake of translucent cloud beyond the water lake: the
first unruffled, and the second wind-stirred. The sun pushed up,

a flattened red ball, from the lake of steel ripples to the lake of
calm clouds. Nearer, a schooner with its sails down stood black
as ebony between two bars of light drawn across the water,
which lay dull and bleak towards the shore. The addition of a
schooner to the scattered fleet of sailboats, bateaux, and birch
canoes made Jenieve laugh. It must have arrived from Sault Ste.
Marie[16] in the night. She had hopes of getting rid of Michel Pensonneau that very day. Since he was going to Cahokia, she felt
stinging regret for the way she had treated him before the whole
village; yet her mother could not be sacrificed to politeness. Except his capacity for marrying, there was really no harm in the
old fellow, as Monsieur Crooks had said.

The humid blockhouse[17] and walls of the fort high above the
bay began to glisten in emerging sunlight, and Jenieve determined not to be hard on Mama Lalotte that day. If Michel came
to say good-by, she would shake his hand herself. It was not
agreeable for a woman so fond of company to sit in the house
with nobody but her daughter. Mama Lalotte did not love the
pine woods, or any place where she would be alone. But Jenieve
could sit and spin in solitude all day, and think of that chill silver
face she had seen at Pontiac's Lookout, and the floating away of
the figure, a phosphorescent bar through the trees, and of that
spoken word which had denounced the French and Indians as
good for nothing. She decided to tell the priest, even if he rebuked her. It did not seem any stranger to Jenieve than many
things which were called natural, such as the morning miracles
in the eastern sky, and the growth of the boys, her dear tor-
ments. To Jenieve's serious eyes, trained by her grandmother, it
was not as strange as the sight of Mama Lalotte, a child in ma-
turity, always craving amusement, and easily led by any chance
hand.

The priest had come to Mackinac in the schooner during the
night. He combined this parish with others more or less distant,
and he opened the chapel and began his duties as soon as he
arrived. Mama Lalotte herself offered to dress the boys for confession. She put their best clothes on them, and then she took
out all her own finery. Jenieve had no suspicion while the little
figure preened and burnished itself, making up for the lack of a
mirror by curves of the neck to look itself well over. Mama

Lalotte thought a great deal about what she wore. She was pleased, and her flaxen curls danced. She kissed Jenieve on both cheeks, as if there had been no quarrel, though unpleasant things never lingered in her memory. And she made the boys kiss Jenieve; and while they were saddened by clothes, she also made them say they were sorry about the shoes.

By sunset, the schooner, which had sat in the straits all day, hoisted its sails and rounded the hooked point of the opposite island. The gun at the fort was like a parting salute, and a shout was raised by coureurs-de-bois thronging the log wharf. They trooped up to the fur warehouse, and the sound of a fiddle and the thump of softshod feet were soon heard; for the French were ready to celebrate any occasion with dancing. Laughter and the high excited voices of women also came from the little ball-room, which was only the office of the Fur Company.

Here the engagés felt at home. The fiddler sat on the top of the desk, and men lounging on a row of benches around the walls sprang to their feet and began to caper at the violin's first invitation. Such maids and wives as were nearest the building were haled in, laughing, by their relations; and in the absence of the agents, and of that awe which goes with making your cross-mark[18] on a paper, a quick carnival was held on the spot where so many solemn contracts had been signed. An odor of furs came from the packing-rooms around, mixed with gums and incense-like whiffs. Added to this was the breath of the general store kept by the agency. Tobacco and snuff, rum, chocolate, calico, blankets, wood and iron utensils, firearms, West India[19] sugar and rice,—all sifted their invisible essences on the air. Unceiled joists showed heavy and brown overhead. But there was no fire-place, for when the straits stood locked in ice and the island was deep in snow, no engagé claimed admission here. He would be a thousand miles away, toiling on snowshoes with his pack of furs through the trees, or bargaining with trappers for his contribution to this month of enormous traffic.

Clean buckskin legs and brand-new belted hunting-shirts whirled on the floor, brightened by sashes of crimson or kerchiefs of orange. Indians from the reservation on Round Island, who happened to be standing, like statues, in front of the building, turned and looked with lenient eye on the performance of

their French brothers. The fiddler was a nervous little Frenchman with eyes like a weasel, and he detected Jenieve Lalotte
putting her head into the room. She glanced from figure to figure
of the dancers, searching through the twilight for what she could
not find; but before he could call her she was off. None of the
men, except a few Scotch-French, were very tall, but they were
a handsome, muscular race, fierce in enjoyment, yet with a languor which prolonged it, and gave grace to every picturesque
pose. Not one of them wanted to pain Lalotte's girl, but, as they
danced, a joyful fellow would here and there spring high above
the floor and shout, "Good voyage to Michel Pensonneau and
his new family!" They had forgotten the one who amused them
yesterday, and remembered only the one who amused them
today.

Jenieve struck on Jean Bati' McClure's door, and faced his
wife, speechless, pointing to the schooner ploughing southward.

"Yes, she's gone," said Jean Bati' McClure's wife, "and the
boys with her."

The confidante came out on the step, and tried to lay her hand
on Jenieve's shoulder, but the girl moved backward from her.

"Now let me tell you, it is a good thing for you, Jenieve
Lalotte. You can make a fine match of your own to-morrow. It
is not natural for a girl to live as you have lived. You are better
off without them."

"But my mother has left me!"

"Well, I am sorry for you; but you were hard on her."

"I blame you, madame!"

"You might as well blame the priest, who thought it best not
to let them go unmarried. And she has taken a much worse man
than Michel Pensonneau in her time."

"My mother and my brothers have left me here alone," repeated Jenieve; and she wrung her hands and put them over her
face. The trouble was so overwhelming that it broke her down
before her enemy.

"Oh, don't take it to heart," said Jean Bati' McClure's wife,
with ready interest in the person nearest at hand. "Come and
eat supper with my man and me to-night, and sleep in our house
if you are afraid."

Jenieve leaned her forehead against the hut, and made no reply to these neighborly overtures.

"Did she say nothing at all about me, madame?"

"Yes; she was afraid you would come at the last minute and take her by the arm and walk her home. You were too strict with her, and that is the truth. She was glad to get away to Cahokia. They say it is fine in the Illinois Territory. You know she is fond of seeing the world."

The young supple creature trying to restrain her shivers and sobs of anguish against the bark house side was really a moving sight; and Jean Bati' McClure's wife, flattening a masculine upper lip with resolution, said promptly,—

"I am going this moment to the Fur Company's quarters to send young Monsieur Crooks after you."

At that Jenieve fled along the beach and took to the bushes. As she ran, weeping aloud like a child, she watched the lessening schooner; and it seemed a monstrous thing, out of nature, that her mother was on that little ship, fleeing from her, with a thoughtless face set smiling towards a new world. She climbed on, to keep the schooner in sight, and made for Pontiac's Lookout, reckless of what she had seen there.

The distant canvas became one leaning sail, and then a speck, and then nothing. There was an afterglow on the water which turned it to a wavering pavement of yellow-pink sheen. In that clear, high atmosphere, mainland shores and islands seemed to throw out the evening purples from themselves, and thus to slowly reach for one another and form darkness. Jenieve had lain on the grass, crying, "O Mama—François—Toussaint—Gabriel!" But she sat up at last, with her dejected head on her breast, submitting to the pettiness and treachery of what she loved. Bats flew across the open place. A sudden rankness of sweetbrier, taking her breath away by its icy puff, reminded her of other things, and she tried to get up and run. Instead of running she seemed to move sidewise out of herself, and saw Pontiac standing on the edge of the cliff. His head turned from St. Ignace to the reviving fires on Round Island, and slowly back again from Round Island to St. Ignace. Jenieve felt as if she were choking, but again she asked out of her heart to his,—

"Monsieur the chief Pontiac, what ails the French and Indians?"

He floated around to face her, the high ridges of his bleached features catching light; but this time he showed only dim dead eyes. His head sunk on his breast, and Jenieve could see the fronds of the feathers he wore traced indistinctly against the sky. The dead eyes searched for her and could not see her; he whispered hoarsely to himself, "Malatat!"

The voice of the living world calling her name sounded directly afterwards in the woods, and Jenieve leaped as if she were shot. She had the instinct that her lover must not see this thing, for there were reasons of race and religion against it. But she need not have feared that Pontiac would show himself, or his long and savage mourning for the destruction of the red man, to any descendant of the English. As the bushes closed behind her she looked back: the phosphoric blur was already so far in the west that she could hardly be sure she saw it again. And the young agent of the Fur Company, breaking his way among leaves, met her with both hands; saying gayly, to save her the shock of talking about her mother:—

"Come home, come home, my sweetbrier maid. No wonder you smell of sweetbrier. I am rank with it myself, rubbing against the dewy bushes."

ALEXANDER LAWRENCE POSEY

1873–1908

THE CREEK JOURNALIST, editor, and political humorist Alexander Posey was born in the Creek nation of mixed heritage—his mother was Chickasaw and Creek and his father was white—and did not speak English until the age of fourteen, when he enrolled in the Creek national school at Eufala, Oklahoma, then part of Indian Territory. Posey went on to attend Bacone Indian University, where he began to write stories, some featuring Chinnubbie Harjo, the witty trickster of Creek legend who provided Posey with a pen name. In addition to Indian tradition, however, Posey was influenced by American and English writers, including Thoreau and Emerson. In the 1890s he wrote mostly poetry, some of which was published posthumously in 1910. After a brief time as superintendent of Creek schools, Posey became owner and editor of the Eufala *Indian Journal* in 1902. Rather than writing editorials he chose to write letters to the editor using the name Fus Fixico. These letters, written in a Creek English dialect, describe the responses of a host of Creek characters—Hotgun, Tookpafka Micco, and others—to major issues facing the Creek community, including Oklahoma statehood and the federally mandated allotment policy designed to break up Creek lands. Published from 1902 to 1908, Posey's Fus Fixico letters became quite popular. Indeed, Posey received requests to write for papers throughout the country, but unlike Finley Peter Dunne, to whom he can be compared as a dialect humorist and journalist, Posey preferred to continue writing, as he did until his death in 1908, for a local, Creek audience.

LETTER NO. 18
INDIAN JOURNAL, APRIL 24, 1903

Well, so Big Man at Washington was made another rule like that one about making the Injin cut his hair off short like a prize fighter or saloon keeper. Big Man he was say this time the Injin was had to change his name just like if the marshal was had a writ for him.[1] So, if the Injin's name is Wolf Warrior, he was had to call himself John Smith, or maybe so Bill Jones, so nobody else could get his mail out of the postoffice. Big Man say Injin name like Sitting Bull or Tecumseh was too hard to remember and don't sound civilized like General Cussed Her or old Grand Pa Harry's Son.[2]

Hotgun he say the Big Man's rule was heap worse than allotment,[3] and Crazy Snake he say he was hear white man say all time you could take everything away from a him but you couldn't steal his good name.[4]

Guess so that was all right 'cause they was nothing to a name nohow if you can't borrow some money on it at the bank. Tookpafka Micco he say he was druther had a deed to his land than a big name in the newspaper. When I ask him what he do after he sell his land, he say he don't know, like Bob Ingersoll.[5] Then he say he was let the future take care of its own self like a calf when it was get too old to suck. Guess so Tookpafka Micco was made up his mind to drink sofky[6] and eat sour bread and be glad like a young cat with a ball a yarn before the fire place in the winter time.

Well, so we hear lots a talk about big progress in Creek nation[7] and read about it in the newspaper before breakfast time. They was good news all time about long stride and development and things like that till you can't make a crop and get out of the hole if you was try to hear all of it. Hotgun he say he think he was had to put beeswax in his ears like Few Leases (Ulysses)[8] in olden time.

But look like you don't hear nothing about fullblood Injins

'way back behind the hills that was had they sofky patch and cabin on land that was done filed on by some half-breed or maybe so white man that was had a right. We don't hear nothing about them kind a Injin at all. But we hear all time about some fellow that was find a coal mine with a post auger,[9] or maybe so some other fellow that was strike oil that was shoot up like a squirrel gun soon as he touch it.

Must be the Big Man that was look out for Injin was look out for himself too much. Hotgun he say it was natural for the Big Man to do that way 'cause he was had the chance. Maybe so, Hotgun he say, that was the only law civilized man don't want to break.

LETTER NO. 54

MUSKOGEE DAILY PHOENIX,

APRIL 16, 1905

"Well, so," Hotgun he say, "Colonel Clarence B. Duglast, he was dee-lighted and Chief P. Porter, he was dee-lighted, and Charley Gibson he was dee-lighted, and Alice M. Lobbysome she was dee-lighted too."[10]

And Tookpafka Micco he was look down his old pipe-stem and say, "Well, so what for?"

And Hotgun he go on and say, "Well, so 'cause the Great White Father from Washington was suffered 'em to come unto 'im[11] on the grand stand, while he was showing his teeth and shaking the Big Stick before the multitude up to Muskogee."[12]

Then Tookpafka Micco he spit out in the yard and say, "Well, so what kind of a thing's the Big Stick,[13] anyhow?"

And Hotgun he look wise, like the supreme court, and explain it, "Well so the Big Stick was the symbol of power, like a policeman's billy. In the jungles a Afriky it was called a war-club; and in the islands a the sea, like Australia, it was called a boomer-rang; and among us fullblood Injins we call it a ball-stick; and if it was fall in the hands a the women folks, it was called a rolling-pin, or maybe so, a broom-handle. It was had lots a different names, like breakfast food. Over in Europe a king was had precious stones put in it, to make it more ornamental than useful, and call it a scepter. The brass-knucks was the latest improvement on it. In olden time Samson[14] was had a Big Stick made out of a jaw-bone of a ass, and was made a great hit with it among the Philistines. Same way when the Great White Father was want to show his influence all he had to do was to flourish the Big Stick and everybody was get out from under it."

(Wolf Warrior and Kono Harjo they was grunt and Took-pafka Micco he was pay close attention and spit out in the yard again.)

Then Hotgun he smoke slow and go on and say, "Well, so, like I first start to say, Colonel Clarence B. Duglast he was dee-lighted and Chief P. Porter he was dee-lighted, and Charley Gibson he was dee-lighted and Alice M. Lobbysome she was dee-lighted too. They was all butt in before the reception committee could see if they badges was on straight. They was put the Great White Father on they shoulders and histed 'im upon the grand stand, and he was made a talk to the multitude. He say, 'Well, so I was mighty glad to see you all and hope you was all well. I couldn't complain and I was left Secretary Its-cocked[15] enjoying good health. (Big cheers and somebody out in the crowd say, Bully for Itscocked!) Look like you all was had a fine country down here. You all ought to had statehood[16] and let Oklahoma show you how to run it. (Colonel Clarence B. Duglast, he pay close attention and listen for some word 'bout 'imself.) I want everybody to had a square deal down here. (Lots more big cheers and everybody smiling but the Snake Injin.) You all was had a fine town here too. You could run flat boats up to it from Ft. Smith,[17] and deliver the goods over lots of railroads, and pump out oil, and develop salt-licks and float bee-courses.[18] But I didn't had time to talk any more, 'cause I couldn't stop here but two minutes and I have been here put near five. So long.'

"Then the special train was kick up a cloud of dust and hide behind it, and the multitude was climb down off the houses and telegraph poles and go tell they neighbors 'bout it. Colonel Clarence B. Duglast he go and tell his friends the President think he was ten cents straight, and Chief P. Porter he go and tell his friends the President say he was the greatest living Injin, and Charley Gibson he go and write a 'Rifle Shot' 'bout giving the

President a fan made out a tame turkey feathers instead of eagle plumes, and Alice M. Lobbysome she go and buy the platform the President stood on for a souvenir. Maybe so she was made a bedstead out of it and distribute the sawdust and shavings among the full-bloods to look at."

And Tookpafka Micco he say, "Well, so I might need some kindling next winter and the keepsakes was come in handy."

(Wolf Warrior and Kono Harjo they was give another big grunt.)

Then Hotgun he go on and say, "Well, so the next stop the Great White Father make was out in Oklahoma in a big pasture, where they was lots of cayotes. He was got after one a horseback and crowd it over the prairies till he was get good results and captured it alive. He was had lots of fun with it before he was run it down. The President was a great hunter and was kill big game well as a cayote or jackrabbit. So he was go on to the Rocky Mountains to beard the bear and lion in they den."

And Tookpafka Micco he say, "Well, so this time the Lord better help the grizzly."

THE CHICAGO WRITER Finley Peter Dunne was a journalist by profession, beginning his newspaper career at the Chicago *Post*, where he introduced his "Mr. Dooley" columns, and later joining the staff of the New York *Morning Telegraph*. Although he eventually worked at the *American Magazine* and became editor of *Collier's* magazine, he is known primarily for his Mr. Dooley newspaper columns. Told from the point of view of an Irish Chicago saloon-keeper, these columns remarked on the historical events and social issues of the day in a humorous and frequently satirical style; appealing to a broad section of American society, the Mr. Dooley columns were enjoyed not only by thousands of newspaper subscribers but also by writers such as Henry Adams and Henry James. Dunne wrote over 700 Mr. Dooley pieces, collecting some in a series of books, beginning with *Mr. Dooley in Peace and War* in 1898 and continuing until 1919. Although, as a journalist, he is not usually regarded as a local colorist, Dunne shows the widespread popularity of a type of writing rooted in the landscape and dialect of a particular community—in this case, the Irish immigrant community. His columns both contributed to and reflected the public awareness of immigration as a force that was radically changing the urban United States at the turn of the century.

FROM THE PREFACE TO
MR. DOOLEY IN PEACE AND WAR

Archey Road stretches back for many miles from the heart of an ugly city to the cabbage gardens that gave the maker of the seal his opportunity to call the city "urbs in horto." Somewhere

between the two—that is to say, forninst[1] th' gas-house and be-
yant Healey's slough and not far from the polis station—lives
Martin Dooley, doctor of philosophy.

There was a time when Archey Road was purely Irish. But
the Huns,[2] turned back from the Adriatic[3] and the stock-yards
and overrunning Archey Road, have nearly exhausted the original population—not driven them out as they drove out less
vigorous races, with thick clubs and short spears, but edged them
out with the more biting weapons of modern civilization—over-
worked and under-eaten them into more languid surroundings
remote from the tanks of the gas-house and the blast furnaces
of the rolling mill.[4]

But Mr. Dooley remains, and enough remain with him to save
the Archey Road. In this community you can hear all the various
accents of Ireland, from the awkward brogue of the "far-
downer"[5] to the mild and aisy Elizabethan English of the southern Irishman, and all the exquisite variations to be heard between
Armagh[6] and Bantry Bay,[7] with the difference that would naturally arise from substituting cinders and sulphuretted hydrogen
for soft misty air and peat smoke. Here also you can see the
wakes and christenings, the marriages and funerals, and the other
fêtes of the ol' counthry somewhat modified and darkened by
American usage. The Banshee has been heard many times in Archey Road. On the eve of All Saints' Day[8] it is well known that
here alone the pookies[9] play thricks in cabbage gardens. In 1893
it was reported that Malachi Dempsey was called "by the other
people," and disappeared west of the tracks, and never came
back.

A simple people! "Simple, says ye!" remarked Mr. Dooley.
"Simple like th' air or th' deep sea. Not complicated like a watch
that stops whin th' shoot iv clothes ye got it with wears out.
Whin Father Butler wr-rote a book he niver finished, he said
simplicity was not wearin' all ye had on ye'er shirt-front, like a
tin-horn[10] gambler with his di'mon' stud. An' 'tis so."

The barbarians around them are moderately but firmly gov-
erned, encouraged to passionate votings for the ruling race, but
restrained from the immoral pursuit of office.

The most generous, thoughtful, honest, and chaste people in
the world are these friends of Mr. Dooley—knowing and in-

nocent; moral, but giving no heed at all to patented political moralities.

Among them lives and prospers the traveller, archaeologist, historian, social observer, saloon-keeper, economist, and philosopher, who has not been out of the ward for twenty-five years "but twict." He reads the newspapers with solemn care, heartily hates them, and accepts all they print for the sake of drowning Hennessy's rising protests against his logic. From the cool heights of life in the Archey Road, uninterrupted by the jarring noises of crickets and cows, he observes the passing show, and meditates thereon. His impressions are transferred to the desensitized plate of Mr. Hennessy's mind, where they can do no harm.

*   *   *

IMMIGRATION

"Well, I see Congress has got to wurruk again," said Mr. Dooley.

"The Lord save us fr'm harm," said Mr. Hennessy.

"Yes, sir," said Mr. Dooley, "Congress has got to wurruk again, an' manny things that seems important to a Congressman 'll be brought up befure thim. 'Tis sthrange that what's a big thing to a man in Wash'nton, Hinnissy, don't seem much account to me. Divvle a bit do I care whether they dig th' Nicaragoon Canal[11] or cross th' Isthmus[12] in a balloon; or whether th' Monroe docthrine[13] is enfoorced or whether it ain't; or whether th' thrusts is abolished as Teddy Rosenfelt wud like to have thim or encouraged to go on with their neefaryous but magnificent entherprises as th' Prisidint wud like;[14] or whether th' water is poured into th' ditches to reclaim th' arid lands iv th' West[15] or th' money f'r thim to fertilize th' arid pocket-books iv th' conthractors; or whether th' Injun is threated like a depindant an' miserable thribesman or like a free an' indepindant dog;[16] or whether we restore th' merchant marine to th' ocean[17] or whether we lave it to restore itsilf. None iv these here questions inthrests me, an' be me I mane you an' be you I mane ivrybody. What we want to know is, ar-re we goin' to have coal

enough in th' hod whin th' cold snap comes; will th' plumbin'
hold out, an' will th' job last.

"But they'se wan question that Congress is goin' to take up
that you an' me are intherested in. As a pilgrim father that missed
th' first boats, I must raise me claryon voice again' th' invasion
iv this fair land be th' paupers an' arnychists iv effete Europe.
Ye bet I must—because I'm here first. 'Twas diff'rent whin I
was dashed high on th' stern an' rockbound coast.[18] In thim days
America was th' refuge iv th' oppressed iv all th' wurruld. They
cud come over here an' do a good job iv oppressin' thimsilves.
As I told ye I come a little late. Th' Rosenfelts an' th' Lodges[19]
bate me be at laste a boat lenth, an' be th' time I got here they
was stern an' rockbound thimsilves. So I got a gloryous raycip-
tion as soon as I was towed off th' rocks. Th' stars an' sthripes
whispered a welcome in th' breeze an' a shovel was thrust into
me hand an' I was pushed into a sthreet excyvatin' as though
I'd been born here. Th' pilgrim father who bossed th' job was a
fine ol' puritan be th' name iv Doherty, who come over in th'
Mayflower[20] about th' time iv th' potato rot[21] in Wexford,[22] an'
he made me think they was a hole in th' breakwather iv th' haven
iv refuge an' some iv th' wash iv th' seas iv opprission had got
through. He was a stern an' rockbound la-ad himsilf, but I was
a good hand at loose stones an' wan day—but I'll tell ye about
that another time.

"Annyhow, I was rayceived with open arms that sometimes
ended in a clinch. I was afraid I wasn't goin' to assimilate with
th' airlyer pilgrim fathers an' th' instichoochions iv th' counthry,
but I soon found that a long swing iv th' pick made me as good
as another man an' it didn't require a gr-reat intellect, or sometimes anny at all, to vote th' dimmycrat ticket, an' befure I was
here a month, I felt enough like a native born American to burn
a witch. Wanst in a while a mob iv intilligint collajeens, whose
grandfathers had bate me to th' dock, wud take a shy at me
Pathrick's Day procission or burn down wan iv me churches,
but they got tired iv that befure long; 'twas too much like
wurruk.

"But as I tell ye, Hinnissy, 'tis diff'rent now. I don't know
why 'tis diff'rent but 'tis diff'rent. 'Tis time we put our back
again' th' open dure an' keep out th' savage horde. If that cousin

iv ye'ers expects to cross, he'd betther tear f'r th' ship. In a few
minyits th' gates 'll be down an' whin th' oppressed wurruld
comes hikin' acrost to th' haven iv refuge, they'll do well to put
a couplin' pin undher their hats, f'r th' Goddess iv Liberty[23] 'll
meet thim at th' dock with an axe in her hand. Congress is goin'
to fix it. Me frind Shaughnessy says so. He was in yisterdah an'
says he: ''Tis time we done something to make th' immigration
laws sthronger,' says he. 'Thrue f'r ye, Miles Standish,'[24] says I;
'but what wud ye do?' 'I'd keep out th' offscourin's iv Europe,'
says he. 'Wud ye go back?' says I. 'Have ye'er joke,' says he.
''Tis not so seeryus as it was befure ye come,' says I. 'But what
ar-re th' immygrants doin' that's roonous to us?' I says. 'Well,'
says he, 'they're arnychists,' he says; 'they don't assymilate with
th' counthry,' he says. 'Maybe th' counthry's digestion has gone
wrong fr'm too much rich food,' says I; 'perhaps now if we'd
lave off thryin' to digest Rockyfellar an' thry a simple diet like
Schwartzmeister, we wudden't feel th' effects iv our vittels,' I
says. 'Maybe if we'd season th' immygrants a little or cook thim
thurly, they'd go down betther,' I says.

" 'They're arnychists, like Parsons,' he says. 'He wud've been
an immygrant if Texas hadn't been admitted to th' Union,'[25] I
says. 'Or Snolgosh,' he says. 'Has Mitchigan seceded?' I says.
'Or Gittoo,' he says. 'Who come fr'm th' effete monarchies iv
Chicago, west iv Ashland Av'noo,' I says. 'Or what's-his-name,
Wilkes Booth,'[26] he says. 'I don't know what he was—maybe a
Boolgharyen,' says I. 'Well, annyhow,' says he, 'they're th' scum
iv th' earth.' 'They may be that,' says I; 'but we used to think
they was th' cream iv civilization,' I says. 'They're off th' top
annyhow. I wanst believed 'twas th' best men iv Europe come
here, th' la-ads that was too sthrong and indepindant to be
kicked around be a boorgomasther[27] at home an' wanted to dig
out f'r a place where they cud get a chanst to make their way
to th' money. I see their sons fightin' into politics an' their
daughters tachin' young American idee how to shoot too high
in th' public school, an' I thought they was all right. But I see
I was wrong. Thim boys out there towin' wan heavy foot afther
th' other to th' rowlin' mills is all arnychists. There's warrants
out f'r all names endin' in 'inski, an' I think I'll board up me
windows, f'r,' I says, 'if immygrants is as dangerous to this coun-

thry as ye an' I an' other pilgrim fathers believe they are, they'se enough iv thim sneaked in already to make us aborigines about as infloointial as the prohibition vote in th' Twenty-ninth Ward. They'll dash again' our stern an' rock-bound coast till they bust it,' says I.

"'But I ain't so much afraid as ye ar-re. I'm not afraid iv me father an' I'm not afraid iv mesilf. An' I'm not afraid iv Schwartzmeister's father or Hinnery Cabin Lodge's grandfather. We all come over th' same way, an' if me ancestors were not what Hogan calls rigicides, 'twas not because they were not ready an' willin', on'y a king niver come their way. I don't believe in killin' kings, mesilf. I niver wud've sawed th' block off that curly-headed potintate that I see in th' pitchers down town, but, be hivins, Presarved Codfish Shaughnessy, if we'd begun a few years ago shuttin' out folks that wudden't mind handin' a bomb to a king, they wudden't be enough people in Mattsachoosetts to make a quorum f'r th' Anti-Impeeryal S'ciety,'[28] says I. 'But what wud ye do with th' offscourin' iv Europe?' says he. 'I'd scour thim some more,' says I.

"An' so th' meetin' iv th' Plymouth Rock Assocyation[29] come to an end. But if ye wud like to get it together, Deacon Hinnissy, to discuss th' immygration question, I'll sind out a hurry call f'r Schwartzmeister an' Mulcahey an' Ignacio Sbarbaro an' Nels Larsen an' Petrus Gooldvink, an' we 'll gather to-night at Fanneilnoviski Hall at th' corner iv Sheridan an' Sigel sthreets. All th' pilgrim fathers is rayquested f'r to bring interpreters."

"Well," said Mr. Hennessy, "divvle th' bit I care, on'y I'm here first, an' I ought to have th' right to keep th' bus fr'm bein' overcrowded."

"Well," said Mr. Dooley, "as a pilgrim father on me gran' nephew's side, I don't know but ye're right. An' they'se wan sure way to keep thim out."

"What's that?" asked Mr. Hennessy.

"Teach thim all about our instichoochions befure they come," said Mr. Dooley.

BORN IN CAMDEN, Ohio, Sherwood Anderson spent his early
life traveling, taking a variety of jobs and serving in the army in
the Spanish-American War. He returned to Ohio, married, and
had children, but eventually left his family to move to Chicago.
There Anderson worked as an advertising copywriter and met
Carl Sandburg, Theodore Dreiser, and other authors. With their
encouragement, Anderson began to write; his first two novels
were unsuccessful, but he achieved fame with *Winesburg, Ohio*
in 1919. This collection of stories, set in a small town, takes a
naturalist view of rebellion against social conventions; it was
popular among young people but was later criticized for its sentimentality by Hemingway, among others. Anderson went on to
publish several volumes of memoirs and many works of poetry
and fiction, of which the best known is *Dark Laughter* (1925),
a best-selling novel which, developing the primitivist strand of
white American modernism, portrays African Americans in ste-
reotyped terms as spiritual and unrepressed. His later work
never matched the success of *Winesburg, Ohio*.

HANDS

Upon the half-decayed veranda of a small frame house that stood
near the edge of a ravine near the town of Winesburg, Ohio, a
fat little old man walked nervously up and down. Across a long
field that had been seeded for clover but that had produced only
a dense crop of yellow mustard weeds, he could see the public
highway along which went a wagon filled with berry pickers
returning from the fields. The berry pickers, youths and maidens, laughed and shouted boisterously. A boy clad in a blue shirt

leaped from the wagon and attempted to drag after him one of the maidens who screamed and protested shrilly. The feet of the boy in the road kicked up a cloud of dust that floated across the face of the departing sun. Over the long field came a thin girlish voice. "Oh, you Wing Biddlebaum, comb your hair, it's falling into your eyes," commanded the voice to the man, who was bald and whose nervous little hands fiddled about the bare white forehead as though arranging a mass of tangled locks.

Wing Biddlebaum, forever frightened and beset by a ghostly band of doubts, did not think of himself as in any way a part of the life of the town where he had lived for twenty years. Among all the people of Winesburg but one had come close to him. With George Willard, son of Tom Willard, the proprietor of the new Willard House, he had formed something like a friendship. George Willard was the reporter on the *Winesburg Eagle* and sometimes in the evenings he walked out along the highway to Wing Biddlebaum's house. Now as the old man walked up and down on the veranda, his hands moving nervously about, he was hoping that George Willard would come and spend the evening with him. After the wagon containing the berry pickers had passed, he went across the field through the tall mustard weeds and climbing a rail fence peered anxiously along the road to the town. For a moment he stood thus, rubbing his hands together and looking up and down the road, and then, fear overcoming him, ran back to walk again upon the porch on his own house.

In the presence of George Willard, Wing Biddlebaum, who for twenty years had been the town mystery, lost something of his timidity, and his shadowy personality, submerged in a sea of doubts, came forth to look at the world. With the young reporter at his side, he ventured in the light of day into Main Street or strode up and down on the rickety front porch of his own house, talking excitedly. The voice that had been low and trembling became shrill and loud. The bent figure straightened. With a kind of wriggle, like a fish returned to the brook by the fisherman, Biddlebaum the silent began to talk, striving to put into words the ideas that had been accumulated by his mind during long years of silence.

Wing Biddlebaum talked much with his hands. The slender

expressive fingers, forever active, forever striving to conceal themselves in his pockets or behind his back, came forth and became the piston rods of his machinery of expression.

The story of Wing Biddlebaum is a story of hands. Their restless activity, like unto the beating of the wings of an imprisoned bird, had given him his name. Some obscure poet of the town had thought of it. The hands alarmed their owner. He wanted to keep them hidden away and looked with amazement at the quiet inexpressive hands of other men who worked beside him in the fields, or passed, driving sleepy teams on country roads.

When he talked to George Willard, Wing Biddlebaum closed his fists and beat with them upon a table or on the walls of his house. The action made him more comfortable. If the desire to talk came to him when the two were walking in the fields, he sought out a stump or the top board of a fence and with his hands pounding busily talked with renewed ease.

The story of Wing Biddlebaum's hands is worth a book in itself. Sympathetically set forth it would tap many strange, beautiful qualities in obscure men. It is a job for a poet. In Winesburg the hands had attracted attention merely because of their activity. With them Wing Biddlebaum had picked as high as a hundred and forty quarts of strawberries in a day. They became his distinguishing feature, the source of his fame. Also they made more grotesque an already grotesque and elusive individuality. Winesburg was proud of the hands of Wing Biddlebaum in the same spirit in which it was proud of Banker White's new stone house and Wesley Moyer's bay stallion, Tony Tip, that had won the two-fifteen trot at the fall races in Cleveland.

As for George Willard, he had many times wanted to ask about the hands. At times an almost overwhelming curiosity had taken hold of him. He felt that there must be a reason for their strange activity and their inclination to keep hidden away and only a growing respect for Wing Biddlebaum kept him from blurting out the questions that were often in his mind.

Once he had been on the point of asking. The two were walking in the fields on a summer afternoon and had stopped to sit upon a grassy bank. All afternoon Wing Biddlebaum had talked as one inspired. By a fence he had stopped and beating like a giant woodpecker upon the top board had shouted at George Willard, condemning his tendency to be too much influenced by the people about him. "You are destroying yourself," he cried. "You have the inclination to be alone and to dream and you are afraid of dreams. You want to be like others in town here. You hear them talk and you try to imitate them."

On the grassy bank Wing Biddlebaum had tried again to drive his point home. His voice became soft and reminiscent, and with a sigh of contentment he launched into a long rambling talk, speaking as one lost in a dream.

Out of the dream Wing Biddlebaum made a picture for George Willard. In the picture men lived again in a kind of pastoral golden age. Across a green open country came clean-limbed young men, some afoot, some mounted upon horses. In crowds the young men came to gather about the feet of an old man who sat beneath a tree in a tiny garden and who talked to them.

Wing Biddlebaum became wholly inspired. For once he forgot the hands. Slowly they stole forth and lay upon George Willard's shoulders. Something new and bold came into the voice that talked. "You must try to forget all you have learned," said the old man. "You must begin to dream. From this time on you must shut your ears to the roaring of the voices."

Pausing in his speech, Wing Biddlebaum looked long and earnestly at George Willard. His eyes glowed. Again he raised the hands to caress the boy and then a look of horror swept over his face.

With a convulsive movement of his body, Wing Biddlebaum sprang to his feet and thrust his hands deep into his trousers pockets. Tears came to his eyes. "I must be getting along home. I can talk no more with you," he said nervously.

Without looking back, the old man had hurried down the hillside and across a meadow, leaving George Willard perplexed and frightened upon the grassy slope. With a shiver of dread the boy arose and went along the road toward town. "I'll not ask him about his hands," he thought, touched by the memory of the terror he had seen in the man's eyes. "There's something wrong, but I don't want to know what it is. His hands have something to do with his fear of me and of everyone."

And George Willard was right. Let us look briefly into the

story of the hands. Perhaps our talking of them will arouse the
poet who will tell the hidden wonder story of the influence for
which the hands were but fluttering pennants of promise.

In his youth Wing Biddlebaum had been a school teacher in
a town in Pennsylvania. He was not then known as Wing Biddlebaum, but went by the less euphonic name of Adolph Myers.
As Adolph Myers he was much loved by the boys of his school.

Adolph Myers was meant by nature to be a teacher of youth.
He was one of those rare, little-understood men who rule by a
power so gentle that it passes as a lovable weakness. In their
feeling for the boys under their charge such men are not unlike
the finer sort of women in their love of men.

And yet that is but crudely stated. It needs the poet there.
With the boys of his school, Adolph Myers had walked in the
evening or had sat talking until dusk upon the schoolhouse steps
lost in a kind of dream. Here and there went his hands, caressing
the shoulders of the boys, playing about the tousled heads. As
he talked his voice became soft and musical. There was a caress
in that also. In a way the voice and the hands, the stroking of
the shoulders and the touching of the hair was a part of the
schoolmaster's effort to carry a dream into the young minds. By
the caress that was in his fingers he expressed himself. He was
one of those men in whom the force that creates life is diffused,
not centralized. Under the caress of his hands doubt and disbelief went out of the minds of the boys and they began also to
dream.

And then the tragedy. A half-witted boy of the school became
enamored of the young master. In his bed at night he imagined
unspeakable things and in the morning went forth to tell his
dreams as facts. Strange hideous accusations fell from his loose-
hung lips. Through the Pennsylvania town went a shiver. Hidden, shadowy doubts that had been in men's minds concerning
Adolph Myers were galvanized into beliefs.

The tragedy did not linger. Trembling lads were jerked out
of bed and questioned. "He put his arms about me," said one.
"His fingers were always playing in my hair," said another.

One afternoon a man of the town, Henry Bradford, who kept
a saloon, came to the schoolhouse door. Calling Adolph Myers
into the school yard he began to beat him with his fists. As his

hard knuckles beat down into the frightened face of the school-master, his wrath became more and more terrible. Screaming with dismay, the children ran here and there like disturbed in-sects. "I'll teach you to put your hands on my boy, you beast," roared the saloon keeper, who, tired of beating the master, had begun to kick him about the yard.

Adolph Myers was driven from the Pennsylvania town in the night. With lanterns in their hands a dozen men came to the door of the house where he lived alone and commanded that he dress and come forth. It was raining and one of the men had a rope in his hands. They had intended to hang the schoolmaster, but something in his figure, so small, white, and pitiful, touched their hearts and they let him escape. As he ran away into the darkness they repented of their weakness and ran after him, swearing and throwing sticks and great balls of soft mud at the figure that screamed and ran faster and faster into the darkness.

For twenty years Adolph Myers had lived alone in Wines-burg. He was but forty but looked sixty-five. The name of Bid-dlebaum he got from a box of goods seen at a freight station as he hurried through an eastern Ohio town. He had an aunt in Winesburg, a black-toothed old woman who raised chickens, and with her he lived until she died. He had been ill for a year after the experience in Pennsylvania, and after his recovery worked as a day laborer in the fields, going timidly about and striving to conceal his hands. Although he did not understand what had happened he felt that the hands must be to blame. Again and again the fathers of the boys had talked of the hands. "Keep your hands to yourself," the saloon keeper had roared, dancing with fury in the schoolhouse yard.

Upon the veranda of his house by the ravine, Wing Biddle-baum continued to walk up and down until the sun had disap-peared and the road beyond the field was lost in the gray shadows. Going into his house he cut slices of bread and spread honey upon them. When the rumble of the evening train that took away the express cars loaded with the day's harvest of ber-ries had passed and restored the silence of the summer night, he went again to walk upon the veranda. In the darkness he could not see the hands and they became quiet. Although he still hun-gered for the presence of the boy, who was the medium through which he expressed his love of man, the hunger became again a part of his loneliness and his waiting. Lighting a lamp, Wing Biddlebaum washed the few dishes soiled by his simple meal and, setting up a folding cot by the screen door that led to the porch, prepared to undress for the night. A few stray white bread crumbs lay on the cleanly washed floor by the table; putting the lamp on a low stool he began to pick up the crumbs, carrying them to his mouth one by one with unbelievable rapidity. In the dense blotch of light beneath the table, the kneeling figure looked like a priest engaged in some service of his church. The nervous expressive fingers, flashing in and out of the light, might well have been mistaken for the fingers of the devotee going swiftly through decade after decade of his rosary.

NORTHEAST

MARY E. WILKINS FREEMAN

1852–1930

BORN IN RANDOLPH, Massachusetts, Mary E. Wilkins Freeman attended high school in Brattleboro, Vermont, as well as Mount Holyoke Seminary and Glenwood Seminary. In 1883 she returned to Brattleboro, and lived with friends after the death of her parents. She married Charles Manning Freeman in 1902 and moved to New Jersey; she separated from him in 1921. In the early 1880s Freeman established herself as a children's author and began writing short stories, typically using the setting and dialect of rural white New England. Her stories frequently address the repression and poverty of rural life and the stubbornness of local people. Freeman published a number of stories in *Harper's Bazaar* and *Harper's Weekly*, but it was her first collections of stories, *A Humble Romance* (1887) and *A New England Nun* (1891), that firmly established her reputation as a regionalist. As her popularity increased, she experimented with other forms, including historical romances, like *Pembroke* (1894), and a play, *Giles Corey, Yeoman* (1893) about the Salem witch trials.

A NEW ENGLAND NUN

It was late in the afternoon, and the light was waning. There was a difference in the look of the tree shadows out in the yard. Somewhere in the distance cows were lowing and a little bell was tinkling; now and then a farm-wagon tilted by, and the dust flew; some blue-shirted laborers with shovels over their shoulders plodded past; little swarms of flies were dancing up and down before the peoples' faces in the soft air. There seemed to be a gentle stir arising over everything for the mere sake of subsidence—a very premonition of rest and hush and night.

This soft diurnal commotion was over Louisa Ellis also. She had been peacefully sewing at her sitting-room window all the afternoon. Now she quilted her needle carefully into her work, which she folded precisely, and laid in a basket with her thimble and thread and scissors. Louisa Ellis could not remember that ever in her life she had mislaid one of these little feminine appurtenances, which had become, from long use and constant association, a very part of her personality.

Louisa tied a green apron round her waist, and got out a flat straw hat with a green ribbon. Then she went into the garden with a little blue crockery bowl, to pick some currants for her tea. After the currants were picked she sat on the back doorstep and stemmed them, collecting the stems carefully in her apron, and afterwards throwing them into the hen-coop. She looked sharply at the grass beside the step to see if any had fallen there.

Louisa was slow and still in her movements; it took her a long time to prepare her tea; but when ready it was set forth with as much grace as if she had been a veritable guest to her own self. The little square table stood exactly in the centre of the kitchen, and was covered with a starched linen cloth whose border pattern of flowers glistened. Louisa had a damask napkin on her tea-tray, where were arranged a cut-glass tumbler full of teaspoons, a silver cream-pitcher, a china sugar-bowl, and one pink china cup and saucer. Louisa used china every day—something which none of her neighbors did. They whispered about it among themselves. Their daily tables were laid with common crockery, their sets of best china stayed in the parlor closet, and Louisa Ellis was no richer nor better bred than they. Still she would use the china. She had for her supper a glass dish full of sugared currants, a plate of little cakes, and one of light white biscuits. Also a leaf or two of lettuce, which she cut up daintily. Louisa was very fond of lettuce, which she raised to perfection in her little garden. She ate quite heartily, though in a delicate, pecking way; it seemed almost surprising that any considerable bulk of the food should vanish.

After tea she filled a plate with nicely baked thin corncakes, and carried them out into the back-yard.

"Caesar!" she called. "Caesar! Caesar!"

There was a little rush, and the clank of a chain, and a large yellow-and-white dog appeared at the door of his tiny hut, which was half hidden among the tall grasses and flowers. Louisa patted him and gave him the corn-cakes. Then she returned to the house and washed the tea-things, polishing the china carefully. The twilight had deepened; the chorus of the frogs floated in at the open window wonderfully loud and shrill, and once in a while a long sharp drone from a tree-toad pierced it. Louisa took off her green gingham apron, disclosing a shorter one of pink-and-white print. She lighted her lamp, and sat down again with her sewing.

In about half an hour Joe Dagget came. She heard his heavy step on the walk, and rose and took off her pink-and-white apron. Under that was still another—white linen with a little cambric edging on the bottom; that was Louisa's company apron. She never wore it without her calico sewing apron over it unless she had a guest. She had barely folded the pink-and-white one with methodical haste and laid it in a table-drawer when the door opened and Joe Dagget entered.

He seemed to fill up the whole room. A little yellow canary that had been asleep in his green cage at the south window woke up and fluttered wildly, beating his little yellow wings against the wires. He always did so when Joe Dagget came into the room.

"Good-evening," said Louisa. She extended her hand with a kind of solemn cordiality.

"Good-evening, Louisa," returned the man, in a loud voice.

She placed a chair for him, and they sat facing each other, with the table between them. He sat bolt-upright, toeing out his heavy feet squarely, glancing with a good-humored uneasiness around the room. She sat gently erect, folding her slender hands in her white-linen lap.

"Been a pleasant day," remarked Dagget.

"Real pleasant," Louisa assented, softly. "Have you been haying?" she asked, after a little while.

"Yes, I've been haying all day, down in the ten-acre lot. Pretty hot work."

"It must be."

"Yes, it's pretty hot work in the sun."

"Is your mother well to-day?"

"Yes, mother's pretty well."

"I suppose Lily Dyer's with her now?"

Dagget colored. "Yes, she's with her," he answered, slowly.

He was not very young, but there was a boyish look about his large face. Louisa was not quite as old as he, her face was fairer and smoother, but she gave people the impression of being older.

"I suppose she's a good deal of help to your mother," she said, further.

"I guess she is; I don't know how mother'd get along without her," said Dagget, with a sort of embarrassed warmth.

"She looks like a real capable girl. She's pretty-looking too," remarked Louisa.

"Yes, she is pretty fair looking."

Presently Dagget began fingering the books on the table. There was a square red autograph album, and a Young Lady's Gift-Book which had belonged to Louisa's mother. He took them up one after the other and opened them; then laid them down again, the album on the Gift-Book.

Louisa kept eyeing them with mild uneasiness. Finally she rose and changed the position of the books, putting the album underneath. That was the way they had been arranged in the first place.

Dagget gave an awkward little laugh. "Now what difference did it make which book was on top?" said he.

Louisa looked at him with a deprecating smile. "I always keep them that way," murmured she.

"You do beat everything," said Dagget, trying to laugh again. His large face was flushed.

He remained about an hour longer, then rose to take leave. Going out, he stumbled over a rug, and trying to recover himself, hit Louisa's work-basket on the table, and knocked it on the floor.

He looked at Louisa, then at the rolling spools; he ducked

himself awkwardly toward them, but she stopped him. "Never mind," said she; "I'll pick them up after you're gone."

She spoke with a mild stiffness. Either she was a little disturbed, or his nervousness affected her, and made her seem constrained in her effort to reassure him.

When Joe Dagget was outside he drew in the sweet evening air with a sigh, and felt much as an innocent and perfectly well-intentioned bear might after his exit from a china shop.

Louisa, on her part, felt much as the kind-hearted, long-suffering owner of the china shop might have done after the exit of the bear.

She tied on the pink, then the green apron, picked up all the scattered treasures and replaced them in her work-basket, and straightened the rug. Then she set the lamp on the floor, and began sharply examining the carpet. She even rubbed her fingers over it, and looked at them.

"He's tracked in a good deal of dust," she murmured. "I thought he must have."

Louisa got a dust-pan and brush, and swept Joe Dagget's track carefully.

If he could have known it, it would have increased his perplexity and uneasiness, although it would not have disturbed his loyalty in the least. He came twice a week to see Louisa Ellis, and every time, sitting there in her delicately sweet room, he felt as if surrounded by a hedge of lace. He was afraid to stir lest he should put a clumsy foot or hand through the fairy web, and he had always the consciousness that Louisa was watching fearfully lest he should.

Still the lace and Louisa commanded perforce his perfect respect and patience and loyalty. They were to be married in a month, after a singular courtship which had lasted for a matter of fifteen years. For fourteen out of the fifteen years the two had not once seen each other, and they had seldom exchanged letters. Joe had been all those years in Australia, where he had gone to make his fortune, and where he had stayed until he made it. He would have stayed fifty years if it had taken so long, and come home feeble and tottering, or never come home at all, to marry Louisa.

But the fortune had been made in the fourteen years, and he

had come home now to marry the woman who had been pa-
tiently and unquestioningly waiting for him all that time.

Shortly after they were engaged he had announced to Louisa
his determination to strike out into new fields, and secure a competency before they should be married. She had listened and
assented with the sweet serenity which never failed her, not even
when her lover set forth on that long and uncertain journey. Joe,
buoyed up as he was by his sturdy determination, broke down
a little at the last, but Louisa kissed him with a mild blush, and
said good-by.

"It won't be for long," poor Joe had said, huskily; but it was
for fourteen years.

In that length of time much had happened. Louisa's mother
and brother had died, and she was all alone in the world. But
greatest happening of all—a subtle happening which both were
too simple to understand—Louisa's feet had turned into a path,
smooth maybe under a calm, serene sky, but so straight and
unswerving that it could only meet a check at her grave, and so
narrow that there was no room for any one at her side.

Louisa's first emotion when Joe Dagget came home (he had
not apprised her of his coming) was consternation, although she
would not admit it to herself, and he never dreamed of it. Fifteen
years ago she had been in love with him—at least she considered
herself to be. Just at that time, gently acquiescing with and falling
into the natural drift of girlhood, she had seen marriage ahead
as a reasonable feature and a probable desirability of life. She
had listened with calm docility to her mother's views upon the
subject. Her mother was remarkable for her cool sense and
sweet, even temperament. She talked wisely to her daughter
when Joe Dagget presented himself, and Louisa accepted him
with no hesitation. He was the first lover she had ever had.

She had been faithful to him all these years. She had never
dreamed of the possibility of marrying any one else. Her life,
especially for the last seven years, had been full of a pleasant
peace, she had never felt discontented nor impatient over her
lover's absence; still she had always looked forward to his return
and their marriage as the inevitable conclusion of things. However, she had fallen into a way of placing it so far in the future

that it was almost equal to placing it over the boundaries of another life.

When Joe came she had been expecting him, and expecting to be married for fourteen years, but she was as much surprised and taken aback as if she had never thought of it.

Joe's consternation came later. He eyed Louisa with an instant confirmation of his old admiration. She had changed but little. She still kept her pretty manner and soft grace, and was, he considered, every whit as attractive as ever. As for himself, his stent was done; he had turned his face away from fortune-seeking, and the old winds of romance whistled as loud and sweet as ever through his ears. All the song which he had been wont to hear in them was Louisa; he had for a long time a loyal belief that he heard it still, but finally it seemed to him that although the winds sang always that one song, it had another name. But for Louisa the wind had never more than murmured; now it had gone down, and everything was still. She listened for a little while with half-wistful attention; then she turned quietly away and went to work on her wedding clothes.

Joe had made some extensive and quite magnificent alterations in his house. It was the old homestead; the newly-married couple would live there, for Joe could not desert his mother, who refused to leave her old home. So Louisa must leave hers. Every morning, rising and going about among her neat maidenly possessions, she felt as one looking her last upon the faces of dear friends. It was true that in a measure she could take them with her, but, robbed of their old environments, they would appear in such new guises that they would almost cease to be themselves. Then there were some peculiar features of her happy solitary life which she would probably be obliged to relinquish altogether. Sterner tasks than these graceful but half-needless ones would probably devolve upon her. There would be a large house to care for; there would be company to entertain; there would be Joe's rigorous and feeble old mother to wait upon; and it would be contrary to all thrifty village traditions for her to keep more than one servant. Louisa had a little still, and she used to occupy herself pleasantly in summer weather with distilling the sweet and aromatic essences from roses and peppermint and spearmint. By-and-by her still must be laid away. Her store of essences was already considerable, and there would be no time for her to distil for the mere pleasure of it. Then Joe's mother would think it foolishness; she had already hinted her opinion in the matter. Louisa dearly loved to sew a linen seam, not always for use, but for the simple, mild pleasure which she took in it. She would have been loath to confess how more than once she had ripped a seam for the mere delight of sewing it together again. Sitting at her window during long sweet afternoons, drawing her needle gently through the dainty fabric, she was peace itself. But there was small chance of such foolish comfort in the future. Joe's mother, domineering, shrewd old matron that she was even in her old age, and very likely even Joe himself, with his honest masculine rudeness, would laugh and frown down all these pretty but senseless old maiden ways.

Louisa had almost the enthusiasm of an artist over the mere order and cleanliness of her solitary home. She had throbs of genuine triumph at the sight of the window-panes which she had polished until they shone like jewels. She gloated gently over her orderly bureau-drawers, with their exquisitely folded contents redolent with lavender and sweet clover and very purity. Could she be sure of the endurance of even this? She had visions, so startling that she half repudiated them as indelicate, of coarse masculine belongings strewn about in endless litter; of dust and disorder arising necessarily from a coarse masculine presence in the midst of all this delicate harmony.

Among her forebodings of disturbance, not the least was with regard to Caesar. Caesar was a veritable hermit of a dog. For the greater part of his life he had dwelt in his secluded hut, shut out from the society of his kind and all innocent canine joys. Never had Caesar since his early youth watched at a woodchuck's hole; never had he known the delights of a stray bone at a neighbor's kitchen door. And it was all on account of a sin committed when hardly out of his puppyhood. No one knew the possible depth of remorse of which this mild-visaged, altogether innocent-looking old dog might be capable; but whether or not he had encountered remorse, he had encountered a full measure of righteous retribution. Old Caesar seldom lifted up his voice in a growl or a bark; he was fat and sleepy; there were yellow rings which looked like spectacles around his dim old eyes; but there was a neighbor who bore on his hand the imprint of several of Caesar's sharp white youthful teeth, and for that he had lived at the end of a chain, all alone in a little hut, for fourteen years. The neighbor, who was choleric[1] and smarting with the pain of his wound, had demanded either Caesar's death or complete ostracism. So Louisa's brother, to whom the dog had belonged, had built him his little kennel and tied him up. It was now fourteen years since, in a flood of youthful spirits, he had inflicted that memorable bite, and with the exception of short excursions, always at the end of the chain, under the strict guardianship of his master or Louisa, the old dog had remained a close prisoner. It is doubtful if, with his limited ambition, he took much pride in the fact, but it is certain that he was possessed of considerable cheap fame. He was regarded by all the children in the village and by many adults as a very monster of ferocity. St. George's dragon[2] could hardly have surpassed in evil repute Louisa Ellis's old yellow dog. Mothers charged their children with solemn emphasis not to go too near to him, and the children listened and believed greedily, with a fascinated appetite for terror, and ran by Louisa's house stealthily, with many sidelong and backward glances at the terrible dog. If perchance he sounded a hoarse bark, there was a panic. Wayfarers chancing into Louisa's yard eyed him with respect, and inquired if the chain were stout. Caesar at large might have seemed a very ordinary dog, and excited no comment whatever; chained, his reputation overshadowed him, so that he lost his own proper outlines and looked darkly vague and enormous. Joe Dagget, however, with his good-humored sense and shrewdness, saw him as he was. He strode valiantly up to him and patted him on the head, in spite of Louisa's soft clamor of warning, and even attempted to set him loose. Louisa grew so alarmed that he desisted, but kept announcing his opinion in the matter quite forcibly at intervals. "There ain't a better-natured dog in town," he would say, "and it's downright cruel to keep him tied up there. Some day I'm going to take him out."

Louisa had very little hope that he would not, one of these days, when their interests and possessions should be more completely fused in one. She pictured to herself Caesar on the ram-

page through the quiet and unguarded village. She saw innocent
children bleeding in his path. She was herself very fond of the
old dog, because he had belonged to her dead brother, and he
was always very gentle with her; still she had great faith in his
ferocity. She always warned people not to go too near him. She
fed him on ascetic fare of corn-mush and cakes, and never fired
his dangerous temper with heating and sanguinary diet of flesh
and bones. Louisa looked at the old dog munching his simple
fare, and thought of her approaching marriage and trembled. Still
no anticipation of disorder and confusion in lieu of sweet peace
and harmony, no forebodings of Caesar on the rampage, no wild
fluttering of her little yellow canary, were sufficient to turn her
a hair's-breadth. Joe Dagget had been fond of her and working
for her all these years. It was not for her, whatever came to pass,
to prove untrue and break his heart. She put the exquisite little
stitches into her wedding-garments, and the time went on until
it was only a week before her wedding day. It was a Tuesday
evening, and the wedding was to be a week from Wednesday.

There was a full moon that night. About nine o'clock Louisa
strolled down the road a little way. There were harvest-fields on
either hand, bordered by low stone walls. Luxuriant clumps of
bushes grew beside the wall, and trees—wild cherry and old
apple-trees—at intervals. Presently Louisa sat down on the wall
and looked about her with mildly sorrowful reflectiveness. Tall
shrubs of blueberry and meadow-sweet, all woven together and
tangled with blackberry vines and horsebriers, shut her in on
either side. She had a little clear space between them. Opposite
her, on the other side of the road, was a spreading tree; the moon
shone between its boughs, and the leaves twinkled like silver.
The road was bespread with a beautiful shifting dapple of silver
and shadow; the air was full of a mysterious sweetness. "I wonder if it's wild grapes?" murmured Louisa. She sat there some
time. She was just thinking of rising, when she heard footsteps
and low voices, and remained quiet. It was a lonely place, and
she felt a little timid. She thought she would keep still in the
shadow and let the persons, whoever they might be, pass her.

But just before they reached her the voices ceased, and the
footsteps. She understood that their owners had also found seats
upon the stone wall. She was wondering if she could not steal

away unobserved, when the voice broke the stillness. It was Joe Dagget's. She sat still and listened.

The voice was announced by a loud sigh, which was as familiar as itself. "Well," said Dagget, "you've made up your mind, then, I suppose?"

"Yes," returned another voice; "I'm going day after to-morrow."

"That's Lily Dyer," thought Louisa to herself. The voice embodied itself in her mind. She saw a girl tall and full-figured, with a firm, fair face, looking fairer and firmer in the moonlight, her strong yellow hair braided in a close knot. A girl full of a calm rustic strength and bloom, with a masterful way which might have beseemed a princess. Lily Dyer was a favorite with the village folk; she had just the qualities to arouse the admiration. She was good and handsome and smart. Louisa had often heard her praises sounded.

"Well," said Joe Dagget, "I ain't got a word to say."

"I don't know what you could say," returned Lily Dyer.

"Not a word to say," repeated Joe, drawing out the words heavily. Then there was a silence. "I ain't sorry," he began at last, "that that happened yesterday—that we kind of let on how we felt to each other. I guess it's just as well we knew. Of course I can't do anything any different. I'm going right on an' get married next week. I ain't going back on a woman that's waited for me fourteen years, an' break her heart."

"If you should jilt her to-morrow, I wouldn't have you," spoke up the girl, with sudden vehemence.

"Well, I ain't going to give you the chance," said he; "but I don't believe you would, either."

"You'd see I wouldn't. Honor's honor, an' right's right. An' I'd never think anything of any man that went against 'em for me or any other girl; you'd find that out, Joe Dagget."

"Well, you'll find out fast enough that I ain't going against 'em for you or any other girl," returned he. Their voices sounded almost as if they were angry with each other. Louisa was listening eagerly.

"I'm sorry you feel as if you must go away," said Joe, "but I don't know but it's best."

"Of course it's best. I hope you and I have got common-sense."

"Well, I suppose you're right." Suddenly Joe's voice got an undertone of tenderness. "Say, Lily," said he, "I'll get along well enough myself, but I can't bear to think—You don't suppose you're going to fret much over it?"

"I guess you'll find out I sha'n't fret much over a married man."

"Well, I hope you won't—I hope you won't, Lily. God knows I do. And—I hope—one of these days—you'll—come across somebody else—"

"I don't see any reason why I shouldn't." Suddenly her tone changed. She spoke in a sweet, clear voice, so loud that she could have been heard across the street. "No, Joe Dagget," said she, "I'll never marry any other man as long as I live. I've got good sense, an' I ain't going to break my heart nor make a fool of myself; but I'm never going to be married, you can be sure of that. I ain't that sort of a girl to feel this way twice."

Louisa heard an exclamation and a soft commotion behind the bushes; then Lily spoke again—the voice sounded as if she had risen. "This must be put a stop to," said she. "We've stayed here long enough. I'm going home."

Louisa sat there in a daze, listening to their retreating steps. After a while she got up and slunk softly home herself. The next day she did her housework methodically; that was as much a matter of course as breathing; but she did not sew on her wedding-clothes. She sat at her window and meditated. In the evening Joe came. Louisa Ellis had never known that she had any diplomacy in her, but when she came to look for it that night she found it, although meek of its kind, among her little feminine weapons. Even now she could hardly believe that she had heard aright, and that she would not do Joe a terrible injury should she break her troth-plight. She wanted to sound him without betraying too soon her own inclinations in the matter. She did it successfully, and they finally came to an understanding; but it was a difficult thing, for he was as afraid of betraying himself as she.

She never mentioned Lily Dyer. She simply said that while she had no cause of complaint against him, she had lived so long in one way that she shrank from making a change.

"Well, I never shrank, Louisa," said Dagget. "I'm going to

be honest enough to say that I think maybe it's better this way; but if you'd wanted to keep on, I'd have stuck to you till my dying day. I hope you know that."

"Yes, I do," said she.

That night she and Joe parted more tenderly than they had done for a long time. Standing in the door, holding each other's hands, a last great wave of regretful memory swept over them.

"Well, this ain't the way we've thought it was all going to end, is it, Louisa?" said Joe.

She shook her head. There was a little quiver on her placid face.

"You let me know if there's ever anything I can do for you," said he. "I ain't ever going to forget you, Louisa." Then he kissed her, and went down the path.

Louisa, all alone by herself that night, wept a little, she hardly knew why; but the next morning, on waking, she felt like a queen who, after fearing lest her domain be wrested away from her, sees it firmly insured in her possession.

Now the tall weeds and grasses might cluster around Caesar's little hermit hut, the snow might fall on its roof year in and year out, but he never would go on a rampage through the unguarded village. Now the little canary might turn itself into a peaceful yellow ball night after night, and have no need to wake and flutter with wild terror against its bars. Louisa could sew linen seams, and distil roses, and dust and polish and fold away in lavender, as long as she listed.[3] That afternoon she sat with her needle-work at the window, and felt fairly steeped in peace. Lily Dyer, tall and erect and blooming, went past; but she felt no qualm. If Louisa Ellis had sold her birthright she did not know it, the taste of the pottage was so delicious, and had been her sole satisfaction for so long.[4] Serenity and placid narrowness had become to her as the birthright itself. She gazed ahead through a long reach of future days strung together like pearls in a rosary, every one like the others, and all smooth and flawless and innocent, and her heart went up in thankfulness. Outside was the fervid summer afternoon; the air was filled with the sounds of the busy harvest of men and birds and bees; there were halloos, metallic clatterings, sweet calls, and long hummings. Louisa sat, prayerfully numbering her days, like an uncloistered nun.

SARAH ORNE JEWETT

1849–1909

PREEMINENT among New England local color writers, Sarah Orne Jewett enjoyed a long and prolific career and became a mentor to other white women writers, including Willa Cather. Jewett was born in South Berwick, Maine; her father was a doctor and professor of medicine at Bowdoin College. She attended Berwick Academy in Maine intermittently because of poor health. When Jewett was nineteen, the *Atlantic Monthly* accepted one of her stories for publication, and in 1873 it published "The Shore House," the first of the *Deephaven* stories which established Jewett's literary reputation. She did not marry but lived with her partner and friend, Annie Adams Fields; the two traveled frequently to Boston, where they participated in a literary circle that included William Dean Howells, John Greenleaf Whittier, and James Russell Lowell. In addition to collections of stories, including *A White Heron* (1886), Jewett published novels, including *A Country Doctor* (1884) and *A Marsh Island* (1885), as well as poems and children's books. Her best-known work, *The Country of the Pointed Firs* (1896), offers a series of interwoven stories, largely about women and set in a declining Maine seaport town. Jewett's stories, frequently describing familiar Maine communities, were known in the late nineteenth century for their descriptive detail; indeed, Lowell called her literary style "narrow in compass, like a gem-cutter's."

I

The coast of Maine was in former years brought so near to foreign shores by its busy fleet of ships that among the older men
and women one still finds a surprising proportion of travelers.
Each seaward-stretching headland with its high-set houses, each
island of a single farm, has sent its spies to view many a Land
of Eshcol;[1] one may see plain, contented old faces at the windows, whose eyes have looked at far-away ports and known the
splendors of the Eastern world. They shame the easy voyager of
the North Atlantic and the Mediterranean; they have rounded
the Cape of Good Hope and braved the angry seas of Cape
Horn in small wooden ships; they have brought up their hardy
boys and girls on narrow decks; they were among the last of the
Northmen's children to go adventuring to unknown shores.
More than this one cannot give to a young State for its enlight-
enment; the sea captains and the captains' wives of Maine knew
something of the wide world, and never mistook their native
parishes for the whole instead of a part thereof; they knew not
only Thomaston and Castine and Portland,[2] but London and
Bristol and Bordeaux,[3] and the strange-mannered harbors of the
China Sea.[4]

One September day, when I was nearly at the end of a summer spent in a village called Dunnet Landing, on the Maine
coast, my friend Mrs. Todd, in whose house I lived, came home
from a long, solitary stroll in the wild pastures, with an eager
look as if she were just starting on a hopeful quest instead of
returning. She brought a little basket with blackberries enough
for supper, and held it towards me so that I could see that there
were also some late and surprising raspberries sprinkled on top,
but she made no comment upon her wayfaring. I could tell
plainly that she had something very important to say.

"You have n't brought home a leaf of anything," I ventured
to this practiced herb-gatherer. "You were saying yesterday that
the witch hazel might be in bloom."

"I dare say, dear," she answered in a lofty manner; "I ain't goin' to say it was n't; I ain't much concerned either way 'bout the facts o' witch hazel. Truth is, I've been off visitin'; there's an old Indian footpath leadin' over towards the Back Shore through the great heron swamp that anybody can't travel over all summer. You have to seize your time some day just now, while the low ground's summer-dried as it is to-day, and before the fall rains set in. I never thought of it till I was out o' sight o' home, and I says to myself, 'To-day 's the day, certain!' and stepped along smart as I could. Yes, I've been visitin'. I did get into one spot that was wet underfoot before I noticed; you wait till I get me a pair o' dry woolen stockings, in case of cold, and I'll come an' tell ye."

Mrs. Todd disappeared. I could see that something had deeply interested her. She might have fallen in with either the sea-serpent or the lost tribes of Israel,[5] such was her air of mystery and satisfaction. She had been away since just before mid-morning, and as I sat waiting by my window I saw the last red glow of autumn sunshine flare along the gray rocks of the shore and leave them cold again, and touch the far sails of some coast-wise[6] schooners so that they stood like golden houses on the sea.

I was left to wonder longer than I liked. Mrs. Todd was making an evening fire and putting things in train for supper; presently she returned, still looking warm and cheerful after her long walk.

"There 's a beautiful view from a hill over where I've been," she told me; "yes, there's a beautiful prospect of land and sea. You would n't discern the hill from any distance, but 't is the pretty situation of it that counts. I sat there a long spell, and I did wish for you. No, I did n't know a word about goin' when I set out this morning" (as if I had openly reproached her!); "I only felt one o' them travelin' fits comin' on, an' I ketched up my little basket; I did n't know but I might turn and come back time for dinner. I thought it wise to set out your luncheon for you in case I did n't. Hope you had all you wanted; yes, I hope you had enough."

"Oh, yes, indeed," said I. My landlady was always peculiarly bountiful in her supplies when she left me to fare for myself, as if she made a sort of peace-offering or affectionate apology.

"You know that hill with the old house right on top, over beyond the heron swamp? You'll excuse me for explainin'," Mrs. Todd began, "but you ain't so apt to strike inland as you be to go right along shore. You know that hill; there's a path leadin' right over to it that you have to look sharp to find nowadays; it belonged to the up-country Indians when they had to make a carry to the landing here to get to the out' islands. I've heard the old folks say that there used to be a place across a ledge where they'd worn a deep track with their moccasin feet, but I never could find it. 'T is so overgrown in some places that you keep losin' the path in the bushes and findin' it as you can; but it runs pretty straight considerin' the lay o' the land, and I keep my eye on the sun and the moss that grows one side o' the tree trunks. Some brook's been choked up and the swamp's bigger than it used to be. Yes; I did get in deep enough, one place!"

I showed the solicitude that I felt. Mrs. Todd was no longer young, and in spite of her strong, great frame and spirited behavior, I knew that certain ills were apt to seize upon her, and would end some day by leaving her lame and ailing.

"Don't you go to worryin' about me," she insisted, "settin' still 's the only way the Evil One 'll ever get the upper hand o' me. Keep me movin' enough, an' I 'm twenty year old summer an' winter both. I don't know why 't is, but I 've never happened to mention the one I 've been to see. I don't know why I never happened to speak the name of Abby Martin, for I often give her a thought, but 't is a dreadful out-o'-the-way place where she lives, and I have n't seen her myself for three or four years. She 's a real good interesting woman, and we 're well acquainted; she 's nigher mother's age than mine, but she 's very young feeling. She made me a nice cup o' tea, and I don't know but I should have stopped all night if I could have got word to you not to worry."

Then there was a serious silence before Mrs. Todd spoke again to make a formal announcement.

"She is the Queen's Twin," and Mrs. Todd looked steadily to see how I might bear the great surprise.

"The Queen's Twin?" I repeated.

"Yes, she 's come to feel a real interest in the Queen, and anybody can see how natural 't is. They were born the very same

day, and you would be astonished to see what a number o' other
things have corresponded. She was speaking o' some o' the facts
to me to-day, an' you 'd think she 'd never done nothing but
read history. I see how earnest she was about it as I never did
before. I 've often and often heard her allude to the facts, but
now she 's got to be old and the hurry 's over with her work,
she 's come to live a good deal in her thoughts, as folks often
do, and I tell you 't is a sight o' company for her. If you want
to hear about Queen Victoria,[7] why Mis' Abby Martin 'll tell
you everything. And the prospect from that hill I spoke of is as
beautiful as anything in this world; 't is worth while your goin'
over to see her just for that."

"When can you go again?" I demanded eagerly.

"I should say to-morrow," answered Mrs. Todd; "yes, I
should say to-morrow; but I expect 't would be better to take
one day to rest, in between. I considered that question as I was
comin' home, but I hurried so that there wa'n't much time to
think. It's a dreadful long way to go with a horse; you have to
go 'most as far as the old Bowden place an' turn off to the left,
a master long, rough road, and then you have to turn right round
as soon as you get there if you mean to get home before nine
o'clock at night. But to strike across country from here, there 's
plenty o' time in the shortest day, and you can have a good hour
or two's visit beside; 't ain't but a very few miles, and it 's pretty
all the way along. There used to be a few good families over
there, but they 've died and scattered, so now she 's far from
neighbors. There, she really cried, she was so glad to see anybody comin'. You 'll be amused to hear her talk about the
Queen, but I thought twice or three times as I set there 't was
about all the company she 'd got."

"Could we go day after to-morrow?" I asked eagerly.

" 'T would suit me exactly," said Mrs. Todd.

II

One can never be so certain of good New England weather as
in the days when a long easterly storm has blown away the warm
late-summer mists, and cooled the air so that however bright the

sunshine is by day, the nights come nearer and nearer to frost-iness. There was a cold freshness in the morning air when Mrs. Todd and I locked the house-door behind us; we took the key of the fields into our own hands that day, and put out across country as one puts out to sea. When we reached the top of the ridge behind the town it seemed as if we had anxiously passed the harbor bar and were comfortably in open sea at last.

"There, now!" proclaimed Mrs. Todd, taking a long breath, "now I do feel safe. It 's just the weather that 's liable to bring somebody to spend the day; I 've had a feeling of Mis' Elder Caplin from North Point bein' close upon me ever since I waked up this mornin', an' I did n't want to be hampered with our present plans. She 's a great hand to visit; she 'll be spendin' the day somewhere from now till Thanksgivin', but there 's plenty o' places at the Landin' where she goes, an' if I ain't there she 'll just select another. I thought mother might be in, too, 'tis so pleasant; but I run up the road to look off this mornin' before you was awake, and there was no sign o' the boat. If they had n't started by that time they would n't start, just as the tide is now; besides, I see a lot o' mackerel-men headin' Green Island[8] way, and they 'll detain William. No, we're safe now, an' if mother should be comin' in tomorrow we 'll have all this to tell her. She an' Mis' Abby Martin 's very old friends."

We were walking down the long pasture slopes towards the dark woods and thickets of the low ground. They stretched away northward like an unbroken wilderness; the early mists still dulled much of the color and made the uplands beyond look like a very far-off country.

"It ain't so far as it looks from here," said my companion reassuringly, "but we 've got no time to spare either," and she hurried on, leading the way with a fine sort of spirit in her step; and presently we struck into the old Indian footpath, which could be plainly seen across the long-unploughed turf of the pastures, and followed it among the thick, low-growing spruces. There the ground was smooth and brown under foot, and the thin-stemmed trees held a dark and shadowy roof overhead. We walked a long way without speaking; sometimes we had to push aside the branches, and sometimes we walked in a broad aisle where the trees were larger. It was a solitary wood, birdless and beastless; there was not even a rabbit to be seen, or a crow high in air to break the silence.

"I don't believe the Queen ever saw such a lonesome trail as this," said Mrs. Todd, as if she followed the thoughts that were in my mind. Our visit to Mrs. Abby Martin seemed in some strange way to concern the high affairs of royalty. I had just been thinking of English landscapes, and of the solemn hills of Scotland with their lonely cottages and stone-walled sheepfolds, and the wandering flocks on high cloudy pastures. I had often been struck by the quick interest and familiar allusion to certain members of the royal house which one found in distant neighborhoods of New England; whether some old instincts of personal loyalty have survived all changes of time and national vicissitudes, or whether it is only that the Queen's own character and disposition have won friends for her so far away, it is impossible to tell. But to hear of a twin sister was the most surprising proof of intimacy of all, and I must confess that there was something remarkably exciting to the imagination in my morning walk. To think of being presented at Court in the usual way was for the moment quite commonplace.

III

Mrs. Todd was swinging her basket to and fro like a schoolgirl as she walked, and at this moment it slipped from her hand and rolled lightly along the ground as if there were nothing in it. I picked it up and gave it to her, whereupon she lifted the cover and looked in with anxiety.

" 'T is only a few little things, but I don't want to lose 'em," she explained humbly. " 'T was lucky you took the other basket if I was goin' to roll it round. Mis' Abby Martin complained o' lacking some pretty pink silk to finish one o' her little frames, an' I thought I 'd carry her some, and I had a bunch o' gold thread that had been in a box o' mine this twenty year. I never was one to do much fancy work, but we 're all liable to be swept away by fashion. And then there 's a small packet o' very choice herbs that I gave a good deal of attention to; they 'll smarten her up and give her the best of appetites, come spring. She was tellin' me that spring weather is very wiltin' an' tryin' to her, and she was beginnin' to dread it already. Mother 's just the same way; if I could prevail on mother to take some o' these remedies in good season 't would make a world o' difference, but she gets all down hill before I have a chance to hear of it, and then William comes in to tell me, sighin' and bewailin', how feeble mother is. 'Why can't you remember 'bout them good herbs that I never let her be without?' I say to him—he does provoke me so; and then off he goes, sulky enough, down to his boat. Next thing I know, she comes in to go to meetin', wantin' to speak to everybody and feelin' like a girl. Mis' Martin's case is very much the same; but she's nobody to watch her. William 's kind o' slow-moulded; but there, any William 's better than none when you get to be Mis' Martin's age."

"Had n't she any children?" I asked.

"Quite a number," replied Mrs. Todd grandly, "but some are gone and the rest are married and settled. She never was a great hand to go about visitin'. I don't know but Mis' Martin might be called a little peculiar. Even her own folks has to make company of her; she never slips in and lives right along with the rest as if 't was at home, even in her own children's houses. I heard one o' her sons' wives say once she 'd much rather have the Queen to spend the day if she could choose between the two, but I never thought Abby was so difficult as that. I used to love to have her come; she may have been sort o' ceremonious, but very pleasant and sprightly if you had sense enough to treat her her own way. I always think she 'd know just how to live with great folks, and feel easier 'long of them an' their ways. Her son's wife 's a great driver with farm-work, boards a great tableful o' men in hayin' time, an' feels right in her element. I don't say but she 's a good woman an' smart, but sort o' rough. Anybody that's gentle-mannered an' precise like Mis' Martin would be a sort o' restraint.

"There 's all sorts o' folks in the country, same 's there is in the city," concluded Mrs. Todd gravely, and I as gravely agreed. The thick woods were behind us now, and the sun was shining clear overhead, the morning mists were gone, and a faint blue haze softened the distance; as we climbed the hill where we were to see the view, it seemed like a summer day. There was an old house on the height, facing southward,—a mere forsaken shell of an old house, with empty windows that looked like blind eyes. The frost-bitten grass grew close about it like brown fur, and there was a single crooked bough of lilac holding its green leaves close by the door.

"We 'll just have a good piece of bread-an'-butter now," said the commander of the expedition, "and then we 'll hang up the basket on some peg inside the house out o' the way o' the sheep, and have a han'some entertainment as we're comin' back. She 'll be all through her little dinner when we get there, Mis' Martin will; but she 'll want to make us some tea, an' we must have our visit an' be startin' back pretty soon after two. I don't want to cross all that low ground again after it 's begun to grow chilly. An' it looks to me as if the clouds might begin to gather late in the afternoon."

Before us lay a splendid world of sea and shore. The autumn colors already brightened the landscape; and here and there at the edge of a dark tract of pointed firs stood a row of bright swamp-maples like scarlet flowers. The blue sea and the great tide inlets were untroubled by the lightest winds.

"Poor land, this is!" sighed Mrs. Todd as we sat down to rest on the worn doorstep. "I 've known three good hard-workin' families that come here full o' hope an' pride and tried to make something o' this farm, but it beat 'em all. There 's one small field that 's excellent for potatoes if you let half of it rest every year; but the land 's always hungry. Now, you see them little peakéd-topped spruces an' fir balsams comin' up over the hill all green an' hearty; they 've got it all their own way! Seems sometimes as if wild Natur' got jealous over a certain spot, and wanted to do just as she 'd a mind to. You' ll see here; she 'll do her own ploughin' an' harrowin' with frost an' wet, an' plant just what she wants and wait for her own crops. Man can't do nothin' with it, try as he may. I tell you those little trees means business!"

I looked down the slope, and felt as if we ourselves were likely to be surrounded and overcome if we lingered too long. There was a vigor of growth, a persistence and savagery about the sturdy little trees that put weak human nature at complete defiance. One felt a sudden pity for the men and women who had been worsted after a long fight in that lonely place; one felt a sudden fear of the unconquerable, immediate forces of Nature, as in the irresistible moment of a thunderstorm.

"I can recollect the time when folks were shy o' these woods we just come through," said Mrs. Todd seriously. "The men-folks themselves never 'd venture into 'em alone; if their cattle got strayed they 'd collect whoever they could get, and start off all together. They said a person was liable to get bewildered in there alone, and in old times folks had been lost. I expect there was considerable fear left over from the old Indian times, and the poor days o' witchcraft; anyway, I 've seen bold men act kind o' timid. Some women o' the Asa Bowden family went out one afternoon berryin' when I was a girl, and got lost and was out all night; they found 'em middle o' the mornin' next day, not half a mile from home, scared most to death, an' sayin' they 'd heard wolves and other beasts sufficient for a caravan. Poor creatur's! they'd strayed at last into a kind of low place amongst some alders, an' one of 'em was so overset she never got over it, an' went off in a sort o' slow decline. 'T was like them victims that drowns in a foot o' water; but their minds did suffer dreadful. Some folks is born afraid of the woods and all wild places, but I must say they 've always been like home to me."

I glanced at the resolute, confident face of my companion. Life was very strong in her, as if some force of Nature were personified in this simple-hearted woman and gave her cousin-ship to the ancient deities. She might have walked the primeval fields of Sicily; her strong gingham skirts might at that very mo-ment bend the slender stalks of asphodel and be fragrant with trodden thyme,[9] instead of the brown wind-brushed grass of New England and frost-bitten goldenrod. She was a great soul, was Mrs. Todd, and I her humble follower, as we went our way to visit the Queen's Twin, leaving the bright view of the sea behind us, and descending to a lower country-side through the dry pastures and fields.

The farms all wore a look of gathering age, though the set-tlement was, after all, so young. The fences were already fragile, and it seemed as if the first impulse of agriculture had soon spent itself without hope of renewal. The better houses were always those that had some hold upon the riches of the sea; a house that could not harbor a fishing-boat in some neighboring inlet was far from being sure of every-day comforts. The land alone was not enough to live upon in that stony region; it belonged by right to the forest, and to the forest it fast returned. From the top of the hill where we had been sitting we had seen prosperity in the dim distance, where the land was good and the sun shone upon fat barns, and where warm-looking houses with three or four chimneys apiece stood high on their solid ridge above the bay.

As we drew nearer to Mrs. Martin's it was sad to see what poor bushy fields, what thin and empty dwelling-places had been left by those who had chosen this disappointing part of the northern country for their home. We crossed the last field and came into a narrow rain-washed road, and Mrs. Todd looked eager and expectant and said that we were almost at our journey's end. "I do hope Mis' Martin 'll ask you into her best room where she keeps all the Queen's pictures. Yes, I think likely she will ask you; but 't ain't everybody she deems worthy to visit 'em, I can tell you!" said Mrs. Todd warningly. "She's been collectin' 'em an' cuttin' 'em out o' newspapers an' magazines time out o' mind, and if she heard of anybody sailin' for an English port she 'd contrive to get a little money to 'em and ask to have the last likeness there was. She 's most covered her best-room wall now; she keeps that room shut up sacred as a meetin'-house! 'I won't say but I have my favorites amongst 'em,' she told me t' other day, 'but they 're all beautiful to me as they can be!' And she 's made some kind o' pretty little frames for 'em all—you know there 's always a new fashion o' frames comin' round; first 't was shell-work, and then 't was pine-cones, and bead-work 's had its day, and now she 's much concerned with perforated cardboard worked with silk. I tell you that best room 's a sight to see! But you must n't look for anything elegant," continued Mrs. Todd, after a moment's reflection. "Mis' Martin 's always been in very poor, strugglin' circumstances. She had ambition for her children, though they took right after their father an' had little for themselves; she wa'n't over an' above well married, however kind she may see fit to speak. She 's been patient an' hard-workin' all her life, and always high above makin' mean complaints of other folks. I expect all this business about the Queen has buoyed her over many a shoal place in life. Yes, you might say that Abby 'd been a slave, but there ain't any slave but has some freedom."

IV

Presently I saw a low gray house standing on a grassy bank close to the road. The door was at the side, facing us, and a tangle of snowberry bushes and cinnamon roses grew to the level of the window-sills. On the doorstep stood a bent-shouldered, little old woman; there was an air of welcome and of unmistakable dignity about her.

"She sees us coming," exclaimed Mrs. Todd in an excited whisper. "There, I told her I might be over this way again if the weather held good, and if I came I'd bring you. She said right off she 'd take great pleasure in havin' a visit from you; I was surprised, she 's usually so retirin'."

Even this reassurance did not quell a faint apprehension on our part; there was something distinctly formal in the occasion, and one felt that consciousness of inadequacy which is never easy for the humblest pride to bear. On the way I had torn my dress in an unexpected encounter with a little thornbush, and I could now imagine how it felt to be going to Court and forgetting one's feathers or her Court train.

The Queen's Twin was oblivious of such trifles; she stood waiting with a calm look until we came near enough to take her kind hand. She was a beautiful old woman, with clear eyes and a lovely quietness and genuineness of manner; there was not a trace of anything pretentious about her, or high-flown, as Mrs. Todd would say comprehensively. Beauty in age is rare enough in women who have spent their lives in the hard work of a farmhouse; but autumnlike and withered as this woman may have looked, her features had kept, or rather gained, a great refinement. She led us into her old kitchen and gave us seats, and took one of the little straight-backed chairs herself and sat a short distance away, as if she were giving audience to an ambassador. It seemed as if we should all be standing; you could not help feeling that the habits of her life were more ceremonious, but that for the moment she assumed the simplicities of the occasion.

Mrs. Todd was always Mrs. Todd, too great and self-possessed a soul for any occasion to ruffle. I admired her calmness, and presently the slow current of neighborhood talk carried one easily along; we spoke of the weather and the small adventures of the way, and then, as if I were after all not a stranger, our hostess turned almost affectionately to speak to me.

"The weather will be growing dark in London now. I expect that you've been in London, dear?" she said.

"Oh, yes," I answered. "Only last year."

"It is a great many years since I was there, along in the forties," said Mrs. Martin. " 'T was the only voyage I ever made; most of my neighbors have been great travelers. My brother was master of a vessel, and his wife usually sailed with him; but that year she had a young child more frail than the others, and she dreaded the care of it at sea. It happened that my brother got a chance for my husband to go as super-cargo,[10] being a good accountant, and came one day to urge him to take it; he was very ill-disposed to the sea, but he had met with losses, and I saw my own opportunity and persuaded them both to let me go too. In those days they did n't object to a woman's being aboard to wash and mend, the voyages were sometimes very long. And that was the way I come to see the Queen."

Mrs. Martin was looking straight in my eyes to see if I showed any genuine interest in the most interesting person in the world.

"Oh, I am very glad you saw the Queen," I hastened to say. "Mrs. Todd has told me that you and she were born the very same day."

"We were indeed, dear!" said Mrs. Martin, and she leaned back comfortably and smiled as she had not smiled before. Mrs. Todd gave a satisfied nod and glance, as if to say that things were going on as well as possible in this anxious moment.

"Yes," said Mrs. Martin again, drawing her chair a little nearer, " 't was a very remarkable thing; we were born the same day, and at exactly the same hour, after you allowed for all the difference in time. My father figured it out sea-fashion. Her Royal Majesty and I opened our eyes upon this world together; say what you may, 't is a bond between us."

Mrs. Todd assented with an air of triumph, and untied her hat-strings and threw them back over her shoulders with a gallant air.

"And I married a man by the name of Albert, just the same as she did, and all by chance, for I did n't get the news that she had an Albert too till a fortnight afterward; news was slower coming then than it is now. My first baby was a girl, and I called her Victoria after my mate; but the next one was a boy, and my husband wanted the right to name him, and took his own name and his brother Edward's, and pretty soon I saw in the paper that the little Prince o' Wales had been christened just the same. After that I made excuse to wait till I knew what she 'd named her children. I did n't want to break the chain, so I had an Alfred, and my darling Alice that I lost long before she lost hers, and there I stopped. If I 'd only had a dear daughter to stay at home with me, same 's her youngest one, I should have been so thankful! But if only one of us could have a little Beatrice, I 'm glad 't was the Queen; we 've both seen trouble, but she 's had the most care."

I asked Mrs. Martin if she lived alone all the year, and was told that she did except for a visit now and then from one of her grandchildren, "the only one that really likes to come an' stay quiet 'long o' grandma. She always says quick as she 's through her schoolin' she 's goin' to live with me all the time, but she 's very pretty an' has taking ways,"[11] said Mrs. Martin, looking both proud and wistful, "so I can tell nothing at all about it! Yes, I 've been alone most o' the time since my Albert was taken away, and that 's a great many years; he had a long time o' failing and sickness first." (Mrs. Todd's foot gave an impatient scuff on the floor.) "An' I 've always lived right here. I ain't like the Queen's Majesty, for this is the only palace I 've got," said the dear old thing, smiling again. "I 'm glad of it too, I don't like changing about, an' our stations in life are set very different. I don't require what the Queen does, but sometimes I 've thought 't was left to me to do the plain things she don't have time for. I expect she's a beautiful housekeeper, nobody could n't have done better in her high place, and she 's been as good a mother as she 's been a queen."

"I guess she has, Abby," agreed Mrs. Todd instantly. "How

was it you happened to get such a good look at her? I meant to ask you again when I was here t' other day."

"Our ship was layin' in the Thames,[12] right there above Wapping.[13] We was dischargin' cargo, and under orders to clear as quick as we could for Bordeaux to take on an excellent freight o' French goods," explained Mrs. Martin eagerly. "I heard that the Queen was goin' to a great review of her army, and would drive out o' her Buckin'ham Palace about ten o'clock in the mornin', and I run aft to Albert, my husband, and brother Horace where they was standin' together by the hatchway, and told 'em they must one of 'em take me. They laughed, I was in such a hurry, and said they could n't go; and I found they meant it and got sort of impatient when I began to talk, and I was 'most broken-hearted; 't was all the reason I had for makin' that hard voyage. Albert could n't help often reproachin' me, for he did so resent the sea, an' I'd known how 't would be before we sailed; but I'd minded nothing all the way till then, and I just crep' back to my cabin an' begun to cry. They was disappointed about their ship's cook, an' I'd cooked for fo'c's'le an' cabin[14] myself all the way over; 't was dreadful hard work, specially in rough weather; we 'd had head winds an' a six weeks' voyage. They 'd acted sort of ashamed o' me when I pled so to go ashore, an' that hurt my feelin's most of all. But Albert come below pretty soon; I 'd never given way so in my life, an' he begun to act frightened, and treated me gentle just as he did when we was goin' to be married, an' when I got over sobbin' he went on deck and saw Horace an' talked it over what they could do; they really had their duty to the vessel, and could n't be spared that day. Horace was real good when he understood everything, and he come an' told me I 'd more than worked my passage an' was goin' to do just as I liked now we was in port. He'd engaged a cook, too, that was comin' aboard that mornin', and he was goin' to send the ship's carpenter with me—a nice fellow from up Thomaston way; he 'd gone to put on his ashore clothes as quick 's he could. So then I got ready, and we started off in the small boat and rowed up river. I was afraid we were too late, but the tide was setting up very strong, and we landed an' left the boat to a keeper, and I run all the way up those great streets and across a park. 'T was a great day, with sights o' folks everywhere, but 't was just as if they was nothin' but wax images[15] to me. I kep' askin' my way an' runnin' on, with the carpenter comin' after as best he could, and just as I worked to the front o' the crowd by the palace, the gates was flung open and out she came; all prancin' horses and shinin' gold, and in a beautiful carriage there she sat; 't was a moment o' heaven to me. I saw her plain, and she looked right at me so pleasant and happy, just as if she knew there was somethin' different between us from other folks."

There was a moment when the Queen's Twin could not go on and neither of her listeners could ask a question.

"Prince Albert was sitting right beside her in the carriage," she continued. "Oh, he was a beautiful man! Yes, dear, I saw 'em both together just as I see you now, and then she was gone out o' sight in another minute, and the common crowd was all spread over the place pushin' an' cheerin'. 'T was some kind o' holiday, an' the carpenter and I got separated, an' then I found him again after I did n't think I should, an' he was all for makin' a day of it, and goin' to show me all the sights; he 'd been in London before, but I did n't want nothin' else, an' we went back through the streets down to the waterside an' took the boat. I remember I mended an old coat o' my Albert's as good as I could, sittin' on the quarter-deck in the sun all that afternoon, and 't was all as if I was livin' in a lovely dream. I don't know how to explain it, but there has n't been no friend I 've felt so near to me ever since."

One could not say much—only listen. Mrs. Todd put in a discerning question now and then, and Mrs. Martin's eyes shone brighter and brighter as she talked. What a lovely gift of imagination and true affection was in this fond old heart! I looked about the plain New England kitchen, with its wood-smoked walls and homely braided rugs on the worn floor, and all its simple furnishings. The loud-ticking clock seemed to encourage us to speak; at the other side of the room was an early newspaper portrait of Her Majesty the Queen of Great Britain and Ireland. On a shelf below were some flowers in a little glass dish, as if they were put before a shrine.

"If I could have had more to read, I should have known 'most everything about her," said Mrs. Martin wistfully. "I 've made the most of what I did have, and thought it over and over till it came clear. I sometimes seem to have her all my own, as if we 'd lived right together. I 've often walked out into the woods alone and told her what my troubles was, and it always seemed as if she told me 't was all right, an' we must have patience. I 've got her beautiful book about the Highlands; 't was dear Mis' Todd here that found out about her printing it and got a copy for me, and it's been a treasure to my heart, just as if 't was written right to me. I always read it Sundays now, for my Sunday treat. Before that I used to have to imagine a good deal, but when I come to read her book, I knew what I expected was all true. We do think alike about so many things," said the Queen's Twin with affectionate certainty. "You see, there is something between us, being born just at the same time; 't is what they call a birthright. She 's had great tasks put upon her, being the Queen, an' mine has been the humble lot; but she 's done the best she could, nobody can say to the contrary, and there 's something between us; she 's been the great lesson I 've had to live by. She's been everything to me. An' when she had her Jubilee,[16] oh, how my heart was with her!"

"There, 't would n't play the part in her life it has in mine," said Mrs. Martin generously, in answer to something one of her listeners had said. "Sometimes I think now she 's older, she might like to know about us. When I think how few old friends anybody has left at our age, I suppose it may be just the same with her as it is with me; perhaps she would like to know how we came into life together. But I 've had a great advantage in seeing her, an' I can always fancy her goin' on, while she don't know nothin' yet about me, except she may feel my love stayin' her heart sometimes an' not know just where it comes from. An' I dream about our being together out in some pretty fields, young as ever we was, and holdin' hands as we walk along. I 'd like to know if she ever has that dream too. I used to have days when I made believe she did know, an' was comin' to see me," confessed the speaker shyly, with a little flush on her cheeks; "and I 'd plan what I could have nice for supper, and I was n't goin' to let anybody know she was here havin' a good rest, except I 'd wish you, Almira Todd, or dear Mis' Blackett would happen in, for you 'd know just how to talk with her. You see, she likes to be up in Scotland, right out in the wild country, better than she does anywhere else."

"I 'd really love to take her out to see mother at Green Island," said Mrs. Todd with a sudden impulse.

"Oh, yes! I should love to have you," exclaimed Mrs. Martin, and then she began to speak in a lower tone. "One day I got thinkin' so about my dear Queen," she said, "an' livin' so in my thoughts, that I went to work an' got all ready for her, just as if she was really comin'. I never told this to a livin' soul before, but I feel you 'll understand. I put my best fine sheets and blankets I spun an' wove myself on the bed, and I picked some pretty flowers and put 'em all round the house, an' I worked as hard an' happy as I could all day, and had as nice a supper ready as I could get, sort of telling myself a story all the time. She was comin' an' I was goin' to see her again, an' I kep' it up until nightfall; an' when I see the dark an' it come to me I was all alone, the dream left me, an' I sat down on the doorstep an' felt all foolish an' tired. An', if you 'll believe it, I heard steps comin', an' an old cousin o' mine come wanderin' along, one I was apt to be shy of. She was n't all there, as folks used to say, but harmless enough and a kind of poor old talking body. And I went right to meet her when I first heard her call, 'stead o' hidin' as I sometimes did, an' she come in dreadful willin', an' we sat down to supper together; 't was a supper I should have had no heart to eat alone."

"I don't believe she ever had such a splendid time in her life as she did then. I heard her tell all about it afterwards," exclaimed Mrs. Todd compassionately. "There, now I hear all this it seems just as if the Queen might have known and could n't come herself, so she sent that poor old creatur' that was always in need!"

Mrs. Martin looked timidly at Mrs. Todd and then at me. " 'T was childish o' me to go an' get supper," she confessed.

"I guess you wa'n't the first one to do that," said Mrs. Todd. "No, I guess you wa'n't the first one who's got supper that way, Abby," and then for a moment she could say no more.

Mrs. Todd and Mrs. Martin had moved their chairs a little so that they faced each other, and I, at one side, could see them both.

"No, you never told me o' that before, Abby," said Mrs. Todd gently. "Don't it show that for folks that have any fancy in 'em, such beautiful dreams is the real part o' life? But to most folks the common things that happens outside 'em is all in all."

Mrs. Martin did not appear to understand at first, strange to say, when the secret of her heart was put into words; then a glow of pleasure and comprehension shone upon her face. "Why, I believe you 're right, Almira!" she said, and turned to me.

"Would n't you like to look at my pictures of the Queen?" she asked, and we rose and went into the best room.

V

The mid-day visit seemed very short; September hours are brief to match the shortening days. The great subject was dismissed for a while after our visit to the Queen's pictures, and my companions spoke much of lesser persons until we drank the cup of tea which Mrs. Todd had foreseen. I happily remembered that the Queen herself is said to like a proper cup of tea, and this at once seemed to make her Majesty kindly join so remote and reverent a company. Mrs. Martin's thin cheeks took on a pretty color like a girl's. "Somehow I always have thought of her when I made it extra good," she said. "I've got a real china cup that belonged to my grandmother, and I believe I shall call it hers now."

"Why don't you?" responded Mrs. Todd warmly, with a delightful smile.

Later they spoke of a promised visit which was to be made in the Indian summer to the Landing and Green Island, but I observed that Mrs. Todd presented the little parcel of dried herbs, with full directions, for a cure-all in the spring, as if there were no real chance of their meeting again first. As we looked back from the turn of the road the Queen's Twin was still standing on the doorstep watching us away, and Mrs. Todd stopped, and stood still for a moment before she waved her hand again.

"There's one thing certain, dear," she said to me with great discernment; "it ain't as if we left her all alone!"

Then we set out upon our long way home over the hill, where we lingered in the afternoon sunshine, and through the dark woods across the heron-swamp.

THE FOREIGNER

I

One evening, at the end of August, in Dunnet Landing, I heard Mrs. Todd's firm footstep crossing the small front entry outside my door, and her conventional cough which served as a herald's trumpet, or a plain New England knock, in the harmony of our fellowship.

"Oh, please come in!" I cried, for it had been so still in the house that I supposed my friend and hostess had gone to see one of her neighbors. The first cold northeasterly storm of the season was blowing hard outside. Now and then there was a dash of great raindrops and a flick of wet lilac leaves against the window, but I could hear that the sea was already stirred to its dark depths, and the great rollers were coming in heavily against the shore. One might well believe that Summer was coming to a sad end that night, in the darkness and rain and sudden access of autumnal cold. It seemed as if there must be danger offshore among the outer islands.

"Oh, there!" exclaimed Mrs. Todd, as she entered. "I know nothing ain't ever happened out to Green Island since the world began, but I always do worry about mother in these great gales. You know those tidal waves occur sometimes down to the West Indies, and I get dwellin' on 'em so I can't set still in my chair, nor knit a common row to a stocking. William might get moon-ing, out in his small bo't, and not observe how the sea was mak-ing, an' meet with some accident. Yes, I thought I'd come in and set with you if you wa'n't busy. No, I never feel any concern about 'em in winter 'cause then they're prepared, and all ashore and everything snug. William ought to keep help, as I tell him; yes, he ought to keep help."

I hastened to reassure my anxious guest by saying that Elijah

Tilley had told me in the afternoon, when I came along the shore past the fish houses, that Johnny Bowden and the Captain were out at Green Island; he had seen them beating[1] up the bay, and thought they must have put into Burnt Island cove, but one of the lobstermen brought word later that he saw them hauling out at Green Island as he came by, and Captain Bowden pointed ashore and shook his head to say that he did not mean to try to get in. "The old Miranda just managed it, but she will have to stay at home a day or two and put new patches in her sail," I ended, not without pride in so much circumstantial evidence.

Mrs. Todd was alert in a moment. "Then they'll all have a very pleasant evening," she assured me, apparently dismissing all fears of tidal waves and other sea-going disasters. "I was urging Alick Bowden to go ashore some day and see mother before cold weather. He's her own nephew; she sets a great deal by him. And Johnny's a great chum o' William's; don't you know the first day we had Johnny out 'long of us, he took an' give William his money to keep for him that he'd been a-savin', and William showed it to me an' was so affected I thought he was goin' to shed tears? 'Twas a dollar an' eighty cents; yes, they'll have a beautiful evenin' all together, and like's not the sea'll be flat as a doorstep come morning."

I had drawn a large wooden rocking-chair before the fire, and Mrs. Todd was sitting there jogging herself a little, knitting fast, and wonderfully placid of countenance. There came a fresh gust of wind and rain, and we could feel the small wooden house rock and hear it creak as if it were a ship at sea.

"Lord, hear the great breakers!" exclaimed Mrs. Todd. "How they pound!—there, there! I always run of an idea that the sea knows anger these nights and gets full o' fight. I can hear the rote[2] o' them old black ledges way down the thoroughfare. Calls up all those stormy verses in the Book o' Psalms; David he knew how the old sea-goin' folks have to quake at the heart."

I thought as I had never thought before of such anxieties. The families of sailors and coastwise adventurers by sea must always be worrying about somebody, this side of the world or the other. There was hardly one of Mrs. Todd's elder acquaintances, men or women, who had not at some time or other made a sea voyage, and there was often no news until the voyagers themselves came back to bring it.

"There's a roaring high overhead, and a roaring in the deep sea," said Mrs. Todd solemnly, "and they battle together nights like this. No, I couldn't sleep; some women folks always goes right to bed an' to sleep, so's to forget, but 'tain't my way. Well, it's a blessin' we don't all feel alike; there's hardly any of our folks at sea to worry about, nowadays, but I can't help my feel-in's, an' I got thinking of mother all alone, if William had happened to be out lobsterin' and couldn't make the cove gettin' back."

"They will have a pleasant evening," I repeated. "Captain Bowden is the best of good company."

"Mother'll make him some pancakes for his supper, like's not," said Mrs. Todd, clicking her knitting needles and giving a pull at her yarn. Just then the old cat pushed open the unlatched door and came straight toward her mistress's lap. She was regarded severely as she stepped about and turned on the broad expanse, and then made herself into a round cushion of fur, but was not openly admonished. There was another great blast of wind overhead, and a puff of smoke came down the chimney.

"This makes me think o' the night Mis' Cap'n Tolland died," said Mrs. Todd, half to herself. "Folks used to say these gales only blew when somebody's a-dyin', or the devil was a-comin' for his own, but the worst man I ever knew died a real pretty mornin' in June."

"You have never told me any ghost stories," said I; and such was the gloomy weather and the influence of the night that I was instantly filled with reluctance to have this suggestion followed. I had not chosen the best of moments; just before I spoke we had begun to feel as cheerful as possible. Mrs. Todd glanced doubtfully at the cat and then at me, with a strange absent look, and I was really afraid that she was going to tell me something that would haunt my thoughts on every dark stormy night as long as I lived.

"Never mind now; tell me to-morrow by daylight, Mrs. Todd," I hastened to say, but she still looked at me full of doubt and deliberation.

"Ghost stories!" she answered. "Yes, I don't know but I've heard a plenty of 'em first an' last. I was just sayin' to myself that this is like the night Mis' Cap'n Tolland died. 'Twas the great line storm[3] in September all of thirty, or maybe forty, year ago. I ain't one that keeps much account o' time."

"Tolland? That's a name I have never heard in Dunnet," I said.

"Then you haven't looked well about the old part o' the buryin' ground, no'theast corner," replied Mrs. Todd. "All their women folks lies there; the sea's got most o' the men. They were a known family o' shipmasters in early times. Mother had a mate, Ellen Tolland, that she mourns to this day; died right in her bloom with quick consumption,[4] but the rest o' that family was all boys but one, and older than she, an' they lived hard seafarin' lives an' all died hard. They were called very smart seamen. I've heard that when the youngest went into one o' the old shippin' houses in Boston, the head o' the firm called out to him: 'Did you say Tolland from Dunnet? That's recommendation enough for any vessel!' There was some o' them old shipmasters as tough as iron, an' they had the name o' usin' their crews very severe, but there wa'n't a man that wouldn't rather sign with 'em an' take his chances, than with the slack ones that didn't know how to meet accidents."

II

There was so long a pause, and Mrs. Todd still looked so absent-minded, that I was afraid she and the cat were growing drowsy together before the fire, and I should have no reminiscences at all. The wind struck the house again, so that we both started in our chairs and Mrs. Todd gave a curious, startled look at me. The cat lifted her head and listened too, in the silence that followed, while after the wind sank we were more conscious than ever of the awful roar of the sea. The house jarred now and then, in a strange, disturbing way.

"Yes, they'll have a beautiful evening out to the island," said Mrs. Todd again; but she did not say it gayly. I had not seen her before in her weaker moments.

"Who was Mrs. Captain Tolland?" I asked eagerly, to change the current of our thoughts.

"I never knew her maiden name; if I ever heard it, I've gone an' forgot; 'twould mean nothing to me," answered Mrs. Todd.

"She was a foreigner, an' he met with her out in the island o' Jamaica. They said she'd been left a widow with property. Land knows what become of it; she was French born, an' her first husband was a Portugee, or somethin'."

I kept silence now, a poor and insufficient question being worse than none.

"Cap'n John Tolland was the least smartest of any of 'em, but he was full smart enough, an' commanded a good brig at the time, in the sugar trade; he'd taken out a cargo o' pine lumber to the islands from somewheres up the river, an' had been loadin' for home in the port o' Kingston, an' had gone ashore that afternoon for his papers, an' remained afterwards 'long of three friends o' his, all shipmasters. They was havin' their suppers together in a tavern; 'twas late in the evenin' an' they was more lively than usual, an' felt boyish; and over opposite was another house full o' company, real bright and pleasant lookin', with a lot o' lights, an' they heard somebody singin' very pretty to a guitar. They wa'n't in no go-to-meetin' condition, an' one of 'em, he slapped the table an' said, 'Le's go over an' hear that lady sing!' an' over they all went, good honest sailors, but three sheets in the wind,[5] and stepped in as if they was invited, an' made their bows inside the door an' asked if they could hear the music; they were all respectable well-dressed men. They saw the woman that had the guitar, an' there was a company a-listin', regular highbinders[6] all of 'em; an' there was a long table all spread out with big candlesticks like little trees o' light, and a sight o' glass an' silver ware; an' part o' the men was young officers in uniform, an' the colored folks was steppin' round servin' 'em, an' they had the lady singin'. 'Twas a wasteful scene, an' a loud talkin' company, an' though they was three sheets in the wind themselves there wa'n't one o' them cap'ns but had sense to perceive it. The others had pushed back their chairs, an' their decanters an' glasses was standin' thick about, an' they was teasin' the one that was singin' as if they'd just got her in to amuse 'em. But they quieted down; one o' the young officers had beautiful manners, an' invited the four cap'ns to join 'em, very polite; 'twas a kind of public house, and after they'd all heard another song, he come to consult with 'em whether they wouldn't git up and dance a hornpipe or somethin' to the lady's music.

"They was all elderly men an' shipmasters, and owned property; two of 'em was church members in good standin'," continued Mrs. Todd loftily, "an' they wouldn't lend theirselves to no such kick-shows[7] as that, an' spite o' bein' three sheets in the wind, as I have once observed; they waved aside the tumblers of wine the young officer was pourin' out for 'em so freehanded,[8] and said they should rather be excused. An' when they all rose, still very dignified, as I've been well informed, and made their partin' bows and was goin' out, them young sports got round 'em an' tried to prevent 'em, and they had to push an' strive considerable, but out they come. There was this Cap'n Tolland, and two Cap'n Bowdens, and the fourth was my own father." (Mrs. Todd spoke slowly, as if to impress the value of her authority.) "Two of them was very religious, upright men, but they would have their night off sometimes, all o' them old-fashioned cap'ns, when they was free of business and ready to leave port.

"An' they went back to their tavern an' got their bills paid, an' set down kind o' mad with everybody by the front windows, mistrusting some o' their tavern charges, like's not, by that time, an' when they got tempered down, they watched the house over across, where the party was.

"There was a kind of a grove o' trees between the house an' the road, an' they heard the guitar a-goin' an' a-stoppin' short by turns, and pretty soon somebody began to screech, an' they saw a white dress come runnin' out through the bushes, an' tumbled over each other in their haste to offer help; an' out she come, with the guitar, cryin' into the street, and they just walked off four square[9] with her amongst 'em, down toward the wharves where they felt more to home. They couldn't make out at first what 'twas she spoke,—Cap'n Lorenzo Bowden was well acquainted in Havre an' Bordeaux, an' spoke a poor quality o' French, an' she knew a little mite o' English, but not much; and they come somehow or other to discern that she was in real distress. Her husband and her children had died o' yellow fever;

they'd all come up to Kingston[10] from one o' the far Wind'ard
Islands[11] to get passage on a steamer to France, an' a Negro had
stole their money off her husband while he lay sick o' the fever,
an' she had been befriended some, but the folks that knew about
her had died too; it had been a dreadful run o' the fever that
season, an' she fell at last to playin' an' singin' for hire, and for
what money they'd throw to her round them harbor houses.

" 'Twas a real hard case, an' when them cap'ns made out
about it, there wa'n't one that meant to take leave without
helpin' of her. They was pretty mellow, an' whatever they might
lack o' prudence they more'n made up with charity: they didn't
want to see nobody abused, an' she was sort of a pretty woman,
an' they stopped in the street then an' there an' drew lots who
should take her aboard, bein' all bound home. An' the lot fell
to Cap'n Jonathan Bowden who did act discouraged; his vessel
had but small accommodations, though he could stow a big
freight, an' she was a dreadful slow sailer through bein' square
as a box, an' his first wife, that was livin' then, was a dreadful
jealous woman. He threw himself right onto the mercy o' Cap'n
Tolland."

Mrs. Todd indulged herself for a short time in a season of
calm reflection.

"I always thought they'd have done better, and more reasonable, to give her some money to pay her passage home to France,
or wherever she may have wanted to go," she continued.

I nodded and looked for the rest of the story.

"Father told mother," said Mrs. Todd confidentially, "that
Cap'n Jonathan Bowden an' Cap'n John Tolland had both taken
a little more than usual; I wouldn't have you think, either, that
they both wasn't the best o' men, an' they was solemn as owls,
and argued the matter between 'em, an' waved aside the other
two when they tried to put their oars in. An' spite o' Cap'n
Tolland's bein' a settled old bachelor they fixed it that he was
to take the prize on his brig; she was a fast sailer, and there was
a good spare cabin or two where he'd sometimes carried passengers, but he'd filled 'em with bags o' sugar on his own account
an' was loaded very heavy beside. He said he'd shift the sugar
an' get along somehow, an' the last the other three cap'ns saw
of the party was Cap'n John handing the lady into his bo't,

guitar and all, an' off they all set tow'ds their ships with their
men rowin' 'em in the bright moonlight down to Port Royal[12]
where the anchorage was, an' where they all lay, goin' out with
the tide an' mornin' wind at break o' day. An' the others thought
they heard music of the guitar, two o' the bo'ts kept well together, but it may have come from another source."

"Well; and then?" I asked eagerly after a pause. Mrs. Todd
was almost laughing aloud over her knitting and nodding emphatically. We had forgotten all about the noise of the wind and
sea.

"Lord bless you! he come sailing into Portland[13] with his
sugar, all in good time, an' they stepped right afore a justice o'
the peace, and Cap'n John Tolland came paradin' home to Dunnet Landin' a married man. He owned one o' them thin, narrow-
lookin' houses with one room each side o' the front door, and
two slim black spruces spindlin' up against the front windows
to make it gloomy inside. There was no horse nor cattle of
course, though he owned pasture land, an' you could see rifts o'
light right through the barn as you drove by. And there was a
good excellent kitchen, but his sister reigned over that; she had
a right to two rooms, and took the kitchen an' a bedroom that
led out of it; an' bein' given no rights in the kitchen had angered
the cap'n so they weren't on no kind o' speakin' terms. He preferred his old brig for comfort, but now and then, between voyages, he'd come home for a few days, just to show he was master
over his part o' the house, and show Eliza she couldn't commit
no trespass.

"They stayed a little while; 'twas pretty spring weather, an' I
used to see Cap'n John rollin' by with his arms full o' bundles
from the store, lookin' as pleased and important as a boy; an'
then they went right off to sea again, an' was gone a good many
months. Next time he left her to live there alone, after they'd
stopped at home together some weeks, an' they said she suffered
from bein' at sea, but some said that the owners wouldn't have
a woman aboard. 'Twas before father was lost on that last voyage
of his, an' he and mother went up once or twice to see them.
Father said there wa'n't a mite o' harm in her, but somehow or
other a sight o' prejudice arose; it may have been caused by the
remarks of Eliza an' her feelin's tow'ds her brother. Even my

mother had no regard for Eliza Tolland. But mother asked the
cap'n's wife to come with her one evenin' to a social circle that
was down to the meetin'-house vestry, so she'd get acquainted
a little, an' she appeared very pretty until they started to have
some singin' to the melodeon.[14] Mari' Harris an' one o' the
younger Caplin girls undertook to sing a duet, an' they sort o'
flatted, an' she put her hands right up to her ears, and give a
little squeal, an' went quick as could be an' give 'em the right
notes, for she could read the music like plain print an' made 'em
try it over again. She was real willin' an' pleasant, but that didn't
suit, an' she made faces when they got it wrong. An' then there
fell a dead calm, an' we was all settin' round prim as dishes, an'
my mother, that never expects ill feelin', asked her if she
wouldn't sing somethin', an' up she got,—poor creatur', it all
seems so different to me now,—an' sung a lovely little song
standin' in the floor; it seemed to have something gay about it
that kept a-repeatin', an' nobody could help keepin' time, an' all
of a sudden she looked round at the tables and caught up a tin
plate that somebody'd fetched a Washin'ton pie in, an' she begun
to drum on it with her fingers like one o' them tambourines, an'
went right on singin' faster an' faster, and next minute she begun
to dance a little pretty dance between the verses, just as light
and pleasant as a child. You couldn't help seein' how pretty
'twas; we all got to trottin' a foot, an' some o' the men clapped
their hands quite loud, a-keepin' time, 'twas so catchin', an'
seemed so natural to her. There wa'n't one of 'em but enjoyed
it; she just tried to do her part, and some urged her on, till she
stopped with a little twirl of her skirts an' went to her place
again by mother. And I can see mother now, reachin' over an'
smilin' an' pattin' her hand.

"But next day there was an awful scandal goin' in the parish,
an' Mari' Harris reproached my mother to her face, an' I never
wanted to see her since, but I've had to a good many times. I
said Mis' Tolland didn't intend no impropriety,—I reminded her
of David's dancin' before the Lord;[15] but she said such a man as
David would never have thought o' dancin' right there in the
Orthodox vestry, and she felt I spoke with irreverence.

"And next Sunday Mis' Tolland came walkin' into our meeting, but I must say she acted like a cat in a strange garret, and

went right out down the aisle with her head in air, from the pew Deacon Caplin had showed her into. 'Twas just in the beginning of the long prayer. I wish she'd stayed through, whatever her reasons were. Whether she'd expected somethin' different, or misunderstood some o' the pastor's remarks, or what 'twas, I don't really feel able to explain, but she kind o' declared war, at least folks thought so, an' war 'twas from that time. I see she was cryin', or had been, as she passed by me; perhaps bein' in meetin' was what had power to make her feel homesick and strange.

"Cap'n John Tolland was away fittin' out; that next week he come home to see her and say farewell. He was lost with his ship in the Straits of Malacca,[16] and she lived there alone in the old house a few months longer till she died. He left her well off; 'twas said he hid his money about the house and she knew where 'twas. Oh, I expect you've heard—that story told over an' over twenty times, since you've been here at the Landin'?"

"Never one word," I insisted.

"It was a good while ago," explained Mrs. Todd with reassurance. "Yes, it all happened a great while ago."

III

At this moment, with a sudden flaw of the wind, some wet twigs outside blew against the window panes and made a noise like a distressed creature trying to get in. I started with sudden fear, and so did the cat, but Mrs. Todd knitted away and did not even look over her shoulder.

"She was a good-looking woman; yes, I always thought Mis' Tolland was good-looking, though she had, as was reasonable, a sort of foreign cast, and she spoke very broken English, no better than a child. She was always at work about her house, or settin' at a front window with her sewing; she was a beautiful hand to embroider. Sometimes, summer evenings, when the windows was open she'd set an' drum on her guitar, but I don't know as I ever heard her sing but once after the cap'n went away. She appeared very happy about havin' him, and took on dreadful at partin' when he was down here on the wharf, going back to Portland by boat to take ship for that last v'y'ge. He

acted kind of ashamed, Cap'n John did; folks about here ain't
so much accustomed to show their feelings. The whistle had
blown an' they was waitin' for him to get aboard, an' he was
put to it to know what to do and treated her very affectionate
in spite of all impatience; but mother happened to be there and
she went an' spoke, and I remember what a comfort she seemed
to be. Mis' Tolland clung to her then, and she wouldn't give a
glance after the boat when it had started, though the captain was
very eager a-wavin' to her. She wanted mother to come home
with her and wouldn't let go her hand, and mother had just come
in to stop all night with me an' had plenty o' time ashore, which
didn't always happen, so they walked off together, an' 'twas
some considerable time before she got back.

"'I want you to neighbor with that poor lonesome creatur','
says mother to me, lookin' reproachful. 'She's a stranger in a
strange land,'[17] says mother. 'I want you to make her have a
sense that somebody feels kind to her.'

"'Why, since that time she flaunted out o' meetin', folks have
felt she liked other ways better'n our'n,' says I. I was provoked
because I'd had a nice supper ready, an' mother'd let it wait so
long 'twas spoiled. 'I hope you'll like your supper!' I told her.
I was dreadful ashamed afterward of speakin' so to mother.

"'What consequence is my supper?' says she to me; mother
can be very stern,—'or your comfort or mine, beside letting a
foreign person an' a stranger feel so desolate; she's done the best
a woman could do in her lonesome place, and she asks nothing
of anybody except a little common kindness. Think if 'twas you
in a foreign land!'

"And mother set down to drink her tea, an' I set down humbled enough over by the wall to wait till she finished. An' I did
think it all over, an' next day I never said nothin', but I put on
my bonnet, and went to see Mis' Cap'n Tolland, if 'twas only
for mother's sake. 'Twas about three quarters of a mile up the
road here, beyond the schoolhouse. I forgot to tell you that the
cap'n had bought out his sister's right at three or four times what
'twas worth, to save trouble, so they'd got clear o' her, an' I
went round into the side yard sort o' friendly an' sociable, rather
than stop an' deal with the knocker an' the front door. It looked
so pleasant an' pretty I was glad I come; she had set a little table

for supper, though 'twas still early, with a white cloth on it, right out under an old apple tree close by the house. I noticed 'twas same as with me at home, there was only one plate. She was just coming out with a dish; you couldn't see the door nor the table from the road.

"In the few weeks she'd been there she'd got some bloomin' pinks an' other flowers next the doorstep. Somehow it looked as if she'd known how to make it homelike for the cap'n. She asked me to set down; she was very polite, but she looked very mournful, and I spoke of mother, an' she put down her dish and caught holt o' me with both hands an' said my mother was an angel. When I see the tears in her eyes 'twas all right between us, and we were always friendly after that, and mother had us come out and make a little visit that summer; but she come a foreigner and she went a foreigner, and never was anything but a stranger among our folks. She taught me a sight o' things about herbs I never knew before nor since; she was well acquainted with the virtues o' plants. She'd act awful secret about some things too, an' used to work charms for herself sometimes, an' some o' the neighbors told to an' fro after she died that they knew enough not to provoke her, but 'twas all nonsense; 'tis the believin' in such things that causes 'em to be any harm, an' so I told 'em," confided Mrs. Todd contemptuously. "That first night I stopped to tea with her she'd cooked some eggs with some herb or other sprinkled all through, and 'twas she that first led me to discern mushrooms; an' she went right down on her knees in my garden here when she saw I had my different of-ficious herbs. Yes, 'twas she that learned me the proper use o' parsley too; she was a beautiful cook."

Mrs. Todd stopped talking, and rose, putting the cat gently in the chair, while she went away to get another stick of apple-tree wood. It was not an evening when one wished to let the fire go down, and we had a splendid bank of bright coals. I had always wondered where Mrs. Todd had got such an unusual knowledge of cookery, of the varieties of mushrooms, and the use of sorrel as a vegetable, and other blessings of that sort. I had long ago learned that she could vary her omelettes like a child of France, which was indeed a surprise in Dunnet Landing.

IV

All these revelations were of the deepest interest, and I was ready
with a question as soon as Mrs. Todd came in and had well
settled the fire and herself and the cat again.

"I wonder why she never went back to France, after she was
left alone?"

"She come here from the French islands," explained Mrs.
Todd. "I asked her once about her folks, an' she said they were
all dead; 'twas the fever took 'em. She made this her home, lonesome as 'twas; she told me she hadn't been in France since she
was 'so small,' and measured me off a child o' six. She'd lived
right out in the country before, so that part wa'n't unusual to
her. Oh yes, there was something very strange about her, and
she hadn't been brought up in high circles nor nothing o' that
kind. I think she'd been really pleased to have the cap'n marry
her an' give her a good home, after all she'd passed through, and
leave her free with his money an' all that. An' she got over bein'
so strange-looking to me after a while, but 'twas a very singular
expression: she wore a fixed smile that wa'n't a smile; there
wa'n't no light behind it, same's a lamp can't shine if it ain't lit.
I don't know just how to express it, 'twas a sort of made
countenance."

One could not help thinking of Sir Philip Sidney's phrase, "A
made countenance,[18] between simpering and smiling."

"She took it hard, havin' the captain go off on that last voyage," Mrs. Todd went on. "She said somethin' told her when
they was partin' that he would never come back. He was lucky
to speak a home-bound ship this side o' the Cape o' Good Hope,
an' got a chance to send her a letter, an' that cheered her up.
You often felt as if you was dealin' with a child's mind, for all
she had so much information that other folks hadn't. I was a
sight younger than I be now, and she made me imagine new
things, and I got interested watchin' her an' findin' out what she
had to say, but you couldn't get to no affectionateness with her.
I used to blame me sometimes; we used to be real good comrades
goin' off for an afternoon, but I never give her a kiss till the day

she laid in her coffin and it come to my heart there wa'n't no one else to do it."

"And Captain Tolland died," I suggested after a while.

"Yes, the cap'n was lost," said Mrs. Todd, "and of course word didn't come for a good while after it happened. The letter come from the owners to my uncle, Cap'n Lorenzo Bowden, who was in charge of Cap'n Tolland's affairs at home, and he come right up for me an' said I must go with him to the house. I had known what it was to be a widow, myself, for near a year, an' there was plenty o' widow women along this coast that the sea had made desolate, but I never saw a heart break as I did then.

" 'Twas this way: we walked together along the road, me an' uncle Lorenzo. You know how it leads straight from just above the schoolhouse to the brook bridge, and their house was just this side o' the brook bridge on the left hand; the cellar's there now, and a couple or three good-sized gray birches growin' in it. And when we come near enough I saw that the best room, this way, where she most never set, was all lighted up, and the curtains up so that the light shone bright down the road, and as we walked, those lights would dazzle and dazzle in my eyes, and I could hear the guitar a-goin', an' she was singin'. She heard our steps with her quick ears and come running to the door with her eyes a-shinin', an' all that set look gone out of her face, an' begun to talk French, gay as a bird, an' shook hands and behaved very pretty an' girlish, sayin' 'twas her fête day. I didn't know what she meant then. And she had gone an' put a wreath o' flowers on her hair an' wore a handsome gold chain that the cap'n had given her; an' there she was poor creatur', makin' believe have a party all alone in her best room; 'twas prim enough to discourage a person, with too many chairs set close to the walls, just as the cap'n's mother had left it, but she had put sort o' long garlands on the walls, droopin' very graceful, and a sight of green boughs in the corners, till it looked lovely, and all lit up with a lot o' candles."

"Oh dear!" I sighed. "Oh, Mrs. Todd, what did you do?"

"She beheld our countenances," answered Mrs. Todd solemnly. "I expect they was telling everything plain enough, but Cap'n Lorenzo spoke the sad words to her as if he had been her father; and she wavered a minute and then over she went on the floor before we could catch hold of her, and then we tried to bring her to herself and failed, and at last we carried her upstairs, an' I told uncle to run down and put out the lights, and then go fast as he could for Mrs. Begg, being very experienced in sickness, an' he so did. I got off her clothes and her poor wreath, and I cried as I done it. We both stayed there that night, and the doctor said 'twas a shock when he come in the morning; he'd been over to Black Island an' had to stay all night with a very sick child."

"You said that she lived alone some time after the news came," I reminded Mrs. Todd then.

"Oh yes, dear," answered my friend sadly, "but it wa'n't what you'd call livin'; no, it was only dyin', though at a snail's pace. She never went out again those few months, but for a while she could manage to get about the house a little, and do what was needed, an' I never let two days go by without seein' her or hearin' from her. She never took much notice as I came an' went except to answer if I asked her anything. Mother was the one who gave her the only comfort."

"What was that?" I asked softly.

"She said that anybody in such trouble ought to see their minister, mother did, and one day she spoke to Mis' Tolland, and found that the poor soul had been believin' all the time that there weren't any priests here. We'd come to know she was a Catholic by her beads and all, and that had set some narrow minds against her. And mother explained it just as she would to a child; and uncle Lorenzo sent word right off somewheres up river by a packet that was bound up the bay, and the first o' the week a priest come by the boat, an' uncle Lorenzo was on the wharf 'tendin' to some business; so they just come up for me, and I walked with him to show him the house. He was a kind-hearted old man; he looked so benevolent an' fatherly I could ha' stopped an' told him my own troubles; yes, I was satisfied when I first saw his face, an' when poor Mis' Tolland beheld him enter the room, she went right down on her knees and clasped her hands together to him as if he'd come to save her life, and he lifted her up and blessed her, an' I left 'em together, and slipped out into the open field and walked there in sight so if they needed to call me, and I had my own thoughts. At last I saw him at the door; he had to catch the return boat. I meant to walk back with him and offer him some supper, but he said no, and said he was comin' again if needed, and signed me to go into the house to her, and shook his head in a way that meant he understood everything. I can see him now; he walked with a cane, rather tired and feeble; I wished somebody would come along, so's to carry him down to the shore.

"Mis' Tolland looked up at me with a new look when I went in, an' she even took hold o' my hand and kept it. He had put some oil on her forehead, but nothing anybody could do would keep her alive very long; 'twas his medicine for the soul rather'n the body. I helped her to bed, and next morning she couldn't get up to dress her, and that was Monday, and she began to fail, and 'twas Friday night she died." (Mrs. Todd spoke with unusual haste and lack of detail.) "Mrs. Begg and I watched with her, and made everything nice and proper, and after all the ill will there was a good number gathered to the funeral. 'Twas in Reverend Mr. Bascom's day, and he done very well in his prayer, considering he couldn't fill in with mentioning all the near connections by name as was his habit. He spoke very feeling about her being a stranger and twice widowed, and all he said about her being reared among the heathen was to observe that there might be roads leadin' up to the New Jerusalem[19] from various points. I says to myself that I guessed quite a number must ha' reached there that wa'n't able to set out from Dunnet Landin'!"

Mrs. Todd gave an odd little laugh as she bent toward the firelight to pick up a dropped stitch in her knitting, and then I heard a heartfelt sigh.

" 'Twas most forty years ago," she said; "most everybody's gone a'ready that was there that day."

V

Suddenly Mrs. Todd gave an energetic shrug of her shoulders, and a quick look at me, and I saw that the sails of her narrative were filled with a fresh breeze.

"Uncle Lorenzo, Cap'n Bowden that I have referred to"—

"Certainly!" I agreed with eager expectation.

"He was the one that had been left in charge of Cap'n John Tolland's affairs, and had now come to be of unforeseen importance.

"Mrs. Begg an' I had stayed in the house both before an' after Mis' Tolland's decease, and she was now in haste to be gone, having affairs to call her home; but uncle come to me as the exercises was beginning, and said he thought I'd better remain at the house while they went to the buryin' ground. I couldn't understand his reasons, an' I felt disappointed, bein' as near to her as most anybody; 'twas rough weather, so mother couldn't get in, and didn't even hear Mis' Tolland was gone till next day. I just nodded to satisfy him, 'twa'n't no time to discuss anything. Uncle seemed flustered; he'd gone out deep-sea fishin' the day she died, and the storm I told you of rose very sudden, so they got blown off way down the coast beyond Monhegan,[20] and he'd just got back in time to dress himself and come.

"I set there in the house after I'd watched her away down the straight road far's I could see from the door; 'twas a little short walkin' funeral an' a cloudy sky, so everything looked dull an' gray, an' it crawled along all in one piece, same's walking funerals do, an' I wondered how it ever come to the Lord's mind to let her begin down among them gay islands all heat and sun, and end up here among the rocks with a north wind blowin'. 'Twas a gale that begun the afternoon before she died, and had kept blowin' off an' on ever since. I'd thought more than once how glad I should be to get home an' out o' sound o' them black spruces a-beatin' an' scratchin' at the front windows.

"I set to work pretty soon to put the chairs back, an' set outdoors some that was borrowed, an' I went out in the kitchen, an' I made up a good fire in case somebody come an' wanted a cup o' tea; but I didn't expect anyone to travel way back to the house unless 'twas uncle Lorenzo. 'Twas growin' so chilly that I fetched some kindlin' wood and made fires in both the fore rooms. Then I set down an' begun to feel as usual, and I got my knittin' out of a drawer. You can't be sorry for a poor creature that's come to the end o' all her troubles; my only discomfort was I thought I'd ought to feel worse at losin' her than I did; I was younger then than I be now. And as I set there, I begun to hear some long notes o' dronin' music from upstairs that chilled me to the bone."

Mrs. Todd gave a hasty glance at me.

"Quick's I could gather me, I went right upstairs to see what 'twas," she added eagerly, "an' 'twas just what I might ha' known. She'd always kept her guitar hangin' right against the wall in her room; 'twas tied by a blue ribbon, and there was a window left wide open; the wind was veerin' a good deal, an' it slanted in and searched the room. The strings was jarrin' yet.

" 'Twas growin' pretty late in the afternoon, an' I begun to feel lonesome as I shouldn't now, and I was disappointed at having to stay there, the more I thought it over, but after a while I saw Cap'n Lorenzo polin' back up the road all alone, and when he come nearer I could see he had a bundle under his arm and had shifted his best black clothes for his everyday ones. I run out and put some tea into the teapot and set it back on the stove to draw, an' when he come in I reached down a little jug o' spirits—Cap'n Tolland had left his house well provisioned as if his wife was goin' to put to sea same's himself, an' there she'd gone an' left it. There was some cake that Mis' Begg an' I had made the day before. I thought that uncle an' me had a good right to the funeral supper, even if there wa'n't anyone to join us. I was lookin' forward to my cup o' tea; 'twas beautiful tea out of a green lacquered chest that I've got now."

"You must have felt very tired," said I, eagerly listening.

"I was 'most beat out, with watchin' an' tendin' and all," answered Mrs. Todd, with as much sympathy in her voice as if she were speaking of another person. "But I called out to uncle as he came in, 'Well, I expect it's all over now, an' we've all done what we could. I thought we'd better have some tea or somethin' before we go home. Come right out in the kitchen, sir,' say I, never thinking but we only had to let the fires out and lock up everything safe an' eat our refreshment, an' go home.

" 'I want both of us to stop here tonight,' says uncle, looking at me very important.

" 'Oh, what for?' says I, kind o' fretful.

" 'I've got proper reasons,' says uncle. 'I'll see you well sat-isfied, Almira. Your tongue ain't so easy-goin' as some 'o the women folks, an' there's property here to take charge of that you don't know nothin' at all about.'

" 'What do you mean?' says I.

" 'Cap'n Tolland acquainted me with his affairs; he hadn't no sort o' confidence in nobody but me an' his wife, after he was tricked into signin' that Portland note, an' lost money. An' she didn't know nothin' about business; but what he didn't take to sea to be sunk with him he's hid somewhere in this house. I expect Mis' Tolland may have told you where she kept things?' said uncle.

"I see he was dependin' a good deal on my answer," said Mrs. Todd, "but I had to disappoint him; no, she had never said nothin' to me.

" 'Well, then, we've got to make a search,' says he, with considerable relish; but he was all tired and worked up, and we set down to the table, an' he had somethin', an' I took my desired cup o' tea, and then I begun to feel more interested.

" 'Where you goin' to look first?' says I, but he give me a short look an' made no answer, and begun to mix me a very small portion out of the jug, in another glass. I took it to please him; he said I looked tired, speakin' real fatherly, and I did feel better for it, and we set talkin' a few minutes, an' then he started for the cellar, carrying an old ship' lantern he fetched out o' the stairway an' lit.

" 'What are you lookin' for, some kind of a chist?' I inquired, and he said yes. All of a sudden it come to me to ask who was the heirs; Eliza Tolland, Cap'n John's own sister, had never demeaned herself to come near the funeral, and uncle Lorenzo faced right about and begun to laugh, sort o' pleased. I thought queer of it; 'twa'n't what he'd taken, which would be nothin' to an old weathered sailor like him.

" 'Who's the heir?' sayd I the second time.

" 'Why, it's *you*, Almiry,' says he; and I was so took aback I set right down on the turn o' the cellar stairs.

" 'Yes 'tis,' said uncle Lorenzo. 'I'm glad of it too. Some thought she didn't have no sense but foreign sense, an' a poor stock o' that, but she said you was friendly to her, an' one day after she got news of Tolland's death, an' I had fetched up his will that left everything to her, she said she was goin' to make a writin', so's you could have things after she was gone, an' she give five hundred to me for bein' executor. Square Pease fixed up the paper, an' she signed it; it's all accordin' to law.' There, I begun to cry," said Mrs. Todd; "I couldn't help it. I wished I had her back again to do somethin' for, an' to make her know I felt sisterly to her more'n I'd ever showed, an' it come over me 'twas all too late, an' I cried the more, till uncle showed impatience, an' I got up an' stumbled along down cellar with my apern to my eyes the greater part of the time.

" 'I'm goin' to have a clean search,' says he; 'you hold the light.' An' I held it, and he rummaged in the arches an' under the stairs, an' over in some old closet where he reached out bottles an' stone jugs an' canted some kags an' one or two casks, an' chuckled well when he heard there was somethin' inside,—but there wa'n't nothin' to find but things usual in a cellar, an' then the old lantern was givin' out an' we come away.

" 'He spoke to me of a chist, Cap'n Tolland did,' says uncle in a whisper. 'He said a good sound chist was as safe a bank as there was, an' I beat him out of such nonsense, 'count o' fire an' other risks.' 'There's no chist in the rooms above,' says I; 'no, uncle, there ain't no sea-chist, for I've been here long enough to see what there was to be seen.' Yet he couldn't feel contented till he'd mounted up into the toploft; 'twas one o' them single, hip-roofed houses that don't give proper accommodation for a real garret, like Cap'n Littlepage's down here at the Landin'. There was broken furniture and rubbish, an' he let down a terrible sign o' dust into the front entry, but sure enough there wasn't no chist. I had it all to sweep up next day.

" 'He must have took it away to sea,' says I to the cap'n, an' even then he didn't want to agree, but we was both beat out. I told him where I'd always seen Mis' Tolland get her money from, and we found much as a hundred dollars there in an old red morocco wallet. Cap'n John had been gone a good while a'ready, and she had spent what she needed. 'Twas in an old desk o' his in the settin' room that we found the wallet."

"At the last minute he may have taken his money to sea," I suggested.

"Oh, yes," agreed Mrs. Todd. "He did take considerable to make his venture to bring home, as was customary, an' that was

drowned with him as uncle agreed; but he had other property
in shipping, and a thousand dollars invested in Portland in a
cordage shop, but 'twas about the time shipping begun to decay,
and the cordage shop failed, and in the end I wa'n't so rich as I
thought I was goin' to be for those few minutes on the cellar
stairs. There was an auction that accumulated something. Old
Mis' Tolland, the cap'n's mother, had heired some good furniture from a sister: there was above thirty chairs in all, and they're
apt to sell well. I got over a thousand dollars when we come to
settle up, and I made uncle take his five hundred; he was getting
along in years and had met with losses in navigation, and he left
it back to me when he died, so I had a real good lift. It all lays
in the bank over to Rockland,[21] and I draw my interest fall an'
spring, with the little Mr. Todd was able to leave me; but that's
kind o' sacred money; 'twas earnt and saved with the hope o'
youth, an' I'm very particular what I spend it for. Oh yes, what
with ownin' my house, I've been enabled to get along very well,
with prudence!" said Mrs. Todd contentedly.

"But there was the house and land," I asked,—"What became
of that part of the property?"

Mrs. Todd looked into the fire, and a shadow of disapproval
flitted over her face.

"Poor old uncle!" she said, "he got childish about the matter.
I was hoping to sell at first, and I had an offer, but he always
run of an idea that there was more money hid away, and kept
wanting me to delay; an' he used to go up there all alone and
search, and dig in the cellar, empty an' bleak as 'twas in winter
weather or any time. An' he'd come and tell me he'd dreamed
he found gold behind a stone in the cellar wall, or somethin'.
And one night we all see the light o' fire up that way, an' the
whole Landin' took the road, and run to look, and the Tolland
property was all in a light blaze. I expect the old gentleman had
dropped the fire about; he said he'd been up there to see if everything was safe in the afternoon. As for the land, 'twas so poor
that every body used to have a joke that the Tolland boys preferred to farm the sea instead. It's 'most all grown up to bushes
now, where it ain't poor water grass in the low places. There's
some upland that has a pretty view, after you cross the brook
bridge. Years an' years after she died, there was some o' her

flowers used to come up an' bloom in the door garden. I brought
two or three that was unusual down here; they always come up
and remind me of her, constant as the spring. But I never did
want to fetch home that guitar, some way or 'nother; I wouldn't
let it go at the auction, either. It was hangin' right there in the
house when the fire took place. I've got some o' her other little
things scattered about the house: that picture on the mantelpiece
belonged to her."

I had often wondered where such a picture had come from,
and why Mrs. Todd had chosen it; it was a French print of the
statue of the Empress Josephine[22] in the Savane at old Fort
Royal, in Martinique.[23]

VI

Mrs. Todd drew her chair closer to mine; she held the cat and
her knitting with one hand as she moved, but the cat was so
warm and so sound asleep that she only stretched a lazy paw in
spite of what must have felt like a slight earthquake. Mrs. Todd
began to speak almost in a whisper.

"I ain't told you all," she continued; "no, I haven't spoken
of all to but very few. The way it came was this," she said solemnly, and then stopped to listen to the wind, and sat for a
moment in deferential silence, as if she waited for the wind, to
speak first. The cat suddenly lifted her head with quick excitement and gleaming eyes, and her mistress was leaning forward
toward the fire with an arm laid on either knee, as if they were
consulting the glowing coals for some augury. Mrs. Todd looked
like an old prophetess as she sat there with the firelight shining
on her strong face; she was posed for some great painter. The
woman with the cat was as unconscious and as mysterious as
any sibyl of the Sistine Chapel.[24]

"There, that's the last struggle o' the gale," said Mrs. Todd,
nodding her head with impressive certainty and still looking into
the bright embers of the fire. "You'll see!" She gave me another
quick glance, and spoke in a low tone as if we might be
overheard.

" 'Twas such a gale as this the night Mis' Tolland died. She
appeared more comfortable the first o' the evenin'; and Mrs.

Begg was more spent than I, bein' older, and a beautiful nurse that was the first to see and think of everything, but perfectly quiet an' never asked a useless question. You remember her funeral when you first come to the Landing? And she consented to goin' an' havin' a good sleep while she could, and left me one o' those good little pewter lamps that burnt whale oil an' made plenty o' light in the room, but not too bright to be disturbin'.

"Poor Mis' Tolland had been distressed the night before, an' all that day, but as night come on she grew more and more easy, an' was layin' there asleep; 'twas like settin' by any sleepin' person, and I had none but usual thoughts. When the wind lulled and the rain, I could hear the seas, though more distant than this, and I don' know's I observed any other sound than what the weather made; 'twas a very solemn feelin' night. I set close by the bed; there was times she looked to find somebody when she was awake. The light was on her face, so I could see her plain; there was always times when she wore a look that made her seem a stranger you'd never set eyes on before. I did think what a world it was that her an' me should have come together so, and she have nobody but Dunnet Landin' folks about her in her extremity. 'You're one o' the stray ones, poor creatur',' I said. I remember those very words passin' through my mind, but I saw reason to be glad she had some comforts, and didn't lack friends at the last, though she'd seen misery an' pain. I was glad she was quiet; all day she'd been restless, and we couldn't understand what she wanted from her French speech. We had the window open to give her air, an' now an' then a gust would strike that guitar that was on the wall and set it swinging by the blue ribbon, and soundin' as if somebody begun to play it. I come near takin' it down, but you never know what'll fret a sick person an' put 'em on the rack,[25] an' that guitar was one o' the few things she'd brought with her."

I nodded assent, and Mrs. Todd spoke still lower.

"I set there close by the bed; I'd been through a good deal for some days back, and I thought I might's well be droppin' asleep too, bein' a quick person to wake. She looked to me as if she might last a day longer, certain, now she'd got more comfortable, but I was real tired, an' sort o' cramped as watchers will get, an' a fretful feeling begun to creep over me such as they often do have. If you give way, there ain't no support for the sick person; they can't count on no composure o' their own. Mis' Tolland moved then; a little restless, an' I forgot me quick enough, an' begun to hum out a little part of a hymn tune just to make her feel everything was as usual an' not wake up into a poor uncertainty. All of a sudden she set right up in bed with her eyes wide open, an' I stood an' put my arm behind her; she hadn't moved like that for days. And she reached out both her arms toward the door, an' I looked the way she was lookin', an' I see someone was standin' there against the dark. No, 'twa'n't Mis' Begg; 'twas somebody a good deal shorter than Mis' Begg. The lamplight struck across the room between us. I couldn't tell the shape, but 'twas a woman's dark face lookin' right at us; 'twa'n't but an instant I could see. I felt dreadful cold, and my head begun to swim; I thought the light went out; 'twa'n't but an instant, as I say, an' when my sight come back I couldn't see nothing there. I was one that didn't know what it was to faint away, no matter what happened; time was I felt above it in others, but 'twas somethin' that made poor human natur' quail. I saw very plain while I could see; 'twas a pleasant enough face, shaped somethin' like Mis' Tolland's, and a kind of expectin' look.

"No, I don't expect I was asleep," Mrs. Todd assured me quietly, after a moment's pause, though I had not spoken. She gave a heavy sigh before she went on. I could see that the recollection moved her in the deepest way.

"I suppose if I hadn't been so spent an' quavery with long watchin', I might have kept my head an' observed much better," she added humbly; "but I see all I could bear. I did try to act calm, an' I laid Mis' Tolland down on her pillow, an' I was a-shakin' as I done it. All she did was look up to me so satisfied and sort o' questioning, an' I looked back to her.

" 'You saw her, didn't you?' she says to me, speakin' perfectly reasonable. ' 'Tis my mother,' she says again, very feeble, but lookin' straight up at me, kind of surprised with the pleasure, and smiling as if she saw I was overcome, an' would have said more if she could, but we had hold of hands. I see then her change was comin', but I didn't call Mis' Begg, nor make no uproar. I felt calm then, an' lifted to somethin' different as I never was since. She opened her eyes just as she was goin'—

" 'You saw her, didn't you?' she said the second time, an' I says, *Yes, dear, I did; you ain't never goin' to feel strange an' lonesome no more.*' An' then in a few quiet minutes 'twas all over. I felt they'd gone away together. No, I wa'n't alarmed afterward; 'twas just that one moment I couldn't live under, but I never called it beyond reason I should see the other watcher. I saw plain enough there was somebody there with me in the room.

VII

" 'Twas just such a night as this Mis' Tolland died," repeated Mrs. Todd, returning to her usual tone and leaning back comfortably in her chair as she took up her knitting. " 'Twas just such a night as this. I've told the circumstances to but very few; but I don't call it beyond reason. When folks is goin' 'tis all natural, and only common things can jar upon the mind. You know plain enough there's somethin' beyond this world; the doors stand wide open. 'There's somethin' of us that must still live on; we've got to join both worlds together an' live in one but for the other.' The doctor said that to me one day, an' I never could forget it; he said 'twas in one o' his old doctor's books."

We sat together in silence in the warm little room; the rain dropped heavily from the eaves, and the sea still roared, but the high wind had done blowing. We heard the far complaining fog horn of a steamer up the Bay.

"There goes the Boston boat out, pretty near on time," said Mrs. Todd with satisfaction. "Sometimes these late August storms'll sound a good deal worse than they really be. I do hate to hear the poor steamers callin' when they're bewildered in thick nights in winter, comin' on the coast. Yes, there goes the boat; they'll find it rough at sea, but the storm's all over."

ABRAHAM CAHAN

1860–1951

LIKE MANY AUTHORS of regionalist fiction, including Alexander Posey, Sui Sin Far, and Joel Chandler Harris, Abraham Cahan made his career in journalism, editing an important Yiddish paper in New York for almost fifty years. Born in Lithuania, Cahan graduated from Vilna Teachers' Institute in 1881; as a socialist involved in an anti-czarist group, he was threatened by the Russian police, and he immigrated to the United States in 1882. Settling in the Yiddish community in New York City, Cahan worked as a labor organizer, a reporter for the *New York Commercial Advertiser*, and a teacher. In 1897 he founded the Yiddish socialist newspaper the *Jewish Daily Forward* and served as its editor from 1903 to 1951. After publishing a number of stories both in Yiddish and English, Cahan wrote his first novel, *Yekl: A Tale of the New York Ghetto*, which was favorably reviewed by William Dean Howells in 1896. In addition to works in Yiddish that have not been translated, Cahan went on to publish several works of fiction dealing with themes of immigration and assimilation, such as the short stories collected in *The Imported Bridegroom and Other Stories of the New York Ghetto* (1898), and the novels *The White Terror and the Red: A Novel of Revolutionary Russia* (1905) and *The Rise of David Levinsky* (1917).

I

"So this is America, and I am a Jewess no longer!" brooded Michalina, as she looked at the stretch of vegetable gardens across the road from the threshold where she sat. "They say farm-hands work shorter hours on Saturdays, yet God knows when Wincas will get home." Her slow, black eyes returned to the stocking and the big darning-needle in her hands.

She was yearning for her Gentile husband and their common birthplace, and she was yearning for her father's house and her Jewish past. Wincas kept buzzing in her ear that she was a Catholic, but he did not understand her. She was a *meshumedeste*— a convert Jewess, an apostate, a renegade, a traitoress, something beyond the vituperative resources of Gentile speech. The bonfires of the Inquisition[1] had burned into her people a point of view to which Wincas was a stranger. Years of religious persecution and enforced clannishness had taught them to look upon the Jew who deserts his faith for that of his oppressors with a horror and a loathing which the Gentile brain could not conceive. Michalina's father had sat seven days shoeless on the ground, as for the dead, but death was what he naturally invoked upon the "defiled head," as the lesser of the two evils. Atheism would have been a malady; *shmad* (conversion to a Gentile creed) was far worse than death. Michalina felt herself buried alive. She was a meshumedeste. She shuddered to think what the word meant.

At first she seemed anxious to realize the change she had undergone. "You are a Jewess no longer—you are a Gentile woman," she would say to herself. But the words were as painful as they were futile, and she turned herself adrift on the feeling that she was the same girl as of old, except that something terrible had befallen her. "God knows where it will all end," she would whisper. She had a foreboding that something far more terrible, a great crushing blow that was to smite her, was gathering force somewhere.

Hatred would rise in her heart at such moments—hatred for her "sorceress of a stepmother," whose cruel treatment of Michalina had driven her into the arms of the Gentile lad and to America. It was owing to her that Rivka (Rebecca) had become a Michalina, a meshumedeste.

The Long Island village (one of a dozen within half an hour's walk from one another) was surrounded by farms which yielded the Polish peasants their livelihood. Their pay was about a dollar a day, but potatoes were the principal part of their food, and this they got from their American employers free. Nearly every peasant owned a fiddle or a banjo. A local politician had humorously dubbed the settlement Chego-Chegg (this was his phonetic summary of the Polish language), and the name clung.

Wincas and Michalina had been only a few days in the place, and although they spoke Polish as well as Lithuanian, they were shy of the other peasants and felt lonely. Michalina had not seen any of her former coreligionists since she and her husband had left the immigrant station, and she longed for them as one for the first time in mid-ocean longs for a sight of land. She had heard that there were two Jewish settlements near by. Often she would stand gazing at the horizon, wondering where they might be; whereupon her vague image of them at once allured and terrified her.

The sun shone dreamily, like an old man smiling at his own drowsiness. It was a little world of blue, green, gray, and gold, heavy with sleep. A spot of white and a spot of red came gleaming down the road. Rabbi Nehemiah was on his way home from Greyton, where he had dined with the "finest householder" and "said some law" to the little congregation at the afternoon service. For it was Sabbath, and that was why his unstarched shirt-collar was so fresh and his red bandana was tied around the waist of his long-skirted coat. Carrying things on the seventh day being prohibited, Rabbi Nehemiah *wore* his handkerchief.

The door of the general store (it was also the inn), overlooking the cross-roads from a raised platform, was wide open. A Polish peasant in American trousers and undershirt, but with a Warsaw pipe dangling from his mouth, sat on a porch, smoking quietly. A barefooted boy was fast asleep in the grass across the road, a soldier's cap by his side, like a corpse on the battle-field.

As Michalina glanced up the gray road to see if Wincas was not coming, her eye fell upon Rabbi Nehemiah. A thrill ran through her. She could tell by his figure, his huge white collar, and the handkerchief around his waist that he was a pious, learned Jew. As he drew near she saw that his face was overgrown with wisps of silken beard of a yellowish shade, and that he was a man of about twenty-seven.

As he walked along he gesticulated and murmured to himself. It was one of his bickerings with Satan.

"It's labor lost, Mr. Satan!" he said, with a withering smile. "You won't catch me again, if you burst. Go try your tricks on somebody else. If you hope to get me among your regular customers you are a very poor business man, I tell you that. Nehemiah is as clever as you, depend upon it. Go, mister, go!"

All this he said quite audibly, in his velvety, purring bass, which set one wondering where his voice came from.

As he came abreast of Michalina he stopped short in consternation.

"Woe is me, on the holy Sabbath!" he exclaimed in Yiddish, dropping his hands to his sides.

The color rushed to Michalina's face. She stole a glance at the Pole down the road. He seemed to be half asleep. She lowered her eyes and went on with her work.

"Will you not stop this, my daughter? Come, go indoors and dress in honor of the Sabbath," he purred on, with a troubled, appealing look.

"I don't understand what you say, sir," she answered, in Lithuanian, without raising her eyes.

The devout man started. "I thought she was a child of Israel!" he exclaimed, in his native tongue, as he hastily resumed his way. "Fie upon her! But what a pretty Gentile maiden!—just like a Jewess—" Suddenly he interrupted himself. "You are at it again, are n't you?" he burst out upon Satan. "Leave me alone, will you?"

Michalina's face was on fire. She was following the pious man with her glance. He was apparently going to one of those two Jewish villages. Every step he took gave her a pang, as if he were tied to her heart. As he disappeared on a side road behind some trees she hastily took her darning indoors and set out after him.

II

About three quarters of an hour had passed when, following the pious little man, she came in sight of a new town that looked as if it had sprung up overnight. It was Burkdale, the newest off-shoot of an old hamlet, and it owed its existence to the "Land Improvement Company," to the president of which, Madison Burke, it owed its name. Some tailoring contractors had moved their "sweat-shops"[2] here, after a prolonged strike in New York, and there were, besides, some fifty or sixty peddlers who spent the week scouring the island for custom[3] and who came here for the two Sabbath days—their own and that of their Christian patrons. The improvised little town was lively with the whir of sewing-machines and the many-colored display of shop windows.

As the man with the red girdle made his appearance, a large, stout woman in a black wig greeted him from across the street.

"Good Sabbath, Rabbi Nehemiah!" she called out to him, with a faint smile.

"A good Sabbath and a good year!" he returned.

Michalina was thrilled once more. She was now following close behind the pious man. She ran the risk of attracting his attention, but she no longer cared. Seeing a boy break some twigs, Rabbi Nehemiah made a dash at him, as though to rescue him from death, and seizing him by the arms, he shook the sticks out of his hands. Then, stroking the urchin's swarthy cheeks, he said fondly:

"It is prohibited, my son. God will give one a lashing for desecrating the Sabbath. Oh, what a lashing!"

A sob rose to Michalina's throat.

A short distance farther on Rabbi Nehemiah paused to re-monstrate with a group of young men who stood smoking cig-arettes and chatting by a merchandise wagon.

"Woe! Woe! Woe!" he exclaimed. "Do throw it away, pray! Are you not children of Israel? Do drop your cigarettes."

"Rabbi Nehemiah is right," said a big fellow, with a wink, concealing his cigarette behind him. The others followed his ex-ample, and Rabbi Nehemiah, flushed with his easy victory, went on pleading for a life of piety and divine study. He spoke from the bottom of his heart, and his face shone, but this did not prevent his plea from being flavored with a certain humor, for the most part at his own expense.

"The world to come is the tree, while this world is only the shadow it casts," he said in his soft, thick voice. "Smoking on the Sabbath, staying away from the synagogue, backbiting, cheating in business, dancing with maidens, or ogling somebody else's wife—all this is a great pleasure, is it not? Well, the sages of this world, the dudes, the educated, and even a high-priced adornment like myself, think it is. We hunt for these delights. Behold, we have caught them. Close your fist tight! Hold the precious find with might and main, Rabbi Nehemiah! Presently, hark! the Angel of Death is coming. 'Please, open your hand, Rabbi Nehemiah. Let us see what you have got.' Alas! it's empty, empty, empty—*Ai-ai!*" he suddenly shrieked in a frightened, piteous voice. While he was speaking the big fellow had stolen up behind him and clapped his enormous high hat over his eyes. The next moment another young man slipped up to Rabbi Nehemiah's side, snatched off his bandana, and set it on fire.

"Woe is me! Woe is me! On the holy Sabbath!" cried the devout man, in despair.

Michalina, who had been looking on at a distance, every minute making ready to go home, rushed up to Rabbi Nehemiah's side.

"Don't—pray don't!" she begged his tormentors, in Yiddish. "You know he did not touch you; why should you hurt him?"

A crowd gathered. The learned man was looking about him with a perplexed air, when along came Sorah-Elka, the bewigged tall woman who had saluted him a short while ago. The young men made way for her.

"What's the matter? Gota licking again?" she inquired, between a frown and a smile, and speaking in phlegmatic, articulate accents. Her smile was like her voice—pleasingly cold. She was the cleverest, the most pious, and the most ill-natured woman in the place. "Serves you right, Rabbi Nehemiah. You look for trouble and you get it. What more do you want? What did they do to him, the scamps?"

"Nothing. They only knocked his hat over his eyes. They were fooling," answered a little boy.

Sorah-Elka's humor and her calm, authoritative manner won Michalina's heart. Oh, if she were one of this Jewish crowd! She wished she could speak to them. Well, who knew her here? As to Rabbi Nehemiah, he did not seem to recognize her, so she ventured to say, ingratiatingly:

"He did n't do them anything. He only talked to them and they hit him on the head."

Many eyes were leveled at the stranger. The young fellow who had burned Rabbi Nehemiah's handkerchief was scanning her face.

Suddenly he exclaimed:

"I sha'n't live till next week if she is not the meshumedeste of Chego-Chegg! I peddle over there."

The terrible untranslatable word, the most loathsome to the Yiddish ear, struck Michalina cold. She wondered whether this was the great calamity which her heart had been predicting. Was it the beginning of her end? Rabbi Nehemiah recognized her. With a shriek of horror, and drawing his skirts about him, as if for fear of contamination, he proceeded to describe his meeting with Michalina at the Polish village.

"What! this plague the meshumedeste who has a peasant for a husband!" said Sorah-Elka, as she swept the young woman with contemptuous curiosity. "May all the woes that are to befall me, you, or any good Jew—may they all strike the head of this horrid thing—fie upon her!" And the big woman spat with the same imperturbable smile with which she had drawled out her malediction.

Michalina went off toward Chego-Chegg. When the crowd was a few yards behind her somebody shouted:

"Meshumedeste! Meshumedeste!"

The children and some full-grown rowdies took up the cry:

"Meshumedeste! Meshumedeste! Meshumedeste!" they sang in chorus, running after her and pelting her with stones.

Michalina was frightened to death. And yet her pursuers and the whole Jewish town became dearer to her heart than ever.

"Where have you been?" Wincas asked, shaking her furiously.

"Don't! Don't! People are looking!" she protested, in her quietly strenuous way.

The village was astir. Children were running about; women sat on the porches, gossiping; two fiddles were squeaking themselves hoarse in the tavern. A young negro, lank, tattered, and grinning, was twanging a banjo to a crowd of simpering Poles. He it was who got the peasants to forsake their accordions, or even fiddles, for banjos. He was the civilizing and Americanizing genius of the place, although he had learned to jabber Polish long before any of his pupils picked up a dozen English words.

"Tell me where you have been," raged Wincas.

"Suppose I don't? Am I afraid of you? I felt lonesome—so lonesome! I thought I would die of loneliness, so I went for a walk and lost my way. Are you satisfied?"

They went indoors, where their landlady had prepared for them a meal of herring, potatoes, and beef-stew.

Half an hour later they were seated on the lawn, conversing in whispers amid the compact blackness of the night. The two tavern windows gleamed like suspended sheets of gold. Diving out of these into the sea of darkness was a frisky host of banjo notes.

"How dark it is!" whispered Michalina.

"Are you afraid of devils?"

"No—why?"

"I thought you might be," he said.

After a pause he suddenly pointed at his heart.

"Does it hurt you?" he asked.

"What do you mean, darling?" she demanded, interlacing her fingers over his shoulder and peering into his beardless face.

"Something has got into me. It's right here. It's pulling me to pieces, Michalinka!"

"That's nothing," she said. "It's only homesickness. It will wear off."

Wincas complained of his employer, the queer ways of American farming, the tastelessness of American food.

"God has cursed this place and taken the life out of everything," he said. "I suppose it's all because the people here are so wicked. Everything looks as it should, but you just try to put it into your mouth, and you find out the swindle. Look here,

Michalinka, maybe it is the Jewish god getting even on me?"

She was bent upon her own thoughts and made no reply. Presently she began to caress him as she would a sick baby.

"Don't worry, my love," she comforted him. "America is a good country. Everybody says so. Wait till we get used to it. Then you won't go, even if you are driven with sticks from here."

They sat mutely clinging to each other, their eyes on the bright tavern windows, when a fresh, fragrant breeze came blowing upon them. Wincas fell to inhaling it thirstily. The breeze brought his native village to his nostrils.

"Mi-Michalinka darling!" he suddenly sobbed out, clasping her to his heart.

III

When Michalina, pale, weak, and beautiful, lay in bed, and the midwife bade her look at her daughter, the young mother opened her flashing black eyes and forthwith shut them again. The handful of flesh and her own splitting headache seemed one and the same thing. After a little, as her agonizing sleep was broken and her torpid gaze found the baby by the wall, she was overcome with terror and disgust. It was a *shikse* (Gentile girl), a heap of defilement. What was it doing by her side?

She had not nursed the baby a week before she grew attached to it. By the time little Marysia was a month old, she was dearer than her own life to her.

The little railroad-station about midway between the two settlements became Michalina's favorite resort. Her neighbors she shunned. She had been brought up to look down upon their people as "a race like unto an ass." At home she could afford to like them. Now that she was one of them, they were repugnant to her. They, in their turn, often mocked her and called her "Jew woman." And so she would often go to spend an hour or two in the waiting-room of the station or on the platform outside. Some of the passengers were Jews, and these would eye her curiously, as if they had heard of her. She blushed under their glances, yet she awaited them impatiently each time a train was due.

One morning a peddler, bending under his pack, stopped to look at her. When he had dropped his burden his face seemed familiar to Michalina. He was an insignificant little man, clean-shaven, with close-clipped yellowish hair, and he wore a derby hat and a sack-coat.

All at once his face broke into a broad, affectionate smile.

"How do you do?" he burst out in a deep, mellow voice which she recognized instantly. "I once spoke to you in Chego-Chegg, do you remember? I see you are amazed to see me in a short coat and without beard and side-locks."

"You look ten years younger," she said in a daze of embarrassment.

"I am Rabbi Nehemiah no longer," he explained bashfully. "They call me Nehemiah the Atheist now."

"Another sinner!" Michalina thought, with a little thrill of pleasure.

Nehemiah continued, with a shamefaced smile:

"When my coat and my side-locks were long my sight was short, while now—why, now I am so saturated with wisdom that pious Jews keep away from me for fear of getting wet, don't you know? Well, joking aside, I had ears, but could not hear because of my ear-locks; I had eyes, and could not see because they were closed in prayer. Now I am cured of my idiocy. And how are you? How are you getting along in America?"

His face beamed. Michalina's wore a pained look. She was bemoaning the fall of an idol.

"I am all right, thank you. Don't the Burkdale people trouble you?" she asked, reddening violently.

"Men will be men and rogues will be rogues. Do you remember that Saturday? It was not the only beating I got, either. They regaled me quite often—the oxen! However, I bear them no ill will. Who knows but it was their cuffs and buffets that woke me up? The one thing that gives me pain is this: the same fellows who used to break my bones for preaching religion now beat me because I expose its idiocies. I am like the great rabbi who had once been a chief of highwaymen. 'What of it?' he used to say. 'I was a leader then, and a leader I am now.' I was whipped when I was Rabbi Nehemiah, and now that I am Nehemiah the Atheist I am whipped again. By the way, do you remember how they hooted you? There's nothing to blush about, missus. Religion is all humbug. There are no Jews and no Gentiles, missus. This is America. All are noblemen here, and all are brothers—children of one mother—Nature, dear little missus." The word was apparently a tidbit to his tongue. He uttered it with relish, peering admiringly into Michalina's face. "Go forth, dear little missus! Go forth, O thou daughter of Zion, and proclaim to all those who are groveling in the mire of Judaism—"

"S-s-s-sh!" she interrupted imploringly. "Why should you speak like that? Don't—oh, don't!"

He began a long and heated argument. She could not follow him.

Marysia was asleep in her arms, munching her little lips and smiling. As Michalina stole a glance at her, she could not help smiling, too. She gazed at the child again and again, pretending to listen. For the twentieth time she noticed that in the upper part of her face Marysia bore a striking resemblance to Wincas.

Michalina and Nehemiah often met. All she understood of his talk was that it was in Yiddish, and this was enough. Though he preached atheism, to her ear his words were echoes from the world of synagogues, rabbis, purified meat, blessed Sabbath lights. Another thing she gathered from his monologues was that he was a fellow-outcast. Of herself she never spoke. Being a mystery to him made her a still deeper mystery to herself, and their secret interviews had an irresistible charm for her.

One day Michalina found him clean-shaven and in a new necktie.

"Good morning!" he said, with unusual solemnity. And drawing a big red apple from his pocket, he shamefacedly placed it in her hand.

"What was it you wanted to tell me?" she inquired, blushing.

"Oh, nothing. I meant it for fun. It's only a story I read. It's about a great man who was in love with a beautiful woman all his life. She was married to another man and true to him, yet the stranger loved her. His soul was bewitched. He sang of her, he dreamed of her. The man's name was Petrarca and the woman's was Laura."[4]

"I don't know what you mean by your story," she said, with an embarrassed shrug of her shoulders.

"How do you know it is only a story?" he rejoined, his eye on the glistening rail. "Maybe it is only a parable? Maybe you are Laura? Laura mine!" he whispered.

"Stop that!" she cried, with a pained gesture.

At that moment he was repulsive.

"Hush, don't eat your heart, little kitten. I was only joking."

IV

Michalina ventured to visit Burkdale once again. This time she was not bothered. Only here and there some one would whisper, "Here comes the apostate of Chego-Chegg." Little by little she got to making most of her purchases in the Jewish town. Wincas at first stormed, and asked whether it was true that the Jew had bedeviled his wife's heart; but before long she persuaded him to go with her on some of her shopping expeditions. Michalina even decided that her husband should learn to press coats, which was far more profitable than working on a farm; but after trying it for a few days, he stubbornly gave it up. The soil called him back, he said, and if he did not obey it, it might get square on him when he was dead and buried in it.

By this time they had moved into a shanty on the outskirts of the village, within a short distance from Burkdale.

At first Michalina forbade Wincas to write to his father, but he mailed a letter secretly. The answer inclosed a note from Michalina's father, in Yiddish, which Wincas, having in his ecstasy let out his secret, handed her.

Your dear father-in-law [the old man wrote] goes about mocking me about you and his precious son. "Will you send her your love?" he asked. "Very well, I will," said I. And here it is, Rivka. May eighty toothaches disturb your peace even as you have disturbed the peace of your mother in her grave. God grant that your impure limbs be hurled from one end of the world to the other, as your damned soul will be when you are dead like a vile cur. Your dear father-in-law (woe to you, Rivka!) asks me what I am writing. "A blessing," say I. May similar blessings strew your path, accursed meshumedeste. That's all.

"What does he write?" asked Wincas.

"Nothing. He is angry," she muttered. In her heart she asked herself: "Who is this Gentile? What is he doing here?" At this moment she felt sure that her end was near.

Nehemiah and Michalina had taken root in the little town as the representatives of two inevitable institutions. Burkdale without an atheist and a convert seemed as impossible as it would have been without a marriage-broker, a synagogue, or a bath-house "for all daughters of Israel."

Nehemiah continued his frenzied agitation. Neglecting his business, half-starved, and the fair game of every jester, but plumed with some success, the zealot went on scouting religious ceremonies, denouncing rabbis, and preaching assimilation with the enlightened Gentiles. Nehemiah was an incurably religious man, and when he had lost his belief disbelief became his religion.

And so the two were known as the *appikoros* (atheist) and the meshumedeste. Between the two there was, however, a wide difference. Disclaim Judaism as Nehemiah would, he could not get the Jews to disclaim him, when Michalina was more alien to the Mosaic community than any of its Christian neighbors. With her child in her arms she moved about among the people of the place like a low shadow. Nehemiah was a Jew who "sinned and led others to sin"; she was not a Jewess who had transgressed, but a living stigma all the more accursed because she had only been a Jewess.

Some of the Jewish women were friendly to her. Zelda the Busybody exchanged little favors with her, but even she stopped at cooking-utensils, for Michalina's food was *treife*[5] and all her dishes were contaminated. One day, when the dumpy little woman called at the lonely hovel, the convert offered her a wedge of her first lemon-pie. It was Zelda who had taught her to make it, and in her exultation and shamefacedness Michalina forgot the chasm that separated her from her caller.

"Taste it and tell me what is wrong about it," she said, blushing.

Zelda became confused.

"No, thank you. I've just had dinner, as true as I'm living," she stammered.

The light in Michalina's eyes went out. For a moment she

stood with the saucer containing the piece of pie in her hand. When the Burkdale woman was gone she threw the pie away.

She bought a special set of dishes which she kept *kosher*,[6] according to the faith of the people of Burkdale. Sometimes she would buy her meat of a Jewish butcher and, on coming home, she would salt and purify it. Not that she expected this to be set to her credit in the world to come, for there was no hope for her soul, but she could not help, at least, playing the Jewess. It both soothed and harrowed her to prepare food or to bless Sabbath light as they did over in Burkdale. But her Sabbath candles burned so stern, so cold, so unhallowed. As she embraced the space about them and with a scooping movement brought her hands together over her shut eyes and fell to whispering the benediction, her heart beat fast. She felt like a thief.

"Praised be Thou, O Lord, King of the world, who hast sanctified us by Thy commandments and commanded us to kindle the light of Sabbath."

When she attempted to recite this she could not speak after the third word.

Michalina received another letter from her father. The old man's heart was wrung with compunction and yearning. He was panting to write to her, but, alas! who ever wrote a meshumedeste except to curse her?

It is to gladden your treacherous heart that I am writing again [ran the letter]. Rejoice, accursed apostate, rejoice! We cannot raise our heads for shame, and our eyes are darkened with disgrace. God give that your eyes become so dark that they behold neither your cur of a husband nor your vile pup. May you be stained in the blood of your own heart even as you have stained the name of our family.

Written by me, who curse the moment when I became your father.

Michalina was in a rage. "We cannot raise our heads"? Who are "we"? He and his sorceress of a wife? First she makes him drive his own daughter to "the impurity" of the Gentile faith, and then she gets him to curse this unhappy child of his for the disgrace she brought on her head! What are they worrying about? Is it that they are afraid it will be hard for Michalina's stepsister to get a husband because there is a meshumedeste in the family? Ah, she is writhing and twitching with pain, the sorceress, is n't she? Writhe away, murderess! Let her taste some of the misery she has heaped on her stepdaughter. "Rejoice, apostate, rejoice!" Michalina did rejoice. She was almost glad to be a meshumedeste.

"But why should it have come out like this?" Michalina thought. "Suppose I had never become a meshumedeste, and Nehemiah, or some handsomer Jew, had married me at home. . . . Would not the sorceress and her daughter burst with envy! Or suppose I became a Jewess again, and married a pious, learned, and wealthy Jew who fainted with love for me, and my stepmother heard of it, and I sent my little brother lots of money— would n't she burst, the sorceress! . . . And I should live in Burkdale, and Sorah-Elka and the other Jews and Jewesses would call at my house, and eat, and drink. On Saturdays I should go to the synagogue with a big prayer-book, and on meeting me on the road people would say, 'Good Sabbath!' and I should answer, 'A good Sabbath and a good year!'"

Michalina began to cry.

v

Spring was coming. The air was mild, pensive, yearning. Michalina was full of tears.

"Don't rail at the rabbis—don't!" she said, with unusual irritation, to Nehemiah at her house. "Do you think I can bear to hear it?"

She cried. Nehemiah's eyes also filled with tears.

"Don't, little kitten," he said; "I did n't mean to hurt you. Are you sorry you became a Christian?" he added, in an embarrassed whisper.

For the first time she recounted her story to him. When she had finished the atheist was walking up and down.

"*Ai-ai-ai! Ai-ai!*" All at once he stopped. "So it was out of revenge for your stepmother that you married Wincas!" he exclaimed. Then he dropped his voice to a shamefaced undertone. "I thought you had fallen in love with him."

"What's that got to do with him?" she flamed out.

His face changed. She went on:

"Anyhow, he is my husband, and I am his wife and a Gentile woman, an accursed soul, doomed to have no rest either in this world or in the other. May the sorceress have as much darkness on her heart as I have on mine!"

"Why should you speak like that, little kitten? Of course I am an atheist, and religion is humbug, but you are grieving for nothing. According to the Jewish law, you are neither his wife nor a Gentile woman. You are a Jewess. Mind, I don't believe in the Talmud; but, according to the Talmud, your marriage does not count. Yes, you are unmarried!" he repeated, noting her interest. "You are a maiden, free as the birds in the sky, my kitten. You can marry a Jew 'according to the laws of Moses and Israel,' and be happy."

His voice died away.

"Lau-au-ra!" he wailed, as he seized her hand and began to kiss its fingers.

"Stop—oh, stop! What has come to you!" she shrieked. Her face was crimson. After an awkward silence, she sobbed out: "Nobody will give me anything but misery—nobody, nobody, nobody! What shall I do? Oh, what shall I do?"

Under the pretense of consulting a celebrated physician, Michalina had obtained Wincas's permission to go to New York. In a secluded room, full of dust and old books, on the third floor of an Orchard street tenement-house, she found a gray-bearded man with a withered face. Before him were an open folio and a glass half filled with tea. His rusty skullcap was pushed back on his head.

The blood rushed to her face as she stepped to the table. She could not speak. "A question of law?" asked the rabbi. "Come, my daughter, what is the trouble?"

Being addressed by the venerable man as a Jewess melted her embarrassment and her fear into tears.

"I have married a Gentile," she murmured, with bowed head.

"A Gentile! Woe is me!" exclaimed the rabbi, with a look of dismay and pity.

"And I have been baptized, too."

Here an old bonnetless woman came in with a chicken. The rabbi was annoyed. After hastily inspecting the fowl, he cried:

"Kosher! Kosher! You may eat it in good health."

When the old woman was gone he leaped up from his seat and bolted the door.

"Well, do you want to do penance?" he demanded, adjusting his skullcap.

She nodded ruefully.

"Well, where is the hindrance? Go ahead, my daughter; and if you do it from a pure heart, the Most High will help you."

"But how am I to become a Jewess again? Rabbi, a man told me I never ceased to be one. Is it true?"

"Foolish young woman! What, then, are you? A Frenchwoman? The God of Israel is not in the habit of refunding one's money. Oh, no! 'Once a Jew, forever a Jew'—that's the way he does business."

"But I am married to a Gentile," she urged, with new light in her black eyes.

"Married? Not in the eye of our faith, my child. You were born a Jewess, and a Jewess cannot marry a Gentile. Now, if your marriage is no marriage—what, then, is it? A sin! Leave the Gentile, if you want to return to God. Cease sinning, and live like a daughter of Israel. Of course—of course the laws of the land—of America—do you understand?—they look upon you as a married woman, and they must be obeyed. But the laws of our faith say you are not married, and were a Jew to put the ring of dedication on your finger, you would be his wife. Do you understand, my child?"

"And how about the baby, rabbi? Suppose I wanted to make a proselyte⁷ of her?"

"A proselyte! Your learning does not seem to go very far," laughed the old man. "Why, your little girl is even a better Jewess than you have been, for she has not sinned, while you have."

"But her father—"

"Her father! What of him? Did *he* go through the throes of childbirth when the girl was born to you? Don't be uneasy, my daughter. According to our faith, children follow their mother. You are a Jewess, and so is she. She is a pure child of Israel. What is her name? Marysia? Well, call her some Jewish name—say Mindele or Shayndele. What does it amount to?"

As Michalina was making her way down the dingy staircase, she hugged the child and kissed her convulsively.

"Sheindele! Sheindele! Pure child of Israel," she said between sobs, for the first time addressing her in Yiddish. "A Jewish girlie! A Jewish girlie!"

VI

The charitable souls who had joined to buy the steamship tickets were up with the larks. At seven o'clock Sorah-Elka's apartments on the second floor of a spick-and-span frame-house were full of pious women come to behold their "good deed" in the flesh. It was the greatest event in the eventful history of Burkdale. Michalina, restored to her Hebrew name, was, of course, the center of attention. Sorah-Elka and Zelda addressed her in the affectionate diminutive; the other women, in the most dignified form of the name; and so "Rievele dear" and "Rieva, if you please" flew thick and fast.

Nehemiah kept assuring everybody that he was an atheist, and that it was only to humor Rebecca that he was going to marry her according to the laws of Moses and Israel. But then nobody paid any heed to him. The pious souls were all taken up with the young woman they were "rescuing from the impurity."

Rebecca was polite, grateful, smiling, and nervous. Sorah-Elka was hovering about, flushed and morose.

"You have kissed her enough," she snarled at Zelda. "Kisses won't take her to the ship. You had better see about the lemons. As long as the ship is in harbor I won't be sure of the job. For one thing, too many people are in the secret. I wish we were in New York, at least."

The preparations were delayed by hitch after hitch. Besides, a prosperous rescuer bethought herself at the eleventh hour that she had a muff, as good as new, which might be of service to Rebecca; and then another rescuer, as prosperous and as pious, remembered that her jar of preserved cherries would be a god-send to Rebecca on shipboard. Still, the train was due fully an hour later; the English steamer would not sail before two o'clock, so there was plenty of time.

As to Wincas, he had gone to work at five in the morning and would not be back before seven in the evening.

Zelda was frisking about with the little girl, whom she exultantly addressed as Shayndele; and so curious was it to call a former Gentile child by a Yiddish name that the next minute everybody in the room was shouting: "Shayndele, come to me!" "Shayndele, look!" "Shayndele going to London to be a pious Jewess!" or "Shayndele, a health to your head, arms, and feet!"

"Never fear, Nehemiah will be a good father to her, won't you, Nehemiah?" said one matron.

Suddenly a woman who stood by the window gave a start.

"Her husband!" she gasped.

There was a panic. Sorah-Elka was excitedly signing to the others to be cool. Rebecca, pale and wild-eyed, burst into the bedroom, whence she presently emerged on tiptoe, flushed and biting her lip.

"What can he be doing here at this hour? I told him I was going to the New York professor," she said under her breath. Concealing herself behind the window-frame, she peeped down into the street.

"Get away from there!" whizzed Sorah-Elka, gnashing her teeth and waving her arms violently.

Rebecca lingered. She saw the stalwart figure of her husband, his long blond hair curling at the end, and his pale, oval face. He was trudging along aimlessly, gaping about him in a perplexed, forlorn way.

"He is wandering about like a cow in search of her calf," Michalina remarked, awkwardly.

"Let him go whistle!" snapped Sorah-Elka. "We shall have to tuck you away somewhere. When the coast is clear again, I'll take you to the other railroad station. Depend upon it, we'll get you over to New York and on board the ship before his pumpkin-head knows what world he is in. But I said that too many people were in the secret."

Sorah-Elka was a fighter. She was mistaken, however, as to the cause of Wincas's sudden appearance. Even the few Poles who worked in the Burkdale sweat-shops knew nothing of the great conspiracy. Water and oil won't swap secrets even when in the same bottle. It was Michalina's manner during the last few days, especially on parting with him this morning, which had kindled suspicion in the peasant's breast. What had made her weep so bitterly, clinging to him and kissing him as he was leaving? As the details of it came back to him, anxiety and an overpowering sense of loneliness had gripped his heart. He could not go on with his work.

There was a cowardly stillness in Sorah-Elka's parlor. Nehemiah was rubbing his hands and gazing at Rebecca like a prisoner mutely praying for his life. Her eye was on the window.

"What can he be doing here at such an early hour?" she muttered, sheepishly. "Maybe he has lost his job."

"And what if he did? Is it any business of yours? Let him hang and drown himself!" declared Sorah-Elka.

"Why should you curse him like that? Where is his fault?" Rebecca protested feebly.

"Look at her—look at her! She *is* dead stuck on the lump of uncleanliness, is n't she? Well, hurry up, Rievela darling. Zelda will see to the express. Come, Rievela, come!"

Rebecca tarried.

"What has got into you? Why don't you get a move on you? You know one minute may cost us the whole game."

There was a minute of suspense. All at once Rebecca burst out sobbing:

"I cannot! I cannot!" she said, with her fists at her temples. "Curse me; I deserve it. I know I am doomed to have no rest either in this world or in the other, but I cannot leave him—I cannot. Forgive me, Nehemiah, but I cannot. What shall I do? Oh, what shall I do?"

The gathering was dumfounded. Sorah-Elka dropped her immense arms. For several moments she stood bewildered. Then she said:

"A pain on my head! The good women have spent so much on the tickets!"

"I'll pay it all back—every cent—every single cent of it," pleaded Michalina. Again her own Yiddish sounded like a foreign tongue to her.

"You pay back! From the treasures of your beggarly peasant

husband, perhaps? May you spend on doctor's bills a thousand dollars for every cent you have cost us, plaguy[8] meshumedeste that you are!"

A bedlam of curses let itself loose. Michalina fled.

"Let her go to all the eighty dark, bitter, and swampy years!" Sorah-Elka concluded, as the door closed upon the apostate. "A meshumedeste will be a meshumedeste."

PAULINE HOPKINS

1859–1930

BORN IN PORTLAND, Maine, Pauline Hopkins was educated in Boston public schools. Following her first ambition to be a playwright, she wrote two musical dramas produced in the Boston area in the 1870s: *Colored Aristocracy* (1877) and *Slaves' Escape; or the Underground Railroad* (1879). Hopkins herself performed in the latter and in other shows with the Boston Colored Troubadours, earning the name of "Boston's Favorite Colored Soprano." She supported herself by working as a stenographer, including appointments at the Massachusetts Bureau of Statistics and at MIT. In 1900 her first novel—and her only book-length publication—appeared, entitled *Contending Forces, A Romance Illustrative of Negro Life North and South* (1900). Like much of her fiction, this romance, set in the African American community in Boston after the Civil War, is concerned with social and political issues facing African Americans: women's roles, lynching, disenfranchisement, miscegenation, and the rise of the black middle class.

In 1900 Hopkins helped to found the *Colored American Magazine*, where for four years she served as literary editor. Her novels *Hagar's Daughter: A Story of Southern Caste Prejudice*, *Winona: A Tale of Negro Life in the South and Southwest*, and *Of One Blood; or, The Hidden Self* were serialized in the *Colored American* between 1901 and 1903; her later works include a sociological text, *The Dark Races of the Twentieth Century* (1905), and many short stories. Hopkins left the *Colored American* in 1904 and went on to write for other African American magazines, including the *New Era Magazine*, which she cofounded with Walter Wallace in 1916. The project was unsuccessful, however, and Hopkins returned to working as a stenographer.

The Canterbury Club of Boston was holding its regular monthly meeting at the palatial Beacon-street residence of Dr. William Thornton, expert medical practitioner and specialist. All the members were present, because some rare opinions were to be aired by men of profound thought on a question of vital importance to the life of the Republic, and because the club celebrated its anniversary in a home usually closed to society. The Doctor's winters, since his marriage, were passed at his summer home near his celebrated sanatorium. This winter found him in town with his wife and two boys. We had heard much of the beauty of the former, who was entirely unknown to social life, and about whose life and marriage we felt sure a romantic interest attached. The Doctor himself was too bright a luminary of the professional world to remain long hidden without creating comment. We had accepted the invitation to dine with alacrity, knowing that we should be welcomed to a banquet that would feast both eye and palate; but we had not been favored by even a glimpse of the hostess. The subject for discussion was: "Expansion; Its Effect upon the Future Development of the Anglo-Saxon throughout the World."

Dinner was over, but we still sat about the social board discussing the question of the hour. The Hon. Herbert Clapp, eminent jurist and politician, had painted in glowing colors the advantages to be gained by the increase of wealth and the exalted position which expansion would give the United States in the councils of the great governments of the world. In smoothly flowing sentences marshalled in rhetorical order, with compact ideas, and incisive argument, he drew an effective picture with all the persuasive eloquence of the trained orator.

Joseph Whitman, the theologian of world-wide fame, accepted the arguments of Mr. Clapp, but subordinated all to the great opportunity which expansion would give to the religious enthusiast. None could doubt the sincerity of this man, who looked once into the idealized face on which heaven had set the seal of consecration.

Various opinions were advanced by the twenty-five men present, but the host said nothing; he glanced from one to another with a look of amusement in his shrewd gray-blue eyes. "Wonderful eyes," said his patients who came under their magic spell. "A wonderful man and a wonderful mind," agreed his contemporaries, as they heard in amazement of some great cure of chronic or malignant disease which approached the supernatural.

"What do you think of this question, Doctor?" finally asked the president, turning to the silent host.

"Your arguments are good; they would convince almost anyone."

"But not Doctor Thornton," laughed the theologian.

"I acquiesce which ever way the result turns. Still, I like to view both sides of a question. We have considered but one tonight. Did you ever think that in spite of our prejudices against amalgamation, some of our descendants, indeed many of them, will inevitably intermarry among those far-off tribes of dark-skinned peoples, if they become a part of this great Union?"

"Among the lower classes that may occur, but not to any great extent," remarked a college president.

"My experience teaches me that it will occur among all classes, and to an appalling extent," replied the Doctor.

"You don't believe in intermarriage with other races?"

"Yes, most emphatically, when they possess decent moral development and physical perfection, for then we develop a superior being in the progeny born of the intermarriage. But if we are not ready to receive and assimilate the new material which will be brought to mingle with our pure Anglo-Saxon stream, we should call a halt in our expansion policy."

"I must confess, Doctor, that in the idea of amalgamation you present a new thought to my mind. Will you not favor us with a few of your main points?" asked the president of the club, breaking the silence which followed the Doctor's remarks.

"Yes, Doctor, give us your theories on the subject. We may not agree with you, but we are all open to conviction."

The Doctor removed the half-consumed cigar from his lips, drank what remained in his glass of the choice Burgundy, and leaning back in his chair contemplated the earnest faces before him.

We may make laws, but laws are but straws in the hands of Omnipotence.

> "There's a divinity that shapes our ends,
> Rough-hew them how we will."[1]

And no man may combat fate. Given a man, propinquity,[2] opportunity, fascinating femininity, and there you are. Black, white, green, yellow—nothing will prevent intermarriage. Position, wealth, family, friends—all sink into insignificance before the God-implanted instinct that made Adam, awakening from a deep sleep and finding the woman beside him, accept Eve as bone of his bone; he cared not nor questioned whence she came. So it is with the sons of Adam ever since, through the law of heredity which makes us all one common family. And so it will be with us in our re-formation of this old Republic. Perhaps I can make my meaning clearer by illustration, and with your permission I will tell you a story which came under my observation as a practitioner.

Doubtless all of you heard of the terrible tragedy which occurred at Gordonville, Mass., some years ago, when Capt. Jonathan Gordon, his wife and little son were murdered. I suppose that I am the only man on this side the Atlantic, outside of the police, who can tell you the true story of that crime.

I knew Captain Gordon well; it was through his persuasions that I bought a place in Gordonville and settled down to spending my summers in that charming rural neighborhood. I had rendered the Captain what he was pleased to call valuable medical help, and I became his family physician. Captain Gordon was a retired sea captain, formerly engaged in the East India[3] trade. All his ancestors had been such; but when the bottom fell out of that business he established the Gordonville Mills with his first wife's money, and settled down as a money-making manufacturer of cotton cloth. The Gordons were old New England Puritans who had come over in the "Mayflower"; they had owned Gordon Hall for more than a hundred years. It was a baronial-like pile of granite with towers, standing on a hill which commanded a superb view of Massachusetts Bay and the surrounding country. I imagine the Gordon star was under a cloud about the time Captain Jonathan married his first wife, Miss Isabel Franklin of Boston, who brought to him the money which mended the broken fortunes of the Gordon house, and restored this old Puritan stock to its rightful position. In the person of Captain Gordon the austerity of manner and indomitable will-power that he had inherited were combined with a temper that brooked no contradiction.

The first wife died at the birth of her third child, leaving him two daughters, Jeannette and Talma. Very soon after her death the Captain married again. I have heard it rumored that the Gordon girls did not get on very well with their stepmother. She was a woman with no fortune of her own, and envied the large portion left by the first Mrs. Gordon to her daughters.

Jeannette was tall, dark, and stern like her father; Talma was like her dead mother, and possessed of great talent, so great that her father sent her to the American Academy at Rome, to develop the gift. It was the hottest of July days when her friends were bidden to an afternoon party on the lawn and a dance in the evening, to welcome Talma Gordon among them again. I watched her as she moved about among her guests, a fairylike blonde in floating white draperies, her face a study in delicate changing tints, like the heart of a flower, sparkling in smiles about the mouth to end in merry laughter in the clear blue eyes. There were all the subtle allurements of birth, wealth and culture about the exquisite creature:

> "Smiling, frowning evermore,
>   Thou art perfect in love-lore,
>   Ever varying Madeline,"

quoted a celebrated writer as he stood apart with me, gazing upon the scene before us. He sighed as he looked at the girl.

"Doctor, there is genius and passion in her face. Sometime our little friend will do wonderful things. But is it desirable to be singled out for special blessings by the gods? Genius always carries with it intense capacity for suffering: 'Whom the gods love die young.' "[4]

"Ah," I replied, "do not name death and Talma Gordon together. Cease your dismal croakings; such talk is rank heresy."

The dazzling daylight dropped slowly into summer twilight. The merriment continued; more guests arrived; the great dancing pagoda built for the occasion was lighted by myriads of Japanese lanterns. The strains from the band grew sweeter and sweeter, and "all went merry as a marriage bell."[5] It was a rare treat to have this party at Gordon Hall, for Captain Jonathan was not given to hospitality. We broke up shortly before midnight, with expressions of delight from all the guests.

I was a bachelor then, without ties. Captain Gordon insisted upon my having a bed at the Hall. I did not fall asleep readily; there seemed to be something in the air that forbade it. I was still awake when a distant clock struck the second hour of the morning. Suddenly the heavens were lighted by a sheet of ghastly light; a terrific midsummer thunderstorm was breaking over the sleeping town. A lurid flash lit up all the landscape, painting the trees in grotesque shapes against the murky sky, and defining clearly the sullen blackness of the waters of the bay breaking in grandeur against the rocky coast. I had arisen and put back the draperies from the windows, to have an unobstructed view of the grand scene. A low muttering coming nearer and nearer, a terrific roar, and then a tremendous downpour. The storm had burst.

Now the uncanny howling of a dog mingled with the rattling volleys of thunder. I heard the opening and closing of doors; the servants were about looking after things. It was impossible to sleep. The lightning was more vivid. There was a blinding flash of a greenish-white tinge mingled with the crash of falling timbers. Then before my startled gaze arose columns of red flames reflected against the sky. "Heaven help us!" I cried; "it is the left tower; it has been struck and is on fire!"

I hurried on my clothes and stepped into the corridor; the girls were there before me. Jeannette came up to me instantly with anxious face. "Oh, Doctor Thornton, what shall we do? papa and mamma and little Johnny are in the old left tower. It is on fire. I have knocked and knocked, but get no answer."

"Don't be alarmed," said I soothingly. "Jenkins, ring the alarm bell," I continued, turning to the butler who was standing near; "the rest follow me. We will force the entrance to the Captain's room."

Instantly, it seemed to me, the bell boomed out upon the now silent air, for the storm had died down as quickly as it arose; and as our little procession paused before the entrance to the old left tower, we could distinguish the sound of the fire engines already on their way from the village.

The door resisted all our efforts; there seemed to be a barrier against it which nothing could move. The flames were gaining headway. Still the same deathly silence within the rooms.

"Oh, will they never get here?" cried Talma, ringing her hands in terror. Jeannette said nothing, but her face was ashen. The servants were huddled together in a panic-stricken group. I can never tell you what a relief it was when we heard the first sound of the firemen's voices, saw their quick movements, and heard the ringing of the axes with which they cut away every obstacle to our entrance to the rooms. The neighbors who had just enjoyed the hospitality of the house were now gathered around offering all the assistance in their power. In less than fifteen minutes the fire was out, and the men began to bear the unconscious inmates from the ruins. They carried them to the pagoda so lately the scene of mirth and pleasure, and I took up my station there, ready to assume my professional duties. The Captain was nearest me; and as I stooped to make the necessary examination I reeled away from the ghastly sight which confronted me—*gentlemen, across the Captain's throat was a deep gash that severed the jugular vein!*

The Doctor paused, and the hand with which he refilled his glass trembled violently.

"What is it, Doctor?" cried the men, gathering about me.

"Take the women away; this is murder!"

"Murder!" cried Jeannette, as she fell against the side of the pagoda.

"Murder!" screamed Talma, staring at me as if unable to grasp my meaning.

I continued my examination of the bodies, and found that the same thing had happened to Mrs. Gordon and to little Johnny.

The police were notified; and when the sun rose over the dripping town he found them in charge of Gordon Hall, the servants standing in excited knots talking over the crime, the friends of the family confounded, and the two girls trying to comfort each other and realize the terrible misfortune that had overtaken them.

Nothing in the rooms of the left tower seemed to have been disturbed. The door of communication between the rooms of the husband and wife was open, as they had arranged it for the night. Little Johnny's crib was placed beside his mother's bed. In it he was found as though never awakened by the storm. It was quite evident that the assassin was no common ruffian. The chief gave strict orders for a watch to be kept on all strangers or suspicious characters who were seen in the neighborhood. He made inquiries among the servants, seeing each one separately, but there was nothing gained from them. No one had heard anything suspicious; all had been awakened by the storm. The chief was puzzled. Here was a triple crime for which no motive could be assigned.

"What do you think of it?" I asked him, as we stood together on the lawn.

"It is my opinion that the deed was committed by one of the higher classes, which makes the mystery more difficult to solve. I tell you, Doctor, there are mysteries that never come to light, and this, I think, is one of them."

While we were talking Jenkins, the butler, an old and trusted servant, came up to the chief and saluted respectfully. "Want to speak with me, Jenkins?" he asked. The man nodded, and they walked away together.

The story of the inquest was short, but appalling. It was shown that Talma had been allowed to go abroad to study because she and Mrs. Gordon did not get on well together. From the testimony of Jenkins it seemed that Talma and her father had quarrelled bitterly about her lover, a young artist whom she had met at Rome, who was unknown to fame, and very poor. There had been terrible things said by each, and threats even had passed, all of which now rose up in judgment against the unhappy girl. The examination of the family solicitor revealed the fact that Captain Gordon intended to leave his daughters only a small annuity, the bulk of the fortune going to his son Jonathan, junior. This was a monstrous injustice, as everyone felt. In vain Talma protested her innocence. Someone must have done it. No one would be benefited so much by these deaths as she and her sister. Moreover, the will, together with other papers, was nowhere to be found. Not the slightest clue bearing upon the disturbing elements in this family, if any there were, was to be found. As the only surviving relatives, Jeannette and Talma became joint heirs to an immense fortune, which only for the bloody tragedy just enacted would, in all probability, have passed them by. Here was the motive. The case was very black against Talma. The foreman stood up. The silence was intense: We "find that Capt. Jonathan Gordon, Mary E. Gordon and Jonathan Gordon, junior, all deceased, came to their deaths by means of a knife or other sharp instrument in the hands of Talma Gordon." The girl was like one stricken with death. The flower-like mouth was drawn and pinched; the great sapphire-blue eyes were black with passionate anguish, terror and despair. She was placed in jail to await her trial at the fall session of the criminal court. The excitement in the hitherto quiet town rose to fever heat. Many points in the evidence seemed incomplete to thinking men. The weapon could not be found, nor could it be divined what had become of it. No reason could be given for the murder except the quarrel between Talma and her father and the ill will which existed between the girl and her stepmother.

When the trial was called Jeannette sat beside Talma in the prisoner's dock; both were arrayed in deepest mourning. Talma was pale and careworn, but seemed uplifted, spiritualized, as it were. Upon Jeannette the full realization of her sister's peril seemed to weigh heavily. She had changed much too: hollow cheeks, tottering steps, eyes blazing with fever, all suggestive of rapid and premature decay. From far-off Italy Edward Turner, growing famous in the art world, came to stand beside his girl-love in this hour of anguish.

The trial was a memorable one. No additional evidence had been collected to strengthen the prosecution; when the attorney-general rose to open the case against Talma he knew, as everyone else did, that he could not convict solely on the evidence ad-

duced. What was given did not always bear upon the case, and
brought out strange stories of Captain Jonathan's methods. Tales
were told of sailors who had sworn to take his life, in revenge
for injuries inflicted upon them by his hand. One or two clues
were followed, but without avail. The judge summed up the evidence impartially, giving the prisoner the benefit of the doubt.
The points in hand furnished valuable collateral evidence, but
were not direct proof. Although the moral presumption was
against the prisoner, legal evidence was lacking to actually convict. The jury found the prisoner "Not Guilty," owing to the
fact that the evidence was entirely circumstantial. The verdict
was received in painful silence; then a murmur of discontent ran
through the great crowd.

"She must have done it," said one; "who else has been benefited by the horrible deed?"

"A poor woman would not have fared so well at the hands
of the jury, nor a homely one either, for that matter," said
another.

The great Gordon trial was ended; innocent or guilty, Talma
Gordon could not be tried again. She was free; but her liberty,
with blasted prospects and fair fame gone forever, was valueless
to her. She seemed to have but one object in her mind: to find
the murderer or murderers of her parents and half-brother. By
her direction the shrewdest of detectives were employed and
money flowed like water, but to no purpose; the Gordon tragedy remained a mystery. I had consented to act as one of the
trustees of the immense Gordon estates and business interests,
and by my advice the Misses Gordon went abroad. A year later
I received a letter from Edward Turner, saying that Jeannette
Gordon had died suddenly at Rome, and that Talma, after refusing all his entreaties for an early marriage, had disappeared,
leaving no clue as to her whereabouts. I could give the poor
fellow no comfort, although I had been duly notified of the
death of Jeannette by Talma, in a letter telling me where to forward her remittances, and at the same time requesting me to keep
her present residence secret, especially from Edward.

I had established a sanitarium for the cure of chronic diseases
at Gordonville, and absorbed in the cares of my profession I

gave little thought to the Gordons. I seemed fated to be involved in mysteries.

A man claiming to be an Englishman, and fresh from the California gold fields, engaged board and professional service at my retreat. I found him suffering in the grasp of the tubercle-fiend[6]—the last stages. He called himself Simon Cameron. Seldom have I seen so fascinating and wicked a face. The lines of the mouth were cruel, the eyes cold and sharp, the smile mocking and evil. He had money in plenty but seemed to have no friends, for he had received no letters and had had no visitors in the time he had been with us. He was an enigma to me; and his nationality puzzled me, for of course I did not believe his story of being English. The peaceful influence of the house seemed to soothe him in a measure, and make his last steps to the mysterious valley as easy as possible. For a time he improved, and would sit or walk about the grounds and sing sweet songs for the pleasure of the other inmates. Strange to say, his malady only affected his voice at times. He sang quaint songs in a silvery tenor of great purity and sweetness that was delicious to the listening ear:

> "A wet sheet and a flowing sea,
>   A wind that follows fast,
> And fills the white and rustling sail
>   And bends the gallant mast;
> And bends the gallant mast, my boys;
>   While like the eagle free,
> Away the good ship flies, and leaves
>   Old England on the lea."[7]

There are few singers on the lyric stage who could surpass Simon Cameron.

One night, a few weeks after Cameron's arrival, I sat in my office making up my accounts when the door opened and closed; I glanced up, expecting to see a servant. A lady advanced toward me. She threw back her veil, and then I saw that Talma Gordon, or her ghost, stood before me. After the first excitement of our meeting was over, she told me she had come direct from Paris, to place herself in my care. I had studied her attentively during the first moments of our meeting, and I felt that she was right; unless something unforeseen happened to arouse her from the stupor into which she seemed to have fallen, the last Gordon was doomed to an early death. The next day I told her I had cabled Edward Turner to come to her.

"It will do no good; I cannot marry him," was her only comment.

"Have you no feeling of pity for that faithful fellow?" I asked her sternly, provoked by her seeming indifference. I shall never forget the varied emotions depicted on her speaking face. Fully revealed to my gaze was the sight of a human soul tortured beyond the point of endurance; suffering all things, enduring all things, in the silent agony of despair.

In a few days Edward arrived, and Talma consented to see him and explain her refusal to keep her promise to him. "You must be present, Doctor; it is due your long, tried friendship to know that I have not been fickle, but have acted from the best and strongest motives."

I shall never forget that day. It was directly after lunch that we met in the library. I was greatly excited, expecting I knew not what. Edward was agitated, too. Talma was the only calm one. She handed me what seemed to be a letter, with the request that I would read it. Even now I think I can repeat every word of the document, so indelibly are the words engraved upon my mind:

MY DARLING SISTER TALMA: When you read these lines I shall be no more, for I shall not live to see your life blasted by the same knowledge that has blighted mine.

One evening, about a year before your expected return from Rome, I climbed into a hammock in one corner of the veranda outside the breakfast-room windows, intending to spend the twilight hours in lazy comfort, for it was very hot, enervating August weather. I fell asleep. I was awakened by voices. Because of the heat the rooms had been left in semi-darkness. As I lay there, lazily enjoying the beauty of the perfect summer night, my wandering thoughts were arrested by words spoken by our father to Mrs. Gordon, for they were the occupants of the breakfast-room.

"Never fear, Mary; Johnny shall have it all—money, houses, land and business."

"But if you do go first, Jonathan, what will happen if the girls contest the will? People will think that they ought to have the money as it appears to be theirs by law. I never could survive the terrible disgrace of the story."

"Don't borrow trouble; all you would need to do would be to show them papers I have drawn up, and they would be glad to take their annuity and say nothing. After all, I do not think it is so bad. Jeannette can teach; Talma can paint; six hundred dollars a year is quite enough for them."

I had been somewhat mystified by the conversation until now. This last remark solved the riddle. What could he mean? teach, paint, six hundred a year! With my usual impetuosity I sprang from my resting-place, and in a moment stood in the room confronting my father, and asking what he meant. I could see plainly that both were disconcerted by my unexpected appearance.

"Ah, wretched girl! you have been listening. But what could I expect of your mother's daughter?"

At these words I felt the indignant blood rush to my head in a torrent. So it had been all my life. Before you could remember, Talma, I had felt my little heart swell with anger at the disparaging hints and slurs concerning our mother. Now was my time. I determined that tonight I would know why she was looked upon as an outcast, and her children subjected to every humiliation. So I replied to my father in bitter anger:

"I was not listening; I fell asleep in the hammock. What do you mean by a paltry six hundred a year each to Talma and to me? 'My mother's daughter' demands an explanation from you, sir, of the meaning of the monstrous injustice that you have always practised toward my sister and me."

"Speak more respectfully to your father, Jeannette," broke in Mrs. Gordon.

"How is it, madam, that you look for respect from one whom you have delighted to torment ever since you came into this most unhappy family?"

"Hush, both of you," said Captain Gordon, who seemed to have recovered from the dismay into which my sudden appear-

ance and passionate words had plunged him. "I think I may as
well tell you as to wait. Since you know so much, you may
as well know the whole miserable story." He motioned me to a
seat. I could see that he was deeply agitated. I seated myself in
a chair he pointed out, in wonder and expectation,—expectation
of I knew not what. I trembled. This was a supreme moment in
my life; I felt it. The air was heavy with the intense stillness that
had settled over us as the common sounds of day gave place to
the early quiet of the rural evening. I could see Mrs. Gordon's
face as she sat within the radius of the lighted hallway. There
was a smile of triumph upon it. I clinched my hands and bit my
lips until the blood came, in the effort to keep from screaming.
What was I about to hear? At last he spoke:

"I was disappointed at your birth, and also at the birth of
Talma. I wanted a male heir. When I knew that I should again
be a father I was torn by hope and fear, but I comforted myself
with the thought that luck would be with me in the birth of the
third child. When the doctor brought me word that a son was
born to the house of Gordon, I was wild with delight, and did
not notice his disturbed countenance. In the midst of my joy he
said to me:

" 'Captain Gordon, there is something strange about this
birth. I want you to see this child.'

"Quelling my exultation I followed him to the nursery, and
there, lying in the cradle, I saw a child dark as a mulatto, with
the characteristic features of the Negro! I was stunned. Gradually it dawned upon me that there was something radically
wrong. I turned to the doctor for an explanation.

" 'There is but one explanation, Captain Gordon; there is Negro blood in this child.'

" 'There is no Negro blood in my veins,' I said proudly. Then
I paused—*the mother!*—I glanced at the doctor. He was watching me intently. The same thought was in his mind. I must have
lived a thousand years in that cursed five seconds that I stood
there confronting the physician and trying to think. 'Come,'
said I to him, 'let us end this suspense.' Without thinking of
consequences, I hurried away to your mother and accused her
of infidelity to her marriage vows. I raved like a madman. Your
mother fell into convulsions; her life was despaired of. I sent for

Mr. and Mrs. Franklin, and then I learned the truth. They were childless. One year while on a Southern tour, they befriended an octoroon[8] girl who had been abandoned by her white lover. Her child was a beautiful girl baby. They, being Northern born, thought little of caste distinction because the child showed no trace of Negro blood. They determined to adopt it. They went abroad, secretly sending back word to their friends at a proper time, of the birth of a little daughter. No one doubted the truth of the statement. They made Isabel their heiress, and all went well until the birth of your brother. Your mother and the unfortunate babe died. This is the story which, if known, would bring dire disgrace upon the Gordon family.

"To appease my righteous wrath, Mr. Franklin left a codicil to his will by which all the property is left at my disposal save a small annuity to you and your sister."

I sat there after he had finished his story, stunned by what I had heard. I understood, now, Mrs. Gordon's half contemptuous toleration and lack of consideration for us both. As I rose from my seat to leave the room I said to Captain Gordon:

"Still, in spite of all, sir, I am a Gordon, legally born. I will not tamely give up my birthright."

I left that room a broken-hearted girl, filled with a desire for revenge upon this man, my father, who by his manner disowned us without a regret. Not once in that remarkable interview did he speak of our mother as his wife; he quietly repudiated her and us with all the cold cruelty of relentless caste prejudice. I heard the treatment of your lover's proposal: I knew why Captain Gordon's consent to your marriage was withheld.

The night of the reception and dance was the chance for which I had waited, planned and watched. I crept from my window into the ivy-vines, and so down, down, until I stood upon the window-sill of Captain Gordon's room in the old left tower. How did I do it, you ask? I do not know. The house was silent after the revel; the darkness of the gathering storm favored me, too. The lawyer was there that day. The will was signed and put safely away among my father's papers. I was determined to have the will and the other documents bearing upon the case, and I would have revenge, too, for the cruelties we had suffered. With the old East Indian dagger firmly grasped I entered the room and found—that my revenge had been forestalled! The horror of the discovery I made that night restored me to reason and a realization of the crime I meditated. Scarce knowing what I did, I sought and found the papers, and crept back to my room as I had come. Do you wonder that my disease is past medical aid?

I looked at Edward as I finished. He sat, his face covered with his hands. Finally he looked up with a glance of haggard despair: "God! Doctor, but this is too much. I could stand the stigma of murder, but add to that the pollution of Negro blood! No man is brave enough to face such a situation."

"It is as I thought it would be," said Talma sadly, while the tears poured over her white face. "I do not blame you, Edward."

He rose from his chair, wrung my hand in a convulsive clasp, turned to Talma and bowed profoundly, with his eyes fixed upon the floor, hesitated, turned, paused, bowed again and abruptly left the room. So those two who had been lovers, parted. I turned to Talma, expecting her to give way. She smiled a pitiful smile, and said: "You see, Doctor, I knew best."

From that on she failed rapidly. I was restless. If only I could rouse her to an interest in life, she might live to old age. So rich, so young, so beautiful, so talented, so pure; I grew savage thinking of the injustice of the world. I had not reckoned on the power that never sleeps. Something was about to happen.

On visiting Cameron next morning I found him approaching the end. He had been sinking for a week very rapidly. As I sat by the bedside holding his emaciated hand, he fixed his bright, wicked eyes on me, and asked: "How long have I got to live?"

"Candidly, but a few hours."

"Thank you; well, I want death; I am not afraid to die. Doctor, Cameron is not my name."

"I never supposed it was."

"No? You are sharper than I thought. I heard all your talk yesterday with Talma Gordon. Curse the whole race!"

He clasped his bony fingers around my arm and gasped: "*I murdered the Gordons!*"

Had I the pen of a Dumas[9] I could not paint Cameron as he told his story. It is a question with me whether this wheeling planet, home of the suffering, doubting, dying, may not hold worse agonies on its smiling surface than those of the conventional hell. I sent for Talma and a lawyer. We gave him stimulants, and then with broken intervals of coughing and prostration we got the story of the Gordon murder. I give it to you in a few words:

"I am an East Indian, but my name does not matter, Cameron is as good as any. There is many a soul crying in heaven and hell for vengeance on Jonathan Gordon. Gold was his idol; and many a good man walked the plank, and many a gallant ship was stripped of her treasure, to satisfy his lust for gold. His blackest crime was the murder of my father, who was his friend, and had sailed with him for many a year as mate. One night these two went ashore together to bury their treasure. My father never returned from that expedition. His body was afterward found with a bullet through the heart on the shore where the vessel stopped that night. It was the custom then among pirates for the captain to kill the men who helped bury their treasure. Captain Gordon was no better than a pirate. An East Indian never forgets, and I swore by my mother's deathbed to hunt Captain Gordon down until I had avenged my father's murder. I had the plans of the Gordon estate, and fixed on the night of the reception in honor of Talma as the time for my vengeance. There is a secret entrance from the shore to the chambers where Captain Gordon slept; no one knew of it save the Captain and trusted members of his crew. My mother gave me the plans, and entrance and escape were easy."

So the great mystery was solved. In a few hours Cameron was no more. We placed the confession in the hands of the police, and there the matter ended.

"But what became of Talma Gordon?" questioned the president. "Did she die?"

"Gentlemen," said the Doctor, rising to his feet and sweeping the faces of the company with his eagle gaze, "gentlemen, if you will follow me to the drawing-room, I shall have much pleasure in introducing you to my wife—*nee* Talma Gordon."

BRO'R ABR'M JIMSON'S WEDDING

A CHRISTMAS STORY

It was a Sunday in early spring the first time that Caramel Johnson dawned on the congregation of —— Church in a populous New England city.

The Afro-Americans of that city are well-to-do, being of a frugal nature, and considering it a lasting disgrace for any man among them, desirous of social standing in the community, not to make himself comfortable in this world's goods against the coming time, when old age creeps on apace and renders him unfit for active business.

Therefore the members of the said church had not waited to be exhorted by reformers to own their unpretentious homes and small farms outside the city limits, but they vied with each other in efforts to accumulate a small competency urged thereto by a realization of what pressing needs the future might bring, or it might have been because of the constant example of white neighbors, and a due respect for the dignity which *their* foresight had brought to the superior race.

Of course, these small Vanderbilts and Astors[1] of a darker hue must have a place of worship in accord with their worldly prosperity, and so it fell out that —— Church was the richest plum in the ecclesiastical pudding, and greatly sought by scholarly divines as a resting place for four years,—the extent of the time-limit allowed by conference to the men who must be provided with suitable charges according to the demands of their energy and scholarship.

The attendance was unusually large for morning service, and a restless movement was noticeable all through the sermon. How strange a thing is nature; the change of the seasons announces itself in all humanity as well as in the trees and flowers, the grass, and in the atmosphere. Something within us responds instantly to the touch of kinship that dwells in all life.

The air, soft and balmy, laden with rich promise for the future, came through the massive, half-open windows, stealing in refreshing waves upon the congregation. The sunlight fell through the colored glass of the windows in prismatic hues, and dancing all over the lofty star-gemmed ceiling, painted the hue of the broad vault of heaven, creeping down in crinkling shadows to touch the deep garnet cushions of the sacred desk, and the rich wood of the altar with a hint of gold.

The offertory[2] was ended. The silvery cadences of a rich soprano voice still lingered on the air, "O, Worship the Lord in the beauty of holiness." There was a suppressed feeling of expectation, but not the faintest rustle as the minister rose in the pulpit, and after a solemn pause, gave the usual invitation:

"If there is anyone in this congregation desiring to unite with this church, either by letter or on probation, please come forward to the altar."

The words had not died upon his lips when a woman started from her seat near the door and passed up the main aisle. There was a sudden commotion on all sides. Many heads were turned—it takes so little to interest a church audience. The girls in the choir-box leaned over the rail, nudged each other and giggled, while the men said to one another, "She's a stunner, and no mistake."

The candidate for membership, meanwhile, had reached the altar railing and stood before the man of God, to whom she had handed her letter from a former Sabbath home, with head decorously bowed as became the time and the holy place. There was no denying the fact that she was a pretty girl; brown of skin, small of feature, with an ever-lurking gleam of laughter in eyes coal black. Her figure was slender and beautifully moulded, with a seductive grace in the undulating walk and erect carriage. But the chief charm of the sparkling dark face lay in its intelligence, and the responsive play of facial expression which was enhanced by two mischievous dimples pressed into the rounded cheeks by the caressing fingers of the god of Love.

The minister whispered to the candidate, coughed, blew his nose on his snowy clerical handkerchief, and, finally, turned to the expectant congregation:

"Sister Chocolate Caramel Johnson—"

He was interrupted by a snicker and a suppressed laugh, again from the choir-box, and an audible whisper which sounded distinctly throughout the quiet church,—

"I'd get the Legislature to change that if it was mine, 'deed I would!" then silence profound caused by the reverend's stern glance of reproval bent on the offenders in the choir-box.

"Such levity will not be allowed among the members of the choir. If it occurs again, I shall ask the choir master for the names of the offenders and have their places taken by those more worthy to be gospel singers."

Thereupon Mrs. Tilly Anderson whispered to Mrs. Nancy Tobias that, "them choir gals is the mos' deceivines' hussies in the church, an' for my part, I'm glad the pastor called 'em down. That sister's too good lookin' fer 'em, an' they'll be after her like er pack o' houn's, min' me, Sis' Tobias."

Sister Tobias ducked her head in her lap and shook her fat sides in laughing appreciation of the sister's foresight.

Order being restored the minister proceeded:

"Sister Chocolate Caramel Johnson brings a letter to us from our sister church in Nashville, Tennessee. She has been a member in good standing for ten years, having been received into fellowship at ten years of age. She leaves them now, much to their regret, to pursue the study of music at one of the large conservatories in this city, and they recommend her to our love and care. You know the contents of the letter. All in favor of giving Sister Johnson the right hand of fellowship, please manifest the same by a rising vote." The whole congregation rose.

"Contrary minded? None. The ayes have it. Be seated, friends. Sister Johnson it gives me great pleasure to receive you into this church. I welcome you to its joys and sorrows. May God bless you, Brother Jimson?" (Brother Jimson stepped from his seat to the pastor's side.) "I assign this sister to your class. Sister Johnson, this is Brother Jimson, your future spiritual teacher."

Brother Jimson shook the hand of his new member, warmly, and she returned to her seat. The minister pronounced the benediction over the waiting congregation; the organ burst into richest melody. Slowly the crowd of worshippers dispersed.

Abraham Jimson had made his money as a janitor for the wealthy people of the city. He was a bachelor, and when reproved by some good Christian brother for still dwelling in single blessedness always offered as an excuse that he had been too

busy to think of a wife, but that now he was "well fixed," pe-
cuniarily, he would begin to "look over" his lady friends for a
suitable companion.

He owned a house in the suburbs and a fine brick dwelling-
house in the city proper. He was a trustee of prominence in the
church; in fact, its "solid man," and his opinion was sought and
his advice acted upon by his associates on the Board. It was felt
that any lady in the congregation would be proud to know herself his choice.

When Caramel Johnson received the right hand of fellowship,
her aunt, the widow Maria Nash, was ahead in the race for the
wealthy class-leader. It had been neck-and-neck for a while between her and Sister Viney Peters, but, finally it had settled
down to Sister Maria with a hundred to one, among the sporting
members of the Board, that she carried off the prize, for Sister
Maria owned a house adjoining Brother Jimson's in the suburbs,
and property counts these days.

Sister Nash had "no idea" when she sent for her niece to
come to B. that the latter would prove a rival; her son Andy was
as good as engaged to Caramel. But it is always the unexpected
that happens. Caramel came, and Brother Jimson had no eyes
for the charms of other women after he had gazed into her coal
black orbs, and watched her dimples come and go.

Caramel decided to accept a position as housemaid in order
to help defray the expenses of her tuition at the conservatory,
and Brother Jimson interested himself so warmly in her behalf
that she soon had a situation in the home of his richest patron
where it was handy for him to chat with her about the business
of the church, and the welfare of her soul, in general. Things
progressed very smoothly until the fall, when one day Sister
Maria had occasion to call, unexpectedly, on her niece and found
Brother Jimson basking in her smiles while he enjoyed a sump-
tuous dinner of roast chicken and fixings.

To say that Sister Maria was "set way back" would not accurately describe her feelings; but from that time Abraham Jimson knew that he had a secret foe in the Widow Nash.

Before many weeks had passed it was publicly known that
Brother Jimson would lead Caramel Johnson to the altar "come
Christmas." There was much sly speculation as to the "widder's

gittin' left," and how she took it from those who had cast hopeless glances toward the chief man of the church. Great preparations were set on foot for the wedding festivities. The bride's
trousseau was a present from the groom and included a white
satin wedding gown and a costly gold watch. The town house
was refurnished, and a trip to New York was in contemplation.

"Hump!" grunted Sister Nash when told the rumors, "there's
no fool like an ol' fool. Car'mel's a han'ful he'll fin', ef he gits
her."

"I reckon he'll git her all right, Sis' Nash," laughed the neighbor, who had run in to talk over the news.

"I've said my word an' I ain't goin' change it, Sis'r. Min' me.
I says, *ef he gits her,* an, I mean it."

Andy Nash was also a member of Brother Jimson's class; he
possessed, too, a strong sweet baritone voice which made him
of great value to the choir. He was an immense success in the
social life of the city, and had created sad havoc with the hearts
of the colored girls; he could have his pick of the best of them
because of his graceful figure and fine easy manners. Until Caramel had been dazzled by the wealth of her elderly lover, she
had considered herself fortunate as the lady of his choice.

It was Sunday, three weeks before the wedding that Andy
resolved to have it out with Caramel.

"She's been hot an' she's been col', an' now she's luke warm,
an' today ends it before this gent-man sleeps," he told himself
as he stood before the glass and tied his pale blue silk tie in a
stunning knot, and settled his glossy tile at a becoming angle.

Brother Jimson's class was a popular one and had a large
membership; the hour spent there was much enjoyed, even by
visitors. Andy went into the vestry early resolved to meet Caramel if possible. She was there, at the back of the room sitting
alone on a settee. Andy immediately seated himself in the vacant
place by her side. There were whispers and much head-shaking
among the few early worshippers, all of whom knew the story
of the young fellow's romance and his disappointment.

As he dropped into the seat beside her, Caramel turned her
large eyes on him intently, speculatively, with a doubtful sort of
curiosity suggested in her expression, as to how he took her
flagrant desertion.

"Howdy, Car'mel?" was his greeting without a shade of resentment.

"I'm well; no need to ask how you are," was the quick response. There was a mixture of cordiality and coquetry in her manner. Her eyes narrowed and glittered under lowered lids, as she gave him a long side-glance. How could she help showing her admiration for the supple young giant beside her? "Surely," she told herself, "I'll have long time enough to git sick of old rheumatics,"[3] her pet name for her elderly lover.

"I ain't sick much," was Andy's surly reply.

He leaned his elbow on the back of the settee and gave his recent sweetheart a flaming glance of mingled love and hate, oblivious to the presence of the assembled class-members.

"You ain't over friendly these days, Car'mel, but I gits news of your capers 'roun' 'bout some of the members."

"My—Yes?" she answered as she flashed her great eyes at him in pretended surprise. He laughed a laugh not good to hear.

"Yes," he drawled. Then he added with sudden energy, "Are you goin' to tie up to old Rheumatism sure 'nuff, come Chris'mas?"

"Come Chris'mas, Andy, I be. I hate to tell you but I have to do it."

He recoiled as from a blow. As for the girl, she found a keen relish in the situation; it flattered her vanity.

"How comes it you've changed your mind, Car'mel, 'bout you an' me? You've tol' me often that I was your first choice."

"We—ll," she drawled, glancing uneasily about her and avoiding her aunt's gaze, which she knew was bent upon her every movement, "I did reckon once I would. But a man with money suits me best, an' you ain't got a cent."

"No more have you. You ain't no better than other women to work an' help a man along, is you?"

The color flamed an instant in her face turning the dusky skin to a deep, dull red.

"Andy Nash, you always was a fool, an' as ignerunt as a wil' Injun. I mean to have a sure nuff brick house an' plenty of money. That makes people respec' you. Why don' you quit bein' so shifless and save your money. You ain't worth your salt."

"Your head's turned with pianorer-playin' an' livin' up

North. Ef you'll turn *him* off an' come back home, I'll turn over a new leaf, Car'mel," his voice was soft and persuasive enough now.

She had risen to her feet; her eyes flashed, her face was full of pride.

"I won't. I've quit likin' you, Andy Nash."

"Are you in earnest?" he asked, also rising from his seat.

"Dead earnes'."

"Then there's no more to be said."

He spoke calmly, not raising his voice above a whisper. She stared at him in surprise. Then he added as he swung on his heel preparatory to leaving her:

"You ain't got him yet, my gal. But remember, I'm waitin' for you when you need me."

While this whispered conference was taking place in the back part of the vestry, Brother Jimson had entered, and many an anxious glance he cast in the direction of the couple. Andy made his way slowly to his mother's side as Brother Jimson rose in his place to open the meeting. There was a commotion on all sides as the members rustled down on their knees for prayer. Widow Nash whispered to her son as they knelt side by side:

"How did you make out, Andy?"

"Didn't make out at all, mammy; she's as obstinate as a mule."

"Well, then, there's only one thing mo' to do."

Andy was unpleasant company for the remainder of the day. He sought, but found nothing to palliate Caramel's treachery. He had only surly, bitter words for his companions who ventured to address him, as the outward expression of inward tumult. The more he brooded over his wrongs the worse he felt. When he went to work on Monday morning he was feeling vicious. He had made up his mind to do something desperate. The wedding should not come off. He would be avenged.

Andy went about his work at the hotel in gloomy silence unlike his usual gay hilarity. It happened that all the female help at the great hostelry was white, and on that particular Monday morning it was the duty of Bridget McCarthy's watch to clean the floors. Bridget was also not in the best of humors, for Pat McClosky, her special company, had gone to the priest's with her rival, Kate Connerton, on Sunday afternoon, and Bridget had not yet got over the effects of a strong rum punch taken to quiet her nerves after hearing the news.

Bridget had scrubbed a wide swath of the marble floor when Andy came through with a rush order carried in scientific style high above his head, balanced on one hand. Intent upon satisfying the guest who was princely in his "tips," Andy's unwary feet became entangled in the maelstrom of brooms, scrubbing-brushes and pails. In an instant the "order" was sliding over the floor in a general mix-up.

To say Bridget was mad wouldn't do her state justice. She forgot herself and her surroundings and relieved her feelings in elegant Irish, ending a tirade of abuse by calling Andy a "wall-eyed, bandy-legged nagur."[4]

Andy couldn't stand that from "common, po' white trash," so calling all his science into play he struck out straight from the shoulder with his right, and brought her a swinging blow on the mouth, which seated her neatly in the five-gallon bowl of freshly made lobster salad which happened to be standing on the floor behind her.

There was a wail from the kitchen force that reached to every department. It being the busiest hour of the day when they served dinner, the dish-washers and scrubbers went on a strike against the "nagur who struck Bridget McCarthy, the baste,"[5] mingled with cries of "lynch him!" Instantly the great basement floor was a battle ground. Every colored man seized whatever was handiest and ranged himself by Andy's side, and stood ready to receive the onslaught of the Irish brigade. For the sake of peace, and sorely against his inclinations, the proprietor surrendered Andy to the police on a charge of assault and battery.

On Wednesday morning of that eventful week, Brother Jimson wended his way to his house in the suburbs to collect the rent. Unseen by the eye of man, he was wrestling with a problem that had shadowed his life for many years. No one on earth suspected him unless it might be the widow. Brother Jimson boasted of his consistent Christian life—rolled his piety like a sweet morsel beneath his tongue, and had deluded himself into thinking that *he* could do no sin. There were scoffers in the church who doubted the genuineness of his pretensions, and he believed that there was a movement on foot against his power led by Widow Nash.

Brother Jimson groaned in bitterness of spirit. His only fear was that he might be parted from Caramel. If he lost her he felt that all happiness in life was over for him, and anxiety gave him a sickening feeling of unrest. He was tormented, too, by jealousy; and when he was called upon by Andy's anxious mother to rescue her son from the clutches of the law, he had promised her fair enough, but in reality resolved to do nothing but—tell the judge that Andy was a dangerous character whom it was best to quell by severity. The pastor and all the other influential members of the church were at court on Tuesday, but Brother Jimson was conspicuous by his absence.

Today Brother Jimson resolved to call on Sister Nash, and, as he had heard nothing of the outcome of the trial, make cautious inquiries concerning that, and also sound her on the subject nearest his heart.

He opened the gate and walked down the side path to the back door. From within came the rhythmic sound of a rubbing board. The brother knocked, and then cleared his throat with a preliminary cough.

"Come," called a voice within. As the door swung open it revealed the spare form of the widow, who with sleeves rolled above her elbows stood at the tub cutting her way through piles of foaming suds.

"Mornin', Sis' Nash! How's all?"

"That you, Bro'r Jimson? How's yourself? Take a cheer an' make yourself to home."

"Cert'nly, Sis' Nash; don' care ef I do," and the good brother scanned the sister with an eagle eye. "Yas'm, I'm purty tol'rable these days, thank God. Bleeg'd to you, Sister, I jes' will stop an' res' myself befo' I repair myself back to the city." He seated himself in the most comfortable chair in the room, tilted it on the two back legs against the wall, lit his pipe and with a grunt of satisfaction settled back to watch the white rings of smoke curl about his head.

"These are mighty ticklish times, Sister. How's you continue on the journey? Is you strong in the faith?"

"I've got the faith, my brother, but I ain't on no mountain

top this week. I'm way down in the valley; I'm jes' coaxin' the Lord to keep me sweet," and Sister Nash wiped the suds from her hands and prodded the clothes in the boiler with the clothes-stick, added fresh pieces and went on with her work.

"This is a worl' strewed with wrecks an' floatin' with tears. It's the valley of tribulation. May your faith continue. I hear Jim Jinkins has bought a farm up Taunton[6] way."

"Wan' ter know!"

"Doctor tells me Bro'r Waters is comin' after Chris-mus. They do say as how he's stirrin' up things turrible; he's easin' his min' on this lynchin' business, an' it's high time—high time."

"Sho! Don' say so! What you reck'n he's goin' tell us now, Brother Jimson?"

"Suthin' 'stonishin', Sister; it'll stir the country from end to end. Yes'm, the Council is powerful strong as an organ'zation."

"Sho! sho!" and the "thrub, thrub" of the board could be heard a mile away.

The conversation flagged. Evidently Widow Nash was not in a talkative mood that morning. The brother was disappointed.

"Well, it's mighty comfort'ble here, but I mus' be goin'."

"What's your hurry, Brother Jimson?"

"Business, Sister, business," and the brother brought his chair forward preparatory to rising. "Where's Andy? How'd he come out of that little difficulty?"

"Locked up."

"You don' mean to say he's in jail?"

"Yes; he's in jail 'tell I git's his bail."

"What might the sentence be, Sister?"

"Twenty dollars fine or six months at the Islan'." There was silence for a moment, broken only by the "thrub, thrub" of the washboard, while the smoke curled upward from Brother Jimson's pipe as he enjoyed a few last puffs.

"These are mighty ticklish times, Sister. Po' Andy, the way of the transgressor is hard."

Sister Nash took her hands out of the tub and stood with arms akimbo, a statue of Justice carved in ebony. Her voice was like the trump of doom.

"Yes; an' men like you is the cause of it. You leadin' men with money an' chances don' do your duty. I arst you, I arst you fair, to go down to the jedge an' bail that po' chile out. Did you go? No; you hard-faced old devil, you lef him be there, an' I had to git the money from my white folks. Yes, an' I'm breakin' my back now, over that pile of clo's to pay that twenty dollars. Um! all the trouble comes to us women."

"That's so, Sister; that's the livin' truth," murmured Brother Jimson furtively watching the rising storm and wondering where the lightning of her speech would strike next.

"I tell you what it is our receiptfulness to each other is the reason we don' prosper an' God's a-punishin' us with fire an' with sward 'cause we's so jealous an' snaky to each other."

"That's so, Sister; that's the livin' truth."

"Yes, sir; a nigger's boun' to be a nigger 'tell the trump of doom. You kin skin him, but he's a nigger still. Broadcloth, biled shirts an' money won' make him more or less, no, sir."

"That's so, Sister; that's jes' so."

"A nigger can't holp himself. White folks can run agin the law all the time an' they never gits caught, but a nigger! Every time he opens his mouth he puts his foot in it—got to hit that po' white trash gal in the mouth an' git jailed, an' leave his po'r ol' mother to work her fingers to the secon' jint to get him out. Um!"

"These are mighty ticklish times, Sister. Man's boun' to sin; it's his nat'ral state. I hope this will teach Andy humility of the sperit."

"A little humility'd be good for yourself, Abra'm Jimson." Sister Nash ceased her sobs and set her teeth hard.

"Lord, Sister Nash, what compar'son is there 'twixt me an' a worthless nigger like Andy? My business is with the salt of the earth, an' so I have dwelt ever since I was consecrated."

"Salt, of the earth! But ef the salt have los' its saver how you goin' salt it ergin'? No, sir, you cain't do it; it mus' be cas' out an' trodded under foot of men. That's who's goin' happen you Abe Jimson, hyar me? An' I'd like to trod on you with my foot, an' every ol' good fer nuthin' bag o' salt like you," shouted Sister Nash. "You're a snake in the grass; you done stole the boy's gal an' then try to git him sent to the Islan'. You cain't deny it, fer the jedge done tol' me all you said, you ol' rhinoceros-hided hypercrite. Salt of the earth! You!"

Brother Jimson regretted that Widow Nash had found him out. Slowly, he turned, settling his hat on the back of his head.

"Good mornin', Sister Nash. I ain't no hard feelin's agains' you. I'm too near to the kindom to let trifles jar me. My bowels of compassion yearns over you, Sister, a pilgrim an' a stranger in this unfriendly worl'."

No answer from Sister Nash. Brother Jimson lingered.

"Good mornin', Sister," still no answer.

"I hope to see you at the weddin', Sister."

"Keep on hopin'; I'll be there. That gal's my own sister's chile. What in time she wants of a rheumatic ol' sap-head like you for, beats me. I wouldn't marry you for no money, myself; no, sir; it's my belief that you've done goophered[7] her."

"Yes, Sister; I've hearn tell of people refusin' befo' they was ask'd," he retorted, giving her a sly look.

For answer the widow grabbed the clothes-stick and flung it at him in speechless rage.

"My, what a temper it's got," remarked Brother Jimson soothingly as he dodged the shovel, the broom, the coalhod and the stove-covers. But he sighed with relief as he turned into the street and caught the faint sound of the washboard now resumed.

* * *

To a New Englander the season of snow and ice with its clear biting atmosphere, is the ideal time for the great festival. Christmas morning dawned in royal splendor; the sun kissed the snowy streets and turned the icicles into brilliant stalactites. The bells rang a joyous call from every steeple, and soon the churches were crowded with eager worshippers—eager to hear again the oft-repeated, the wonderful story on which the heart of the whole Christian world feeds its faith and hope. Words of tender faith, marvelous in their simplicity fell from the lips of a world-renowned preacher, and touched the hearts of the listening multitude:

"The winter sunshine is not more bright and clear than the atmosphere of living joy, which stretching back between our eyes and that picture of Bethlehem, shows us its beauty in unstained freshness. And as we open once again those chapters of the gospel in which the ever fresh and living picture stands, there seems from year to year always to come some newer, brighter meaning into the words that tell the tale.

"St. Matthew says that when Jesus was born in Bethlehem the wise men came from the East to Jerusalem. The East means man's search after God; Jerusalem means God's search after man. The East means the religion of the devout soul; Jerusalem means the religion of the merciful God. The East means Job's cry, 'Oh, that I knew where I might find him!' Jerusalem means 'Immanuel—God with us.' "

Then the deep-toned organ joined the grand chorus of human voices in a fervent hymn of praise and thanksgiving:

> "Lo! the Morning Star appeareth,
>   O'er the world His beams are cast;
> He the Alpha and Omega,
>   He, the Great, the First the Last!
> Hallelujah! hallelujah!
>   Let the heavenly portal ring!
> Christ is born, the Prince of glory!
>   Christ the Lord, Messiah, King!"

Everyone of prominence in church circles had been bidden to the Jimson wedding. The presents were many and costly. Early after service on Christmas morning the vestry room was taken in hand by leading sisters to prepare the tables for the supper, for on account of the host of friends bidden to the feast, the reception was to be held in the vestry.

The tables groaned beneath their loads of turkey, salads, pies, puddings, cakes and fancy ices.

Yards and yards of evergreen wreaths encircled the granite pillars; the altar was banked with potted plants and cut flowers. It was a beautiful sight. The main aisle was roped off for the invited guests, with white satin ribbons.

Brother Jimson's patrons were to be present in a body, and they had sent the bride a solid silver service so magnificent that the sisters could only sigh with envy.

The ceremony was to take place at seven sharp. Long before that hour the ushers in full evening dress were ready to receive the guests. Sister Maria Nash was among the first to arrive, and even the Queen of Sheba[8] was not arrayed like unto her. At fifteen minutes before the hour, the organist began an elaborate instrumental performance. There was an expectant hush and much head-turning when the music changed to the familiar strains of the "Wedding March." The minister took his place inside the railing ready to receive the party. The groom waited at the altar.

First came the ushers, then the maids of honor, then the flower girl—daughter of a prominent member—carrying a basket of flowers which she scattered before the bride, who was on the arm of the best man. In the bustle and confusion incident to the entrance of the wedding party no one noticed a group of strangers accompanied by Andy Nash, enter and occupy seats near the door.

The service began. All was quiet. The pastor's words fell clearly upon the listening ears. He had reached the words:

"If any man can show just cause, etc.," when like a thunderclap came a voice from the back part of the house—an angry excited voice, and a woman of ponderous avoirdupois[9] advanced up the aisle.

"Hol' on thar, pastor, hol'on! A man cain't have but one wife 'cause it's agin' the law. I'm Abe Jimson's lawful wife, an' hyars his six children—all boys—to pint out their daddy." In an instant the assembly was in confusion.

"My soul," exclaimed Viney Peters, "the ol' sarpen'! An' to think how near I come to takin' up with him. I'm glad I ain't Car'mel."

Sis'r Maria said nothing, but a smile of triumph lit up her countenance.

"Brother Jimson, is this true?" demanded the minister, sternly. But Abraham Jimson was past answering. His face was ashen, his teeth chattering, his hair standing on end. His shaking limbs refused to uphold his weight; he sank upon his knees on the steps of the altar.

But now a hand was laid upon his shoulder and Mrs. Jimson hauled him up on his feet with a jerk.

"Abe Jimson, you know me. You run'd 'way from me up North fifteen years ago, an' you hid yourself like a groun' hog in a hole, but I've got you. There'll be no new wife in the Jimson family this week. I'm yer fus' wife an' I'll be yer las' one. Git up hyar now, you mis'able sinner an' tell the pastor who I be." Brother Jimson meekly obeyed the clarion voice. His sanctified air had vanished; his pride humbled into the dust.

"Pastor," came in trembling tones from his quivering lips. "These are mighty ticklish times." He paused. A deep silence followed his words. "I'm a weak-kneed, mis'able sinner. I have fallen under temptation. This is Ma' Jane, my wife, an' these hyar boys is my sons, God forgive me."

The bride, who had been forgotten now, broke in:

"Abraham Jimson, you ought to be hung. I'm goin' to sue you for breach of promise." It was a fatal remark. Mrs. Jimson turned upon her.

"You will, will you? Sue him, will you? I'll make a choc'late Car'mel of you befo' I'm done with you, you 'ceitful hussy, hoodooin'[10] hones' men from thar wives."

She sprang upon the girl, tearing, biting, rendering. The satin gown and gossamar veil were reduced to rags. Caramel emitted a series of ear-splitting shrieks, but the biting and tearing went on. How it might have ended no one can tell if Andy had not sprang over the backs of the pews and grappled with the infuriated woman.

The excitement was intense. Men and women struggled to get out of the church. Some jumped from the windows and others crawled under the pews, where they were secure from violence. In the midst of the melee, Brother Jimson disappeared and was never seen again, and Mrs. Jimson came into possession of his property by due process of law.

In the church Abraham Jimson's wedding and his fall from grace is still spoken of in eloquent whispers.

*   *   *

In the home of Mrs. Andy Nash a motto adorns the parlor walls worked in scarlet wool and handsomely framed in gilt. The text reads: "Ye are the salt of the earth; there is nothing hidden that shall not be revealed."[11]

W. E. B. DU BOIS

1868–1963

ALTHOUGH the prominent African American writer, speaker, sociologist, and historian W. E. B. Du Bois taught at a number of universities in the United States and published many works of fiction and nonfiction, he is best known for his 1903 book *The Souls of Black Folk*, an analysis of African American life, politics, and philosophy at the turn of the century. Born in Great Barrington, Massachusetts, Du Bois attended Fisk University, a historically black university in Nashville, and later studied at the University of Berlin and received his Ph.D. at Harvard University. Among his books are the sociological study *The Philadelphia Negro* (1899); the historical text *Black Reconstruction* (1935), which worked to correct white histories of the Reconstruction period; a history of Africa titled *The World and Africa* (1947); several novels, including *Dark Princess* (1928); and an autobiography published in 1968.

Initially known for his opposition to Booker T. Washington's accommodationist views, Du Bois formed the Niagara Movement in 1905 and was among the founders of the NAACP in 1909. He later became editor of the NAACP's journal, *The Crisis*, from 1919 to 1932. Though differences of opinion made his work with the NAACP discontinuous, he served on and off until 1948, meanwhile continuing his writing and research. In 1949, Du Bois was vice-chairman of the Council on African Affairs and helped to found the Peace Information Center; for this activity as well as for his socialist views he was indicted by the United States as a subversive agent but was acquitted. He died in 1963 in Ghana, where he had emigrated two years earlier.

ON BEING CRAZY

It was one o'clock and I was hungry. I walked into a restaurant, seated myself and reached for the bill-of-fare. My table companion rose.

"Sir," said he, "do you wish to force your company on those who do not want you?"

No, said I, I wish to eat.

"Are you aware, Sir, that this is social equality?"[1]

Nothing of the sort, Sir, it is hunger,—and I ate.

The day's work done, I sought the theatre. As I sank into my seat, the lady shrank and squirmed.

I beg pardon, I said.

"Do you enjoy being where you are not wanted?" she asked coldly.

Oh no, I said.

"Well you are not wanted here."

I was surprised. I fear you are mistaken, I said. I certainly want the music and I like to think the music wants me to listen to it.

"Usher," said the lady, "this is social equality."

No, madame, said the usher, it is the second movement of Beethoven's Fifth Symphony.

After the theatre, I sought the hotel where I had sent my baggage. The clerk scowled.

"What do you want?" he asked.

Rest, I said.

"This is a white hotel," he said.

I looked around. Such a color scheme requires a great deal of cleaning, I said, but I don't know that I object.

"We object," said he.

Then why—, I began, but he interrupted.

"We don't keep 'niggers,'" he said, "we don't want social equality."

Neither do I. I replied gently, I want a bed.

I walked thoughtfully to the train. I'll take a sleeper[2] through Texas. I'm a bit dissatisfied with this town.

"Can't sell you one."

I only want to hire it, said I, for a couple of nights.

"Can't sell you a sleeper in Texas," he maintained. "They consider that social equality."

I consider it barbarism, I said, and I think I'll walk.

Walking, I met a wayfarer who immediately walked to the other side of the road where it was muddy. I asked his reasons.

" 'Niggers' is dirty," he said.

So is mud, said I. Moreover I added, I am not as dirty as you—at least, not yet.

"But you're a 'nigger,' ain't you?" he asked.

My grandfather was so-called.

"Well then!" he answered triumphantly.

Do you live in the South? I persisted, pleasantly.

"Sure," he growled, "and starve there."

I should think you and the Negroes might get together and vote out starvation.

"We don't let them vote."

We? Why not? I said in surprise.

" 'Niggers' is too ignorant to vote."

But, I said, I am not so ignorant as you.

"But you're a 'nigger.' "

Yes, I'm certainly what you mean by that.

"Well then!" he returned, with that curiously inconsequential note of triumph. "Moreover," he said, "I don't want my sister to marry a nigger."

I had not seen his sister, so I merely murmured, let her say, no.

"By God you shan't marry her, even if she said yes."

But,—but I don't want to marry her, I answered a little perturbed at the personal turn.

"Why not!" he yelled, angrier than ever.

Because I'm already married and I rather like my wife.

"Is she a 'nigger'?" he asked suspiciously.

Well, I said again, her grandmother—was called that.

"*Well then!*" he shouted in that oddly illogical way.

I gave up. Go on, I said, either you are crazy or I am.

"We both are," he said as he trotted along in the mud.

WEST

BRET HARTE

1836–1902

BRET HARTE, the white western local color writer perhaps most responsible for popularizing the genre, moved from his birthplace of Albany, New York, to San Francisco in 1852. After a failed attempt at gold mining, he became a journalist and writer, contributing to the *Golden Era*, the *Californian*, and the *Overland Monthly*, where he also served as editor. After his collection of local color tales *The Luck of Roaring Camp and Other Stories* brought him national fame in 1870, Harte moved to Boston to accept a contract with the *Atlantic Monthly*, which offered $10,000 for a year's writing. The magazine did not renew his contract, however, and his popularity declined. Faced with financial difficulties throughout his later life, Harte served as U.S. consul in Europe and continued to publish stories, poems, short novels (*Gabriel Conroy* in 1876 and *Jeff Briggs's Love Story* in 1880), and plays (*Two Men of Sandy Bar* in 1876 and *Ah Sin* in 1877). Harte is best known for his early sketches of the West such as "The Outcast of Poker Flats" and "The Luck of Roaring Camp," with their mixture of sentimentality and realism, attention to local dialect, and regional humor.

AN INGÉNUE OF THE SIERRAS

I

We all held our breath as the coach rushed through the semidarkness of Galloper's Ridge. The vehicle itself was only a huge lumbering shadow; its side-lights were carefully extinguished, and Yuba Bill had just politely removed from the lips of an outside passenger even the cigar with which he had been osten-

tatiously exhibiting his coolness. For it had been rumored that
the Ramon Martinez gang of "road agents"[1] were "laying" for
us on the second grade, and would time the passage of our lights
across Galloper's in order to intercept us in the "brush" beyond.
If we could cross the ridge without being seen, and so get
through the brush before they reached it, we were safe. If they
followed, it would only be a stern chase with the odds in our
favor.

The huge vehicle swayed from side to side, rolled, dipped,
and plunged, but Bill kept the track, as if, in the whispered
words of the Expressman, he could "feel and smell" the road he
could no longer see. We knew that at times we hung perilously
over the edge of slopes that eventually dropped a thousand feet
sheer to the tops of the sugar-pines below, but we knew that
Bill knew it also. The half visible heads of the horses, drawn
wedge-wise together by the tightened reins, appeared to cleave
the darkness like a ploughshare, held between his rigid hands.
Even the hoof-beats of the six horses had fallen into a vague,
monotonous, distant roll. Then the ridge was crossed, and we
plunged into the still blacker obscurity of the brush. Rather we
no longer seemed to move—it was only the phantom night that
rushed by us. The horses might have been submerged in some
swift Lethean[2] stream; nothing but the top of the coach and the
rigid bulk of Yuba Bill arose above them. Yet even in that awful
moment our speed was unslackened; it was as if Bill cared no
longer to *guide* but only to drive, or as if the direction of his
huge machine was determined by other hands than his. An in-
cautious whisperer hazarded the paralyzing suggestion of our
"meeting another team." To our great astonishment Bill overheard it; to our greater astonishment he replied. "It 'ud be only
a neck and neck race which would get to h-ll first," he said
quietly. But we were relieved—for he had *spoken!* Almost si-
multaneously the wider turnpike began to glimmer faintly as a
visible track before us; the wayside trees fell out of line, opened
up, and dropped off one after another; we were on the broader
tableland, out of danger, and apparently unperceived and un-
pursued.

Nevertheless in the conversation that broke out again with
the relighting of the lamps, and the comments, congratulations,

and reminiscences that were freely exchanged, Yuba Bill preserved a dissatisfied and even resentful silence. The most generous praise of his skill and courage awoke no response. "I reckon the old man waz just spilin' for a fight, and is feelin' disappointed," said a passenger. But those who knew that Bill had the true fighter's scorn for any purely purposeless conflict were more or less concerned and watchful of him. He would drive steadily for four or five minutes with thoughtfully knitted brows, but eyes still keenly observant under his slouched hat, and then, relaxing his strained attitude, would give way to a movement of impatience. "You ain't uneasy about anything, Bill, are you?" asked the Expressman confidentially. Bill lifted his eyes with a slightly contemptuous surprise. "Not about anything ter *come*. It's what *hez* happened that I don't exackly *sabe*. I don't see no signs of Ramon's gang ever havin' been out at all, and ef they were out I don't see why they didn't go for us."

"The simple fact is that our ruse was successful," said an outside passenger. "They waited to see our lights on the ridge, and, not seeing them, missed us until we had passed. That's my opinion."

"You ain't puttin' any price on that opinion, air ye?" inquired Bill politely.

"No."

" 'Cos thar's a comic paper in 'Frisco pays for them things, and I've seen worse things in it."

"Come off, Bill," retorted the passenger, slightly nettled by the tittering of his companions. "Then what did you put out the lights for?"

"Well," returned Bill grimly, "it mout have been because I didn't keer to hev you chaps blazin' away at the first bush you *thought* you saw move in your skeer,[3] and bringin' down their fire on us."

The explanation, though unsatisfactory, was by no means an improbable one, and we thought it better to accept it with a laugh. Bill, however, resumed his abstracted manner.

"Who got in at the Summit?" he at last asked abruptly of the Expressman.

"Derrick and Simpson of Cold Spring, and one of the 'Excelsior' boys," responded the Expressman.

"And that Pike County girl from Dow's Flat, with her bundles. Don't forget her," added the outside passenger ironically.

"Does anybody here know her?" continued Bill, ignoring the irony.

"You'd better ask Judge Thompson; he was mighty attentive to her; gettin' her a seat by the off window, and lookin' after her bundles and things."

"Gettin' her a seat by the *window?*" repeated Bill.

"Yes, she wanted to see everything, and wasn't afraid of the shooting."

"Yes," broke in a third passenger, "and he was so d——d civil that when she dropped her ring in the straw, he struck a match agin all your rules, you know, and held it for her to find it. And it was just as we were crossin' through the brush, too. I saw the hull thing through the window, for I was hanging over the wheels with my gun ready for action. And it wasn't no fault of Judge Thompson's if his d——d foolishness hadn't shown us up, and got us a shot from the gang."

Bill gave a short grunt, but drove steadily on without further comment or even turning his eyes to the speaker.

We were now not more than a mile from the station at the crossroads where we were to change horses. The lights already glimmered in the distance, and there was a faint suggestion of the coming dawn on the summits of the ridge to the west. We had plunged into a belt of timber, when suddenly a horseman emerged at a sharp canter from a trail that seemed to be parallel with our own. We were all slightly startled; Yuba Bill alone preserving his moody calm.

"Hullo!" he said.

The stranger wheeled to our side as Bill slackened his speed. He seemed to be a "packer" or freight muleteer.[4]

"Ye didn't get 'held up' on the Divide?" continued Bill cheerfully.

"No," returned the packer, with a laugh; "*I* don't carry treasure. But I see you're all right, too. I saw you crossin' over Galloper's."

"*Saw* us?" said Bill sharply. "We had our lights out."

"Yes, but there was suthin' white—a handkerchief or woman's veil, I reckon—hangin' from the window. It was only a movin' spot agin the hillside, but ez I was lookin' out for ye I knew it was you by that. Good-night!"

He cantered away. We tried to look at each other's faces, and at Bill's expression in the darkness, but he neither spoke nor stirred until he threw down the reins when we stopped before the station. The passengers quickly descended from the roof; the Expressman was about to follow, but Bill plucked his sleeve.

"I'm goin' to take a look over this yer stage and these yer passengers with ye, afore we start."

"Why, what's up?"

"Well," said Bill, slowly disengaging himself from one of his enormous gloves, "when we waltzed down into the brush up there I saw a man, ez plain ez I see you, rise up from it. I thought our time had come and the band was goin' to play, when he sorter drew back, made a sign, and we just scooted past him."

"Well?"

"Well," said Bill, "it means that this yer coach was *passed through free* to-night."

"You don't object to *that*—surely? I think we were deucedly lucky."

Bill slowly drew off his other glove. "I've been riskin' my everlastin' life on this d——d line three times a week," he said with mock humility, "and I'm allus thankful for small mercies. *But*," he added grimly, "when it comes down to being passed free by some pal of a hoss thief, and thet called a speshal Providence, *I ain't in it!* No, sir, I ain't in it!"

II

It was with mixed emotions that the passengers heard that a delay of fifteen minutes to tighten certain screw-bolts had been ordered by the autocratic Bill. Some were anxious to get their breakfast at Sugar Pine, but others were not averse to linger for the daylight that promised greater safety on the road. The Expressman, knowing the real cause of Bill's delay, was nevertheless at a loss to understand the object of it. The passengers were all well known; any idea of complicity with the road agents was wild and impossible, and, even if there was a confederate of the gang among them, he would have been more likely to precipitate a robbery than to check it. Again, the discovery of such a confederate—to whom they clearly owed their safety—and his arrest would have been quite against the Californian sense of justice, if not actually illegal. It seemed evident that Bill's quixotic sense of honor was leading him astray.

The station consisted of a stable, a wagon shed, and a building containing three rooms. The first was fitted up with "bunks" or sleeping berths for the employees; the second was the kitchen; and the third and larger apartment was dining-room or sitting-room, and was used as general waiting-room for the passengers. It was not a refreshment station, and there was no "bar." But a mysterious command from the omnipotent Bill produced a demijohn[5] of whiskey, with which he hospitably treated the company. The seductive influence of the liquor loosened the tongue of the gallant Judge Thompson. He admitted to having struck a match to enable the fair Pike Countian to find her ring, which, however, proved to have fallen in her lap. She was "a fine healthy young woman—a type of the Far West, sir; in fact, quite a prairie blossom! yet simple and guileless as a child." She was on her way to Marysville, he believed, "although she expected to meet friends—a friend, in fact—later on." It was her first visit to a large town—in fact, any civilized centre—since she crossed the plains three years ago. Her girlish curiosity was quite touching, and her innocence irresistible. In fact, in a country whose tendency was to produce "frivolity and forwardness in young girls, he found her a most interesting young person." She was even then out in the stable-yard watching the horses being harnessed, "preferring to indulge a pardonable healthy young curiosity than to listen to the empty compliments of the younger passengers."

The figure which Bill saw thus engaged, without being otherwise distinguished, certainly seemed to justify the Judge's opinion. She appeared to be a well-matured country girl, whose frank gray eyes and large laughing mouth expressed a wholesome and abiding gratification in her life and surroundings. She was watching the replacing of luggage in the boot. A little feminine start, as one of her own parcels was thrown somewhat roughly on the roof, gave Bill his opportunity. "Now there," he growled to the helper, "ye ain't carting stone! Look out, will yer! Some of your things, miss?" he added, with gruff courtesy, turning to her. "These yer trunks, for instance?"

She smiled a pleasant assent, and Bill, pushing aside the helper, seized a large square trunk in his arms. But from excess of zeal, or some other mischance, his foot slipped, and he came down heavily, striking the corner of the trunk on the ground and loosening its hinges and fastenings. It was a cheap, common-looking affair, but the accident discovered in its yawning lid a quantity of white, lace-edged feminine apparel of an apparently superior quality. The young lady uttered another cry and came quickly forward, but Bill was profuse in his apologies, himself girded the broken box with a strap, and declared his intention of having the company "make it good" to her with a new one. Then he casually accompanied her to the door of the waiting-room, entered, made a place for her before the fire by simply lifting the nearest and most youthful passenger by the coat collar from the stool that he was occupying, and, having installed the lady in it, displaced another man who was standing before the chimney, and, drawing himself up to his full six feet of height in front of her, glanced down upon his fair passenger as he took his waybill[6] from his pocket.

"Your name is down here as Miss Mullins?" he said.

She looked up, became suddenly aware that she and her questioner were the centre of interest to the whole circle of passengers, and, with a slight rise of color, returned, "Yes."

"Well, Miss Mullins, I've got a question or two to ask ye. I ask it straight out afore this crowd. It's in my rights to take ye aside and ask it—but that ain't my style; I'm no detective. I needn't ask it at all, but act as ef I knowed the answer, or I might leave it to be asked by others. Ye needn't answer it ef ye don't like; ye've got a friend over ther—Judge Thompson—who is a friend to ye, right or wrong, jest as any other man here is —as though ye'd packed your own jury. Well, the simple question I've got to ask ye is *this:* Did you signal to anybody from the coach when we passed Galloper's an hour ago?"

We all thought that Bill's courage and audacity had reached its climax here. To openly and publicly accuse a "lady" before a group of chivalrous Californians, and that lady possessing the further attractions of youth, good looks, and innocence, was little short of desperation. There was an evident movement of adhesion[7] towards the fair stranger, a slight muttering broke out on the right, but the very boldness of the act held them in stupefied surprise. Judge Thompson, with a bland propitiatory smile began: "Really, Bill, I must protest on behalf of this young lady"—when the fair accused, raising her eyes to her accuser, to the consternation of everybody answered with the slight but convincing hesitation of conscientious truthfulness:—

"*I did.*"

"Ahem!" interposed the Judge hastily, "er—that is—er—you allowed your handkerchief to flutter from the window,—I noticed it myself,—casually—one might say even playfully—but without any particular significance."

The girl, regarding her apologist with a singular mingling of pride and impatience, returned briefly:—

"I signaled."

"Who did you signal to?" asked Bill gravely.

"The young gentleman I'm going to marry."

A start, followed by a slight titter from the younger passengers, was instantly suppressed by a savage glance from Bill.

"What did you signal to him for?" he continued.

"To tell him I was here, and that it was all right," returned the young girl, with a steadily rising pride and color.

"Wot was all right?" demanded Bill.

"That I wasn't followed, and that he could meet me on the road beyond Cass's Ridge Station." She hesitated a moment, and then, with a still greater pride, in which a youthful defiance was still mingled, said: "I've run away from home to marry him. And I mean to! No one can stop me. Dad didn't like him just because he was poor, and dad's got money. Dad wanted me to marry a man I hate, and got a lot of dresses and things to bribe me."

"And you're taking them in your trunk to the other feller?" said Bill grimly.

"Yes, he's poor," returned the girl defiantly.

"Then your father's name is Mullins?" asked Bill.

"It's not Mullins. I—I—took that name," she hesitated, with her first exhibition of self-consciousness.

"Wot *is* his name?"

"Eli Hemmings."

A smile of relief and significance went round the circle. The fame of Eli or "Skinner" Hemmings, as a notorious miser and usurer, had passed even beyond Galloper's Ridge.

"The step that you're taking, Miss Mullins, I need not tell you, is one of great gravity," said Judge Thompson, with a certain paternal seriousness of manner, in which, however, we were glad to detect a glaring affectation; "and I trust that you and your affianced have fully weighed it. Far be it from me to interfere with or question the natural affections of two young people, but may I ask you what you know of the—er—young gentleman for whom you are sacrificing so much, and, perhaps, imperiling your whole future? For instance, have you known him long?"

The slightly troubled air of trying to understand,—not unlike the vague wonderment of childhood,—with which Miss Mullins had received the beginning of this exordium, changed to a relieved smile of comprehension as she said quickly, "Oh yes, nearly a whole year."

"And," said the Judge, smiling, "has he a vocation—is he in business?"

"Oh yes," she returned; "he's a collector."

"A collector?"

"Yes; he collects bills, you know,—money," she went on, with childish eagerness, "not for himself,—*he* never has any money, poor Charley,—but for his firm. It's dreadful hard work, too; keeps him out for days and nights, over bad roads and baddest weather. Sometimes, when he's stole over to the ranch just to see me, he's been so bad he could scarcely keep his seat in the saddle, much less stand. And he's got to take mighty big risks, too. Times the folks are cross with him and won't pay; once they shot him in the arm, and he came to me, and I helped do it up for him. But he don't mind. He's real brave,—jest as brave as he's good." There was such a wholesome ring of truth in this pretty praise that we were touched in sympathy with the speaker.

"What firm does he collect for?" asked the Judge gently.

"I don't know exactly—he won't tell me; but I think it's a Spanish firm. You see"—she took us all into her confidence with a sweeping smile of innocent yet half-mischievous artfulness—

"I only know because I peeped over a letter he once got from his firm, telling him he must hustle up and be ready for the road the next day; but I think the name was Martinez—yes, Ramon Martinez."

In the dead silence that ensued—a silence so profound that we could hear the horses in the distant stable-yard rattling their harness—one of the younger "Excelsior" boys burst into a hysteric laugh, but the fierce eye of Yuba Bill was down upon him, and seemed to instantly stiffen him into a silent, grinning mask. The young girl, however, took no note of it. Following out, with lover-like diffusiveness,[8] the reminiscences thus awakened, she went on:—

"Yes, it's mighty hard work, but he says it's all for me, and as soon as we're married he'll quit it. He might have quit it before, but he won't take no money of me, nor what I told him I could get out of dad! That ain't his style. He's mighty proud —if he is poor—is Charley. Why thar's all ma's money which she left me in the Savin's Bank that I wanted to draw out—for I had the right—and give it to him, but he wouldn't hear of it! Why, he wouldn't take one of the things I've got with me, if he knew it. And so he goes on ridin' and ridin', here and there and everywhere, and gettin' more and more played out and sad, and thin and pale as a spirit, and always so uneasy about his business, and startin' up at times when we're meetin' out in the South Woods or in the far clearin', and sayin': 'I must be goin' now, Polly,' and yet always tryin' to be chiffle[9] and chipper afore me. Why he must have rid miles and miles to have watched for me thar in the brush at the foot of Galloper's tonight, jest to see if all was safe; and Lordy! I'd have given him the signal and showed a light if I'd died for it the next minit. There! That's what I know of Charley—that's what I'm running away from home for—that's what I'm running to him for, and I don't care who knows it! And I only wish I'd done it afore—and I would—if—if—if—he'd only *asked me!* There now!" She stopped, panted, and choked. Then one of the sudden transitions of youthful emotion overtook the eager, laughing face; it clouded up with the swift change of childhood, a lightning quiver of expression broke over it, and—then came the rain!

I think this simple act completed our utter demoralization!

We smiled feebly at each other with that assumption of masculine superiority which is miserably conscious of its own help-
lessness at such moments. We looked out of the window, blew
our noses, said: "Eh—what?" and "I say," vaguely to each
other, and were greatly relieved, and yet apparently astonished,
when Yuba Bill, who had turned his back upon the fair speaker,
and was kicking the logs in the fireplace, suddenly swept down
upon us and bundled us all into the road, leaving Miss Mullins
alone. Then he walked aside with Judge Thompson for a few
moments; returned to us, autocratically demanded of the party
a complete reticence towards Miss Mullins on the subject-matter
under discussion, reëntered the station, reappeared with the
young lady, suppressed a faint idiotic cheer which broke from
us at the spectacle of her innocent face once more cleared and
rosy, climbed the box, and in another moment we were under
way.

"Then she don't know what her lover is yet?" asked the Expressman eagerly.

"No."

"Are *you* certain it's one of the gang?"

"Can't say *for sure.* It mout be a young chap from Yolo who
bucked agin the tiger at Sacramento, got regularly cleaned out
and busted, and joined the gang for a flier. They say thar was a
new hand in that job over at Keeley's,—and a mighty game one,
too; and ez there was some buckshot onloaded that trip, he
might hev got his share, and that would tally with what the girl
said about his arm. See! Ef that's the man, I've heered he was
the son of some big preacher in the States, and a college sharp
to boot, who ran wild in 'Frisco, and played himself for all he
was worth. They're the wust kind to kick when they once get a
foot over the traces. For stiddy, comf'ble kempany," added Bill
reflectively, "give *me* the son of a man that was *hanged!*"

"But what are you going to do about this?"

"That depends upon the feller who comes to meet her."

"But you ain't going to try to take him? That would be playing it pretty low down on them both."

"Keep your hair on, Jimmy! The Judge and me are only going
to rastle with the sperrit of that gay young galoot, when he drops
down for his girl—and exhort him pow'ful! Ef he allows he's

convicted of sin and will find the Lord, we'll marry him and the gal offhand at the next station, and the Judge will officiate himself for nothin'. We're goin' to have this yer elopement done on the square—and our waybill clean—you bet!"

"But you don't suppose he'll trust himself in your hands?"

"Polly will signal to him that it's all square."

"Ah!" said the Expressman. Nevertheless in those few moments the men seemed to have exchanged dispositions. The Expressman looked doubtfully, critically, and even cynically before him. Bill's face had relaxed, and something like a bland smile beamed across it, as he drove confidently and unhesitatingly forward.

Day, meantime, although full blown and radiant on the mountain summits around us, was yet nebulous and uncertain in the valleys into which we were plunging. Lights still glimmered in the cabins and few ranch buildings which began to indicate the thicker settlements. And the shadows were heaviest in a little copse, where a note from Judge Thompson in the coach was handed up to Yuba Bill, who at once slowly began to draw up his horses. The coach stopped finally near the junction of a small crossroad. At the same moment Miss Mullins slipped down from the vehicle, and, with a parting wave of her hand to the Judge, who had assisted her from the steps, tripped down the crossroad, and disappeared in its semi-obscurity. To our surprise the stage waited, Bill holding the reins listlessly in his hands. Five minutes passed—an eternity of expectation, and, as there was that in Yuba Bill's face which forbade idle questioning, an aching void of silence also! This was at last broken by a strange voice from the road:—

"Go on—we'll follow."

The coach started forward. Presently we heard the sound of other wheels behind us. We all craned our necks backward to get a view of the unknown, but by the growing light we could only see that we were followed at a distance by a buggy with two figures in it. Evidently Polly Mullins and her lover! We hoped that they would pass us. But the vehicle, although drawn by a fast horse, preserved its distance always, and it was plain that its driver had no desire to satisfy our curiosity. The Expressman had recourse to Bill.

"Is it the man you thought of?" he asked eagerly.

"I reckon," said Bill briefly.

"But," continued the Expressman, returning to his former skepticism, "what's to keep them both from levanting together now?"

Bill jerked his hand towards the boot with a grim smile.

"Their baggage."

"Oh!" said the Expressman.

"Yes," continued Bill. "We'll hang on to that gal's little frills and fixin's until this yer job's settled, and the ceremony's over, jest as ef we waz her own father. And, what's more, young man," he added, suddenly turning to the Expressman, "*you'll* express them trunks of hers *through to Sacramento* with your kempany's labels, and hand her the receipts and checks for them, so she *can get 'em there.* That'll keep *him* outer temptation and the reach o' the gang, until they get away among white men and civilization again. When your hoary-headed ole grandfather, or, to speak plainer, that partikler old whiskey-soaker known as Yuba Bill, wot sits on this box," he continued, with a diabolical wink at the Expressman, "waltzes in to pervide for a young couple jest startin' in life, thar's nothin' mean about his style, you bet. He fills the bill every time! Speshul Providences take a back seat when he's around."

When the station hotel and straggling settlement of Sugar Pine, now distinct and clear in the growing light, at last rose within rifleshot on the plateau, the buggy suddenly darted swiftly by us, so swiftly that the faces of the two occupants were barely distinguishable as they passed, and keeping the lead by a dozen lengths, reached the door of the hotel. The young girl and her companion leaped down and vanished within as we drew up. They had evidently determined to elude our curiosity, and were successful.

But the material appetites of the passengers, sharpened by the keen mountain air, were more potent than their curiosity, and, as the breakfast-bell rang out at the moment the stage stopped, a majority of them rushed into the dining-room and scrambled for places without giving much heed to the vanished couple or to the Judge and Yuba Bill, who had disappeared also. The through coach to Marysville and Sacramento was likewise waiting, for Sugar Pine was the limit of Bill's ministration, and the coach which we had just left went no farther. In the course of twenty minutes, however, there was a slight and somewhat ceremonious bustling in the hall and on the veranda, and Yuba Bill and the Judge reappeared. The latter was leading, with some elaboration of manner and detail, the shapely figure of Miss Mullins, and Yuba Bill was accompanying her companion to the buggy. We all rushed to the windows to get a good view of the mysterious stranger and probable ex-brigand whose life was now linked with our fair fellow-passenger. I am afraid, however, that we all participated in a certain impression of disappointment and doubt. Handsome and even cultivated-looking, he assuredly was—young and vigorous in appearance. But there was a certain half-shamed, half-defiant suggestion in his expression, yet coupled with a watchful lurking uneasiness which was not pleasant and hardly becoming in a bridegroom—and the possessor of such a bride. But the frank, joyous, innocent face of Polly Mullins, resplendent with a simple, happy confidence, melted our hearts again, and condoned the fellow's shortcomings. We waved our hands; I think we would have given three rousing cheers as they drove away if the omnipotent eye of Yuba Bill had not been upon us. It was well, for the next moment we were summoned to the presence of that soft-hearted autocrat.

We found him alone with the Judge in a private sitting-room, standing before a table on which there was a decanter and glasses. As we filed expectantly into the room and the door closed behind us, he cast a glance of hesitating tolerance over the group.

"Gentlemen," he said slowly, "you was all present at the beginnin' of a little game this mornin', and the Judge thar thinks that you oughter be let in at the finish. *I* don't see that it's any of *your* d——d business—so to speak; but ez the Judge here allows you're all in the secret, I've called you in to take a partin' drink to the health of Mr. and Mrs. Charley Byng—ez is now comf'ably off on their bridal tower. What *you* know or what *you* suspects of the young galoot[10] that's married the gal ain't worth shucks to anybody, and I wouldn't give it to a yaller pup to play with, but the Judge thinks you ought all to promise right here that you'll keep it dark. That's his opinion. Ez far as my opinion goes, gen'l'men," continued Bill, with greater blandness and apparent cordiality, "I wanter simply remark, in a keerless offhand gin'ral way, that ef I ketch any God-forsaken, lop-eared, chuckle-headed blatherin' idjet airin' *his* opinion"—

"One moment, Bill," interposed Judge Thompson with a grave smile; "let me explain. You understand, gentlemen," he said, turning to us, "the singular, and I may say affecting, situation which our good-hearted friend here has done so much to bring to what we hope will be a happy termination. I want to give here, as my professional opinion, that there is nothing in his request which, in your capacity as good citizens and law-abiding men, you may not grant. I want to tell you, also, that you are condoning no offense against the statutes; that there is not a particle of legal evidence before us of the criminal antecedents of Mr. Charles Byng, except that which has been told you by the innocent lips of his betrothed, which the law of the land has now sealed forever in the mouth of his wife, and that our own actual experience of his acts have been in the main exculpatory of any previous irregularity—if not incompatible with it. Briefly, no judge would charge, no jury convict, on such evidence. When I add that the young girl is of legal age, that there is no evidence of any previous undue influence, but rather of the reverse, on the part of the bridegroom, and that I was content, as a magistrate, to perform the ceremony, I think you will be satisfied to give your promise, for the sake of the bride, and drink a happy life to them both."

I need not say that we did this cheerfully, and even extorted from Bill a grunt of satisfaction. The majority of the company, however, who were going with the through coach to Sacramento, then took their leave, and, as we accompanied them to the veranda, we could see that Miss Polly Mullins's trunks were already transferred to the other vehicle under the protecting seals and labels of the all-potent Express Company. Then the whip cracked, the coach rolled away, and the last traces of the adventurous young couple disappeared in the hanging red dust of its wheels.

But Yuba Bill's grim satisfaction at the happy issue of the episode seemed to suffer no abatement. He even exceeded his usual deliberately regulated potations, and, standing comfortably with his back to the centre of the now deserted barroom, was more than usually loquacious with the Expressman. "You see," he said, in bland reminiscence, "when your old Uncle Bill takes hold of a job like this, he puts it straight through without changin' hosses. Yet thar was a moment, young feller, when I thought I was stompt! It was when we'd made up our mind to make that chap tell the gal fust all what he was! Ef she'd rared or kicked in the traces, or hung back only ez much ez that, we'd hev given him jest five minits' law to get up and get and leave her, and we'd hev toted that gal and her fixin's back to her dad again! But she jest gave a little scream and start, and then went off inter hysterics, right on his buzzum, laughing and cryin' and sayin' that nothin' should part 'em. Gosh! if I didn't think *he* woz more cut up than she about it; a minit it looked as ef *he* didn't allow to marry her arter all, but that passed, and they was married hard and fast—you bet! I reckon he's had enough of stayin' out o' nights to last him, and ef the valley settlements hevn't got hold of a very shining member, at least the foothills hev got shut of one more of the Ramon Martinez gang."

"What's that about the Ramon Martinez gang?" said a quiet potential voice.

Bill turned quickly. It was the voice of the Divisional Superintendent of the Express Company,—a man of eccentric determination of character, and one of the few whom the autocratic Bill recognized as an equal,—who had just entered the barroom. His dusty pongee[11] cloak and soft hat indicated that he had that morning arrived on a round of inspection.

"Don't care if I do, Bill," he continued, in response to Bill's invitatory gesture, walking to the bar. "It's a little raw out on the road. Well, what were you saying about Ramon Martinez gang? You haven't come across one of 'em, have you?"

"No," said Bill, with a slight blinking of his eye, as he ostentatiously lifted his glass to the light.

"And you *won't*," added the Superintendent, leisurely sipping his liquor. "For the fact is, the gang is about played out. Not from want of a job now and then, but from the difficulty of disposing of the results of their work. Since the new instructions to the agents to identify and trace all dust and bullion offered to them went into force, you see, they can't get rid of their swag.[12] All the gang are spotted at the offices, and it costs too much for them to pay a fence or a middleman of any standing. Why, all that flaky river gold they took from the Excelsior Company can be identified as easy as if it was stamped with the company's mark. They can't melt it down themselves; they can't get others to do it for them; they can't ship it to the Mint or Assay Offices in Marysville and 'Frisco, for they won't take it without our certificate and seals; and *we* don't take any undeclared freight *within* the lines that we've drawn around their beat, except from people and agents known. Why, *you* know that well enough, Jim," he said, suddenly appealing to the Expressman, "don't you?"

Possibly the suddenness of the appeal caused the Expressman to swallow his liquor the wrong way, for he was overtaken with a fit of coughing, and stammered hastily as he laid down his glass, "Yes—of course—certainly."

"No, sir," resumed the Superintendent cheerfully, "they're pretty well played out. And the best proof of it is that they've lately been robbing ordinary passengers' trunks. There was a freight wagon 'held up' near Dow's Flat the other day, and a lot of baggage gone through. I had to go down there to look into it. Darned if they hadn't lifted a lot o' woman's wedding things from that rich couple who got married the other day out at Marysville. Looks as if they were playing it rather low down, don't it? Coming down to hardpan and the bed rock[13]—eh?"

The Expressman's face was turned anxiously towards Bill, who, after a hurried gulp of his remaining liquor, still stood staring at the window. Then he slowly drew on one of his large gloves. "Ye didn't," he said, with a slow, drawling, but perfectly distinct, articulation, "happen to know old 'Skinner' Hemmings when you were over there?"

"Yes."

"And his daughter?"

"He hasn't got any."

"A sort o' mild, innocent, guileless child of nature?" persisted Bill, with a yellow face, a deadly calm and Satanic deliberation.

"No. I tell you he *hasn't* any daughter. Old man Hemmings is a confirmed old bachelor. He's too mean to support more than one."

"And you didn't happen to know any o' that gang, did ye?" continued Bill, with infinite protraction.

"Yes. Knew 'em all. There was French Pete, Cherokee Bob, Kanaka Joe, One-eyed Stillson, Softy Brown, Spanish Jack, and two or three Greasers."

"And ye didn't know a man by the name of Charley Byng?"

"No," returned the Superintendent, with a slight suggestion of weariness and a distraught glance towards the door.

"A dark, stylish chap, with shifty black eyes and a curled-up merstache?" continued Bill, with dry, colorless persistence.

"No. Look here, Bill, I'm in a little bit of a hurry—but I suppose you must have your little joke before we part. Now, what *is* your little game?"

"Wot you mean?" demanded Bill, with sudden brusqueness.

"Mean? Well, old man, you know as well as I do. You're giving me the very description of Ramon Martinez himself, ha! ha! No—Bill! you didn't play me this time. You're mighty spry and clever, but you didn't catch on just then."

He nodded and moved away with a light laugh. Bill turned a stony face to the Expressman. Suddenly a gleam of mirth came into his gloomy eyes. He bent over the young man, and said in a hoarse, chuckling whisper:—

"But I got even after all!"

"How?"

"He's tied up to that lying little she-devil, hard and fast!"

Sui Sin Far, a journalist, essayist, and fiction writer, is thought to have published the first book-length collection of fiction by a Chinese North American author. Unlike her sister, Winnifred Eaton, who wrote under the name Onoto Watanna and published romantic novels set in Japan, Sui Sin Far claimed her Chinese American heritage; in both fiction and nonfiction, she addressed the negotiation of biracial and multicultural identities and the situation of the Chinese in North America. The daughter of a Chinese mother and an English father, Sui Sin Far was one of fourteen children. She was born in Macclesfield, England, and as a child emigrated with her family to Montreal. In the 1880s and 1890s she worked as a stenographer and journalist in Montreal and began writing short stories, essays, and journalistic articles on Chinese Canadian and Chinese American issues. In 1897 she traveled to Jamaica, then divided her time from 1898 to 1912 between the East and West Coasts of the United States; she never married. Her stories, first published in the California magazine *Land of Sunshine*, were collected in 1912 in a volume titled *Mrs. Spring Fragrance*.

"Its Wavering Image"

I

Pan was a half white, half Chinese girl. Her mother was dead, and Pan lived with her father who kept an Oriental Bazaar on Dupont Street. All her life had Pan lived in Chinatown, and if she were different in any sense from those around her, she gave little thought to it. It was only after the coming of Mark Carson that the mystery of her nature began to trouble her.

They met at the time of the boycott of the Sam Yups by the See Yups. After the heat and dust and unsavoriness of the highways and byways of Chinatown, the young reporter who had been sent to find a story, had stepped across the threshold of a cool, deep room, fragrant with the odor of dried lilies and sandalwood, and found Pan.

She did not speak to him, nor he to her. His business was with the spectacled merchant, who, with a pointed brush, was making up accounts in brown paper books and rolling balls in an abacus box. As to Pan, she always turned from whites. With her father's people she was natural and at home; but in the presence of her mother's she felt strange and constrained, shrinking from their curious scrutiny as she would from the sharp edge of a sword.

When Mark Carson returned to the office, he asked some questions concerning the girl who had puzzled him. What was she? Chinese or white? The city editor answered him, adding: "She is an unusually bright girl, and could tell more stories about the Chinese than any other person in this city—if she would."

Mark Carson had a determined chin, clever eyes, and a tone to his voice which easily won for him the confidence of the unwary. In the reporter's room he was spoken of as "a man who would sell his soul for a story."

After Pan's first shyness had worn off, he found her bewilderingly frank and free with him; but he had all the instincts of a gentleman save one, and made no ordinary mistake about her. He was Pan's first white friend. She was born a Bohemian,[1] exempt from the conventional restrictions imposed upon either the white or Chinese woman; and the Oriental who was her father mingled with his affection for his child so great a respect for and trust in the daughter of the dead white woman, that everything she did or said was right to him. And Pan herself! A white woman might pass over an insult; a Chinese woman fail to see one. But Pan! He would be a brave man indeed who offered one to childish little Pan.

All this Mark Carson's clear eyes perceived, and with delicate tact and subtlety he taught the young girl that, all unconscious until his coming, she had lived her life alone. So well did she learn this lesson that it seemed at times as if her white self must entirely dominate and trample under foot her Chinese.

Meanwhile, in full trust and confidence, she led him about Chinatown, initiating him into the simple mystery and history of many things, for which she, being of her father's race, had a tender regard and pride. For her sake he was received as a brother by the yellow-robed priest in the joss house,[2] the Astrologer of Prospect Place, and other conservative Chinese. The Water Lily Club opened its doors to him when she knocked, and the Sublimely Pure Brothers' organization admitted him as one of its honorary members, thereby enabling him not only to see but to take part in a ceremony in which no American had ever before participated. With her by his side, he was welcomed wherever he went. Even the little Chinese women in the midst of their babies, received him with gentle smiles, and the children solemnly munched his candies and repeated nursery rhymes for his edification.

He enjoyed it all, and so did Pan. They were both young and light-hearted. And when the afternoon was spent, there was always that high room open to the stars, with its China bowls full of flowers and its big colored lanterns, shedding a mellow light.

Sometimes there was music. A Chinese band played three evenings a week in the gilded restaurant beneath them, and the louder the gongs sounded and the fiddlers fiddled, the more delighted was Pan. Just below the restaurant was her father's bazaar. Occasionally Mun You would stroll upstairs and inquire of the young couple if there was anything needed to complete their felicity, and Pan would answer: "Thou only." Pan was very proud of her Chinese father. "I would rather have a Chinese for a father than a white man," she often told Mark Carson. The last time she had said that he had asked whom she would prefer for a husband, a white man or a Chinese. And Pan, for the first time since he had known her, had no answer for him.

II

It was a cool, quiet evening, after a hot day. A new moon was in the sky.

"How beautiful above! How unbeautiful below!" exclaimed Mark Carson involuntarily.

He and Pan had been gazing down from their open retreat into the lantern-lighted, motley-thronged street beneath
them.

"Perhaps it isn't very beautiful," replied Pan, "but it is here
I live. It is my home." Her voice quivered a little.

He leaned towards her suddenly and grasped her hands.

"Pan," he cried, "you do not belong here. You are white—
white."

"No! no!" protested Pan.

"You are," he asserted. "You have no right to be here."

"I was born here," she answered, "and the Chinese people
look upon me as their own."

"But they do not understand you," he went on. "Your real
self is alien to them. What interest have they in the books you
read—the thoughts you think?"

"They have an interest in me," answered faithful Pan. "Oh,
do not speak in that way any more."

"But I must," the young man persisted. "Pan, don't you see
that you have got to decide what you will be—Chinese or
white? You cannot be both."

"Hush! Hush!" bade Pan. "I do not love you when you talk
to me like that."

A little Chinese boy brought tea and saffron cakes. He was a
picturesque little fellow with a quaint manner of speech. Mark
Carson jested merrily with him, while Pan holding a tea-bowl
between her two small hands laughed and sipped.

When they were alone again, the silver stream and the crescent
moon became the objects of their study. It was a very beautiful
evening.

After a while Mark Carson, his hand on Pan's shoulder, sang:

> "And forever, and forever,
>   As long as the river flows,
>   As long as the heart has passions,
>   As long as life has woes,
>   The moon and its broken reflection,
>   And its shadows shall appear,
>   As the symbol of love in heaven,
>   And its wavering image here."

Listening to that irresistible voice singing her heart away, the girl broke down and wept. She was so young and so happy.

"Look up at me," bade Mark Carson. "Oh, Pan! Pan! Those tears prove that you are white."

Pan lifted her wet face.

"Kiss me, Pan," said he. It was the first time.

Next morning Mark Carson began work on the special-feature article which he had been promising his paper for some weeks.

III

"Cursed be his ancestors," bayed Man You.

He cast a paper at his daughter's feet and left the room.

Startled by her father's unwonted passion, Pan picked up the paper, and in the clear passionless light of the afternoon read that which forever after was blotted upon her memory.

"Betrayed! Betrayed! Betrayed to be a betrayer!"

It burnt red hot; agony unrelieved by words, unassuaged by tears.

So till evening fell. Then she stumbled up the dark stairs which led to the high room open to the stars and tried to think it out. Someone had hurt her. Who was it? She raised her eyes. There shone: "Its Wavering Image." It helped her to lucidity. He had done it. Was it unconsciously dealt—that cruel blow? Ah, well did he know that the sword which pierced her through others, would carry with it to her own heart, the pain of all those others. None knew better than he that she, whom he had called "a white girl, a white woman," would rather that her own naked body and soul had been exposed, than that things, sacred and secret to those who loved her, should be cruelly unveiled and ruthlessly spread before the ridiculing and uncomprehending foreigner. And knowing all this so well, so well, he had carelessly sung her heart away, and with her kiss upon his lips, had smilingly turned and stabbed her. She, who was of the race that remembers.

IV

Mark Carson, back in the city after an absence of two months, thought of Pan. He would see her that very evening. Dear little Pan, pretty Pan, clever Pan, amusing Pan; Pan, who was always so frankly glad to have him come to her; so eager to hear all that he was doing; so appreciative, so inspiring, so loving. She would have forgotten that article by now. Why should a white woman care about such things? Her true self was above it all. Had he not taught her *that* during the weeks in which they had seen so much of one another? True, his last lesson had been a little harsh, and as yet he knew not how she had taken it; but even if its roughness had hurt and irritated, there was a healing balm, a wizard's oil which none knew so well as he how to apply.

But for all these soothing reflections, there was an undercurrent of feeling which caused his steps to falter on his way to Pan. He turned into Portsmouth Square and took a seat on one of the benches facing the fountain erected in memory of Robert Louis Stevenson.[3] Why had Pan failed to answer the note he had written telling her of the assignment which would keep him out of town for a couple of months and giving her his address? Would Robert Louis Stevenson have known why? Yes—and so did Mark Carson. But though Robert Louis Stevenson would have boldly answered himself the question, Mark Carson thrust it aside, arose, and pressed up the hill.

"I knew they would not blame you, Pan!"

"Yes."

"And there was no word of you, dear. I was careful about that, not only for your sake, but for mine."

Silence.

"It is mere superstition anyway. These things have got to be exposed and done away with."

Still silence.

Mark Carson felt strangely chilled. Pan was not herself tonight. She did not even look herself. He had been accustomed to seeing her in American dress. Tonight she wore the Chinese costume. But for her clear-cut features she might have been a Chinese girl. He shivered.

"Pan," he asked, "why do you wear that dress?"

Within her sleeves Pan's small hands struggled together; but her face and voice were calm.

"Because I am a Chinese woman," she answered.

"You are not," cried Mark Carson, fiercely. "You cannot say that now, Pan. You are a white woman—white. Did your kiss not promise me that?"

"A white woman!" echoed Pan her voice rising high and clear to the stars above them. "I would not be a white woman for all the world. *You* are a white man. And *what* is a promise to a white man!"

*   *   *

When she was lying low, the element of Fire having raged so fiercely within her that it had almost shriveled up the childish frame, there came to the house of Man You a little toddler who could scarcely speak. Climbing upon Pan's couch, she pressed her head upon the sick girl's bosom. The feel of that little head brought tears.

"Lo!" said the mother of the toddler. "Thou wilt bear a child thyself some day, and all the bitterness of this will pass away."

And Pan, being a Chinese woman, was comforted.

The Wisdom of the New

~~~

I

Old Li Wang, the peddler, who had lived in the land beyond the sea, was wont to declare: "For every cent that a man makes here, he can make one hundred there."

"Then, why," would ask Sankwei, "do you now have to move from door to door to fill your bowl with rice?"

And the old man would sigh and answer:

"Because where one learns how to make gold, one also learns how to lose it."

"How to lose it!" echoed Wou Sankwei. "Tell me all about it."

So the old man would tell stories about the winning and the losing, and the stories of the losing were even more fascinating than the stories of the winning.

"Yes, that was life," he would conclude. "Life, life."

At such times the boy would gaze across the water with wistful eyes. The land beyond the sea was calling to him.

The place was a sleepy little south coast town where the years slipped by monotonously. The boy was the only son of the man who had been the town magistrate.

Had his father lived, Wou Sankwei would have been sent to complete his schooling in another province. As it was he did nothing but sleep, dream, and occasionally get into mischief. What else was there to do? His mother and sister waited upon him hand and foot. Was he not the son of the house? The family income was small, scarcely sufficient for their needs; but there was no way by which he could add to it, unless, indeed, he disgraced the name of Wou by becoming a common fisherman. The great green waves lifted white arms of foam to him, and the fishes gleaming and lurking in the waters seemed to beseech him to draw them from the deep; but his mother shook her head.

"Should you become a fisherman," said she, "your family would lose face. Remember that your father was a magistrate."

When he was about nineteen there returned to the town one who had been absent for many years. Ching Kee, like old Li Wang, had also lived in the land beyond the sea; but unlike old Li Wang he had accumulated a small fortune.

" 'Tis a hard life over there," said he, "but 'tis worth while. At least one can be a man, and can work at what work comes his way without losing face."[1] Then he laughed at Wou Sankwei's flabby muscles, at his soft, dark eyes, and plump, white hands.

"If you lived in America," said he, "you would learn to be ashamed of such beauty."

Whereupon Wou Sankwei made up his mind that he would go to America, the land beyond the sea. Better any life than that of a woman man.

He talked long and earnestly with his mother. "Give me your

blessing," said he. "I will work and save money. What I send home will bring you many a comfort, and when I come back to China, it may be that I shall be able to complete my studies and obtain a degree. If not, my knowledge of the foreign language which I shall acquire, will enable me to take a position which will not disgrace the name of Wou."

His mother listened and thought. She was ambitious for her son whom she loved beyond all things on earth. Moreover, had not Sik Ping, a Canton merchant, who had visited the little town two moons ago, declared to Hum Wah, who traded in palm leaves, that the signs of the times were that the son of a cobbler, returned from America with the foreign language, could easier command a position of consequence than the son of a school-teacher unacquainted with any tongue but that of his motherland?

"Very well," she acquiesced; "but before you go I must find you a wife. Only your son, my son, can comfort me for your loss."

II

Wou Sankwei stood behind his desk, busily entering figures in a long yellow book. Now and then he would thrust the hair pencil with which he worked behind his ears and manipulate with deft fingers a Chinese counting machine. Wou Sankwei was the junior partner and bookkeeper of the firm of Leung Tang Wou & Co. of San Francisco. He had been in America seven years and had made good use of his time. Self-improvement had been his object and ambition, even more than the acquirement of a fortune, and who, looking at his fine, intelligent face and listening to his careful English, could say that he had failed?

One of his partners called his name. Some ladies wished to speak to him. Wou Sankwei hastened to the front of the store. One of his callers, a motherly looking woman, was the friend who had taken him under her wing shortly after his arrival in America. She had come to invite him to spend the evening with her and her niece, the young girl who accompanied her.

After his callers had left, Sankwei returned to his desk and worked steadily until the hour for his evening meal, which he

took in the Chinese restaurant across the street from the bazaar.
He hurried through with this, as before going to his friend's
house, he had a somewhat important letter to write and mail.
His mother had died a year before, and the uncle, to whom he
was writing, had taken his wife and son into his home until such
time as his nephew could send for them. Now the time had
come.

Wou Sankwei's memory of the woman who was his wife was
very faint. How could it be otherwise? She had come to him but
three weeks before the sailing of the vessel which had brought
him to America, and until then he had not seen her face. But
she was his wife and the mother of his son. Ever since he had
worked in America he had sent money for her support, and she
had proved a good daughter to his mother.

As he sat down to write he decided that he would welcome
her with a big dinner to his countrymen.

"Yes," he replied to Mrs. Dean, later on in the evening, "I
have sent for my wife."

"I am so glad," said the lady. "Mr. Wou"—turning to her
niece—"has not seen his wife for seven years."

"Deary me!" exclaimed the young girl. "What a lot of letters
you must have written!"

"I have not written her one," returned the young man somewhat stiffly.

Adah Charlton looked up in surprise. "Why—" she began.

"Mr. Wou used to be such a studious boy when I first knew
him," interrupted Mrs. Dean, laying her hand affectionately
upon the young man's shoulder. "Now, it is all business. But
you won't forget the concert on Saturday evening."

"No, I will not forget," answered Wou Sankwei.

"He has never written to his wife," explained Mrs. Dean
when she and her niece were alone, "because his wife can neither
read nor write."

"Oh, isn't that sad!" murmured Adah Charlton, her own
winsome face becoming pensive.

"They don't seem to think so. It is the Chinese custom to
educate only the boys. At least it has been so in the past. Sankwei
himself is unusually bright. Poor boy! He began life here as a
laundryman, and you may be sure that it must have been hard

on him, for, as the son of a petty Chinese Government official, he had not been accustomed to manual labor. But Chinese character is wonderful; and now after seven years in this country, he enjoys a reputation as a business man amongst his countrymen, and is as up to date as any young American."

"But, Auntie, isn't it dreadful to think that a man should live away from his wife for so many years without any communication between them whatsoever except through others."

"It is dreadful to our minds, but not to theirs. Everything with them is a matter of duty. Sankwei married his wife as a matter of duty. He sends for her as a matter of duty."

"I wonder if it is all duty on her side," mused the girl.

Mrs. Dean smiled. "You are too romantic, Adah," said she. "I hope, however, that when she does come, they will be happy together. I think almost as much of Sankwei as I do of my own boy."

III

Pau Lin, the wife of Wou Sankwei, sat in a corner of the deck of the big steamer, awaiting the coming of her husband. Beside her, leaning his little queued[2] head against her shoulder, stood her six-year-old son. He had been ailing throughout the voyage, and his small face was pinched with pain. His mother, who had been nursing him every night since the ship had left port, appeared very worn and tired. This, despite the fact that with a feminine desire to make herself fair to see in the eyes of her husband, she had arrayed herself in a heavily embroidered purple costume, whitened her forehead and cheeks with powder, and tinted her lips with carmine.[3]

He came at last, looking over and beyond her. There were two others of her countrywomen awaiting the men who had sent for them, and each had a child, so that for a moment he seemed somewhat bewildered. Only when the ship's officer pointed out and named her, did he know her as his. Then he came forward, spoke a few words of formal welcome, and, lifting the child in his arms, began questioning her as to its health.

She answered in low monosyllables. At his greeting she had raised her patient eyes to his face—the face of the husband whom she had not seen for seven long years—then the eager look of expectancy which had crossed her own faded away, her eyelids drooped, and her countenance assumed an almost sullen expression.

"Ah, poor Sankwei!" exclaimed Mrs. Dean, who with Adah Charlton stood some little distance apart from the family group.

"Poor wife!" murmured the young girl. She moved forward and would have taken in her own white hands the ringed ones of the Chinese woman, but the young man gently restrained her. "She cannot understand you," said he. As the young girl fell back, he explained to his wife the presence of the stranger women. They were there to bid her welcome; they were kind and good and wished to be her friends as well as his.

Pau Lin looked away. Adah Charlton's bright face, and the tone in her husband's voice when he spoke to the young girl, aroused a suspicion in her mind—a suspicion natural to one who had come from a land where friendship between a man and woman is almost unknown.

"Poor little thing! How shy she is!" exclaimed Mrs. Dean.

Sankwei was glad that neither she nor the young girl understood the meaning of the averted face.

Thus began Wou Sankwei's life in America as a family man. He soon became accustomed to the change, which was not such a great one after all. Pau Lin was more of an accessory than a part of his life. She interfered not at all with his studies, his business, or his friends, and when not engaged in housework or sewing, spent most of her time in the society of one or the other of the merchants' wives who lived in the flats and apartments around her own. She kept up the Chinese custom of taking her meals after her husband or at a separate table, and observed faithfully the rule laid down for her by her late mother-in-law: to keep a quiet tongue in the presence of her man. Sankwei, on his part, was always kind and indulgent. He bought her silk dresses, hair ornaments, fans, and sweetmeats. He ordered her favorite dishes from the Chinese restaurant. When she wished to go out with her women friends, he hired a carriage, and shortly after her advent erected behind her sleeping room a chapel for the ancestral tablet and gorgeous goddess which she had brought over seas with her.

Upon the child both parents lavished affection. He was a quaint, serious little fellow, small for his age and requiring much care. Although naturally much attached to his mother, he became also very fond of his father who, more like an elder brother than a parent, delighted in playing all kinds of games with him, and whom he followed about like a little dog. Adah Charlton took a great fancy to him and sketched him in many different poses for a book on Chinese children which she was illustrating.

"He will be strong enough to go to school next year," said Sankwei to her one day. "Later on I intend to put him through an American college."

"What does your wife think of a Western training for him?" inquired the young girl.

"I have not consulted her about the matter," he answered. "A woman does not understand such things."

"A woman, Mr. Wou," declared Adah, "understands such things as well as and sometimes better than a man."

"An American woman, maybe," amended Sankwei; "but not a Chinese."

From the first Pau Lin had shown no disposition to become Americanized, and Sankwei himself had not urged it.

"I do appreciate the advantages of becoming westernized," said he to Mrs. Dean whose influence and interest in his studies in America had helped him to become what he was, "but it is not as if she had come here as I came, in her learning days. The time for learning with her is over."

One evening, upon returning from his store, he found the little Yen sobbing pitifully.

"What!" he teased, "A man—and weeping."

The boy tried to hide his face, and as he did so, the father noticed that his little hand was red and swollen. He strode into the kitchen where Pau Lin was preparing the evening meal.

"The little child who is not strong—is there anything he could do to merit the infliction of pain?" he questioned.

Pau Lin faced her husband. "Yes, I think so," said she.

"What?"

"I forbade him to speak the language of the white women, and he disobeyed me. He had words in that tongue with the white boy from the next street."

Sankwei was astounded.

"We are living in the white man's country," said he. "The child will have to learn the white man's language."

"Not my child," answered Pau Lin.

Sankwei turned away from her. "Come, little one," said he to his son, "we will take supper tonight at the restaurant, and afterwards Yen shall see a show."

Pau Lin laid down the dish of vegetables which she was straining and took from a hook a small wrap which she adjusted around the boy.

"Now go with thy father," said she sternly.

But the boy clung to her—to the hand which had punished him. "I will sup with you," he cried, "I will sup with you."

"Go," repeated his mother, pushing him from her. And as the two passed over the threshold, she called to the father: "Keep the wrap around the child. The night air is chill."

Late that night, while father and son were peacefully sleeping, the wife and mother arose, and lifting gently the unconscious boy, bore him into the next room where she sat down with him in a rocker. Waking, he clasped his arms around her neck. Backwards and forwards she rocked him, passionately caressing the wounded hand and crooning and crying until he fell asleep again.

The first chastisement that the son of Wou Sankwei had received from his mother, was because he had striven to follow in the footsteps of his father and use the language of the stranger.

"You did perfectly right," said old Sien Tau the following morning, as she leaned over her balcony to speak to the wife of Wou Sankwei. "Had I again a son to rear, I should see to it that he followed not after the white people."

Sien Tau's son had married a white woman, and his children passed their grandame on the street without recognition.

"In this country, she is most happy who has no child," said Lae Choo, resting her elbow upon the shoulder of Sien Tau. "A Toy, the young daughter of Lew Wing, is as bold and free in her ways as are the white women, and her name is on all the men's tongues. What prudent man of our race would take her as wife?"

"One needs not to be born here to be made a fool of," joined in Pau Lin, appearing at another balcony door. "Think of Hum

Wah. From sunrise till midnight he worked for fourteen years, then a white man came along and persuaded from him every dollar, promising to return doublefold within the moon. Many moons have risen and waned, and Hum Wah still waits on this side of the sea for the white man and his money. Meanwhile, his father and mother, who looked long for his coming, have passed beyond returning."

"The new religion—what trouble it brings!" exclaimed Lae Choo. "My man received word yestereve that the good old mother of Chee Ping—he who was baptized a Christian at the last baptizing in the Mission around the corner—had her head secretly severed from her body by the steadfast people of the village, as soon as the news reached there. 'Twas the first violent death in the records of the place. This happened to the mother of one of the boys attending the Mission corner of my street."

"No doubt, the poor old mother, having lost face, minded not so much the losing of her head," sighed Pau Lin. She gazed below her curiously. The American Chinatown held a strange fascination for the girl from the seacoast village. Streaming along the street was a motley throng made up of all nationalities. The sing-song voices of girls whom respectable merchants' wives shudder to name, were calling to one another from high balconies up shadowy alleys. A fat barber was laughing hilariously at a drunken white man who had fallen into a gutter; a withered old fellow, carrying a bird in a cage, stood at the corner entreating passersby to have a good fortune told; some children were burning punk[4] on the curbstone. There went by a stalwart Chief of the Six Companies engaged in earnest confab with a yellow-robed priest from the joss house. A Chinese dressed in the latest American style and a very blonde woman, laughing immoderately, were entering a Chinese restaurant together. Above all the hubbub of voices was heard the clang of electric cars and the jarring of heavy wheels over cobblestones.

Pau Lin raised her head and looked her thoughts at the old woman, Sien Tau.

"Yes," nodded the dame, " 'tis a mad place in which to bring up a child."

Pau Lin went back into the house, gave little Yen his noonday meal, and dressed him with care. His father was to take him out that afternoon. She questioned the boy, as she braided his queue, concerning the white women whom he visited with his father.

It was evening when they returned—Wou Sankwei and his boy. The little fellow ran up to her in high glee. "See, mother," said he, pulling off his cap, "I am like father now. I wear no queue."

The mother looked down upon him—at the little round head from which the queue, which had been her pride, no longer dangled.

"Ah!" she cried. "I am ashamed of you; I am ashamed!"

The boy stared at her, hurt and disappointed.

"Never mind, son," comforted his father. "It is all right."

Pau Lin placed the bowls of seaweed and chickens' liver before them and went back to the kitchen where her own meal was waiting. But she did not eat. She was saying within herself: "It is for the white woman he has done this; it is for the white woman!"

Later, as she laid the queue of her son within the trunk wherein lay that of his father, long since cast aside, she discovered a picture of Mrs. Dean, taken when the American woman had first become the teacher and benefactress of the youthful laundryman. She ran over with it to her husband. "Here," said she; "it is a picture of one of your white friends."

Sankwei took it from her almost reverently, "That woman," he explained, "has been to me as a mother."

"And the young woman—the one with eyes the color of blue china—is she also as a mother?" inquired Pau Lin gently.

But for all her gentleness, Wou Sankwei flushed angrily.

"Never speak of her," he cried. "Never speak of her!"

"Ha, ha, ha! Ha, ha, ha!" laughed Pau Lin. It was a soft and not unmelodious laugh, but to Wou Sankwei it sounded almost sacrilegious.

Nevertheless, he soon calmed down. Pau Lin was his wife, and to be kind to her was not only his duty but his nature. So when his little boy climbed into his lap and besought his father to pipe him a tune, he reached for his flute and called to Pau Lin to put aside work for that night. He would play her some Chinese music. And Pau Lin, whose heart and mind, undiverted by change, had been concentrated upon Wou Sankwei ever since the day she had become his wife, smothered, for the time being, the bitterness in her heart, and succumbed to the magic of her husband's playing—a magic which transported her in thought to the old Chinese days, the old Chinese days whose impression and influence ever remain with the exiled sons and daughters of China.

IV

That a man should take to himself two wives, or even three, if he thought proper, seemed natural and right in the eyes of Wou Pau Lin. She herself had come from a home where there were two broods of children and where her mother and her father's other wife had eaten their meals together as sisters. In that home there had not always been peace; but each woman, at least, had the satisfaction of knowing that her man did not regard or treat the other woman as her superior. To each had fallen the common lot—to bear children to the man, and the man was master of all.

But, oh! the humiliation and shame of bearing children to a man who looked up to another woman—and a woman of another race—as a being above the common uses of women. There is a jealousy of the mind more poignant than any mere animal jealousy.

When Wou Sankwei's second child was two weeks old, Adah Charlton and her aunt called to see the little one, and the young girl chatted brightly with the father and played merrily with Yen, who was growing strong and merry. The American women could not, of course, converse with the Chinese; but Adah placed beside her a bunch of beautiful flowers, pressed her hand, and looked down upon her with radiant eyes. Secure in the difference of race, in the love of many friends, and in the happiness of her chosen work, no suspicion whatever crossed her mind that the woman whose husband was her aunt's protégé tasted everything bitter because of her.

After the visitors had gone, Pau Lin, who had been watching her husband's face while the young artist was in the room, said to him:

"She can be happy who takes all and gives nothing."

"Takes all and gives nothing," echoed her husband. "What do you mean?"

"She has taken all your heart," answered Pau Lin, "but she has not given you a son. It is I who have had that task."

"You are my wife," answered Wou Sankwei. "And she—oh! how can you speak of her so? She, who is as a pure water-flower—a lily!"

He went out of the room, carrying with him a little painting of their boy, which Adah Charlton had given to him as she bade him goodbye and which he had intended showing with pride to the mother.

It was on the day that the baby died that Pau Lin first saw the little picture. It had fallen out of her husband's coat pocket when he lifted the tiny form in his arms and declared it lifeless. Even in that first moment of loss Pau Lin, stooping to pick up the portrait, had shrunk back in horror, crying: "She would cast a spell! She would cast a spell!"

She set her heel upon the face of the picture and destroyed it beyond restoration.

"You know not what you say and do," sternly rebuked Sankwei. He would have added more, but the mystery of the dead child's look forbade him.

"The loss of a son is as the loss of a limb," said he to his childless partner, as under the red glare of the lanterns they sat discussing the sad event.

"But you are not without consolation," returned Leung Tsao. "Your firstborn grows in strength and beauty."

"True," assented Wou Sankwei, his heavy thoughts becoming lighter.

And Pau Lin, in her curtained balcony overhead, drew closer her child and passionately cried:

"Sooner would I, O heart of my heart, that the light of thine eyes were also quenched, than that thou shouldst be contaminated with the wisdom of the new."

v

The Chinese women friends of Wou Pau Lin gossiped among themselves, and their gossip reached the ears of the American

woman friend of Pau Lin's husband. Since the days of her wid-
owhood Mrs. Dean had devoted herself earnestly and whole-
heartedly to the betterment of the condition and the uplifting of
the young workingmen of Chinese race who came to America.
Their appeal and need, as she had told her niece, was for closer
acquaintance with the knowledge of the Western people, and
that she had undertaken to give them, as far as she was able. The
rewards and satisfactions of her work had been rich in some
cases. Witness Wou Sankwei.

But the gossip had reached and much perturbed her. What
was it that they said Wou Sankwei's wife had declared—that her
little son should not go to an American school nor learn the
American learning. Such bigotry and narrow-mindedness! How
sad to think of! Here was a man who had benefited and profited
by living in America, anxious to have his son receive the benefits
of a Western education—and here was this man's wife opposing
him with her ignorance and hampering him with her unreason-
able jealousy.

Yes, she had heard that too. That Wou Sankwei's wife was
jealous—jealous—and her husband the most moral of men, the
kindest and the most generous.

"Of what is she jealous?" she questioned Adah Charlton.
"Other Chinese men's wives, I have known, have had cause to
be jealous, for it is true some of them are dreadfully immoral
and openly support two or more wives. But not Wou Sankwei.
And this little Pau Lin. She has everything that a Chinese woman
could wish for."

A sudden flash of intuition came to the girl, rendering her for
a moment speechless. When she did find words, she said:

"Everything that a Chinese woman could wish for, you say.
Auntie, I do not believe there is any real difference between the
feelings of a Chinese wife and an American wife. Sankwei is
treating Pau Lin as he would treat her were he living in China.
Yet it cannot be the same to her as if she were in their own
country, where he would not come in contact with American
women. A woman is a woman with intuitions and perceptions,
whether Chinese or American, whether educated or uneducated,
and Sankwei's wife must have noticed, even on the day of her
arrival, her husband's manner towards us, and contrasted it with

his manner towards her. I did not realize this before you told me that she was jealous. I only wish I had. Now, for all her ignorance, I can see that the poor little thing became more of an American in that one half hour on the steamer than Wou Sankwei, for all your pride in him, has become in seven years."

Mrs. Dean rested her head on her hand. She was evidently much perplexed.

"What you say may be, Adah," she replied after a while; "but even so, it is Sankwei whom I have known so long, who has my sympathies. He has much to put up with. They have drifted seven years of life apart. There is no bond of interest or sympathy between them, save the boy. Yet never the slightest hint of trouble has come to me from his own lips. Before the coming of Pau Lin, he would confide in me every little thing that worried him, as if he were my own son. Now he maintains absolute silence as to his private affairs."

"Chinese principles," observed Adah, resuming her work. "Yes, I admit Sankwei has some puzzles to solve. Naturally, when he tries to live two lives—that of a Chinese and that of an American."

"He is compelled to that," retorted Mrs. Dean. "Is it not what we teach these Chinese boys—to become Americans? And yet, they are Chinese, and must, in a sense, remain so."

Adah did not answer.

Mrs. Dean sighed. "Poor, dear children, both of them," mused she. "I feel very low-spirited over the matter. I suppose you wouldn't care to come down town with me. I should like to have another chat with Mrs. Wing Sing."

"I shall be glad of the change," replied Adah, laying down her brushes.

Rows of lanterns suspended from many balconies shed a mellow, moonshiny radiance. On the walls and doors were splashes of red paper inscribed with hieroglyphics. In the narrow streets, booths decorated with flowers, and banners and screens painted with immense figures of josses⁵ diverted the eye; while bands of musicians in gaudy silks, shrilled and banged, piped and fluted.

Everybody seemed to be out of doors—men, women, and children—and nearly all were in holiday attire. A couple of priests, in vivid scarlet and yellow robes, were kotowing before

an altar covered with a rich cloth, embroidered in white and
silver. Some Chinese students from the University of California
stood looking on with comprehending, half-scornful interest;
three girls lavishly dressed in colored silks, with their black hair
plastered back from their faces and heavily bejewelled behind,
chirped and chattered in a gilded balcony above them like birds
in a cage. Little children, their hands full of half-moon-shaped
cakes, were pattering about, with eyes, for all the hour, as bright
as stars.

Chinatown was celebrating the Harvest Moon Festival, and
Adah Charlton was glad that she had an opportunity to see
something of the celebration before she returned East. Mrs.
Dean, familiar with the Chinese people and the mazes of Chinatown, led her around fearlessly, pointing out this and that
object of interest and explaining to her its meaning. Seeing that
it was a gala night, she had abandoned her idea of calling upon
the Chinese friend.

Just as they turned a corner leading up to the street where
Wou Sankwei's place of business and residence was situated, a
pair of little hands grasped Mrs. Dean's skirt and a delighted
little voice piped: "See me! See me!" It was little Yen, resplendent in mauve-colored pantaloons and embroidered vest
and cap. Behind him was a tall man whom both women
recognized.

"How do you happen to have Yen with you?" Adah asked.

"His father handed him over to me as a sort of guide, coun-
sellor, and friend. The little fellow is very amusing."

"See over here," interrupted Yen. He hopped over the alley
to where the priests stood by the altar. The grown people followed him.

"What is that man chanting?" asked Adah. One of the priests
had mounted a table, and with arms outstretched towards the
moon sailing high in the heavens, seemed to be making some
sort of an invocation.

Her friend listened for some moments before replying:

"It is a sort of apotheosis of the moon. I have heard it on a
like occasion in Hankow,[6] and the Chinese *bonze*[7] who officiated
gave me a translation. I almost know it by heart. May I repeat
it to you?"

Mrs. Dean and Yen were examining the screen with the big josses.

"Yes, I should like to hear it," said Adah.

"Then fix your eyes upon Diana."[8]

"Dear and lovely moon, as I watch thee pursuing thy solitary course o'er the silent heavens, heart-easing thoughts steal o'er me and calm my passionate soul. Thou art so sweet, so serious, so serene, that thou causest me to forget the stormy emotions which crash like jarring discords across the harmony of life, and bringest to my memory a voice scarce ever heard amidst the warring of the world—love's low voice.

"Thou art so peaceful and so pure that it seemeth as if naught false or ignoble could dwell beneath thy gentle radiance, and that earnestness—even the earnestness of genius—must glow within the bosom of him on whose head thy beams fall like blessings.

"The magic of thy sympathy disburtheneth me of many sorrows, and thoughts, which, like the songs of the sweetest sylvan singer, are too dear and sacred for the careless ears of day, gush forth with unconscious eloquence when thou art the only listener.

"Dear and lovely moon, there are some who say that those who dwell in the sunlit fields of reason should fear to wander through the moonlit valleys of imagination; but I, who have ever been a pilgrim and a stranger in the realm of the wise, offer to thee the homage of a heart which appreciates that thou graciously shinest—even on the fool."

"Is that really Chinese?" queried Adah.

"No doubt about it—in the main. Of course, I cannot swear to it word for word."

"I should think that there would be some reference to the fruits of the earth—the harvest. I always understood that the Chinese religion was so practical."

"Confucianism is. But the Chinese mind requires two religions. Even the most commonplace Chinese has yearnings for something about everyday life. Therefore, he combines with his Confucianism, Buddhism—or, in this country, Christianity."

"Thank you for the information. It has given me a key to the mind of a certain Chinese in whom Auntie and I are interested."

"And who is this particular Chinese in whom you are interested."

"The father of the little boy who is with us tonight."

"Wou Sankwei! Why, here he comes with Lee Tong Hay. Are you acquainted with Lee Tong Hay?"

"No, but I believe Aunt is. Plays and sings in vaudeville, doesn't he?"

"Yes; he can turn himself into a German, a Scotchman, an Irishman, or an American, with the greatest ease, and is as natural in each character as he is as a Chinaman. Hello, Lee Tong Hay."

"Hello, Mr. Stimson."

While her friend was talking to the lively young Chinese who had answered his greeting, Adah went over to where Wou Sankwei stood speaking to Mrs. Dean.

"Yen begins school next week," said her aunt, drawing her arm within her own. It was time to go home.

Adah made no reply. She was settling her mind to do something quite out of the ordinary. Her aunt often called her romantic and impractical. Perhaps she was.

VI

"Auntie went out of town this morning," said Adah Charlton. "I, 'phoned for you to come up, Sankwei because I wished to have a personal and private talk with you."

"Any trouble, Miss Adah," inquired the young merchant. "Anything I can do for you?"

Mrs. Dean often called upon him to transact little business matters for her or to consult with him on various phases of her social and family life.

"I don't know what I would do without Sankwei's head to manage for me," she often said to her niece.

"No," replied the girl, "you do too much for us. You always have, ever since I've known you. It's a shame for us to have allowed you."

"What are you talking about, Miss Adah? Since I came to America your aunt has made this house like a home to me, and, of course, I take an interest in it and like to do anything for it that a man can. I am always happy when I come here."

"Yes, I know you are, poor old boy," said Adah to herself.

Aloud she said: "I have something to say to you which I would like you to hear. Will you listen, Sankwei?"

"Of course I will," he answered.

"Well then," went on Adah, "I asked you to come here today because I have heard that there is trouble at your house and that your wife is jealous of you."

"Would you please not talk about that, Miss Adah. It is a matter which you cannot understand."

"You promised to listen and heed. I do understand, even though I cannot speak to your wife nor find out what she feels and thinks. I know you, Sankwei, and I can see just how the trouble has arisen. As soon as I heard that your wife was jealous I knew why she was jealous."

"Why?" he queried.

"Because," she answered unflinchingly, "you are thinking far too much of other women."

"Too much of other women?" echoed Sankwei dazedly. "I did not know that."

"No, you didn't. That is why I am telling you. But you are, Sankwei. And you are becoming too Americanized. My aunt encourages you to become so, and she is a good woman, with the best and highest of motives; but we are all liable to make mistakes, and it is a mistake to try and make a Chinese man into an American—if he has a wife who is to remain as she always has been. It would be different if you were not married and were a man free to advance. But you are not."

"What am I to do then, Miss Adah? You say that I think too much of other women besides her, and that I am too much Americanized. What can I do about it now that it is so?"

"First of all you must think of your wife. She has done for you what no American woman would do—came to you to be your wife, love you and serve you without even knowing you —took you on trust altogether. You must remember that for many years she was chained in a little cottage to care for your ailing and aged mother—a hard task indeed for a young girl. You must remember that you are the only man in the world to her, and that you have always been the only one that she has ever cared for. Think of her during all the years you are here, living a lonely hard-working life—a baby and an old woman her only companions. For this, she had left all her own relations. No American woman would have sacrificed herself so.

"And, now, what has she? Only you and her housework. The white woman reads, plays, paints, attends concerts, entertainments, lectures, absorbs herself in the work she likes, and in the course of her life thinks of and cares for a great many people. She has much to make her happy besides her husband. The Chinese woman has him only."

"And her boy."

"Yes, her boy," repeated Adah Charlton, smiling in spite of herself, but lapsing into seriousness the moment after. "There's another reason for you to drop the American for a time and go back to being a Chinese. For sake of your darling little boy, you and your wife should live together kindly and cheerfully. That is much more important for his welfare than that he should go to the American school and become Americanized."

"It is my ambition to put him through both American and Chinese schools."

"But what he needs most of all is a loving mother."

"She loves him all right."

"Then why do you not love her as you should? If I were married I would not think my husband loved me very much if he preferred spending his evenings in the society of other women than in mine, and was so much more polite and deferential to other women than he was to me. Can't you understand now why your wife is jealous?"

Wou Sankwei stood up.

"Goodbye," said Adah Charlton, giving him her hand.

"Goodbye," said Wou Sankwei.

Had he been a white man, there is no doubt that Adah Charlton's little lecture would have had a contrary effect from what she meant it to have. At least, the lectured would have been somewhat cynical as to her sincerity. But Wou Sankwei was not a white man. He was a Chinese, and did not see any reason for insincerity in a matter as important as that which Adah Charlton had brought before him. He felt himself exiled from Paradise, yet it did not occur to him to question, as a white man would have done, whether the angel with the flaming sword had authority for her action. Neither did he lay the blame for things gone wrong upon any woman. He simply made up his mind to make the best of what was.

VII

It had been a peaceful week in the Wou household—the week before little Yen was to enter the American school. So peaceful indeed that Wou Sankwei had begun to think that his wife was reconciled to his wishes with regard to the boy. He whistled softly as he whittled away at a little ship he was making for him. Adah Charlton's suggestions had set coursing a train of thought which had curved around Pau Lin so closely that he had decided that, should she offer any further opposition to the boy's attending the American school, he would not insist upon it. After all, though the American language might be useful during this century, the wheel of the world would turn again, and then it might not be necessary at all. Who could tell? He came very near to expressing himself thus to Pau Lin.

And now it was the evening before the morning that little Yen was to march away to the American school. He had been excited all day over the prospect, and to calm him, his father finally told him to read aloud a little story from the Chinese book which he had given him on his first birthday in America and which he had taught him to read. Obediently the little fellow drew his stool to his mother's side and read in his childish sing-song the story of an irreverent lad who came to great grief because he followed after the funeral of his grandfather and regaled himself on the crisply roasted chickens and loose-skinned oranges which were left on the grave for the feasting of the spirit.

Wou Sankwei laughed heartily over the story. It reminded him of some of his own boyish escapades. But Pau Lin stroked silently the head of the little reader, and seemed lost in reverie.

A whiff of fresh salt air blew in from the Bay. The mother shivered, and Wou Sankwei, looking up from the fastening of the boat's rigging, bade Yen close the door. As the little fellow came back to his mother's side, he stumbled over her knee.

"Oh, poor mother!" he exclaimed with quaint apology. " 'Twas the stupid feet, not Yen."

"So," she replied, curling her arm around his neck, " 'tis always the feet. They are to the spirit as the cocoon to the butterfly. Listen, and I will sing you the song of the Happy Butterfly."

She began singing the old Chinese ditty in a fresh birdlike voice. Wou Sankwei, listening, was glad to hear her. He liked having everyone around him cheerful and happy. That had been the charm of the Dean household.

The ship was finished before the little family retired. Yen examined it, critically at first, then exultingly. Finally, he carried it away and placed it carefully in the closet where he kept his kites, balls, tops, and other treasures. "We will set sail with it tomorrow after school," said he to his father, hugging gratefully that father's arm.

Sankwei rubbed the little round head. The boy and he were great chums.

*   *   *

What was that sound which caused Sankwei to start from his sleep? It was just on the border land of night and day, an unusual time for Pau Lin to be up. Yet, he could hear her voice in Yen's room. He raised himself on his elbow and listened. She was softly singing a nursery song about some little squirrels and a huntsman. Sankwei wondered at her singing in that way at such an hour. From where he lay he could just perceive the child's cot and the silent child figure lying motionless in the dim light. How very motionless! In a moment Sankwei was beside it.

The empty cup with its dark dregs told the tale.

The thing he loved the best in all the world—the darling son who had crept into his heart with his joyousness and beauty—had been taken from him—by her who had given.

Sankwei reeled against the wall. The kneeling figure by the cot arose. The face of her was solemn and tender.

"He is saved," smiled she, "from the Wisdom of the New." [9]

In grief too bitter for words the father bowed his head upon his hands.

"Why! Why!" queried Pau Lin, gazing upon him bewilderedly. "The child is happy. The butterfly mourns not o'er the shed cocoon."

Sankwei put up his shutters and wrote this note to Adah Charlton:

> I have lost my boy through an accident. I am returning to China with my wife whose health requires a change.

JACK LONDON

1876–1916

SAID TO HAVE BEEN the illegitimate son of William Henry Chaney, an itinerant astrologer and spiritualist, Jack London was born in San Francisco. After attending high school he took a variety of jobs, going to sea in 1893, traveling in the United States and Canada, and returning to attend the University of California for a semester in 1896. In 1897 London went to the Klondike to join the gold rush, but moved back to Oakland, California, a year later, having failed as a miner.

On his return London began to publish short stories about the Yukon in the *Overland Monthly* (1898) and the *Atlantic Monthly* (1899); his first book of these Alaska stories, *The Son of the Wolf*, appeared in 1900. Many other successful novels and stories followed, including the novels *The Call of the Wild* (1903) and *The Sea-Wolf* (1904). In addition to these novels and stories, London is also known for his tales about the South Sea islands. He traveled widely, reported on the Russo-Japanese war for the Hearst newspapers, and gave lectures. London was a socialist and admirer of Karl Marx, but also an avid reader of Darwin and Nietzsche; some of his books address class struggle, while others celebrate white masculine ideas of individualism and conquest.

When a man journeys into a far country, he must be prepared to forget many of the things he has learned, and to acquire such customs as are inherent with existence in the new land; he must abandon the old ideals and the old gods, and oftentimes he must reverse the very codes by which his conduct has hitherto been shaped. To those who have the protean faculty of adaptability, the novelty of such change may even be a source of pleasure; but to those who happen to be hardened to the ruts in which they were created, the pressure of the altered environment is unbearable, and they chafe in body and in spirit under the new restrictions which they do not understand. This chafing is bound to act and react, producing divers evils and leading to various misfortunes. It were better for the man who cannot fit himself to the new groove to return to his own country; if he delay too long, he will surely die.

The man who turns his back upon the comforts of an elder civilization, to face the savage youth, the primordial simplicity of the North, may estimate success at an inverse ratio to the quantity and quality of his hopelessly fixed habits. He will soon discover, if he be a fit candidate, that the material habits are the less important. The exchange of such things as a dainty menu for rough fare, of the stiff leather shoe for the soft, shapeless moccasin, of the feather bed for a couch in the snow, is after all a very easy matter. But his pinch will come in learning properly to shape his mind's attitude toward all things, and especially toward his fellow man. For the courtesies of ordinary life, he must substitute unselfishness, forbearance, and tolerance. Thus, and thus only, can he gain that pearl of great price,—true comradeship. He must not say "Thank you"; he must mean it without opening his mouth, and prove it by responding in kind. In short, he must substitute the deed for the word, the spirit for the letter.

When the world rang with the tale of Arctic gold, and the lure of the North gripped the heartstrings of men, Carter Weatherbee threw up his snug clerkship, turned the half of his savings over to his wife, and with the remainder bought an outfit. There was no romance in his nature,—the bondage of commerce had crushed all that; he was simply tired of the ceaseless grind, and wished to risk great hazards in view of corresponding returns. Like many another fool, disdaining the old trails used by the Northland pioneers for a score of years, he hurried to Edmonton[1] in the spring of the year; and there, unluckily for his soul's welfare, he allied himself with a party of men.

There was nothing unusual about this party, except its plans. Even its goal, like that of all other parties, was the Klondike.[2] But the route it had mapped out to attain that goal took away the breath of the hardiest native, born and bred to the vicissitudes of the Northwest. Even Jacques Baptiste, born of a Chippewa woman and a renegade *voyageur*[3] (having raised his first whimpers in a deerskin lodge north of sixty-fifth parallel,[4] and had the same hushed by blissful sucks of raw tallow), was surprised. Though he sold his services to them and agreed to travel even to the never-opening ice, he shook his head ominously whenever his advice was asked.

Percy Cuthfert's evil star must have been in the ascendant, for he, too, joined this company of argonauts.[5] He was an ordinary man, with a bank account as deep as his culture, which is saying a good deal. He had no reason to embark on such a venture,—no reason in the world, save that he suffered from an abnormal development of sentimentality. He mistook this for the true spirit of romance and adventure. Many another man has done the like, and made as fatal a mistake.

The first break-up of spring found the party following the ice-run of Elk River. It was an imposing fleet, for the outfit was large, and they were accompanied by a disreputable contingent of half-breed *voyageurs* with their women and children. Day in and day out, they labored with the bateaux and canoes, fought mosquitoes and other kindred pests, or sweated and swore at the portages. Severe toil like this lays a man naked to the very roots of his soul, and ere Lake Athabasca[6] was lost in the south, each member of the party had hoisted his true colors.

The two shirks and chronic grumblers were Carter Weatherbee and Percy Cuthfert. The whole party complained less of its aches and pains than did either of them. Not once did they volunteer for the thousand and one petty duties of the camp. A bucket of water to be brought, an extra armful of wood to be chopped, the dishes to be washed and wiped, a search to be made through the outfit for some suddenly indispensable article,—and these two effete scions of civilization discovered sprains or blisters requiring instant attention. They were the first to turn in at night, with a score of tasks yet undone; the last to turn out in the morning, when the start should be in readiness before the breakfast was begun. They were the first to fall to at meal-time, the last to have a hand in the cooking; the first to dive for a slim delicacy, the last to discover they had added to their own another man's share. If they toiled at the oars, they slyly cut the water at each stroke and allowed the boat's momentum to float up the blade. They thought nobody noticed; but their comrades swore under their breaths and grew to hate them, while Jacques Baptiste sneered openly and damned them from morning till night. But Jacques Baptiste was no gentleman.

At the Great Slave,[7] Hudson Bay dogs were purchased, and the fleet sank to the guards with its added burden of dried fish and pemmican.[8] Then canoe and bateau answered to the swift current of the Mackenzie,[9] and they plunged into the Great Barren Ground. Every likely-looking "feeder" was prospected, but the elusive "pay-dirt"[10] danced ever to the north. At the Great Bear,[11] overcome by the common dread of the Unknown Lands, their *voyageurs* began to desert, and Fort of Good Hope[12] saw the last and bravest bending to the tow-lines as they bucked the current down which they had so treacherously glided. Jacques Baptiste alone remained. Had he not sworn to travel even to the never-opening ice?

The lying charts, compiled in main from hearsay, were now constantly consulted. And they felt the need of hurry, for the sun had already passed its northern solstice and was leading the winter south again. Skirting the shores of the bay, where the Mackenzie disembogues into the Arctic Ocean, they entered the mouth of the Little Peel River. Then began the arduous upstream toil, and the two Incapables fared worse than ever. Towline and pole, paddle and tump-line,[13] rapids and portages,—such tortures served to give the one a deep disgust for great hazards, and printed for the other a fiery text on the true romance of adventure. One day they waxed mutinous, and being vilely cursed by Jacques Baptiste, turned, as worms sometimes will. But the half-breed thrashed the twain, and sent them, bruised and bleeding, about their work. It was the first time either had been man-handled.

Abandoning their river craft at the headwaters of the Little Peel, they consumed the rest of the summer in the great portage over the Mackenzie watershed to the West Rat. This little stream fed the Porcupine, which in turn joined the Yukon where that mighty highway of the North countermarches on the Arctic Circle. But they had lost in the race with winter, and one day they tied their rafts to the thick eddy-ice and hurried their goods ashore. That night the river jammed and broke several times; the following morning it had fallen asleep for good.

"We can't be more 'n four hundred miles from the Yukon," concluded Sloper, multiplying his thumb nails by the scale of the map. The council, in which the two Incapables had whined to excellent disadvantage, was drawing to a close.

"Hudson Bay Post, long time ago. No use um now." Jacques Baptiste's father had made the trip for the Fur Company in the old days, incidentally marking the trail with a couple of frozen toes.

"Sufferin' cracky!" cried another of the party. "No whites?"

"Nary white," Sloper sententiously affirmed; "but it's only five hundred more up the Yukon to Dawson. Call it a rough thousand from here."

Weatherbee and Cuthfert groaned in chorus.

"How long'll that take, Baptiste?"

The half-breed figured for a moment. "Workum like hell, no man play out, ten—twenty—forty—fifty days. Um babies come" (designating the Incapables), "no can tell. Mebbe when hell freeze over; mebbe not then."

The manufacture of snowshoes and moccasins ceased. Somebody called the name of an absent member, who came out of an ancient cabin at the edge of the camp-fire and joined them. The cabin was one of the many mysteries which lurk in the vast recesses of the North. Built when and by whom, no man could tell. Two graves in the open, piled high with stones, perhaps contained the secret of those early wanderers. But whose hand had piled the stones?

The moment had come. Jacques Baptiste paused in the fitting of a harness and pinned the struggling dog in the snow. The cook made mute protest for delay, threw a handful of bacon into a noisy pot of beans, then came to attention. Sloper rose to his feet. His body was a ludicrous contrast to the healthy physiques of the Incapables. Yellow and weak, fleeing from a South American fever-hole, he had not broken his flight across the zones, and was still able to toil with men. His weight was probably ninety pounds, with the heavy hunting-knife thrown in, and his grizzled hair told of a prime which had ceased to be. The fresh young muscles of either Weatherbee or Cuthfert were equal to ten times the endeavor of his; yet he could walk them into the earth in a day's journey. And all this day he had whipped his stronger comrades into venturing a thousand miles of the stiffest hardship man can conceive. He was the incarnation of the unrest of his race, and the old Teutonic stubbornness, dashed with the quick grasp and action of the Yankee, held the flesh in the bondage of the spirit.

"All those in favor of going on with the dogs as soon as the ice sets, say ay."

"Ay!" rang out eight voices,—voices destined to string a trail of oaths along many a hundred miles of pain.

"Contrary minded?"

"No!" For the first time the Incapables were united without some compromise of personal interests.

"And what are you going to do about it?" Weatherbee added belligerently.

"Majority rule! Majority rule!" clamored the rest of the party.

"I know the expedition is liable to fall through if you don't come," Sloper replied sweetly; "but I guess, if we try real hard, we can manage to do without you. What do you say, boys?"

The sentiment was cheered to the echo.

"But I say, you know," Cuthfert ventured apprehensively; "what's a chap like me to do?"

"Ain't you coming with us?"

"No-o."

"Then do as you damn well please. We won't have nothing to say."

"Kind o' calkilate yuh might settle it with that canoodlin'[14] pardner of yourn," suggested a heavy-going Westerner from the Dakotas, at the same time pointing out Weatherbee. "He'll be shore to ask yuh what yur a-goin' to do when it comes to cookin' an' gatherin' the wood."

"Then we'll consider it all arranged," concluded Sloper. "We'll pull out to-morrow, if we camp within five miles,—just to get everything in running order and remember if we've forgotten anything."

The sleds groaned by on their steel-shod runners, and the dogs strained low in the harnesses in which they were born to die. Jacques Baptiste paused by the side of Sloper to get a last glimpse of the cabin. The smoke curled up pathetically from the Yukon stove-pipe. The two Incapables were watching them from the doorway.

Sloper laid his hand on the other's shoulder.

"Jacques Baptiste, did you ever hear of the Kilkenny cats?"[15]

The half-breed shook his head.

"Well, my friend and good comrade, the Kilkenny cats fought till neither hide, nor hair, nor yowl, was left. You understand? —till nothing was left. Very good. Now, these two men don't like work. They won't work. We know that. They'll be alone in that cabin all winter,—a mighty long, dark winter. Kilkenny cats,—well?"

The Frenchman in Baptiste shrugged his shoulders, but the Indian in him was silent. Nevertheless, it was an eloquent shrug, pregnant with prophecy.

Things prospered in the little cabin at first. The rough badinage of their comrades had made Weatherbee and Cuthfert conscious of the mutual responsibility which had devolved upon them; besides, there was not so much work after all for two healthy men. And the removal of the cruel whip-hand, or in other words the bulldozing half-breed, had brought with it a joyous reaction. At first, each strove to outdo the other, and they performed petty tasks with an unction which would have opened the eyes of their comrades who were now wearing out bodies and souls on the Long Trail.

All care was banished. The forest, which shouldered in upon them from three sides, was an inexhaustible woodyard. A few yards from their door slept the Porcupine,[16] and a hole through its winter robe formed a bubbling spring of water, crystal clear and painfully cold. But they soon grew to find fault with even that. The hole would persist in freezing up, and thus gave them many a miserable hour of ice-chopping. The unknown builders of the cabin had extended the side-logs so as to support a cache at the rear. In this was stored the bulk of the party's provisions. Food there was, without stint, for three times the men who were fated to live upon it. But the most of it was of the kind which built up brawn and sinew, but did not tickle the palate. True, there was sugar in plenty for two ordinary men; but these two were little else than children. They early discovered the virtues of hot water judiciously saturated with sugar, and they prodigally swam their flapjacks and soaked their crusts in the rich, white syrup. Then coffee and tea, and especially the dried fruits, made disastrous inroads upon it. The first words they had were over the sugar question. And it is a really serious thing when two men, wholly dependent upon each other for company, begin to quarrel.

Weatherbee loved to discourse blatantly on politics, while Cuthfert, who had been prone to clip his coupons and let the commonwealth jog on as best it might, either ignored the subject or delivered himself of startling epigrams. But the clerk was too obtuse to appreciate the clever shaping of thought, and this waste of ammunition irritated Cuthfert. He had been used to blinding people by his brilliancy, and it worked him quite a hardship, this loss of an audience. He felt personally aggrieved and unconsciously held his mutton-head[17] companion responsible for it.

Save existence, they had nothing in common,—came in touch on no single point. Weatherbee was a clerk who had known naught but clerking all his life; Cuthfert was a master of arts, a dabbler in oils, and had written not a little. The one was a lower-class man who considered himself a gentleman, and the other was a gentleman who knew himself to be such. From this it may be remarked that a man can be a gentleman without possessing the first instinct of true comradeship. The clerk was as sensuous as the other was aesthetic, and his love adventures, told at great length and chiefly coined from his imagination, affected the supersensitive master of arts in the same way as so many whiffs of sewer gas. He deemed the clerk a filthy, uncultured brute, whose place was in the muck with the swine, and told him so; and he was reciprocally informed that he was a milk-and-water sissy and a cad. Weatherbee could not have defined "cad" for his life; but it satisfied its purpose, which after all seems the main point in life.

Weatherbee flatted every third note and sang such songs as "The Boston Burglar" and "The Handsome Cabin Boy," for hours at a time, while Cuthfert wept with rage, till he could stand it no longer and fled into the outer cold. But there was no escape. The intense frost could not be endured for long at a time, and the little cabin crowded them—beds, stove, table, and all—into a space of ten by twelve. The very presence of either became a personal affront to the other, and they lapsed into sullen silences which increased in length and strength as the days went by. Occasionally, the flash of an eye or the curl of a lip got the better of them, though they strove to wholly ignore each other during these mute periods. And a great wonder sprang up in the breast of each, as to how God had ever come to create the other.

With little to do, time became an intolerable burden to them. This naturally made them still lazier. They sank into a physical lethargy which there was no escaping, and which made them rebel at the performance of the smallest chore. One morning when it was his turn to cook the common breakfast, Weatherbee rolled out of his blankets, and to the snoring of his companion, lighted first the slush-lamp[18] and then the fire. The kettles were frozen hard, and there was no water in the cabin with which to wash. But he did not mind that. Waiting for it to thaw, he sliced the bacon and plunged into the hateful task of breadmaking. Cuthfert had been slyly watching through his half-closed lids. Consequently there was a scene, in which they fervently blessed each other, and agreed, thenceforth, that each do his own cooking. A week later, Cuthfert neglected his morning ablutions, but none the less complacently ate the meal which he had cooked.

Weatherbee grinned. After that the foolish custom of washing passed out of their lives.

As the sugar-pile and other little luxuries dwindled, they began to be afraid they were not getting their proper shares, and in order that they might not be robbed, they fell to gorging themselves. The luxuries suffered in this gluttonous contest, as did also the men. In the absence of fresh vegetables and exercise, their blood became impoverished, and a loathsome, purplish rash crept over their bodies. Yet they refused to heed the warning. Next, their muscles and joints began to swell, the flesh turning black, while their mouths, gums, and lips took on the color of rich cream. Instead of being drawn together by their misery, each gloated over the other's symptoms as the scurvy[19] took its course.

They lost all regard for personal appearance, and for that matter, common decency. The cabin became a pigpen, and never once were the beds made or fresh pine boughs laid underneath. Yet they could not keep to their blankets, as they would have wished; for the frost was inexorable, and the fire box consumed much fuel. The hair of their heads and faces grew long and shaggy, while their garments would have disgusted a ragpicker.[20] But they did not care. They were sick, and there was no one to see; besides, it was very painful to move about.

To all this was added a new trouble,—the Fear of the North. This Fear was the joint child of the Great Cold and the Great Silence, and was born in the darkness of December, when the sun dipped below the southern horizon for good. It affected them according to their natures. Weatherbee fell prey to the grosser superstitions, and did his best to resurrect the spirits which slept in the forgotten graves. It was a fascinating thing, and in his dreams they came to him from out of the cold, and snuggled into his blankets, and told him of their toils and troubles ere they died. He shrank away from the clammy contact as they drew closer and twined their frozen limbs about him, and when they whispered in his ear of things to come, the cabin rang with his frightened shrieks. Cuthfert did not understand,—for they no longer spoke,—and when thus awakened he invariably grabbed for his revolver. Then he would sit up in bed, shivering nervously, with the weapon trained on the unconscious dreamer.

Cuthfert deemed the man going mad, and so came to fear for his life.

His own malady assumed a less concrete form. The mysterious artisan who had laid the cabin, log by log, had pegged a windvane to the ridge-pole. Cuthfert noticed it always pointed south, and one day, irritated by its steadfastness of purpose, he turned it toward the east. He watched eagerly, but never a breath came by to disturb it. Then he turned the vane to the north, swearing never again to touch it till the wind did blow. But the air frightened him with its unearthly calm, and he often rose in the middle of the night to see if the vane had veered,—ten degrees would have satisfied him. But no, it poised above him as unchangeable as fate. His imagination ran riot, till it became to him a fetich. Sometimes he followed the path it pointed across the dismal dominions, and allowed his soul to become saturated with the Fear. He dwelt upon the unseen and the unknown till the burden of eternity appeared to be crushing him. Everything in the Northland had that crushing effect,—the absence of life and motion; the darkness; the infinite peace of the brooding land; the ghastly silence, which made the echo of each heart-beat a sacrilege; the solemn forest which seemed to guard an awful, inexpressible something, which neither word nor thought could compass.

The world he had so recently left, with its busy nations and great enterprises, seemed very far away. Recollections occasionally obtruded,—recollections of marts and galleries and crowded thoroughfares, of evening dress and social functions, of good men and dear women he had known,—but they were dim memories of a life he had lived long centuries agone, on some other planet. This phantasm was the Reality. Standing beneath the wind-vane, his eyes fixed on the polar skies, he could not bring himself to realize that the Southland really existed, that at that very moment it was a-roar with life and action. There was no Southland, no men being born of women, no giving and taking in marriage. Beyond his bleak sky-line there stretched vast solitudes, and beyond these still vaster solitudes. There were no lands of sunshine, heavy with the perfume of flowers. Such things were only old dreams of paradise. The sunlands of the West and the spicelands of the East, the smiling Arcadias[21] and blissful Islands of the Blest,—ha! ha! His laughter split the void and shocked him with its unwonted sound. There was no sun. This was the Universe, dead and cold and dark, and he its only citizen. Weatherbee? At such moments Weatherbee did not count. He was a Caliban,[22] a monstrous phantom, fettered to him for untold ages, the penalty of some forgotten crime.

He lived with Death among the dead, emasculated by the sense of his own insignificance, crushed by the passive mastery of the slumbering ages. The magnitude of all things appalled him. Everything partook of the superlative save himself,—the perfect cessation of wind and motion, the immensity of the snow-covered wilderness, the height of the sky and the depth of the silence. That wind-vane,—if it would only move. If a thunderbolt would fall, or the forest flare up in flame. The rolling up of the heavens as a scroll, the crash of Doom—anything, anything! But no, nothing moved; the Silence crowded in, and the Fear of the North laid icy fingers on his heart.

Once, like another Crusoe,[23] by the edge of the river he came upon a track,—the faint tracery of a snowshoe rabbit on the delicate snow-crust. It was a revelation. There was life in the Northland. He would follow it, look upon it, gloat over it. He forgot his swollen muscles, plunging through the deep snow in an ecstasy of anticipation. The forest swallowed him up, and the brief midday twilight vanished; but he pursued his quest till exhausted nature asserted itself and laid him helpless in the snow. There he groaned and cursed his folly, and knew the track to be the fancy of his brain; and late that night he dragged himself into the cabin on hands and knees, his cheeks frozen and a strange numbness about his feet. Weatherbee grinned malevolently, but made no offer to help him. He thrust needles into his toes and thawed them out by the stove. A week later mortification set in.

But the clerk had his own troubles. The dead men came out of their graves more frequently now, and rarely left him, waking or sleeping. He grew to wait and dread their coming, never passing the twin cairns without a shudder. One night they came to him in his sleep and led him forth to an appointed task. Frightened into inarticulate horror, he awoke between the heaps of stones and fled wildly to the cabin. But he had lain there for some time, for his feet and cheeks were also frozen.

Sometimes he became frantic at their insistent presence, and danced about the cabin, cutting the empty air with an axe, and smashing everything within reach. During these ghostly encounters, Cuthfert huddled into his blankets and followed the madman about with a cocked revolver, ready to shoot him if he came too near. But, recovering from one of these spells, the clerk noticed the weapon trained upon him. His suspicions were aroused, and thenceforth he, too, lived in fear of his life. They watched each other closely after that, and faced about in startled fright whenever either passed behind the other's back. This apprehensiveness became a mania which controlled them even in their sleep. Through mutual fear they tacitly let the slush-lamp burn all night, and saw to a plentiful supply of bacon-grease before retiring. The slightest movement on the part of one was sufficient to arouse the other, and many a still watch their gazes countered as they shook beneath their blankets with fingers on the trigger-guards.

What with the Fear of the North, the mental strain, and the ravages of the disease, they lost all semblance of humanity, taking on the appearance of wild beasts, hunted and desperate. Their cheeks and noses, as an aftermath of the freezing, had turned black. Their frozen toes had begun to drop away at the first and second joints. Every movement brought pain, but the fire box was insatiable, wringing a ransom of torture from their miserable bodies. Day in, day out, it demanded its food,—a veritable pound of flesh,[24]—and they dragged themselves into the forest to chop wood on their knees. Once, crawling thus in search of dry sticks, unknown to each other they entered a thicket from opposite sides. Suddenly, without warning, two peering death's-heads confronted each other. Suffering had so transformed them that recognition was impossible. They sprang to their feet, shrieking with terror, and dashed away on their mangled stumps; and falling at the cabin door, they clawed and scratched like demons till they discovered their mistake.

Occasionally they lapsed normal, and during one of these sane intervals, the chief bone of contention, the sugar, had been divided equally between them. They guarded their separate sacks, stored up in the cache, with jealous eyes; for there were but a few cupfuls left, and they were totally devoid of faith in each other. But one day Cuthfert made a mistake. Hardly able to move, sick with pain, with his head swimming and eyes blinded, he crept into the cache, sugar canister in hand, and mistook Weatherbee's sack for his own.

January had been born but a few days when this occurred. The sun had some time since passed its lowest southern declination, and at meridian now threw flaunting streaks of yellow light upon the northern sky. On the day following his mistake with the sugarbag, Cuthfert found himself feeling better, both in body and in spirit. As noontime drew near and the day brightened, he dragged himself outside to feast on the evanescent glow, which was to him an earnest of the sun's future intentions. Weatherbee was also feeling somewhat better, and crawled out beside him. They propped themselves in the snow beneath the moveless wind-vane, and waited.

The stillness of death was about them. In other climes, when nature falls into such moods, there is a subdued air of expectancy, a waiting for some small voice to take up the broken strain. Not so in the North. The two men had lived seeming aeons in this ghostly peace. They could remember no song of the past; they could conjure no song of the future. This unearthly calm had always been,—the tranquil silence of eternity.

Their eyes were fixed upon the north. Unseen, behind their backs, behind the towering mountains to the south, the sun swept toward the zenith of another sky than theirs. Sole spectators of the mighty canvas, they watched the false dawn slowly grow. A faint flame began to glow and smoulder. It deepened in intensity, ringing the changes of reddish-yellow, purple, and saffron. So bright did it become that Cuthfert thought the sun must surely be behind it,—a miracle, the sun rising in the north! Suddenly, without warning and without fading, the canvas was swept clean. There was no color in the sky. The light had gone out of the day. They caught their breaths in half-sobs. But lo! the air was a-glint with particles of scintillating frost, and there, to the north, the wind-vane lay in vague outline on the snow. A shadow! A shadow! It was exactly midday. They jerked their heads hurriedly to the south. A golden rim peeped over the mountain's snowy shoulder, smiled upon them an instant, then dipped from sight again.

There were tears in their eyes as they sought each other. A strange softening came over them. They felt irresistibly drawn toward each other. The sun was coming back again. It would be with them tomorrow, and the next day, and the next. And it would stay longer every visit, and a time would come when it would ride their heaven day and night, never once dropping below the sky-line. There would be no night. The ice-locked winter would be broken; the winds would blow and the forests answer; the land would bathe in the blessed sunshine, and life renew. Hand in hand, they would quit this horrid dream and journey back to the Southland. They lurched blindly forward, and their hands met,—their poor maimed hands, swollen and distorted beneath their mittens.

But the promise was destined to remain unfulfilled. The Northland is the Northland, and men work out their souls by strange rules, which other men, who have not journeyed into far countries, cannot come to understand.

An hour later, Cuthfert put a pan of bread into the oven, and fell to speculating on what the surgeons could do with his feet when he got back. Home did not seem so very far away now. Weatherbee was rummaging in the cache. Of a sudden, he raised a whirlwind of blasphemy, which in turn ceased with startling abruptness. The other man had robbed his sugar-sack. Still, things might have happened differently, had not the two dead men come out from under the stones and hushed the hot words in his throat. They led him quite gently from the cache, which he forgot to close. That consummation was reached; that something they had whispered to him in his dreams was about to happen. They guided him gently, very gently, to the woodpile, where they put the axe in his hands. Then they helped him shove open the cabin door, and he felt sure they shut it after him,—at least he heard it slam and the latch fall sharply into place. And he knew they were waiting just without, waiting for him to do his task.

"Carter! I say, Carter!"

Percy Cuthfert was frightened at the look on the clerk's face, and he made haste to put the table between them.

Carter Weatherbee followed, without haste and without enthusiasm. There was neither pity nor passion in his face, but rather the patient, stolid look of one who has certain work to do and goes about it methodically.

"I say, what's the matter?"

The clerk dodged back, cutting off his retreat to the door, but never opening his mouth.

"I say, Carter, I say; let's talk. There's a good chap."

The master of arts was thinking rapidly, now, shaping a skillful flank movement on the bed where his Smith & Wesson lay. Keeping his eyes on the madman, he rolled backward on the bunk, at the same time clutching the pistol.

"Carter!"

The powder flashed full in Weatherbee's face, but he swung his weapon and leaped forward. The axe bit deeply at the base of the spine, and Percy Cuthfert felt all consciousness of his lower limbs leave him. Then the clerk fell heavily upon him, clutching him by the throat with feeble fingers. The sharp bite of the axe had caused Cuthfert to drop the pistol, and as his lungs panted for release, he fumbled aimlessly for it among the blankets. Then he remembered. He slid a hand up the clerk's belt to the sheathknife; and they drew very close to each other in that last clinch.

Percy Cuthfert felt his strength leave him. The lower portion of his body was useless. The inert weight of Weatherbee crushed him,—crushed him and pinned him there like a bear under a trap. The cabin became filled with a familiar odor, and he knew the bread to be burning. Yet what did it matter? He would never need it. And there were all of six cupfuls of sugar in the cache, —if he had foreseen this he would not have been so saving the last several days. Would the wind-vane ever move? It might even be veering now. Why not? Had he not seen the sun to-day? He would go and see. No; it was impossible to move. He had not thought the clerk so heavy a man.

How quickly the cabin cooled! The fire must be out. The cold was forcing in. It must be below zero already, and the ice creeping up the inside of the door. He could not see it, but his past experience enabled him to gauge its progress by the cabin's temperature. The lower hinge must be white ere now. Would the tale of this ever reach the world? How would his friends take it? They would read it over their coffee, most likely, and talk it over at the clubs. He could see them very clearly. "Poor Old Cuthfert," they murmured; "not such a bad sort of a chap, after all." He smiled at their eulogies, and passed on in search of a Turkish bath. It was the same old crowd upon the streets. Strange, they did not notice his moosehide moccasins and tattered German socks! He would take a cab. And after the bath a shave would not be bad. No; he would eat first. Steak, and potatoes, and green things,—how fresh it all was! And what was that? Squares of honey, streaming liquid amber! But why did they bring so much? Ha! ha! he could never eat it all. Shine! Why certainly. He put his foot on the box. The bootblack looked curiously up at him, and he remembered his moosehide moccasins and went away hastily.

Hark! The wind-vane must be surely spinning. No; a mere singing in his ears. That was all,—a mere singing. The ice must have passed the latch by now. More likely the upper hinge was covered. Between the moss-chinked roof-poles, little points of frost began to appear. How slowly they grew! No; not so slowly. There was a new one, and there another. Two—three—four; they were coming too fast to count. There were two growing together. And there, a third had joined them. Why, there were no more spots. They had run together and formed a sheet.

Well, he would have company. If Gabriel[25] ever broke the silence of the North, they would stand together, hand in hand, before the great White Throne. And God would judge them, God would judge them!

Then Percy Cuthfert closed his eyes and dropped off to sleep.

TO THE MAN ON TRAIL

"Dump it in."

"But I say, Kid, is n't that going it a little too strong? Whiskey and alcohol's bad enough; but when it comes to brandy and pepper-sauce[1] and"—

"Dump it in. Who's making this punch, anyway?" And Malemute Kid smiled benignantly through the clouds of steam. "By the time you've been in this country as long as I have, my son, and lived on rabbit-tracks and salmon-belly, you'll learn that Christmas comes only once per annum. And a Christmas without punch is sinking a hole to bedrock with nary a pay-streak."[2]

"Stack up on that fer a high cyard,"[3] approved Big Jim Belden, who had come down from his claim on Mazy May to spend Christmas, and who, as every one knew, had been living the two months past on straight moose-meat. "Hain't fergot the *hooch*[4] we-uns made on the Tanana, hev yeh?"

"Well, I guess yes. Boys, it would have done your hearts good to see that whole tribe fighting drunk—and all because of a glorious ferment of sugar and sour dough. That was before your time," Malemute Kid said as he turned to Stanley Prince, a young mining expert who had been in two years. "No white women in the country then, and Mason wanted to get married. Ruth's father was chief of the Tananas,[5] and objected, like the rest of the tribe. Stiff? Why, I used my last pound of sugar; finest work in that line I ever did in my life. You should have seen the chase, down the river and across the portage."

"But the squaw?" asked Louis Savoy, the tall French-Canadian, becoming interested; for he had heard of this wild deed, when at Forty Mile the preceding winter.

Then Malemute Kid, who was a born raconteur,[6] told the unvarnished tale of the Northland Lochinvar.[7] More than one rough adventurer of the North felt his heartstrings draw closer, and experienced vague yearnings for the sunnier pastures of the Southland, where life promised something more than a barren struggle with cold and death.

"We struck the Yukon just behind the first ice-run," he concluded, "and the tribe only a quarter of an hour behind. But that saved us; for the second run broke the jam above and shut them out. When they finally got into Nuklukyeto, the whole Post was ready for them. And as to the foregathering, ask Father Roubeau here: he performed the ceremony."

The Jesuit took the pipe from his lips, but could only express his gratification with patriarchal smiles, while Protestant and Catholic vigorously applauded.

"By gar!" ejaculated Louis Savoy, who seemed overcome by

the romance of it. "La petite squaw; mon Mason brav.[8] By gar!"

Then, as the first tin cups of punch went round, Bettles the Unquenchable sprang to his feet and struck up his favorite drinking song:—

> "There's Henry Ward Beecher[9]
> And Sunday-school teachers,
>   All drink of the sassafras root;[10]
> But you bet all the same,
> If it had its right name,
>   It's the juice of the forbidden fruit."

> "Oh the juice of the forbidden fruit,"

roared out the Bacchanalian chorus,—

> "Oh the juice of the forbidden fruit;
>   But you bet all the same,
>   If it had its right name,
> It's the juice of the forbidden fruit."

Malemute Kid's frightful concoction did its work; the men of the camps and trails unbent in its genial glow, and jest and song and tales of past adventure went round the board. Aliens from a dozen lands, they toasted each and all. It was the Englishman, Prince, who pledged "Uncle Sam, the precocious infant of the New World"; the Yankee, Bettles, who drank to "The Queen, God bless her"; and together, Savoy and Meyers, the German trader, clanged their cups to Alsace and Lorraine.[11]

Then Malemute Kid arose, cup in hand, and glanced at the greased-paper window, where the frost stood full three inches thick. "A health to the man on trail this night; may his grub hold out; may his dogs keep their legs; may his matches never miss fire."

Crack! Crack!—they heard the familiar music of the dogwhip, the whining howl of the Malemutes,[12] and the crunch of a sled as it drew up to the cabin. Conversation languished while they waited the issue.

"An old-timer; cares for his dogs and then himself," whispered Malemute Kid to Prince, as they listened to the snapping jaws and the wolfish snarls and yelps of pain which proclaimed to their practiced ears that the stranger was beating back their dogs while he fed his own.

Then came the expected knock, sharp and confident, and the stranger entered. Dazzled by the light, he hesitated a moment at the door, giving to all a chance for scrutiny. He was a striking personage, and a most picturesque one, in his Arctic dress of wool and fur. Standing six foot two or three, with proportionate breadth of shoulders and depth of chest, his smooth-shaven face nipped by the cold to a gleaming pink, his long lashes and eyebrows white with ice, and the ear and neck flaps of his great wolfskin cap loosely raised, he seemed, of a verity, the Frost King,[13] just stepped in out of the night. Clasped outside his mackinaw jacket,[14] a beaded belt held two large Colt's revolvers and a hunting-knife, while he carried, in addition to the inevitable dogwhip, a smokeless rifle of the largest bore and latest pattern. As he came forward, for all his step was firm and elastic, they could see that fatigue bore heavily upon him.

An awkward silence had fallen, but his hearty "What cheer, my lads?" put them quickly at ease, and the next instant Malemute Kid and he had gripped hands. Though they had never met, each had heard of the other, and the recognition was mutual. A sweeping introduction and a mug of punch were forced upon him before he could explain his errand.

"How long since that basket-sled, with three men and eight dogs, passed?" he asked.

"An even two days ahead. Are you after them?"

"Yes; my team. Run them off under my very nose, the cusses. I've gained two days on them already,—pick them up on the next run."

"Reckon they'll show spunk?" asked Belden, in order to keep up the conversation, for Malemute Kid already had the coffee-pot on and was busily frying bacon and moose-meat.

The stranger significantly tapped his revolvers.

"When 'd yeh leave Dawson?"[15]

"Twelve o'clock."

"Last night?"—as a matter of course.

"To-day."

A murmur of surprise passed round the circle. And well it

might; for it was just midnight, and seventy-five miles of rough river trail was not to be sneered at for a twelve hours' run.

The talk soon became impersonal, however, harking back to the trails of childhood. As the young stranger ate of the rude fare, Malemute Kid attentively studied his face. Nor was he long in deciding that it was fair, honest, and open, and that he liked it. Still youthful, the lines had been firmly traced by toil and hardship. Though genial in conversation, and mild when at rest, the blue eyes gave promise of the hard steel-glitter which comes when called into action, especially against odds. The heavy jaw and square-cut chin demonstrated rugged pertinacity and indomitability. Nor, though the attributes of the lion were there, was there wanting the certain softness, the hint of womanliness, which bespoke the emotional nature.

"So thet's how me an' the ol' woman got spliced,"[16] said Belden, concluding the exciting tale of his courtship. " 'Here we be, dad,' sez she. 'An' may yeh be damned,' sez he to her, an' then to me, 'Jim, yeh—yeh git outen them good duds o' yourn; I want a right peart slice o' thet forty acre ploughed 'fore dinner.' An' then he turns on her an' sez, 'An' yeh, Sal; yeh sail inter them dishes.' An' then he sort o' sniffled an' kissed her. An' I was thet happy,—but he seen me an' roars out, 'Yeh, Jim!' An' yeh bet I dusted fer[17] the barn."

"Any kids waiting for you back in the States?" asked the stranger.

"Nope; Sal died 'fore any come. Thet's why I'm here." Belden abstractedly began to light his pipe, which had failed to go out, and then brightened up with, "How 'bout yerself, stranger,—married man?"

For reply, he opened his watch, slipped it from the thong which served for a chain, and passed it over. Belden pricked up the slush-lamp, surveyed the inside of the case critically, and swearing admiringly to himself, handed it over to Louis Savoy. With numerous "By gars!" he finally surrendered it to Prince, and they noticed that his hands trembled and his eyes took on a peculiar softness. And so it passed from horny hand to horny hand—the pasted photograph of a woman, the clinging kind that such men fancy, with a babe at the breast. Those who had not yet seen the wonder were keen with curiosity; those who had, became silent and retrospective. They could face the pinch of famine, the grip of scurvy, or the quick death by field or flood; but the pictured semblance of a stranger woman and child made women and children of them all.

"Never have seen the youngster yet,—he's a boy, she says, and two years old," said the stranger as he received the treasure back. A lingering moment he gazed upon it, then snapped the case and turned away, but not quick enough to hide the restrained rush of tears.

Malemute Kid led him to a bunk and bade him turn in.

"Call me at four, sharp. Don't fail me," were his last words, and a moment later he was breathing in the heaviness of exhausted sleep.

"By Jove! he's a plucky chap," commented Prince. "Three hours' sleep after seventy-five miles with the dogs, and then the trail again. Who is he, Kid?"

"Jack Westondale. Been in going on three years, with nothing but the name of working like a horse, and any amount of bad luck to his credit. I never knew him, but Sitka Charley told me about him."

"It seems hard that a man with a sweet young wife like his should be putting in his years in this God-forsaken hole, where every year counts two on the outside."

"The trouble with him is clean grit and stubbornness. He's cleaned up twice with a stake, but lost it both times."

Here the conversation was broken off by an uproar from Bettles, for the effect had begun to wear away. And soon the bleak years of monotonous grub and deadening toil were being forgotten in rough merriment. Malemute Kid alone seemed unable to lose himself, and cast many an anxious look at his watch. Once he put on his mittens and beaver-skin cap, and leaving the cabin, fell to rummaging about in the cache.

Nor could he wait the hour designated; for he was fifteen minutes ahead of time in rousing his guest. The young giant had stiffened badly, and brisk rubbing was necessary to bring him to his feet. He tottered painfully out of the cabin, to find his dogs harnessed and everything ready for the start. The company wished him good luck and a short chase, while Father Roubeau, hurriedly blessing him, led the stampede for the cabin; and small wonder, for it is not good to face seventy-four degrees below zero with naked ears and hands.

Malemute Kid saw him to the main trail, and there, gripping his hand heartily, gave him advice.

"You'll find a hundred pounds of salmon-eggs on the sled," he said. "The dogs will go as far on that as with one hundred and fifty of fish, and you can't get dog-food at Pelly,[18] as you probably expected." The stranger started, and his eyes flashed, but he did not interrupt. "You can't get an ounce of food for dog or man till you reach Five Fingers, and that's a stiff two hundred miles. Watch out for open water on the Thirty Mile River, and be sure you take the big cut-off above Le Barge."

"How did you know it? Surely the news can't be ahead of me already?"

"I don't know it; and what's more, I don't want to know it. But you never owned that team you're chasing. Sitka Charley sold it to them last spring. But he sized you up to me as square once, and I believe him. I've seen your face; I like it. And I've seen—why, damn you, hit the high places for salt water and that wife of yours, and"—Here the Kid unmittened and jerked out his sack.

"No; I don't need it," and the tears froze on his cheeks as he convulsively gripped Malemute Kid's hand.

"Then don't spare the dogs; cut them out of the traces as fast as they drop; buy them, and think they're cheap at ten dollars a pound. You can get them at Five Fingers, Little Salmon,[19] and the Hootalinqua. And watch out for wet feet," was his parting advice. "Keep a-traveling up to twenty-five, but if it gets below that, build a fire and change your socks."

Fifteen minutes had barely elapsed when the jingle of bells announced new arrivals. The door opened, and a mounted policeman of the Northwest Territory entered, followed by two half-breed dog-drivers. Like Westondale, they were heavily armed and showed signs of fatigue. The half-breeds had been born to the trail, and bore it easily; but the young policeman was badly exhausted. Still, the dogged obstinacy of his race held him to the pace he had set, and would hold him till he dropped in his tracks.

"When did Westondale pull out?" he asked. "He stopped here, didn't he?" This was supererogatory, for the tracks told their own tale too well.

Malemute Kid had caught Belden's eye, and he, scenting the wind, replied evasively, "A right peart while back."

"Come, my man; speak up," the policeman admonished.

"Yeh seem to want him right smart. Hez he ben gittin' cantankerous down Dawson way?"

"Held up Harry McFarland's for forty thousand; exchanged it at the P. C. store for a check on Seattle; and who's to stop the cashing of it if we don't overtake him? When did he pull out?"

Every eye suppressed its excitement, for Malemute Kid had given the cue, and the young officer encountered wooden faces on every hand.

Striding over to Prince, he put the question to him. Though it hurt him, gazing into the frank, earnest face of his fellow countryman, he replied inconsequentially on the state of the trail.

Then he espied Father Roubeau, who could not lie. "A quarter of an hour ago," the priest answered; "but he had four hours' rest for himself and dogs."

"Fifteen minutes' start, and he's fresh! My God!" The poor fellow staggered back, half fainting from exhaustion and disappointment, murmuring something about the run from Dawson in ten hours and the dogs being played out.

Malemute Kid forced a mug of punch upon him; then he turned for the door, ordering the dog-drivers to follow. But the warmth and promise of rest were too tempting, and they objected strenuously. The Kid was conversant with their French patois, and followed it anxiously.

They swore that the dogs were gone up;[20] that Siwash and Babette would have to be shot before the first mile was covered; that the rest were almost as bad; and that it would be better for all hands to rest up.

"Lend me five dogs?" he asked, turning to Malemute Kid.

But the Kid shook his head.

"I'll sign a check on Captain Constantine for five thousand, —here's my papers,—I'm authorized to draw at my own discretion."

Again the silent refusal.

"Then I'll requisition them in the name of the Queen."

Smiling incredulously, the Kid glanced at his well-stocked arsenal, and the Englishman, realizing his impotency, turned for the door. But the dog-drivers still objecting, he whirled upon them fiercely, calling them women and curs. The swart face of the older half-breed flushed angrily, as he drew himself up and promised in good, round terms that he would travel his leader off his legs, and would then be delighted to plant him in the snow.

The young officer—and it required his whole will—walked steadily to the door, exhibiting a freshness he did not possess. But they all knew and appreciated his proud effort; nor could he veil the twinges of agony that shot across his face. Covered with frost, the dogs were curled up in the snow, and it was almost impossible to get them to their feet. The poor brutes whined under the stinging lash, for the dog-drivers were angry and cruel; nor till Babette, the leader, was cut from the traces, could they break out the sled and get under way.

"A dirty scoundrel and a liar!" "By gar! him no good!" "A thief!" "Worse than an Indian!" It was evident that they were angry—first, at the way they had been deceived; and second, at the outraged ethics of the Northland, where honesty, above all, was man's prime jewel. "An' we gave the cuss a hand, after knowin' what he'd did." All eyes were turned accusingly upon Malemute Kid, who rose from the corner where he had been making Babette comfortable, and silently emptied the bowl for a final round of punch.

"It's a cold night, boys,—a bitter cold night," was the irrelevant commencement of his defense. "You've all traveled trail, and know what that stands for. Don't jump a dog when he's down. You've only heard one side. A whiter[21] man than Jack Westondale never ate from the same pot nor stretched blanket with you or me. Last fall he gave his whole clean-up,[22] forty thousand, to Joe Castrell, to buy in on Dominion. To-day he'd be a millionaire. But while he stayed behind at Circle City, taking care of his partner with the scurvy, what does Castrell do? Goes into McFarland's, jumps the limit,[23] and drops the whole sack. Found him dead in the snow the next day. And poor Jack laying his plans to go out this winter to his wife and the boy he's never seen. You'll notice he took exactly what his partner lost,—forty thousand. Well, he's gone out; and what are you going to do about it?"

The Kid glanced round the circle of his judges, noted the softening of their faces, then raised his mug aloft. "So a health to the man on trail this night; may his grub hold out; may his dogs keep their legs; may his matches never miss fire. God prosper him; good luck go with him; and"—

"Confusion to the Mounted Police!" cried Bettles, to the crash of the empty cups.

MARY AUSTIN

1868–1934

BORN IN CARLINVILLE, Illinois, Mary Hunter graduated from Blackburn College in 1888. That same year, following other white settlers to the West, she moved with her family to California as a homesteader. During the move she began writing, and in 1891 she married Stafford Wallace Austin, but their marriage was troubled. Their efforts at farming were unsuccessful, they moved several times, and their only child was mentally retarded. Austin sold her first story to the *Overland Monthly* in 1892 and later published her work in *Land of Sunshine*. Separating from her husband in 1905, Austin soon moved to Carmel, California, where she became acquainted with Jack London and other writers. She published *Lost Borders* in 1909. Later she traveled to Europe; lived in New York, where her play *The Arrow Maker* was produced in 1910; and participated in the suffrage movement.

After 1910, Austin divided her time between New York and Carmel, publishing thirty-two books and numerous essays and lecturing widely. In 1924 she moved to Santa Fe, New Mexico, where she built a house, "Casa Querida," and worked for Indian rights and the preservation of Indian and Hispanic arts and folklore. Her best-known works include *The Basket Woman* (1904), collections of regional stories; novels such as *Santa Lucia* (1908); environmental writing such as her classic volume *The Land of Little Rain* (1903); an autobiography, *Earth Horizon* (1932); and a critical work on poetry, *The American Rhythm* (1923), which includes an analysis of Native American verse.

East away from the Sierras,[1] south from Panamint[2] and Amar-gosa,[3] east and south many an uncounted mile, is the Country of Lost Borders.

Ute,[4] Paiute, Mojave, and Shoshone inhabit its frontiers, and as far into the heart of it as a man dare go. Not the law, but the land sets the limit. Desert is the name it wears upon the maps, but the Indian's is the better word. Desert is a loose term to indicate land that supports no man; whether the land can be bitted and broken to that purpose is not proven. Void of life it never is, however dry the air and villainous the soil.

This is the nature of that country. There are hills, rounded, blunt, burned, squeezed up out of chaos, chrome and vermilion painted, aspiring to the snowline. Between the hills lie high level-looking plains full of intolerable sun glare, or narrow valleys drowned in a blue haze. The hill surface is streaked with ash drift and black, unweathered lava flows. After rains water ac-cumulates in the hollows of small closed valleys, and, evaporat-ing, leaves hard dry levels of pure desertness that get the local name of dry lakes. Where the mountains are steep and the rains heavy, the pool is never quite dry, but dark and bitter, rimmed about with the efflorescence of alkaline deposits. A thin crust of it lies along the marsh over the vegetating area, which has neither beauty nor freshness. In the broad wastes open to the wind the sand drifts in hummocks about the stubby shrubs, and between them the soil shows saline traces. The sculpture of the hills here is more wind than water work, though the quick storms do sometimes scar them past many a year's redeeming. In all the Western desert edges there are essays in miniature at the famed, terrible Grand Cañon, to which, if you keep on long enough in this country, you will come at last.

Since this is a hill country one expects to find springs, but not to depend upon them; for when found they are often brack-ish and unwholesome, or maddening, slow dribbles in a thirsty soil. Here you find the hot sink of Death Valley, or high rolling districts where the air has always a tang of frost. Here are the long heavy winds and breathless calms on the tilted mesas where dust devils dance, whirling up into a wide, pale sky. Here you have no rain when all the earth cries for it, or quick downpours called cloud-bursts for violence. A land of lost rivers, with little in it to love; yet a land that once visited must be come back to inevitably. If it were not so there would be little told of it.

This is the country of three seasons. From June on to November it lies hot, still, and unbearable, sick with violent unrelieving storms; then on until April, chill, quiescent, drinking its scant rain and scanter snows; from April to the hot season again, blossoming, radiant, and seductive. These months are only approximate; later or earlier the rain-laden wind may drift up the water gate[5] of the Colorado[6] from the Gulf, and the land sets its seasons by the rain.

The desert floras shame us with their cheerful adaptations to the seasonal limitations. Their whole duty is to flower and fruit, and they do it hardly, or with tropical luxurance, as the rain admits. It is recorded in the report of the Death Valley expedition that after a year of abundant rains, on the Colorado desert was found a specimen of Amaranthus[7] ten feet high. A year later the same species in the same place matured in the drought at four inches. One hopes the land may breed like qualities in her human offspring, not tritely to "try," but to do. Seldom does the desert herb attain the full stature of the type. Extreme aridity and extreme altitude have the same dwarfing effect, so that we find in the high Sierras and in Death Valley related species in miniature that reach a comely growth in mean temperatures. Very fertile are the desert plants in expedients to prevent evaporation, turning their foliage edgewise toward the sun, growing silky hairs, exuding viscid gum. The wind, which has a long sweep, harries and helps them. It rolls up dunes about the stocky stems, encompassing and protective, and above the dunes, which may be, as with the mesquite, three times as high as a man, the blossoming twigs flourish and bear fruit.

There are many areas in the desert where drinkable water lies within a few feet of the surface, indicated by the mesquite and the bunch grass (*Sporobolus airoides*). It is this nearness of unimagined help that makes the tragedy of desert deaths. It is related that the final breakdown of that hapless party that gave

Death Valley its forbidding name occurred in a locality where shallow wells would have saved them. But how were they to know that? Properly equipped it is possible to go safely across that ghastly sink, yet every year it takes its toll of death, and yet men find there sun-dried mummies, of whom no trace or rec-ollection is preserved. To underestimate one's thirst, to pass a given landmark to the right or left, to find a dry spring where one looked for running water—there is no help for any of these things.

Along springs and sunken watercourses one is surprised to find such water-loving plants as grow widely in moist ground, but the true desert breeds its own kind, each in its particular habitat. The angle of the slope, the frontage of a hill, the struc-ture of the soil determines the plant. South-looking hills are nearly bare, and the lower tree-line higher here by a thousand feet. Cañons running east and west will have one wall naked and one clothed. Around dry lakes and marshes the herbage pre-serves a set and orderly arrangement. Most species have well-defined areas of growth, the best index the voiceless land can give the traveler of his whereabouts.

If you have any doubt about it, know that the desert begins with the creosote.[8] This immortal shrub spreads down into Death Valley and up to the lower timber-line, odorous and me-dicinal as you might guess from the name, wandlike, with shin-ing fretted foliage. Its vivid green is grateful to the eye in a wilderness of gray and greenish white shrubs. In the spring it exudes a resinous gum which the Indians of those parts know how to use with pulverized rock for cementing arrow points to shafts. Trust Indians not to miss any virtues of the plant world!

Nothing the desert produces expresses it better than the un-happy growth of the tree yuccas.[9] Tormented, thin forests of it stalk drearily in the high mesas, particularly in that triangular slip that fans out eastward from the meeting of the Sierras and coastwise hills where the first swings across the southern end of the San Joaquin Valley.[10] The yucca bristles with bayonet-pointed leaves, dull green, growing shaggy with age, tipped with panicles of fetid, greenish bloom. After death, which is slow, the ghostly hollow network of its woody skeleton, with hardly power to rot, makes the moonlight fearful. Before the yucca has come to flower, while yet its bloom is a creamy cone-shaped bud of the size of a small cabbage, full of sugary sap, the Indians twist it deftly out of its fence of daggers and roast it for their own delectation. So it is that in those parts where man inhabits one sees young plants of *Yucca arborensis* infrequently. Other yuccas, cacti, low herbs, a thousand sorts, one finds journeying east from the coastwise hills. There is neither poverty of soil nor species to account for the sparseness of desert growth, but simply that each plant requires more room. So much earth must be preëmpted to extract so much moisture. The real struggle for existence, the real brain of the plant, is underground; above there is room for a rounded perfect growth. In Death Valley, reputed the very core of desolation, are nearly two hundred identified species.

Above the lower tree-line, which is also the snow-line, mapped out abruptly by the sun, one finds spreading growth of piñon, juniper, branched nearly to the ground, lilac and sage, and scattering white pines.

There is no special preponderance of self-fertilized or wind-fertilized plants, but everywhere the demand for and evidence of insect life. Now where there are seeds and insects there will be birds and small mammals and where these are, will come the slinking, sharp-toothed kind that prey on them. Go as far as you dare in the heart of a lonely land, you cannot go so far that life and death are not before you. Painted lizards slip in and out of rock crevices, and pant on the white hot sands. Birds, hummingbirds even, nest in the cactus scrub; woodpeckers befriend the demoniac yuccas; out of the stark, treeless waste rings the music of the night-singing mockingbird. If it be summer and the sun well down, there will be a burrowing owl to call. Strange, furry, tricksy things dart across the open places, or sit motionless in the conning towers[11] of the creosote. The poet may have "named all the birds without a gun,"[12] but not the fairy-footed, ground-inhabiting, furtive, small folk of the rainless regions. They are too many and too swift; how many you would not believe without seeing the footprint tracings in the sand. They are nearly all night workers, finding the days too hot and white. In mid-desert where there are no cattle, there are no birds of carrion, but if you go far in that direction the chances are that you will find yourself shadowed by their tilted wings. Nothing so large as a man can move unspied upon in that country, and they know well how the land deals with strangers. There are hints to be had here of the way in which a land forces new habits on its dwellers. The quick increase of suns at the end of spring sometimes overtakes birds in their nesting and effects a reversal of the ordinary manner of incubation. It becomes necessary to keep eggs cool rather than warm. One hot, stifling spring in the Little Antelope I had occasion to pass and repass frequently the nest of a pair of meadowlarks, located unhappily in the shelter of a very slender weed. I never caught them sitting except near night, but at midday they stood, or drooped above it, half fainting with pitifully parted bills, between their treasure and the sun. Sometimes both of them together with wings spread and half lifted continued a spot of shade in a temperature that constrained me at last in a fellow feeling to spare them a bit of canvas for permanent shelter. There was a fence in that country shutting in a cattle range, and along its fifteen miles of posts one could be sure of finding a bird or two in every strip of shadow; sometime the sparrow and the hawk, with wings trailed and beaks parted, drooping in the white truce of noon.

If one is inclined to wonder at first how so many dwellers came to be in the loneliest land that ever came out of God's hands, what they do there and why stay, one does not wonder so much after having lived there. None other than this long brown land lays such a hold on the affections. The rainbow hills, the tender bluish mists, the luminous radiance of the spring, have the lotus charm.[13] They trick the sense of time, so that once inhabiting there you always mean to go away without quite realizing that you have not done it. Men who have lived there, miners and cattle-men, will tell you this, not so fluently, but emphatically, cursing the land and going back to it. For one thing there is the divinest, cleanest air to be breathed anywhere in God's world. Some day the world will understand that, and the little oases on the windy tops of hills will harbor for healing its ailing, house-weary broods. There is promise there of great wealth in ores and earths, which is no wealth by reason of being so far removed from water and workable conditions, but men are bewitched by it and tempted to try the impossible.

You should hear Salty Williams tell how he used to drive eighteen and twenty-mule teams from the borax marsh[14] to Mojave,[15] ninety miles, with the trail wagon full of water barrels. Hot days the mules would go so mad for drink that the clank of the water bucket set them into an uproar of hideous, maimed noises, and a tangle of harness chains, while Salty would sit on the high seat with the sun glare heavy in his eyes, dealing out curses of pacification in a level, uninterested voice until the clamor fell off from sheer exhaustion. There was a line of shallow graves along that road; they used to count on dropping a man or two of every new gang of coolies[16] brought out in the hot season. But when he lost his swamper,[17] smitten without warning at the noon halt, Salty quit his job; he said it was "too durn hot." The swamper he buried by the way with stones upon him to keep the coyotes from digging him up, and seven years later I read the penciled lines on the pine headboard, still bright and unweathered.

But before that, driving up on the Mojave stage, I met Salty again crossing Indian Wells, his face from the high seat, tanned and ruddy as a harvest moon, looming through the golden dust above his eighteen mules. The land had called him.

The palpable sense of mystery in the desert air breeds fables, chiefly of lost treasure. Somewhere within its stark borders, if one believes report, is a hill strewn with nuggets; one seamed with virgin silver; an old clayey water-bed where Indians scooped up earth to make cooking pots and shaped them reeking with grains of pure gold. Old miners drifting about the desert edges, weathered into the semblance of the tawny hills, will tell you tales like these convincingly. After a little sojourn in that land you will believe them on their own account. It is a question whether it is not better to be bitten by the little horned snake of the desert that goes sidewise and strikes without coiling, than by the tradition of a lost mine.

And yet—and yet—is it not perhaps to satisfy expectation that one falls into the tragic key in writing of desertness? The more you wish of it the more you get, and in the mean time lose much of pleasantness. In that country which begins at the foot of the east slope of the Sierras and spreads out by less and less lofty hill ranges toward the Great Basin,[18] it is possible to live with great zest, to have red blood and delicate joys, to pass and repass about one's daily performance an area that would make an Atlantic seaboard State, and that with no peril, and, according to our way of thought, no particular difficulty. At any rate, it was not people who went into the desert merely to write it up who invented the fabled Hassayampa,[19] of whose waters, if any drink, they can no more see fact as naked fact, but all radiant with the color of romance. I, who must have drunk of it in my twice seven years' wanderings, am assured that it is worth while.

For all the toll the desert takes of a man it gives compensations, deep breaths, deep sleep, and the communion of the stars. It comes upon one with new force in the pauses of the night that the Chaldeans[20] were a desert-bred people. It is hard to escape the sense of mastery as the stars move in the wide clear heavens to risings and settings unobscured. They look large and near and palpitant; as if they moved on some stately service not needful to declare. Wheeling to their stations in the sky, they make the poor world-fret of no account. Of no account you who lie out there watching, nor the lean coyote that stands off in the scrub from you and howls and howls.

THE SIOUX short story writer and Indian rights activist Zitkala-Ša was born on the Yankton Sioux reservation in South Dakota and spoke no English until age eight, when she went to a Quaker missionary school in Indiana. Though she was unhappy there, she found her return to life on the reservation equally difficult. Going back east, she attended Earlham College in Richmond, Indiana; studied music at the New England Conservatory of Music in Boston; and taught at Carlisle Indian School from 1898 to 1899.

Her autobiographical pieces and short stories, including "Impressions of an Indian Childhood," "The School Days of an Indian Girl," "An Indian Teacher Among Indians," and "Why I Am a Pagan," appeared in the *Atlantic Monthly* and *Harper's* between 1900 and 1902, and in 1901 she published *Old Indian Legends*, a collection of traditional Sioux tales gathered on the reservation. In 1902 Zitkala-Ša married Raymond Talesfase Bonnin, a Sioux who worked for the Indian Service, and moved to the Uintah and Ouray Reservation in Utah. There she devoted her energies to political writing and activism: in 1916 she moved to Washington, D.C., to work as secretary for the Society of American Indians, and later edited the *American Indian Magazine* (1918–19). In 1926 she founded the National Council of American Indians, serving as its president until 1938. She traveled widely, lecturing on Indian rights; often dressed in Sioux costume; and worked to preserve Sioux culture during the era of assimilation. In addition to *Old Indian Legends*, Zitkala-Ša wrote an opera, *Sundance* (1913), a second volume of stories, *American Indian Legends* (1921), and a book on the exploitation of the Oklahoma Indians in 1924.

I

Beside the open fire I sat within our tepee. With my red blanket wrapped tightly about my crossed legs, I was thinking of the coming season, my sixteenth winter. On either side of the wigwam were my parents. My father was whistling a tune between his teeth while polishing with his bare hand a red stone pipe he had recently carved. Almost in front of me, beyond the center fire, my old grandmother sat near the entranceway.

She turned her face toward her right and addressed most of her words to my mother. Now and then she spoke to me, but never did she allow her eyes to rest upon her daughter's husband, my father. It was only upon rare occasions that my grandmother said anything to him. Thus his ears were open and ready to catch the smallest wish she might express. Sometimes when my grandmother had been saying things which pleased him, my father used to comment upon them. At other times, when he could not approve of what was spoken, he used to work or smoke silently.

On this night my old grandmother began her talk about me. Filling the bowl of her red stone pipe with dry willow bark, she looked across at me.

"My grandchild, you are tall and are no longer a little boy." Narrowing her old eyes, she asked, "My grandchild, when are you going to bring here a handsome young woman?" I stared into the fire rather than meet her gaze. Waiting for my answer, she stooped forward and through the long stem drew a flame into the red stone pipe.

I smiled while my eyes were still fixed upon the bright fire, but I said nothing in reply. Turning to my mother, she offered her the pipe. I glanced at my grandmother. The loose buckskin sleeve fell off at her elbow and showed a wrist covered with silver bracelets. Holding up the fingers of her left hand, she named off the desirable young women of our village.

"Which one, my grandchild, which one?" she questioned.

"Hoh!" I said, pulling at my blanket in confusion. "Not yet!" Here my mother passed the pipe over the fire to my father. Then she, too, began speaking of what I should do.

"My son, be always active. Do not dislike a long hunt. Learn to provide much buffalo meat and many buckskins before you bring home a wife." Presently my father gave the pipe to my grandmother, and he took his turn in the exhortations.

"Ho, my son, I have been counting in my heart the bravest warriors of our people. There is not one of them who won his title in his sixteenth winter. My son, it is a great thing for some brave of sixteen winters to do."

Not a word had I to give in answer. I knew well the fame of my warrior father. He had earned the right of speaking such words, though even he himself was a brave only at my age. Refusing to smoke my grandmother's pipe because my heart was too much stirred by their words, and sorely troubled with a fear lest I should disappoint them, I arose to go. Drawing my blanket over my shoulders, I said, as I stepped toward the entranceway: "I go to hobble my pony. It is now late in the night."

II

Nine winters' snows had buried deep that night when my old grandmother, together with my father and mother, designed my future with the glow of a camp fire upon it.

Yet I did not grow up the warrior, huntsman, and husband I was to have been. At the mission school I learned it was wrong to kill. Nine winters I hunted for the soft heart of Christ, and prayed for the huntsmen who chased the buffalo on the plains.

In the autumn of the tenth year I was sent back to my tribe to preach Christianity to them. With the white man's Bible in my hand, and the white man's tender heart in my breast, I returned to my own people.

Wearing a foreigner's dress, I walked, a stranger, into my father's village.

Asking my way, for I had not forgotten my native tongue, an old man led me toward the tepee where my father lay. From my old companion I learned that my father had been sick many moons. As we drew near the tepee, I heard the chanting of a medicine-man within it. At once I wished to enter in and drive from my home the sorcerer of the plains, but the old warrior checked me. "Ho, wait outside until the medicine-man leaves your father," he said. While talking he scanned me from head to feet. Then he retraced his steps toward the heart of the camping-ground.

My father's dwelling was on the outer limits of the round-faced village. With every heart-throb I grew more impatient to enter the wigwam.

While I turned the leaves of my Bible with nervous fingers, the medicine-man came forth from the dwelling and walked hurriedly away. His head and face were closely covered with the loose robe which draped his entire figure.

He was tall and large. His long strides I have never forgot. They seemed to me then the uncanny gait of eternal death. Quickly pocketing my Bible, I went into the tepee.

Upon a mat lay my father, with furrowed face and gray hair. His eyes and cheeks were sunken far into his head. His sallow skin lay thin upon his pinched nose and high cheekbones. Stooping over him, I took his fevered hand. "How, Ate?" I greeted him. A light flashed from his listless eyes and his dried lips parted. "My son!" he murmured, in a feeble voice. Then again the wave of joy and recognition receded. He closed his eyes, and his hand dropped from my open palm to the ground.

Looking about, I saw an old woman sitting with bowed head. Shaking hands with her, I recognized my mother. I sat down between my father and mother as I used to do, but I did not feel at home. The place where my old grandmother used to sit was now unoccupied. With my mother I bowed my head. Alike our throats were choked and tears were streaming from our eyes; but far apart in spirit our ideas and faiths separated us. My grief was for the soul unsaved; and I thought my mother wept to see a brave man's body broken by sickness.

Useless was my attempt to change the faith in the medicine-man to that abstract power named God. Then one day I became righteously mad with anger that the medicine-man should thus ensnare my father's soul. And when he came to chant his sacred songs I pointed toward the door and bade him go! The man's eyes glared upon me for an instant. Slowly gathering his robe about him, he turned his back upon the sick man and stepped out of our wigwam. "Ha, ha, ha! my son, I can not live without the medicine-man!" I heard my father cry when the sacred man was gone.

III

On a bright day, when the winged seeds of the prairie-grass were flying hither and thither, I walked solemnly toward the centre of the camping-ground. My heart beat hard and irregularly at my side. Tighter I grasped the sacred book I carried under my arm. Now was the beginning of life's work.

Though I knew it would be hard, I did not once feel that failure was to be my reward. As I stepped unevenly on the rolling ground, I thought of the warriors soon to wash off their war-paints and follow me.

At length I reached the place where the people had assembled to hear me preach. In a large circle men and women sat upon the dry red grass. Within the ring I stood, with the white man's Bible in my hand. I tried to tell them of the soft heart of Christ.

In silence the vast circle of bareheaded warriors sat under an afternoon sun. At last, wiping the wet from my brow, I took my place in the ring. The hush of the assembly filled me with great hope.

I was turning my thoughts upward to the sky in gratitude, when a stir called me to earth again.

A tall, strong man arose. His loose robe hung in folds over his right shoulder. A pair of snapping black eyes fastened themselves like the poisonous fangs of a serpent upon me. He was the medicine-man. A tremor played about my heart and a chill cooled the fire in my veins.

Scornfully he pointed a long forefinger in my direction and asked:

"What loyal son is he who, returning to his father's people, wears a foreigner's dress?" He paused a moment, and then continued: "The dress of that foreigner of whom a story says he bound a native of our land, and heaping dry sticks around him, kindled a fire at his feet!" Waving his hand toward me, he exclaimed, "Here is the traitor to his people!"

I was helpless. Before the eyes of the crowd the cunning magician turned my honest heart into a vile nest of treachery. Alas! the people frowned as they looked upon me.

"Listen!" he went on. "Which one of you who have eyed the young man can see through his bosom and warn the people of the nest of young snakes hatching there? Whose ear was so acute that he caught the hissing of snakes whenever the young man opened his mouth? This one has not only proven false to you, but even to the Great Spirit who made him. He is a fool! Why do you sit here giving ear to a foolish man who could not defend his people because he fears to kill, who could not bring venison to renew the life of his sick father? With his prayers, let him drive away the enemy! With his soft heart, let him keep off starvation! We shall go elsewhere to dwell upon an untainted ground."

With this he disbanded the people. When the sun lowered in the west and the winds were quiet, the village of cone-shaped tepees was gone. The medicine-man had won the hearts of the people.

Only my father's dwelling was left to mark the fighting-ground.

IV

From a long night at my father's bedside I came out to look upon the morning. The yellow sun hung equally between the snow-covered land and the cloudless blue sky. The light of the new day was cold. The strong breath of winter crusted the snow and fitted crystal shells over the rivers and lakes. As I stood in front of the tepee, thinking of the vast prairies which separated us from our tribe, and wondering if the high sky likewise separated the soft-hearted Son of God from us, the icy blast from the North blew through my hair and skull. My neglected hair had grown long and fell upon my neck.

My father had not risen from his bed since the day the medicine-man led the people away. Though I read from the Bible and prayed beside him upon my knees, my father would not listen. Yet I believed my prayers were not unheeded in heaven.

"Ha, ha, ha! my son," my father groaned upon the first snowfall. "My son, our food is gone. There is no one to bring me meat! My son, your soft heart has unfitted you for everything!" Then covering his face with the buffalo-robe,[1] he said no more. Now while I stood out in that cold winter morning, I was starving. For two days I had not seen any food. But my own cold and hunger did not harass my soul as did the whining cry of the sick old man.

Stepping again into the tepee, I untied my snow-shoes, which were fastened to the tent-poles.

My poor mother, watching by the sick one, and faithfully heaping wood upon the centre fire, spoke to me:

"My son, do not fail again to bring your father meat, or he will starve to death."

"How, Ina," I answered, sorrowfully. From the tepee I started forth again to hunt food for my aged parents. All day I tracked the white level lands in vain. Nowhere, nowhere were there any other footprints but my own! In the evening of this third fast-day I came back without meat. Only a bundle of sticks for the fire I brought on my back. Dropping the wood outside, I lifted the door-flap and set one foot within the tepee.

There I grew dizzy and numb. My eyes swam in tears. Before me lay my old gray-haired father sobbing like a child. In his horny hands he clutched the buffalo-robe, and with his teeth he was gnawing off the edges. Chewing the dry stiff hair and buffalo-skin, my father's eyes sought my hands. Upon seeing them empty, he cried out:

"My son, your soft heart will let me starve before you bring me meat! Two hills eastward stand a herd of cattle. Yet you will see me die before you bring me food!"

Leaving my mother lying with covered head upon her mat, I rushed out into the night.

With a strange warmth in my heart and swiftness in my feet, I climbed over the first hill, and soon the second one. The moonlight upon the white country showed me a clear path to the white man's cattle. With my hand upon the knife in my belt, I leaned heavily against the fence while counting the herd.

Twenty in all I numbered. From among them I chose the best-fattened creature. Leaping over the fence, I plunged my knife into it.

My long knife was sharp, and my hands, no more fearful and slow, slashed off choice chunks of warm flesh. Bending under the meat I had taken for my starving father, I hurried across the prairie.

Toward home I fairly ran with the life-giving food I carried upon my back. Hardly had I climbed the second hill when I heard sounds coming after me. Faster and faster I ran with my load for my father, but the sounds were gaining upon me. I heard the clicking of snowshoes and the squeaking of the leather straps at my heels; yet I did not turn to see what pursued me, for I was intent upon reaching my father. Suddenly like thunder an angry voice shouted curses and threats into my ear! A rough hand wrenched my shoulder and took the meat from me! I stopped struggling to run. A deafening whir filled my head. The moon and stars began to move. Now the white prairie was sky, and the stars lay under my feet. Now again they were turning. At last the starry blue rose up into place. The noise in my ears was still. A great quiet filled the air. In my hand I found my long knife dripping with blood. At my feet a man's figure lay prone in blood-red snow. The horrible scene about me seemed a trick of my senses, for I could not understand it was real. Looking long upon the blood-stained snow, the load of meat for my starving father reached my recognition at last. Quickly I tossed it over my shoulder and started again homeward.

Tired and haunted I reached the door of the wigwam. Carrying the food before me, I entered with it into the tepee.

"Father, here is food!" I cried, as I dropped the meat near my mother. No answer came. Turning about, I beheld my gray-haired father dead! I saw by the unsteady firelight an old gray-haired skeleton lying rigid and stiff.

Out into the open I started, but the snow at my feet became bloody.

v

On the day after my father's death, having led my mother to the camp of the medicine-man, I gave myself up to those who were searching for the murderer of the paleface.

They bound me hand and foot. Here in this cell I was placed four days ago.

The shrieking winter winds have followed me hither. Rattling the bars, they howl unceasingly: "Your soft heart! your soft heart will see me die before bring me food!" Hark! something is clanking the chain on the door. It is being opened. From the dark night without a black figure crosses the threshold. . . . It is the guard. He comes to warn me of my fate. He tells me that tomorrow I must die. In his stern face I laugh aloud. I do not fear death.

Yet I wonder who shall come to welcome me in the realm of strange sight. Will the loving Jesus grant me pardon and give my soul a soothing sleep? or will my warrior father greet me and receive me as his son? Will my spirit fly upward to a happy heaven? or shall I sink into the bottomless pit, an outcast from a God of infinite love?

Soon, soon I shall know, for now I see the east is growing red. My heart is strong. My face is calm. My eyes are dry and eager for new scenes. My hands hang quietly at my side. Serene and brave, my soul awaits the men to perch me on the gallows for another flight. I go.

IKTOMI AND THE DUCKS

Iktomi is a spider fairy. He wears brown deerskin leggins with long soft fringes on either side, and tiny beaded moccasins on his feet. His long black hair is parted in the middle and wrapped with red, red bands. Each round braid hangs over a small brown ear and falls forward over his shoulders.

He even paints his funny face with red and yellow, and draws big black rings around his eyes. He wears a deerskin jacket, with bright colored beads sewed tightly on it. Iktomi dresses like a real Dakota brave. In truth, his paint and deerskins are the best part of him—if ever dress is part of man or fairy.

Iktomi is a wily fellow. His hands are always kept in mischief. He prefers to spread a snare rather than to earn the smallest thing with honest hunting. Why! he laughs outright with wide open mouth when some simple folk are caught in a trap, sure and fast.

He never dreams another lives so bright as he. Often his own conceit leads him hard against the common sense of simpler people.

Poor Iktomi cannot help being a little imp. And so long as he is a naughty fairy, he cannot find a single friend. No one helps him when he is in trouble. No one really loves him. Those who come to admire his handsome beaded jacket and long fringed leggins soon go away sick and tired of his vain, vain words and heartless laughter.

Thus Iktomi lives alone in a cone-shaped wigwam upon the plain. One day he sat hungry within his teepee. Suddenly he rushed out, dragging after him his blanket. Quickly spreading it on the ground, he tore up dry tall grass with both his hands and tossed it fast into the blanket.

Tying all the four corners together in a knot, he threw the light bundle of grass over his shoulder.

Snatching up a slender willow stick with his free left hand, he started off with a hop and a leap. From side to side bounced the bundle on his back, as he ran lightfooted over the uneven ground. Soon he came to the edge of the great level land. On the hilltop he paused for breath. With wicked smacks of his dry parched lips, as if tasting some tender meat, he looked straight into space toward the marshy river bottom. With a thin palm shading his eyes from the western sun, he peered far away into the lowlands, munching his own cheeks all the while. "Ah-ha!" grunted he, satisfied with what he saw.

A group of wild ducks were dancing and feasting in the marshes. With wings outspread, tip to tip, they moved up and down in a large circle. Within the ring, around a small drum, sat the chosen singers, nodding their heads and blinking their eyes.

They sang in unison a merry dance-song, and beat a lively tattoo on the drum.

Following a winding footpath near by, came a bent figure of a Dakota brave. He bore on his back a very large bundle. With a willow cane he propped himself up as he staggered along beneath his burden.

"Ho! who is there?" called out a curious old duck, still bobbing up and down in the circular dance.

Hereupon the drummers stretched their necks till they strangled their song for a look at the stranger passing by.

"Ho, Iktomi! Old fellow, pray tell us what you carry in your blanket. Do not hurry off! Stop! halt!" urged one of the singers.

"Stop! stay! Show us what is in your blanket!" cried out other voices.

"My friends, I must not spoil your dance. Oh, you would not care to see if you only knew what is in my blanket. Sing on! dance on! I must not show you what I carry on my back," answered Iktomi, nudging his own sides with his elbows. This reply broke up the ring entirely. Now all the ducks crowded about Iktomi.

"We must see what you carry! We must know what is in your blanket!" they shouted in both his ears. Some even brushed their wings against the mysterious bundle. Nudging himself again, wily Iktomi said, "My friends, 'tis only a pack of songs I carry in my blanket."

"Oh, then let us hear your songs!" cried the curious ducks.

At length Iktomi consented to sing his songs. With delight all the ducks flapped their wings and cried together, "Hoye! hoye!"

Iktomi, with great care, laid down his bundle on the ground.

"I will build first a round straw house, for I never sing my songs in the open air," said he.

Quickly he bent green willow sticks, planting both ends of each pole into the earth. These he covered thick with reeds and grasses. Soon the straw hut was ready. One by one the fat ducks waddled in through a small opening, which was the only entrance way. Beside the door Iktomi stood smiling, as the ducks, eyeing his bundle of songs, strutted into the hut.

In a strange low voice Iktomi began his queer old tunes. All the ducks sat round-eyed in a circle about the mysterious singer. It was dim in that straw hut, for Iktomi had not forgot to cover up the small entrance way. All of a sudden his song burst into full voice. As the startled ducks sat uneasily on the ground, Iktomi changed his tune into a minor strain. These were the words he sang:

"Ištokmus wacipo, tuwayatunwanpi kinhan išta nišašapi kta,"
which is, "With eyes closed you must dance. He who dares to
open his eyes, forever red eyes shall have."

Up rose the circle of seated ducks and holding their wings
close against their sides began to dance to the rhythm of Iktomi's
song and drum.

With eyes closed they did dance! Iktomi ceased to beat his
drum. He began to sing louder and faster. He seemed to be
moving about in the center of the ring. No duck dared blink a
wink. Each one shut his eyes very tight and danced even harder.
Up and down! Shifting to the right of them they hopped round
and round in that blind dance. It was a difficult dance for the
curious folk.

At length one of the dancers could close his eyes no longer!
It was a Skiska who peeped the least tiny blink at Iktomi within
the center of the circle. "Oh! oh!" squawked he in awful terror!
"Run! fly! Iktomi is twisting your heads and breaking your
necks! Run out and fly! fly!" he cried. Hereupon the ducks
opened their eyes. There beside Iktomi's bundle of songs lay half
of their crowd—flat on their backs.

Out they flew through the opening Skiska had made as he
rushed forth with his alarm.

But as they soared high into the blue sky they cried to one
another: "Oh! your eyes are red-red!" "And yours are red-red!"
For the warning words of the magic minor strain had proven
true. "Ah-ha!" laughed Iktomi, untying the four corners of his
blanket, "I shall sit no more hungry within my dwelling."
Homeward he trudged along with nice fat ducks in his blanket.
He left the little straw hut for the rains and winds to pull down.

Having reached his own teepee on the high level lands, Iktomi
kindled a large fire out of doors. He planted sharp-pointed sticks
around the leaping flames. On each stake he fastened a duck to
roast. A few he buried under the ashes to bake. Disappearing
within his teepee, he came out again with some huge seashells.
These were his dishes. Placing one under each roasting duck, he
muttered, "The sweet fat oozing out will taste well with the
hard-cooked breasts."

Heaping more willows upon the fire, Iktomi sat down on the
ground with crossed shins. A long chin between his knees

pointed toward the red flames, while his eyes were on the browning ducks.

Just above his ankles he clasped and unclasped his long bony fingers. Now and then he sniffed impatiently the savory odor.

The brisk wind which stirred the fire also played with a squeaky old tree beside Iktomi's wigwam.

From side to side the tree was swaying and crying in an old man's voice, "Help! I 'll break! I 'll fall!" Iktomi shrugged his great shoulders, but did not once take his eyes from the ducks. The dripping of amber oil into pearly dishes, drop by drop, pleased his hungry eyes. Still the old tree man called for help. "Hĕ! What sound is it that makes my ear ache!" exclaimed Iktomi, holding a hand on his ear.

He rose and looked around. The squeaking came from the tree. Then he began climbing the tree to find the disagreeable sound. He placed his foot right on a cracked limb without seeing it. Just then a whiff of wind came rushing by and pressed together the broken edges. There in a strong wooden hand Iktomi's foot was caught.

"Oh! my foot is crushed!" he howled like a coward. In vain he pulled and puffed to free himself.

While sitting a prisoner on the tree he spied, through his tears, a pack of gray wolves roaming over the level lands. Waving his hands toward them, he called in his loudest voice, "Hĕ! Gray wolves! Don't you come here! I 'm caught fast in the tree so that my duck feast is getting cold. Don't you come to eat up my meal."

The leader of the pack upon hearing Iktomi's words turned to his comrades and said:

"Ah! hear the foolish fellow! He says he has a duck feast to be eaten! Let us hurry there for our share!" Away bounded the wolves toward Iktomi's lodge.

From the tree Iktomi watched the hungry wolves eat up his nicely browned fat ducks. His foot pained him more and more. He heard them crack the small round bones with their strong long teeth and eat out the oily marrow. Now severe pains shot up from his foot through his whole body. "Hin-hin-hin!" sobbed Iktomi. Real tears washed brown streaks across his red-painted cheeks. Smacking their lips, the wolves began to leave

420 ZITKALA-ŠA [GERTRUDE SIMMONS BONNIN]

the place, when Iktomi cried out like a pouting child, "At least you have left my baking under the ashes!"

"Ho! po!" shouted the mischievous wolves; "he says more ducks are to be found under the ashes! Come! Let us have our fill this once!"

Running back to the dead fire, they pawed out the ducks with such rude haste that a cloud of ashes rose like gray smoke over them.

"Hin-hin-hin!" moaned Iktomi, when the wolves had scampered off. All too late, the sturdy breeze returned, and, passing by, pulled apart the broken edges of the tree. Iktomi was released. But alas! he had no duck feast.

MARÍA CRISTINA MENA

1893–1965

ONE OF THE FIRST WOMEN of Mexican heritage to publish fiction in the United States in English, María Cristina Mena wrote stories that address questions of gender, class, and cultural difference with a mixture of romance and realism. Mena was born in Mexico City, the daughter of a prominent businessman, and enjoyed a privileged education, first at a convent school and later in an English boarding school. In 1907, during the time of unrest that led to the Mexican Revolution in 1910, Mena was sent to New York to live with family friends. At the age of twenty-one she published her first stories, "John of God, the Water-Carrier" and "The Gold Vanity Set," in the *American Magazine* and the *Century Magazine*; she eventually became "the foremost interpreter of Mexican life" for magazines such as *Cosmopolitan* and *Household*. At the invitation of the *Century Magazine*, Mena produced a series of stories set in Mexico, including "Dona Rita's Rivals," her best-known tale, "The Vine-Leaf," and a retelling of the Aztec myth of Huitzilopochtli titled "The Birth of the God of War," all of which appeared between 1913 and 1916.

In New York Mena entered literary circles, becoming a friend of D. H. Lawrence and in 1916 marrying Henry Kellett Chambers, a playwright and journalist. Though she published no more short stories, she went on to write five children's books, as well as a reminiscence of D. H. Lawrence published in 1964. She continued to live in Brooklyn and was active in the Authors Guild of New York and the Catholic Library Association.

The Vine-Leaf

It is a saying in the capital of Mexico that Dr. Malsufrido carries more family secrets under his hat than any archbishop, which applies, of course, to family secrets of the rich. The poor have no family secrets, or none that Dr. Malsufrido would trouble to carry under his hat.

The doctor's hat is, appropriately enough, uncommonly capacious, rising very high, and sinking so low that it seems to be supported by his ears and eyebrows, and it has a furry look, as if it had been brushed the wrong way, which is perhaps what happens to it if it is ever brushed at all. When the doctor takes it off, the family secrets do not fly out like a flock of parrots, but remain nicely bottled up beneath a dome of old and highly polished ivory, which, with its unbroken fringe of dyed black hair, has the effect of a tonsure; and then Dr. Malsufrido looks like one of the early saints. I 've forgotten which one.

So edifying is his personality that, when he marches into a sick-room, the forces of disease and infirmity march out of it, and do not dare to return until he has taken his leave. In fact, it is well known that none of his patients has ever had the bad manners to die in his presence.

If you will believe him, he is almost ninety years old, and everybody knows that he has been dosing[1] good Mexicans for half a century. He is forgiven for being a Spaniard on account of a legend that he physicked[2] royalty in his time, and that a certain princess—but that has nothing to do with this story.

It is sure he has a courtly way with him that captivates his female patients, of whom he speaks as his *penitentes*,[3] insisting on confession as a prerequisite of diagnosis, and declaring that the physician who undertakes to cure a woman's body without reference to her soul is a more abominable kill-healthy than the famous *Dr. Sangrado,* who taught medicine to *Gil Blas.*

"Describe me the symptoms of your conscience, Señora," he will say. "Fix yourself that I shall forget one tenth of what you tell me."

"But what of the other nine tenths, Doctor?" the troubled lady will exclaim.

"The other nine tenths I shall take care not to believe," Dr. Malsufrido will reply, with a roar of laughter. And sometimes he will add:

"Do not confess your neighbor's sins; the doctor will have enough with your own."

When an inexperienced one fears to become a *penitente* lest that terrible old doctor betray her confidence, he reassures her as to his discretion, and at the same time takes her mind off her anxieties by telling her the story of his first patient.

"Figure you my prudence, Señora," he begins, "that, although she was my patient, I did not so much as see her face."

And then, having enjoyed the startled curiosity of his hearer, he continues:

"On that day of two crosses when I first undertook the mending of mortals, she arrived to me beneath a veil as impenetrable as that of a nun, saying:

" 'To you I come, Señor Doctor, because no one knows you.'

" 'Who would care for fame, Señorita,' said I, 'when obscurity brings such excellent fortune?'

"And the lady, in a voice which trembled slightly, returned:

" 'If your knife is as apt as your tongue, and your discretion equal to both, I shall not regret my choice of a surgeon.'

"With suitable gravity I reassured her, and inquired how I might be privileged to serve her. She replied:

" 'By ridding me of a blemish, if you are skilful enough to leave no trace on the skin.'

" 'Of that I will judge, with the help of God, when the señorita shall have removed her veil.'

" 'No, no; you shall not see my face. Praise the saints the blemish is not there!'

" 'Wherever it be,' said I, resolutely, 'my science tells me that it must be seen before it can be well removed.'

"The lady answered with great simplicity that she had no anxiety on that account, but that, as she had neither duenna[4] nor servant with her, I must help her. I had no objection, for a surgeon must needs be something of a lady's maid. I judged from the quality of her garments that she was of an excellent family, and I was ashamed of my clumsy fingers; but she was as patient as marble, caring only to keep her face closely covered. When at last I saw the blemish she had complained of, I was astonished, and said:

" 'But it seems to me a blessed stigma, Señorita, this delicate, wine-red vine-leaf, staining a surface as pure as the petal of any magnolia. With permission, I should say that the god Bacchus[5] himself painted it here in the arch of this chaste back, where only the eyes of Cupid[6] could find it; for it is safely below the line of the most fashionable gown.'

"But she replied:

" 'I have my reasons. Fix yourself that I am superstitious.'

"I tried to reason with her on that, but she lost her patience, and cried:

" 'For favor, good surgeon, your knife!'

"Even in those days I had much sensibility, Señora, and I swear that my heart received more pain from the knife than did she. Neither the cutting nor the stitching brought a murmur from her. Only some strong ulterior thought could have armed a delicate woman with such valor. I beat my brains to construe the case, but without success. A caprice took me to refuse the fee she offered me.

" 'No, Señorita,' I said, 'I have not seen your face, and if I were to take your money, it might pass that I should not see the face of a second patient, which would be a great misfortune. You are my first, and I am as superstitious as you.'

"I would have added that I had fallen in love with her, but I feared to appear ridiculous, having seen no more than her back.

" 'You would place me under an obligation,' she said. I felt that her eyes studied me attentively through her veil. 'Very well, I can trust you the better for that. Adiós, Señor Surgeon.'

"She came once more to have me remove the stitches, as I had told her, and again her face was concealed, and again I refused payment; but I think she knew that the secret of the vine-leaf was buried in my heart."

"But that secret, what was it, Doctor? Did you ever see the mysterious lady again?"

"Chist! Little by little one arrives to the rancho,[7] Señora. Five years passed, and many patients arrived to me, but, although all showed me their faces, I loved none of them better than the first one. Partly through family influence, partly through well-chosen friendships, and perhaps a little through that diligence in the art of Hippocrates[8] for which in my old age I am favored by the most charming of Mexicans, I had prospered, and was no longer unknown.

"At a meeting of a learned society I became known to a certain *marqués* who had been a great traveler in his younger days. We had a discussion on a point of anthropology, and he invited me to his house, to see the curiosities he had collected in various countries. Most of them recalled scenes of horror, for he had a morbid fancy.

"Having taken from my hand the sword with which he had seen five Chinese pirates sliced into small pieces, he led me toward a little door, saying:

" 'Now you shall see the most mysterious and beautiful of my mementos, one which recalls a singular event in our own peaceful Madrid.'

"We entered a room lighted by a skylight, and containing little but an easel on which rested a large canvas. The *marqués* led me where the most auspicious light fell upon it. It was a nude, beautifully painted. The model stood poised divinely, with her back to the beholder, twisting flowers in her hair before a mirror. And there, in the arch of that chaste back, staining a surface as pure as the petal of any magnolia, what did my eyes see? Can you possibly imagine, Señora?"

"*Válgame Dios!*[9] The vine-leaf, Doctor!"

"What penetration of yours, Señora! It was veritably the vine-leaf, wine-red, as it had appeared to me before my knife barbarously extirpated it from the living flesh; but in the picture it seemed unduly conspicuous, as if Bacchus had been angry when he kissed. You may imagine how the sight startled me. But those who know Dr. Malsufrido need no assurance that even in those early days he never permitted himself one imprudent word. No, Señora; I only remarked, after praising the picture in proper terms:

" 'What an interesting moon is that upon the divine creature's back!'

" 'Does it not resemble a young vine-leaf in early spring?' said the *marqués*, who contemplated the picture with the ardor of a connoisseur. I agreed politely, saying:

" 'Now that you suggest it, *Marqués*, it has some of the form and color of a tender vine-leaf. But I could dispense me a better vine-leaf, with many bunches of grapes, to satisfy the curiosity I have to see such a well-formed lady's face. What a misfortune that it does not appear in that mirror, as the artist doubtless intended! The picture was never finished, then?'

" 'I have reason to believe that it was finished,' he replied, 'but that the face painted in the mirror was obliterated. Observe that its surface is an opaque and disordered smudge of many pigments, showing no brush-work, but only marks of a rude rubbing that in some places has overlapped the justly painted frame of the mirror.'

" 'This promises an excellent mystery,' I commented lightly. 'Was it the artist or his model who was dissatisfied with the likeness, *Marqués*?'

" 'I suspect that the likeness was more probably too good than not good enough,' returned the *marqués*. 'Unfortunately, poor Andrade is not here to tell us.'

" 'Andrade! The picture was his work?'

" 'The last his hand touched. Do you remember when he was found murdered in his studio?'

" 'With a knife sticking between his shoulders. I remember it very well.'

"The *marqués* continued:

" 'I had asked him to let me have this picture. He was then working on that rich but subdued background. The figure was finished, but there was no vine-leaf, and the mirror was empty of all but a groundwork of paint, with a mere luminous suggestion of a face.

" 'Andrade, however, refused to name me a price, and tried to put me off with excuses. His friends were jesting about the unknown model, whom no one had managed to see, and all suspected that he designed to keep the picture for himself. That made me the more determined to possess it. I wished to make it a betrothal gift to the beautiful Señorita Lisarda Monte Alegre, who had then accepted the offer of my hand, and who is now the *marquesa*. When I have a desire, Doctor, it bites me, and I make it bite others. That poor Andrade, I gave him no peace.

" 'He fell into one of his solitary fits, shutting himself in his studio, and seeing no one; but that did not prevent me from knocking at his door whenever I had nothing else to do. Well, one morning the door was open.'

" 'Yes, yes!' I exclaimed. 'I remember now, *Marqués,* that it was you who found the body.'

" 'You have said it. He was lying in front of this picture, having dragged himself across the studio. After assuring myself that he was beyond help, and while awaiting the police, I made certain observations. The first thing to strike my attention was this vine-leaf. The paint was fresh, whereas the rest of the figure was comparatively dry. Moreover, its color had not been mixed with Andrade's usual skill. Observe you, Doctor, that the blemish is not of the texture of the skin, or bathed in its admirable atmosphere. It presents itself as an excrescence. And why? Because that color had been mixed and applied with feverish haste by the hand of a dying man, whose one thought was to denounce his assassin—she who undoubtedly bore such a mark on her body, and who had left him for dead, after carefully obliterating the portrait of herself which he had painted in the mirror.'

" '*Ay Dios!* But the police, *Marqués*—they never reported these details so significant?'

" 'Our admirable police are not connoisseurs of the painter's art, my friend. Moreover, I had taken the precaution to remove from the dead man's fingers the empurpled brush with which he had traced that accusing symbol.'

" 'You wished to be the accomplice of an unknown assassin?'

" 'Inevitably, Señor, rather than deliver that lovely body to the hands of the public executioner.'

"The *marqués* raised his lorgnette[10] and gazed at the picture. And I—I was recovering from my agitation, Señora. I said:

" 'It seems to me, *Marqués,* that if I were a woman and loved you, I should be jealous of that picture.'

"He smiled and replied:

" 'It is true that the *marquesa* affects some jealousy on that account, and will not look at the picture. However, she is one who errs on the side of modesty, and prefers more austere objects of contemplation. She is excessively religious.'

" 'I have been called superstitious,' pronounced a voice behind me.

"It was a voice that I had heard before. I turned, Señora, and I ask you to try to conceive whose face I now beheld."

"*Válgame la Virgen,* Dr. Malsufrido, was it not the face of the good *marquesa,* and did she not happen to have been also your first patient?"

"Again such penetration, Señora, confounds me. It was she. The *marqués* did me the honor to present me to her.

" 'I have heard of your talents, Señor Surgeon,' she said.

" 'And I of your beauty, *Marquesa,*' I hastened to reply; 'but that tale was not well told.' And I added, 'If you are superstitious, I will be, too.'

"With one look from her beautiful and devout eyes she thanked me for that prudence which to this day, Señora, is at the service of my *penitentes,* little daughters of my affections and my prayers; and then she sighed and said:

" 'Can you blame me for not loving this questionable lady of the vine-leaf, of whom my husband is such a gallant accomplice?'

" 'Not for a moment,' I replied, 'for I am persuaded, *Marquesa,* that a lady of rare qualities may have power to bewitch an unfortunate man without showing him the light of her face.' "

EXPLANATORY NOTES

NIGHTS WITH UNCLE REMUS
1. *old man Nod:* Sleep.
2. *high-primin':* Showing off.
3. *big house:* The home of the white master and his family on a plantation.
4. *feel his fat:* Possibly *feel his feet;* i.e., be aware of his power.
5. *sane:* A seine net.
6. *wescut:* Waistcoat.
7. *consate:* Possibly *concept.*

DAVE'S NECKLISS
1. *camp-meeting:* An outdoor religious gathering, often lasting several days.
2. *Arcadian:* Peaceful, pastoral.
3. *law against slaves reading:* In most southern states, slaves were prohibited from learning to read.
4. *bockrah:* Buckra; a white man (often derogatory); a cracker.
5. *peart:* Lively, sprightly, smart.
6. *Rockfish:* A river in central Virginia, flowing southeast to the James River.
7. *junesey:* Sweetheart.
8. *double-headed:* Variation of "double-hearted"; i.e., deceitful.
9. *lighterd-knot:* Probably *lighter knot,* a piece of wood used to start a fire.

THE SHERIFF'S CHILDREN
1. *freshet:* The sudden overflowing of a stream.
2. *Sherman's army:* William Tecumseh Sherman (1820–1891), a general of the Union army during the Civil War, took Atlanta in 1864, and, leaving much destruction in his wake, marched with his men to the sea at Savannah, then proceeded north.
3. *bummers:* Beggars, hoboes; in this case stragglers from the army.
4. *Troy:* A town in central North Carolina, southwest of Durham.
5. *Mexico:* The Mexican War (1846–1848) ended with the Treaty of Guadalupe Hidalgo, in which Mexico gave up its claim to Texas.

6. *Gettysburg:* The battle at Gettysburg, Pennsylvania, on July 1–3, 1863, a Union victory, is regarded as the turning point of the Civil War.
7. *mulatto:* A person of mixed European and African ancestry.
8. *butternut trousers:* Overalls of brown homespun cloth.
9. *lynching:* The murder by a mob of someone who has been accused of a crime; an epidemic of white violence against black men in the South from Reconstruction through the early twentieth century.
10. *Chapel Hill:* Town in north central North Carolina, the site of the first state university in the United States, founded in 1795.
11. *oath of allegiance:* Several federal plans for Reconstruction required a percentage of the voters in a southern state to swear allegiance to the Union before a new state government could be established.
12. *wicket:* A small door set in a larger door.

THE PRALINE WOMAN
1. *S'il vous plaît:* [French] Please.
2. *Mais non, maman:* Why no, Mama.
3. *ma bébé, ma petite:* My baby, my little one.
4. *mais brune:* But dark [of complexion].
5. *le bon Dieu:* the good Lord.
6. *Dix sous:* Ten sous. A sou is a copper coin.
7. *lagniappe:* A small present given to a customer with a purchase.
8. *c'est bon:* It's good.
9. *misère:* Misery, unhappiness.
10. *filé:* A powder made from sassafras leaves and used in Creole cooking, especially gumbo.
11. *St. Rocque:* Saint Roch of France (c. 1350–c. 1379), known for his charity and aid to the sick.
12. *no l'argent:* No money.
13. *crivasse:* Also *crevasse;* a break in a river's levee or dike.

THE STONES OF THE VILLAGE
1. *West Indies:* The Caribbean islands.
2. *Red River:* A river flowing southeast through Arkansas and Louisiana into the Mississippi; also a parish in northwest Louisiana south of Shreveport.
3. *Trés bien:* [French] Very well.
4. *Tulane College:* Now Tulane University; founded in New Orleans in 1834.
5. *theatre seats and cars:* The 1896 Supreme Court ruling in *Plessy v.*

Ferguson, with its "separate but equal" doctrine, allowed institutionalized racial segregation throughout the South in schools, modes of transportation, and other public places.

6. *pocketbook:* A man's purse or billfold.
7. *St. Landry parish:* In south central Louisiana, west of Baton Rouge.
8. *banquette:* A raised path or sidewalk.
9. *gas house:* A facility where gas for heating is processed.
10. *"no good could come out of this Nazareth":* See John 1:46: "Can there any good thing come out of Nazareth?"
11. *bête noir:* A person or thing that is particularly feared or disliked.

THE STORY OF AN HOUR
1. *goddess of Victory:* The Goddess of Victory, or Nike of Samothrace, a Greek statue from the third century B.C., was found in 1863 and is now in the Louvre. The female winged figure stands erect with her clothing blowing back.

THE STORM
1. *sacque:* A woman's loose straight dress with no waistline.
2. *harrow:* A tool, pulled by a horse, that break ups, levels, and weeds plowed fields.
3. *Dieu sait:* [French] Heaven only knows.
4. *Bonté:* Goodness.
5. *Assumption:* A Louisiana parish south of Baton Rouge and west of New Orleans.
6. *J'vous réponds:* Take my word for it; I assure you.
7. *Biloxi:* A city in southern Mississippi, on the Gulf of Mexico.

THE DANCIN' PARTY AT HARRISON'S COVE
1. *Alleghenies:* Part of the Appalachian mountain chain in Pennsylvania, Maryland, West Virginia, and Virginia.
2. *Scorpio:* A constellation resembling a scorpion and containing the star Antares.
3. *watering-place:* A resort or spa with springs for bathing or a beach for swimming.
4. *furbelows:* Flounces or ruffles; showy ornamentation.
5. *Castor and Pollux:* In Greek and Roman myth, twin brothers.
6. *germans and kettledrums:* Germans were parties where a dance of the same name was performed; kettledrums were afternoon or evening parties without dancing.
7. *febrifuge:* A medicine or remedy for fever.

8. *circuit-rider:* A traveling minister or preacher.

9. *Terpsichore:* In Greek myth, the muse of dance.

10. *jeans:* A strong cotton cloth in a twill weave.

11. *St. Augustin and his Forty Monks:* Saint Augustine (d. 604), with forty other monks, was sent from Rome to Britain in 596 to convert the Anglo-Saxons to Christianity. He became the first archbishop of Canterbury.

12. *lay-reader:* A nonclergyman authorized to conduct some religious services in the Episcopal church.

13. *the war:* The Civil War (1861–1865).

14. *good Samaritan:* A charitable person; see Luke 10:30–37.

15. *dancing in the fear of the Lord:* See Psalm 111:10: "The fear of the Lord is the beginning of wisdom."

16. *tithing of mint and anise and cummin:* In Matthew 23:23, Christ denounces religious officials who observe the rituals but not the spirit of the faith: "Woe unto you, scribes and Pharisees, hypocrites! for ye pay the tithe of mint and anise and cumin and have omitted the weightier matters of the law, judgement, mercy, and faith."

17. *one catholic and apostolic church:* From the Apostles' Creed in the Episcopal service.

18. *the old Adam:* Personification of natural sin. From the text for baptism of infants in the English *Book of Common Prayer*: "Grant that the old Adam in this Child may be so buried, that the new man may be raised up."

19. *Shiloh:* One of the great battles of the Civil War, fought in 1862 in southwestern Tennessee. It resulted in a victory for the North and large casualties on both sides.

20. *gallopade:* A fast-paced round dance.

SCRAMBLED EGGS

1. *quadroon:* A person of one-fourth African ancestry; also, the term "yellow" refers to a person of mixed African and European heritage.

2. *pasition:* Physician?

3. *janders:* Jaundice.

4. *"Bringing in the sheeps":* The hymn "Bringing in the Sheaves," date unknown; music by George Minor and words by Knowles Shaw.

5. *speculator:* One who bought and sold slaves for profit.

6. *peanut ring:* Also *peanut gallery* [slang]. The upper section of the

theater where the cheapest seats were located; in segregated communities African American patrons were expected to sit there.

7. *blace:* [Illegible in original].
8. *Montgomery:* Capital of Alabama, in the south central part of the state.
9. *lion:* The most prominent or popular person; the celebrity.
10. *their cake was all dough:* Their project had failed.
11. *mammon:* Wealth as an evil, taken as an object of worship.

THE VOICE OF THE RICH PUDDING
1. *land of Nod:* Sleep.
2. *high church or low church:* Two segments of the Episcopal church; the high church emphasizes the priesthood and traditional rituals and doctrines, while the low church emphasizes evangelical activities.
3. *fish on Friday:* The Roman Catholic custom of abstaining from eating meat on Fridays.
4. *rumest:* Strangest; queerest.
5. *happy as a bunch of tops:* [colloquial] "Tops" are members of the highest social class.

UP THE COOLLY
1. *Mississippi River:* River in the central United States, flowing from Minnesota to the Gulf of Mexico.
2. *Wisconsin River:* River flowing south through the center of Wisconsin to join the Mississippi.
3. *Black River:* River in south central Wisconsin, flowing into the Mississippi.
4. *La Crosse:* City in western Wisconsin on the Mississippi River; the surrounding valley.
5. *Brooklyn Bridge:* Bridge erected in New York in 1883, connecting Brooklyn with Manhattan.
6. *battlements:* Roofs.
7. *White Mountains:* Part of the Appalachian mountains in northern New Hampshire.
8. *drummer:* [colloquial] A traveling salesman.
9. *quaits:* A game like horseshoes.
10. *turning out:* Usually *turning in*—going to bed, retiring.
11. *chaff:* Banter; light talk or joking.
12. *Coollies:* Also coulees; in western Canada and the United States, deep ravines formed by rain or melting snow, but dry in summer.

13. *ridge-pole:* The horizontal beam at the peak of a roof.
14. *hickory shirt:* A coarse shirt of cotton twill worn by laborers.
15. *poor as Job's off-ox:* The phrase "poor as Job" is from Shake-speare's *King Henry IV, Part II* (I.ii.145); Job is a figure in the Old Testament whom God tested with great suffering. The off side of a horse, ox, or team is the side away from the driver, but "off-ox" is also used colloquially to mean a clumsy or stubborn person; e.g., "I don't know him from Adam's off-ox" (*OED*).
16. *arabesque frieze:* An ornamental band decorating part of a room, in this case modeled on Arabic art.
17. *Enneking, Brush, Millet:* John Joseph Enneking (1841–1916) was an American landscape painter born in Ohio; George de Forest Brush (1855–1941) was a Tennessee painter known for pictures of Indians; Jean-François Millet (1814–1875) was a French painter of scenes from rustic life.
18. *camphor:* A crystalline substance used to protect clothing from moths and in medicine as a stimulant.
19. *soap-advertising lithographs:* Prints made by a popular nineteenth-century method and distributed to promote products; here used as decoration.
20. *reveille:* A signal that wakes soldiers or sailors in the morning.
21. *negligé:* Informal.
22. *Windsor scarf:* A wide silk necktie tied in a loose bow.
23. *as I'm a jay!:* A jay is a noisy blue bird; or [colloquial] a silly person, a simpleton.
24. *finical:* Finicky; fastidious.
25. *regimentals:* Clothes resembling a military uniform.
26. *kildee:* A small bird.
27. *Ich bin durstig:* [German] I am thirsty.
28. *Ich bin hier geboren:* I was born here.
29. *cabinet organ:* A small portable organ.
30. *chromos:* Chromolithographs; colored pictures printed on a series of plates.
31. *Wo ist ihre goot mann?:* Where is your good husband?
32. *sawed wood:* Attended to his own task; continued to work steadily.
33. *a hard row of stumps:* Variation of "a hard row to hoe." A difficult task; hard times.
34. *diagonals:* Clothing made of fabric woven with diagonal lines; a twill suit.
35. *rig:* Dress or costume, especially an odd or showy kind.
36. *hand-work:* Sewing done by hand, not by machine.

37. *bucolic:* A pastoral poem; in this case, a rustic experience that resembles such a poem.
38. *speculator:* One who buys and sells land for profit.
39. *Honest John:* "Honest John's Jig" was a popular square-dance tune played on a fiddle.
40. *set:* The participants in a country or square dance.
41. *dyspeptic:* Gloomy; bad-tempered.
42. *I see very well the aureole of the dandelions:* From Millet's statement of artistic principles in a letter to Alfred Sensier (May 30, 1863) called his "Confession of Faith" and later that year published in the journal *L'Autographe.*
43. *puff-ball:* A white mushroom that bursts when touched, releasing a brown powder.
44. *Puritans:* The original English settlers of North America, or any group that is excessively strict about morals or religion.
45. *"The Arkansaw Traveller":* A comic American folk song and story about an easterner traveling in Arkansas who requests information, food, and lodging from a rural family. First published in 1847, but earlier an oral tradition.
46. *wammus:* A warm knit jacket similar to a cardigan.

PONTIAC'S LOOKOUT
1. *Mackinac:* An island in the waterway connecting Lake Huron and Lake Michigan.
2. *bateaux:* Lightweight flat-bottomed boats used on rivers in Canada and Louisiana.
3. *Illinois Territory:* Illinois was acquired by the United States in 1783 and became a state in 1818.
4. *Iroquois:* A group of American Indian nations with a shared language and culture who lived in western and northern New York, the lower Great Lakes region, and the Susquehanna River valley in Pennsylvania.
5. *engagés:* Enlisted men.
6. *coureurs-de-bois:* Trappers.
7. *bush-lopers:* Variation of *land-lopers*—i.e., vagabonds; here, woodsmen.
8. *Pontiac:* Chief of the Ottawa Indians, Pontiac (1720–1769) forged alliances among Indian groups and led an unsuccessful rebellion against the British in 1763.
9. *Bois Blanc:* An island southeast of Mackinac Island.
10. *St. Ignace:* A city on the northern shore of the waterway connecting Lake Huron and Lake Michigan, west of Mackinac Island.

11. *Chippewa:* Also *Ojibwa;* a group of Indian tribes living in Michigan, Wisconsin, Minnesota, and North Dakota, and speaking the Algonquin language.

12. *Ottawa:* A tribe of Algonquin-speaking Indians who lived near the mouth of the Ottawa River in southeastern Ontario and in Michigan.

13. *offish:* Standoffish; unapproachable.

14. *squaw:* Term for a Native American woman, now considered derogatory.

15. *portage:* A place where boats and supplies must be carried overland between rivers or lakes.

16. *Sault Ste. Marie:* A city in northern Michigan on the St. Marys River and the city opposite in Canada.

17. *blockhouse:* A wooden fort with a projecting second story.

18. *cross-mark:* The mark made by an illiterate person as a signature.

19. *West India:* The West Indies; the Caribbean islands.

THE FUS FIXICO LETTERS

1. *Indians cutting hair, changing names:* White authorities often cut the hair of Indian prisoners and schoolchildren; federal policies around the turn of the century called for the renaming of Indians to conform with Anglo-American conventions.

2. *Sitting Bull, Tecumseh, Custer, Harrison:* Sitting Bull (1831–1890), a Sioux leader, was involved in the defeat of General George Armstrong Custer (1839–1876) at Little Bighorn in 1876. Tecumseh (1768–1813) was a Shawnee leader. As ninth president of the United States, William Henry Harrison (1773–1841) became famous for the U.S. victory over the Indians at Tippecanoe in 1811.

3. *allotment:* The Dawes Act of 1887 provided for the allotment of tribal lands to individual Indians in order to assimilate them into American patterns of settled farming and break up tribal authority.

4. *steal his good name:* See Shakespeare, *Othello* III.iii.135.

5. *Ingersoll:* Robert Green Ingersoll (1833–1899), an American lawyer and writer who became a noted agnostic lecturer. Posey admired his work.

6. *sofky:* A traditional Creek food made from corn grits.

7. *Creek nation:* Originally located in the mid-South, the Creek Indians were pushed westward after European contact to Indian Territory, now Oklahoma.

8. *Ulysses:* In Homer's Odyssey, Odysseus (Ulysses) puts wax in his ears in order to resist the song of the Sirens.

9. *post auger:* A tool for digging postholes in the ground.

10. *Douglas, Porter, Gibson, Robertson:* Clarence Douglas was editor of the *Muskogee Phoenix*; Pleasant Porter was chief of the Creeks from 1899 to 1907; Charles Gibson, a Creek writer and Posey's friend at the *Indian Journal*, published a column on Creek life titled "Gibson's Rifle Shots"; Alice Mary Robertson (1854–1931) was a teacher and school superintendent in the Creek Nation.

11. *suffer 'em to come unto:* See Mark 10:14.

12. *Muskogee:* A city in eastern Oklahoma on the Arkansas River.

13. *Big Stick:* U.S. President Theodore Roosevelt (1858–1919) became famous for the saying "Speak softly and carry a big stick," which he used in a 1901 speech to describe his aggressive foreign policy.

14. *Samson:* See Judges 15:16.

15. *Secretary Itscocked:* Ethan Allen Hitchcock (1835–1909) served as secretary of the interior (1899–1907) after a career in the railroad and mining businesses.

16. *statehood:* The Curtis Act (1898) provided for the statehood of Indian Territory, but there was ongoing debate over whether it would be joined with the Oklahoma Territory or become a separate state.

17. *Ft. Smith:* A town on the Oklahoma/Arkansas border and on the Arkansas River.

18. *salt-licks and bee-courses:* That is to say, commercial projects of little importance. Salt licks are natural sources of salt; bee courses are trails of bees that could be "floated" or tracked to their hive.

MR. DOOLEY IN PEACE AND WAR

1. *forninst:* Against, facing.

2. *Huns:* A warlike people who invaded central and eastern Europe in the fourth and fifth centuries A.D.; here, any non-Irish resident.

3. *Adriatic:* A sea between Italy and the former Yugoslavia.

4. *rolling mill:* A factory in which metal pieces are rolled out.

5. *far-downer:* An Irish American whose family came from northern Ireland.

6. *Armagh:* A farming county in Ulster province, northern Ireland.

7. *Bantry Bay:* An inlet of the Atlantic Ocean in County Cork, Ireland.

8. *All Saints' Day:* The annual festival that celebrates the saints on November 1, the day after All Hallows' Eve (Halloween).

9. *pookies:* Hobgoblins in Irish folklore.

10. *tin-horn:* [slang] Pretending importance; cheap and showy.

11. *Nicaraguan Canal:* Nicaragua was first favored as the site of a canal across Central America, but in 1902 plans were shifted to Panama.

12. *Isthmus:* In 1903, having supported the Panamanian revolution, the United States made a treaty with the new Republic of Panama to allow construction of a canal linking the Atlantic and Pacific oceans across the Isthmus of Panama; the canal opened in 1914.

13. *Monroe Doctrine:* A tenet of U.S. foreign policy first articulated by President James Monroe in 1823. It promised U.S. protection of all nations of the Western Hemisphere against European colonization. This doctrine became more broadly interpreted, and more influential, after 1870; in 1904 the "Roosevelt Corollary" to the Monroe Doctrine stated that in cases of wrongdoing in Latin America, the United States could intervene in other nations' internal affairs.

14. *Teddy Roosevelt:* Roosevelt was known for his expansionist policies and support for restrictions on immigration.

15. *plan to irrigate West:* Roosevelt campaigned throughout his presidency for conservation and better use of land; he supported the Reclamation Act, passed in 1902, which allowed the federal government to build dams in the western United States to collect water for the irrigation of crops.

16. *Indian policies:* During Roosevelt's presidency, Native American issues were prominent; in 1906 the Burke Act made it possible for Indians who had received land through allotment to sell it quickly, usually to white buyers.

17. *merchant marine:* Beginning in 1901, Roosevelt advocated strengthening the American fleet of merchant ships by subsidizing U.S. shipbuilding.

18. *stern an' rockbound coast:* From a poem by Felicia Hemans (1793–1835), "The Landing of the Pilgrim Fathers in New England":

> The breaking waves dashed high
> On a stern and rock-bound coast,
> And the woods, against a stormy sky,
> Their giant branches tossed.

19. *Roosevelts and Lodges:* Henry Cabot Lodge (1850–1924), a Republican senator, belonged to the Immigration Restriction Association, a group advocating stricter tests for immigrants and limitations on their entry into the United States.

20. *Mayflower:* The ship on which the Pilgrims arrived in America in 1620.

21. *potato rot:* A blight that destroyed crops in Ireland, causing a great famine that led to mass immigration to the United States in the mid-nineteenth century.

22. *Wexford:* A seacoast county of Ireland.

23. *Goddess of Liberty:* Perhaps the Statue of Liberty, erected in 1886 at the entrance to New York Harbor, where many European immigrants arrived in the United States.

24. *Miles Standish:* Standish (c. 1584–1656) was one of the first English settlers who arrived in Massachusetts on the *Mayflower* in 1620.

25. *Texas:* After winning independence from Mexico as an independent republic in 1836, Texas was admitted to the Union as a state in 1845.

26. *Wilkes Booth:* John Wilkes Booth (1838–1865), an unsuccessful American actor, assassinated President Lincoln in 1865.

27. *burgermeister:* [German] A high-ranking member of the municipal government.

28. *Anti-Imperial Society:* Organization founded in 1898 to oppose U.S. expansion, especially the acquisition of the Philippines; it began in Massachusetts and later became a national organization based in Chicago.

29. *Plymouth Rock Association:* Plymouth Rock is the site at Plymouth, Massachusetts, where the Pilgrims are said to have first landed in America.

A NEW ENGLAND NUN

1. *choleric:* Irritable; having a quick temper.

2. *St. George's dragon:* Saint George, a Christian martyr of the fourth century A.D., is said to have killed a dragon; he is regarded as the guardian saint of England.

3. *listed:* Wanted.

4. *birthright/pottage:* In Genesis 25:29–34, Esau, the elder son of Isaac and Rebecca, comes home very hungry and sells his inheritance to his younger brother, Jacob, in exchange for food.

THE QUEEN'S TWIN

1. *Land of Eshcol:* A valley near Hebron in Canaan; the biblical "land of milk and honey." See Numbers 13:23–27.

2. *Thomaston, Castine, Portland:* Towns in southern Maine.

3. *Bristol, Bordeaux:* Bristol and Bordeaux are seaports in southwest England and southwest France, respectively.

4. *China Sea:* Part of the Pacific Ocean east and south of China.

5. *lost tribes of Israel:* A reference to the ten tribes who lived in the

northern kingdom of Israel, which fell to the Assyrians in 722 B.C. These Israelites were exiled to Assyria and there are many legends about their fate. See II Kings 17–23.

6. *coast-wise:* Along the coast.

7. *Queen Victoria:* Victoria (1819–1901) was queen of England from 1837 to 1901.

8. *Green Island:* An island in southern Maine near the entrance to Penobscot Bay.

9. *asphodel/thyme:* A plant of the lily family and an herb of the mint family.

10. *super-cargo:* A person on a merchant ship in charge of the cargo and commercial transactions.

11. *taking ways:* Engaging or charming manners.

12. *Thames:* A river in southern England, flowing through London into the North Sea.

13. *Wapping:* A district of east central London.

14. *fo'c's'le an' cabin:* The forecastle is the part of a ship holding the sailors' quarters; a cabin is a private room on a ship. Together they suggest everyone on the ship, from lowest to highest in station.

15. *wax images:* Wax figures, often representing famous people, exhibited as a public entertainment in the late nineteenth century.

16. *Jubilee:* The British national celebration of the fiftieth anniversary of Queen Victoria's accession to the throne, in 1887.

THE FOREIGNER

1. *beating:* Rowing rhythmically.

2. *rote:* The sound of the sea crashing on the shore.

3. *line storm:* A storm occurring about the time of the equinox in spring or fall.

4. *consumption:* Any wasting away of the body, especially due to tuberculosis.

5. *three sheets in the wind:* Drunk.

6. *highbinders:* Ruffians, gangsters.

7. *kick-shows:* Possibly *kick-shoes,* meaning buffoons.

8. *freehanded:* Generous.

9. *four square:* Unyielding.

10. *Kingston:* Seaport and capital of Jamaica, on its southeastern coast.

11. *Windward Islands:* Group of Caribbean islands in the Lesser Antilles, north of Trinidad.

12. *Port Royal:* A town in Jamaica, at the entrance to Kingston Harbor.

13. *Portland:* Seaport in southeast Maine.

14.   *melodeon:* An early form of the American organ.
15.   *David's dancin' before the Lord:* See II Samuel 6:14.
16.   *Straits of Malacca:* A leading shipping lane between Europe and the Far East, connecting the Pacific Ocean and the South China Sea.
17.   *stranger in a strange land:* See Exodus 2:22.
18.   *A made countenance:* See Sir Philip Sidney's *New Arcadia* (1590), I.35–36.
19.   *New Jerusalem:* See Revelation 21:2.
20.   *Monhegan:* An island in southern Maine.
21.   *Rockland:* A city in southern Maine on the west shore of Penobscot Bay.
22.   *Empress Josephine:* Wife of Napoleon and empress of France (1763–1814).
23.   *Martinique:* Island in the eastern West Indies; a French colony.
24.   *sibyl of the Sistine Chapel:* A figure from the frescoes painted by Michelangelo in the papal chapel in the Vatican in Rome.
25.   *on the rack:* In a state of great suffering, anxiety, or suspense.

THE APOSTATE OF CHEGO-CHEGG

1.   *Inquisition:* The Roman Catholic tribunal formed in the thirteenth century to search out and punish heretics; nonconforming Christians, and Jews as well, were persecuted. Most active in Italy, Spain, and Portugal, the Inquisition became notorious in the sixteenth century for its atrocities.
2.   *sweatshops:* Manufacturing shops where employees work long hours in poor conditions, common in New York around the turn of the century.
3.   *custom:* Customers; regular patrons of a business.
4.   *Petrarch/Laura:* Petrarch (1304–1374), an Italian poet and scholar, is known for his faithful and pure love of Laura, recorded in his sonnets and songs.
5.   *triefe:* Not prepared according to Mosaic law, proscribed, the opposite of kosher [author's note].
6.   *kosher:* Fit to eat according to the Jewish dietary laws.
7.   *proselyte:* A person who has converted from one religion to another.
8.   *plaguy:* [colloquial] Annoying; disagreeable.

TALMA GORDON

1.   *There's a divinity that shapes our ends:* From Shakespeare, *Hamlet* V.ii.10.

2. *propinquity:* Nearness in time, place, or kinship.

3. *East India:* India, the Indochinese peninsula, and the Malay archipelago, as distinguished from the West Indies, the Caribbean islands.

4. *Whom the gods love die young:* From Plautus (c. 254–184 B.C.), *Bacchides* IV, 7:18; or Menander (c. 342–292 B.C.), *The Double Deceiver.*

5. *merry as a marriage bell:* From *Childe Harold's Pilgrimage*, by Lord Byron (1788–1824):

> A thousand hearts beat happily; and when
> Music arose with its voluptuous swell,
> Soft eyes look'd love to eyes which spake again, .
> And all went merry as a marriage bell. (III.21)

6. *tubercle-fiend:* Tuberculosis.

7. *A wet sheet and a flowing sea:* From the song "A Wet Sheet and a Flowing Sea," in the 1825 volume *The Songs of Scotland*, by Allan Cunningham (1784–1842).

8. *octoroon:* A person of one eighth African ancestry.

9. *Dumas:* Alexandre Dumas (1802–1870) was a French novelist and playwright, author of *The Count of Monte Cristo* (1844) and *The Three Musketeers* (1844). Through his grandmother, who was born in Haiti, Dumas could claim African descent.

BRO'R ABR'M JIMSON'S WEDDING

1. *Vanderbilts and Astors:* Members of the white American elite. Cornelius Vanderbilt (1794–1877) made his fortune in shipping and later railroads; John Jacob Astor (1763–1848) became a millionaire after founding the American Fur Company.

2. *offertory:* That part of many Christian church services in which bread and wine are offered to God before they are consecrated at communion. In some traditions, money is also collected from the congregation at this time.

3. *rheumatics:* People suffering from rheumatism, inflammation, and pain in the joints and muscles; elderly persons.

4. *nagur:* [dialect] Nigger. A derogatory term for an African American.

5. *baste:* [dialect] Beast.

6. *Taunton:* City in southeastern Massachusetts.

7. *goophered:* Bewitched; under a spell.

8. *Queen of Sheba:* A biblical queen known for her wealth. See I Kings 10:1–13.

9. *avoirdupois:* Weight.
10. *hoodooin':* Bringing bad luck to. From the African American and African Caribbean spiritual practice of vodoun or voodoo.
11. *Ye are the salt of the earth:* See Matthew 5:13.

ON BEING CRAZY

1. *social equality:* White southerners' defense of segregation in the late nineteenth century through the mid-twentieth century was rooted in the "social equality" argument, which suggested that any integration would lead to the mixing of the races in all aspects of life.
2. *sleeper:* The car of a train equipped with sleeping compartments for passengers.

AN INGÉNUE OF THE SIERRAS

1. *road agents:* Highwaymen along stagecoach routes.
2. *Lethean:* Causing forgetfulness. In Greek myth, Lethe is the place of oblivion.
3. *in your skeer:* That is to say, in your fright.
4. *muleteer:* One who drives a team of mules.
5. *demijohn:* A bottle wrapped in a wicker casing.
6. *waybill:* The list of passengers on the stagecoach.
7. *adhesion:* Attraction or attachment.
8. *diffusiveness:* Outpouring, effusiveness.
9. *chiffle:* Cheerful.
10. *galoot:* A strange or foolish man.
11. *pongee:* A tan-colored fabric.
12. *swag:* Money or valuables, especially stolen goods.
13. *Coming down to hardpan and the bed rock:* Getting down to the fundamental things.

"ITS WAVERING IMAGE"

1. *Bohemian:* A person who lives in an unconventional way.
2. *joss house:* A Chinese temple.
3. *Robert Louis Stevenson:* A Scottish author (1850–1894) best known for *Treasure Island* (1883) and *Dr. Jekyll and Mr. Hyde* (1886).

THE WISDOM OF THE NEW

1. *losing face:* Being humiliated, losing one's reputation.
2. *queued:* Worn in a braid from the back of the head.
3. *carmine:* A red pigment.

4. *punk:* A chemically treated fungus substance shaped into thin sticks and used to light fireworks or other fires.

5. *josses:* Figures of Chinese gods; or joss sticks, sticks of Chinese incense.

6. *Hankow:* Former city in east central China; now merged with Hanyang and Wuchang and called Wuhan.

7. *bonze:* A Buddhist monk.

8. *Diana:* Roman goddess of the moon.

9. *Wisdom of the New:* Possibly an allusion to Sir Francis Bacon's *The Wisdom of the Ancients* (1609).

IN A FAR COUNTRY

1. *Edmonton:* The capital of Alberta, in Canada.

2. *Klondike:* A gold-mining region around the Klondike River in the western Yukon territory of northwestern Canada; site of a gold rush in 1898.

3. *voyageur:* A person employed by the fur companies to transport goods by boat; any woodsman or boatman in rural Canada.

4. *65th parallel:* A measure of latitude, this east/west line roughly bisects Alaska.

5. *argonauts:* People who participated in the California gold rush of 1848–1849; from the Greek myth of Jason and his men, who sailed in search of the golden fleece.

6. *Lake Athabasca:* A lake on the North Alberta–Saskatchewan border in Canada.

7. *Great Slave:* A lake in the southern Mackenzie District of the Northwest Territories, Canada.

8. *pemmican:* Dried meat, suet, or fruit pressed into cakes as food for arctic expeditions.

9. *Mackenzie:* A river in the Northwest Territories of Canada, flowing from Great Slave Lake to the Beaufort Sea.

10. *pay-dirt:* Soil rich in gold for mining.

11. *Great Bear:* A lake in the southern Mackenzie District of the Northwest Territories.

12. *Fort of Good Hope:* A town in the Northwest Territories on the Mackenzie River.

13. *tump-line:* A broad band running across the forehead and over the shoulders to support a pack on the back.

14. *canoodlin':* [slang] Caressing, necking; i.e., not attending to business.

15. *Kilkenny cats:* From an anonymous limerick:

> There once was two cats of Kilkenny,
> Each thought there was one cat too many,
> So they quarreled and they fit,
> They scratched and they bit,
> 'Til instead of two cats, there weren't any.

16. *Porcupine:* A river in the northern Yukon area of Canada, flowing into the Yukon River.
17. *mutton-head:* [slang] A stupid person.
18. *slush-lamp:* A lamp fueled by fat or grease left over from cooking.
19. *scurvy:* A disease caused by a deficiency of vitamin C.
20. *ragpicker:* A person who made his living by collecting and selling rags and other refuse; a shabby or unclean person.
21. *Arcadias:* Places of ideal peace and happiness, named for a district in the ancient Peloponnesus.
22. *Caliban:* A savage native creature in Shakespeare's play *The Tempest* (1611).
23. *Crusoe:* The title character of the novel *Robinson Crusoe* (1719), by Daniel Defoe (1660–1731), who is shipwrecked on a remote island.
24. *pound of flesh:* An extremely cruel penalty; in Shakespeare's *The Merchant of Venice* (1596–1597), Shylock demands a pound of Antonio's flesh as bond for a debt (I.iii).
25. *Gabriel:* One of the seven archangels in the Bible; the herald of good news (Daniel 8:16; Luke 1:26).

TO THE MAN ON TRAIL

1. *pepper-sauce:* A fiery condiment made from red peppers and vinegar.
2. *sinking a hole to bedrock without a pay-streak:* Expending great effort on a mine without finding gold.
3. *Stack up on that for a high card:* To stack a deck of cards is to shuffle dishonestly in order to deal oneself a high card.
4. *hooch:* Alcohol; named for the liquor made by the Alaskan Hoochinoo Indians.
5. *Tananas:* Members of an American Indian nation living around the Tanana River in southeast Alaska.
6. *raconteur:* A skilled storyteller.
7. *Lochinvar:* The hero of a ballad in Sir Walter Scott's *Marmion* (1808).
8. *La petite squaw; mon Mason brav:* [French] The little squaw; my brave Mason.

9. *Henry Ward Beecher:* An American Congregationalist preacher (1813–1887) who opposed slavery and advocated temperance, brother of Harriet Beecher Stowe.

10. *sassafras root:* The root and bark of the North American sassafras tree were used to make medicines, tea, and other beverages.

11. *Alsace and Lorraine:* Two former provinces of France which were under German control from 1871 to 1919.

12. *Malemutes:* [malamute] A large, strong dog, originally bred by the Alaskan Eskimos as a sled dog.

13. *Frost King:* Also Jack Frost; personification of the cold.

14. *mackinaw jacket:* A short, double-breasted plaid wool coat, named for Mackinac Island in the strait connecting Lake Huron and Lake Michigan.

15. *Dawson:* A city in the western Yukon Territory, on the Yukon River; formerly a gold-mining center.

16. *spliced:* [slang] Married.

17. *dusted for:* Took off in a hurry.

18. *Pelly:* A river in the Yukon Territory, feeding into the Yukon River.

19. *Little Salmon:* A lake in the Yukon Territory, feeding into the Yukon River.

20. *gone up:* Weak, used up, beyond hope.

21. *whiter:* More pure or moral.

22. *clean-up:* The process of collecting the yield of a mining operation.

23. *jumps the limit:* To jump a claim is to take possession of land that has been abandoned or is not legally owned by another.

THE LAND OF LITTLE RAIN

1. *Sierras:* The Sierra Nevada mountains in eastern California.

2. *Panamint:* The Panamint mountain range in southeastern California.

3. *Amargosa:* A river in southern Nevada and eastern California, flowing into Death Valley, the desert basin that lies east of the Panamint mountains.

4. *Ute:* A nation of nomadic Shoshonean Indians living in Colorado, Utah, New Mexico, and Arizona.

5. *water gate:* A channel for water; a river's course.

6. *Colorado:* A major river of the southwestern United States, flowing from Colorado State through Utah and Arizona to the Gulf of California.

7. *Amaranthus:* One of a family of plants that includes the tumbleweed; in myth, a plant that never fades or dies.

8. *creosote:* An evergreen shrub found in northern Mexico and the southwestern United States.

9. *tree yuccas:* The yucca is a plant of the agave family, with sword-shaped leaves.

10. *San Joaquin Valley:* The southern part of California's Central Valley, which extends north and south between the Coastal Range and the Sierra Nevadas.

11. *conning towers:* The pilothouses or steering turrets of warships.

12. *named all the birds without a gun:* From the first line of the poem "Forbearance" (1842), by Ralph Waldo Emerson (1803–1882).

13. *the lotus charm:* In an episode of the Odyssey, the Greek sailors visit a land whose lotus fruit causes lethargy and forgetfulness in those who eat it. See also Tennyson's poem "The Lotos-Eaters" (1832).

14. *borax marsh:* Borax is a white, crystalline salt.

15. *Mojave:* A desert in southeastern California.

16. *coolies:* Name given to Chinese laborers, including those who worked building railroads in the western United States. Now considered derogatory.

17. *swamper:* A handyman or helper.

18. *Great Basin:* Region between the Sierra Nevadas and the Wasatch mountains, including eastern California, western Utah, Nevada, and parts of Oregon and Idaho.

19. *Hassayampa:* A river in western Arizona that flows south into the Gila River.

20. *Chaldeans:* The people of Chaldea, an ancient province of Babylonia; associated with astronomy and sorcery.

THE SOFT-HEARTED SIOUX
1. *buffalo-robe:* A robe or blanket made of the skin of a buffalo.

THE VINE-LEAF
1. *dosing:* Giving medicine to.

2. *physicked:* Dosed with medicine; healed.

3. *penitentes:* [Spanish] Those who repent of their sins.

4. *duenna:* An elderly woman who chaperones a young unmarried woman.

5. *Bacchus:* Greek and Roman god of wine and revelry.

6. *Cupid:* Roman god of love, represented as a boy with a bow and arrow.

7. *Little by little one arrives at the* rancho: A *rancho* is a farm house or village; often an inn or stopping place for travelers. Possibly a

version of the Italian proverb "Step by step one gets to Rome."

8. *Hippocrates:* Greek physician (c. 460–c. 370 B.C.); called the Father of Medicine.

9. *Válgame Dios!:* "God help me!"

10. *lorgnette:* Eyeglass(es) such as a monocle or pince-nez.